2003
Feb 5

D0368491

No Escape

No Escape

Hilary Norman

PIATKUS

✿ *Visit the Piatkus website!*

Piatkus publishes a wide range of best-selling fiction and non-fiction, including books on health, mind, body & spirit, sex, self-help, cookery, biography and the paranormal.

If you want to:

- read descriptions of our popular titles
- buy our books over the Internet
- take advantage of our special offers
- enter our monthly competition
- learn more about your favourite Piatkus authors

VISIT OUR WEBSITE AT: www.piatkus.co.uk

Copyright © Hilary Norman 2003

First published in Great Britain in 2003 by
Judy Piatkus (Publishers) Ltd of
5 Windmill Street, London W1T 2JA
email: info@piatkus.co.uk

The moral right of the author has been asserted

A catalogue record for this book is available from the British Library

ISBN 0 7499 0638 3

Set in Times by
Phoenix Photosetting, Chatham, Kent
Printed and bound in Great Britain by
Butler and Tanner, Frome

As always, my gratitude to all those who've taken time and trouble to help, with special thanks to:

Sarah Abel; Koula Antoniou; Howard Barmad; Jennifer Bloch; Ros Chinosky; Sara Fisher; Gillian Green; Peter Johnston; Jonathan Kern; Aleksandar Lazarevic; Herta Norman; Judy Piatkus; Helen Rose; Ann Ryan, South Chingford Library; and Dr Jonathan Tarlow.

For Bernhard Grünwald

Case No. 5/040573

BOLSOVER, L.F.

Study/Review

Pending

Action

Resolved   ✓

1

All through the last week of February, the body lay beneath a pile of sacking on the floor of a neglected shed on an allotment near Claris Green in the London borough of Barnet. Less than a year ago, this tiny plot of land had boasted plums, tomatoes, strawberries and seasonal flowers, but then the allotment holder had died, and in the lengthy wait for a new tenant the plants had withered, become choked by weeds and threaded with cobwebs, and one wall of the shed had been smashed by vandals using it for sport.

It being late winter, with no new holder yet in prospect, the body had thus far remained undiscovered for eight days, though one large, smooth, speckled pebble, chucked through the broken planks of wood by a hooligan with time on his hands, now rested on the sacking directly over the dead woman's left thigh.

The discovery, when it was finally made, would horrify and sicken whoever had the misfortune to stumble upon it. However advanced the state of decomposition of the corpse by then, identification would swiftly be made, for Lynne Frances Bolsover had been reported as a missing person by her husband seven days before, and with no reported sightings since then or usage of her VISA card, concern for her safety had begun to mount. Besides which, while Mrs Bolsover's black leather Marks & Spencer handbag (placed by her killer in a wheelie bin on Franklin Road, less than a mile from the allotment) would never be found, Lynne was still dressed in her Next red pullover and blue jeans with a Siamese cat patch on their right back pocket, and those clothes, supported by the missing woman's dental records, would smooth the way for the police.

Though not, of course, the Bolsover family.

2

The pathologist would, in due course, confirm that the twenty-nine-year-old wife of John Bolsover and mother of Kylie, aged six, and Alex, aged four, had died from a massive brain haemorrhage after her skull had been fractured by three blows to her head. The murder investigation already launched by the Metropolitan Police's Area Major Investigation Team, North West, would pick up a full head of steam – and would, in all probability, be rapidly solved. For the AMIT NW detectives would soon learn that, hoping to alleviate Lynne's prolonged depression after an abortion a year earlier, her GP, Dr Deirdre Miller, had recently prescribed Prozac; that staff at a health shop half a mile from the Bolsovers' semi-detached had often supplied the deceased with arnica for bruising; that, according to Pam Wakefield (Lynne's sister) and Valerie Golding (her next-door-neighbour), Lynne had frequently been bullied, yelled at, and almost certainly hit by John Bolsover, her husband; and that – this from sister Pam – it had been John who had insisted on the termination that had so depressed his wife.

It was likely that Bolsover would be interviewed several times before being arrested and charged with her murder.

Though he would never confess.

Because he was not guilty.

2

Everyone said, regularly, that Lizzie Piper Wade was a very lucky woman.

'Except for poor Jack, of course—' those who knew about her middle child's Duchenne muscular dystrophy would quickly add '—though God knows even that has to be a little easier for her than for other women.'

'Other women' meaning those with the misfortune not to be married to Christopher Wade.

Life had taught Lizzie about counting blessings, and she had learned over the years, despite the cruelty of Jack's diagnosis, to be grateful for many things. She was grateful for Jack's courage and humour, for his intelligence and self-esteem, and, perhaps most vitally, for his unshakable confidence in his family's great love for him. She was boundlessly grateful that twelve-year-old Edward and Sophie, seven in March, were both healthy – though time and testing, perhaps in her teens, would yet tell whether or not Sophie was a carrier of the gene defect that had afflicted ten-year-old Jack.

She was grateful for her work.

'How important—' a journalist interviewing her for one of the Saturday supplements had asked her a year ago '—would you say your career is to you, in the general scheme of things?'

'I know I'm lucky to have it,' Lizzie had answered. 'Lucky to be able to cook and eat and drink, and write about it *and* get paid for it.'

She'd gone on, as she usually did, about her good fortune, saying that though she did actually work fairly hard, it was sometimes difficult to think of what she did as real 'work'. But she had not given the answer that lay uppermost in her mind: the most truthful answer.

Work keeps me sane.

The journalist, knowing about Jack's condition, would probably have assumed that Lizzie was thinking of that. But Lizzie had not spoken the words, neither to that person nor to any other. Not even to Angela Piper, her mother, nor to Gilly Spence, who helped with Jack and the other children and some of the housework – making Gilly another blessing.

Work keeps me sane.

None of them would have truly understood that statement. All of them would have believed that if Lizzie's emotional strength did occasionally teeter a bit, it had to be because of Jack and the constant strain of balancing priorities – and even then, taking all that into account, they would still silently have added a waiver to their very real empathy: *Easier for Lizzie than most.*

Because all her family, friends and colleagues, and anyone who'd read about her in women's magazines or tabloids, felt much the same way about one pivotal aspect of her life; that Lizzie's greatest, head-and-shoulders-above-the-rest, blessing (especially, some privately thought, since though she was a nice enough-looking blue-eyed blonde, she was no great beauty) was that she had Christopher for her husband.

Christopher Edward Julian Wade.

The gifted, renowned, attractive plastic surgeon who regularly donated his services to the needy in European and Third World countries, as well as being the founder and lynchpin of HANDS, a charitable institution dedicated to the physical and psychological aid of disfigured men, women and children.

Dubbed 'Saint Christopher' by several tabloids.

The Wades divided their family life between a large, early Victorian, stucco-fronted house on the Thames near Marlow in Buckinghamshire, and a garden flat in London's Holland Park; both homes having been virtually gutted and reconstructed some years back in order to be able to accommodate Jack's special needs – ramps, a stairlift in the house, widened doorways, modified bathrooms – as they arose, as his strength and abilities gradually waned, and both also possessing working kitchens for Lizzie and studies for her and Christopher.

Add the blessing of wealth.

5

Lizzie had long ago lost count of how many fans had written to tell her how much they envied her – not so much because of her bestselling books and regular appearances as Lizzie Piper in cookery slots on *This Morning* and on the Food and Drink Channel, but because of her life with the fabulous Christopher.

Because none of them knew the truth about him.

They all knew only what Lizzie *wished* them to know, for knowing more would serve no purpose. She would not – could not – contemplate leaving Christopher, no matter what, because of her children. Because of Jack. Because, flawed as her husband was, he was also the most genuinely tender father imaginable.

And because Jack worshipped him.

So, for at least as long as Jack lived (and although Lizzie knew the statistics, knew that despite the hopes for gene and other therapies of the future, her beloved son might still be lucky to survive past his teens or early twenties, she seldom permitted herself to contemplate his death), Lizzie would tell no one. Would allow her family and the world beyond to go on believing, wholeheartedly, in the semi-myth of 'Saint Christopher' Wade.

For Jack.

3

Some people found it hard to trust Robin Allbeury.

A prosperous, successful, Labour-supporting solicitor with offices in Bedford Row and a sumptuous penthouse home in Shad Tower, a sleek building on Bermondsey Riverside near St Saviour's Dock and Butler's Wharf on the south-east side of Tower Bridge, Allbeury was, on the whole, a contented man.

An elegant bachelor of forty-two, not handsome but undeniably attractive, with dark hair threading nicely with silver, and warm brown eyes, he supported the arts but, in his personal taste rankings, placed cinema above theatre, thrillers above literature, jazz above opera. Silence above jazz. Quiet dinners above parties. Friendships with women above men. And his single status above marriage.

'You don't know what you're missing,' David Lerman, one of his partners, blissfully happy with his second wife, had told him more than once. 'Julia's transformed my life.'

'Julia's wonderful,' Allbeury had agreed, 'but you were a miserable sod before you met her, whereas I'm a happy man.'

'So you claim.' Lerman had remained dubious.

'I do.' Allbeury had smiled.

His speciality in law was matrimony, though these days, as head of his own firm, he tended to be highly selective about which cases he took on, leaving either Lerman or one of their associates to deal with the bulk of marital matters, while he supervised and allowed himself time for his 'other' work.

What he did in that spare, private time, was to help rescue women trapped in deeply unhappy marriages; women who, either for financial or other reasons, saw no way out. They seldom came to him. It was usually Allbeury who, learning of their circumstances in any number of ways, volunteered his services to them.

He had built up a grapevine of trusted informants over the years, a disparate bunch spread over Greater London. A telephone operator working for the emergency services, a disillusioned social worker, a probation officer, a police constable, a paramedic, a publican and one west London vicar.

'Anyone finds out I've passed this on to you,' the social worker had agitated at one of his early meetings with Allbeury, 'and I'm fucked.'

'No one's going to find out from me,' Allbeury had told him.

The case in question had concerned a woman suffering from her husband's extreme mental cruelty. Social services had been alerted by neighbours because of the wife's constant loud sobbing, but with no visible bruises or blood, and in the face of her refusal to make any complaint, the social worker had had little choice but to withdraw.

'I feel I've abandoned someone in darkest despair.'

'No chance of her leaving?' Allbeury asked.

'She's sunk too deep to even try,' the young man had said. 'He's a complete control freak. Won't let her cash a cheque without his signature, won't let her have an ATM card, tells her who she can or can't see.'

'Suicide risk, do you think?' Allbeury asked.

'I'd say it's a distinct likelihood.'

Allbeury had been quiet for a moment.

'Tell me all you know.'

He generally worked that way, extracted whatever his informant could offer, then used his own methods to verify the woman's circumstances, after which, if he felt he might be able to help, he made contact via a third party to arrange a first meeting, usually in a public place outside their own environment. Some of the women shied away in alarm, but often they were sufficiently intrigued and bleak enough to take at least that first step.

They tended, in general, to like and to have faith in Allbeury, who was a gentle, diplomatic interrogator, though some were suspicious, especially when he told them there was no need to concern themselves about money.

'I can't pay you any other way either,' more than one had said.

'Nor do I expect you to.'

8

All he was offering, he told them, was a way out. An escape. An end to their marriage, if that was what they decided they ultimately wanted. An end to intimidation or raw vulnerability or actual fear.

'But *why*?' one distrustful wife had asked. 'If you say you don't want money, and I won't risk applying for Legal Aid, why on earth do you want to help?'

He had smiled. 'Call it my missionary complex.'

'Missionaries convert people, don't they?'

'The only thing I want to convert you to,' Robin Allbeury had told her, 'is freedom.'

4

Mike Novak, a private investigator with a struggling agency operating out of a run-down former warehouse in New Smithfield, a
grungy undeveloped cul-de-sac off Dock Street near the old Royal
Mint, had first hooked up with Robin Allbeury five years ago after
Allen Keith, at that time a junior partner in the Bedford Row practice, had hired Novak to check out the allegedly adulterous wife of
a wealthy client. Novak had learned that the shoe had been firmly
on the other foot, and had reported as much. The client had been
enraged and ordered Allen Keith to fire Novak and withhold
payment, but two days later senior partner Robin Allbeury had
come to the agency to apologize.

'I'd rather have my fee,' Novak had told him.

The solicitor with the beautifully-cut hair and suit, and the
younger man with rumpled fair hair, pugnacious nose and mouth
and hostile blue eyes, had taken a good look at one another.

'Your fee plus a bonus.' Allbeury had smiled as he'd written out
the cheque on the spot. 'And my thanks for a job well done.'

'Your client wouldn't agree.'

'Nevertheless,' Allbeury had said.

When, some months later, Novak had read in the *Mirror* that the
client's divorce had been settled with particular fairness to the
wife, he'd wondered if his report and, perhaps, Robin Allbeury
himself, might have played a part in the deal.

The following afternoon, a pair of heavies had jumped Novak
near his flat in Lamb's Conduit Street, advising him that he'd be
smart in future to keep his reports in the interests of those who
paid his bills, then given him a kicking to ram home the point.
Deciding later, nursing a stiff drink and his wounds, that the rather

smoothly charming Robin Allbeury should be made aware of the kind of people he was dealing with, Novak had phoned him, and within hours the solicitor had come to the flat.

'Christ,' Allbeury had said, appalled by his face.

'You didn't need to come.'

The other man had ignored the bolshiness. 'May I come in?' In his left hand, he held a bottle of Jameson's. 'Better than aspirin.'

Novak had hesitated, then let him in and shown him where the glasses were.

'Straight to the point,' Allbeury had said, pouring for them both. 'Okay?'

'Why not?'

'You have my word,' Allbeury said, 'which I hope, in time, you'll come to see is worth something, that my firm will, as of tomorrow, sever all links with the client in question.'

'Judging by this little lot—' Novak felt his ribs gingerly '—he may not like it.'

'Tough,' Allbeury said.

'What about Allen Keith?'

'If Mr Keith has a problem with my decision, he can look for a partnership elsewhere.'

Novak had frowned. 'You sound like you mean that.'

'I never say things I don't mean,' Allbeury had said.

If those thugs had inadvertently helped to bring about the start of a long working relationship with Robin Allbeury, they had also introduced Mike Novak to the love of his life.

Clare Killin had been a nurse on duty in A&E when he'd limped in on the afternoon of his beating to have the nastiest of the gashes on his forehead stitched up. It was one thing, Novak had confessed to her, facing up to the odd angry fist or even boot, but needles were another matter altogether.

'I'll do my best,' she'd assured him, her voice soft and Edinburgh-accented.

'Aren't you going to take the piss?' he'd asked.

'Would it help?'

'Not a bit.'

'Didn't think so.' She'd turned around. 'Want to shut your eyes?'

11

Novak had checked out her calm hazel eyes, sweet mouth and curly red hair, tied off her face, a few stray hairs escaping. 'Think I'll keep them open,' he'd said. 'If you don't mind.'

A fortnight after their first dinner together, Clare had moved into his flat, and three months later they had quietly, joyfully married. Neither had relatives in easy reach, Novak having lost both his Czech-born father and English mother in a plane crash seven years before, and Clare's widowed father, Malcolm Killin, living up in Scotland, but neither had felt any need for family or for anyone else.

The nearest thing to tension Novak had experienced in those blissful early days had been the odd troublesome client or the ongoing challenge of trying to make Novak Investigations pay its way. Clare's stresses, on the other hand, had been on a vastly different level, witnessing, as she did almost daily, the kinds of pain and distress that Novak preferred not even to imagine. When she had finally burned out because, according to a colleague at the hospital, she was too empathetic to survive long-term as an emergency care nurse, Novak feared that he might, in some way, have failed her.

The agency was relegated to second place and business suffered accordingly as he became determined to help Clare back to full strength, but she never went back to A&E, and Novak had backed her decision. The hospital, keen to help, had suggested the possibility of a transfer to another department, and Novak had mooted the idea that she might want to try her hand at private nursing, but Clare had rejected both notions.

'It's A&E or nothing for me,' she'd said. 'The things that made me unwell are the things I loved.' And then she'd looked at him, strangely, searchingly.

'What?' Novak had found the look unsettling. 'What is it, Clare?'

'You must be very disappointed in me.' It was a flat statement.

Dismay hit him hard. 'For God's sake, why would you think that?'

'You married a nurse. A strong, capable woman who took care of people.'

'I married a human being, Clare. A sensitive, caring woman.'

'You still love me then?'

The flatness had gone, but the fragility was back, worrying him.

'More than ever,' he had told her, almost violently. 'More than anything.'

He'd asked her, soon after that, if she might like to consider joining him at the agency, had been both surprised and delighted by her eagerness to agree and, as time passed, greatly impressed by her contribution. Clare had turned out to be both a natural organizer and an ace at spotting flaws. In less than two weeks, she'd been confident enough to take over most administrative and bookkeeping tasks, leaving Novak free to focus on persuading at least a few of his formerly regular clients – two divorce lawyers, one of the big agencies who farmed out work, and Robin Allbeury – that he was back on track.

Enrolling in night school, Clare had completed courses in IT, bookkeeping and business administration. She liked learning, enjoyed using her new skills to reorganize and market the agency while managing to bring down overheads and, to Novak's relief and gratitude, helping them to break even for the first time and, soon after that, to move into profit. Still eager, she had urged her husband into some extracurricular studies of his own so that he might become an ABI member.

'Respectability and contacts,' she'd said, 'can't hurt.'

'That's what Robin says,' Novak told her.

'Oh, well,' Clare said wryly. 'If Robin says so.'

She had never felt entirely certain about Robin Allbeury or convinced by his unusual, unorthodox and apparently altruistic activities, felt that he had to be concealing his true motives. If he was, Novak had told her, he hadn't yet found out what they were, and, to be frank, he wasn't sure that he wanted to find out so long as Allbeury went on helping people.

'Women,' Clare had said.

'He helps us pay our bills,' Novak had pointed out.

She'd had no argument with that.

'And he thinks you're a remarkable person.'

'Why should he think that?'

'Because he's a clever man,' Novak had said.

Two years after that, heartache had returned for them both with the death, at birth, of their longed-for first child. Clare, alone at home and taking a bath, had passed out before being able to

13

summon help, and their son, born with frightening speed, had suffered breathing difficulties and had not survived. Grief had poleaxed them. For a week after Clare's discharge from hospital, neither she nor Novak had moved from the flat, unable to eat or sleep. Robin Allbeury, concerned by the lack of response to his messages, had come to the flat and all but taken over, shopping and cooking, alerting Clare's father to the tragedy (though Malcolm Killin had himself been ill with pneumonia at the time, and unable to help) and helping Novak to organize the small, sad funeral.

After the hideousness of the inquest, they'd picked themselves up with agonizing slowness, had forced themselves to visit a bereavement counsellor but found her of limited help. Work, predictably, had helped the most, and time. Months passed and they began to throw themselves more vigorously into the agency, to build again. But nothing was the same any more, everything felt contaminated by sorrow, shame or fear. If something made them laugh, they felt guilty because their child was in his grave. If they made love, they clung to each other like swimmers close to drowning. If they saw an infant in a pushchair, the force of their envy cut off their ability to breathe.

Yet even that had passed.

'Would you mind,' Clare asked one morning, almost a year after their loss, 'if I took on a part-time nursing job? Just two or three evenings a week.'

Novak had been startled. 'I didn't know you were even thinking about nursing.'

'I wasn't, till Maureen phoned last week.'

Maureen Donnelly, a former colleague of Clare's, had transferred to Waltham General in Essex two years before to be closer to her father, who had Parkinson's disease. Mindful, in the past, not to overdo shop talk when she and Clare got together, Maureen had lately noticed her old friend becoming increasingly keen to listen to A&E news and was happy enough to oblige by talking her through some of the more interesting cases that had come through her department.

Nick Parry was one such case, a twenty-eight-year-old paraplegic who had come in the previous month after his adapted car had been involved in an accident on the North Circular. Struck by the young man's courage and sense of humour, and upon hearing

14

that one of his favourite part-time carers was about to be sent back to New Zealand by the Home Office, Maureen had promised to scout around for a replacement on his behalf.

'Maureen thought we might get on,' Clare told Novak, 'so I went to visit him.'

'Why didn't you tell me?'

'Because I thought you'd either get excited for me and then upset if it didn't work out, or worried about it and upset if it did.'

'Apparently it did,' Novak said. 'Work out.'

'If you don't mind.'

He'd looked at her for a moment. 'Do you still not really know me? I'd never stop you doing anything you wanted to do.' He had paused, then quickly asked the question suddenly uppermost in his mind. 'Do you want to leave the agency?'

'No,' Clare had replied decisively. 'Never. The agency's what healed me.' She had paused 'And you, of course.'

'*You* healed you,' Novak had told her.

Clare had kissed him then, leaned very close and laid her lips gently against his mouth. 'You're the best, Mike,' she said. 'You know that?'

'I just love you,' he said.

5

'So what do you think, Lizzie?'

It was the second Monday of March – two days after Sophie's seventh birthday party – and Andrew France, her agent, had just telephoned Lizzie at the house in Marlow to tell her that Vicuna Press, her publishers, had come through with their very handsome share of an offer – made in conjunction with the Food and Drink Channel – for a new Lizzie Piper book and TV series that would, if she accepted, take her on a European tour, tasting and creating new recipes for publication.

'It sounds marvellous.' Lizzie leaned back in the leather swivel chair in her study. 'I can't quite take it in.'

'It really is quite extraordinarily exciting.' Andrew sounded gratified by her response.

'You haven't said yes?'

'Of course not.' The agent's tone became a touch wary. 'But I must admit I imagined it an almost foregone conclusion.' He paused. 'You do want this, Lizzie, don't you? Christopher certainly seemed sure you'd be leaping up and down.'

Lizzie was silent for an instant. 'When did you speak to Christopher?'

'Less than two hours ago. While you were still out on the school run. I know I asked him to let me give you the news myself, but I felt sure he wouldn't be able to resist saying something.'

Lizzie heard the surprise in Andrew's voice. 'He was called to London before I got back,' she said casually. 'There's probably a note somewhere.'

'That explains it,' Andrew said.

'So what exactly did Christopher say about this offer?'

16

'Not much,' Andrew replied. 'Except that he really was very happy for you. Which, if I may say so, Lizzie, you don't seem to be.'

'Oh, I am.' Lizzie tried to sound it. 'Of course I am.'

'So can I go back to them, clinch it?'

She hesitated. 'Give me a little while, Andrew, please. I can't just say yes to something as big, or at least as time-consuming, as this, without talking to the whole family.' She paused. 'Could you get a few more details for me? When, for instance, and how long, and which countries?'

'Yes, of course,' Andrew said. 'Though naturally all that'll be open for discussion. No one's going to expect you to drop everything and fly off, Lizzie.'

'I couldn't,' she said.

'No,' Andrew said. 'I know you couldn't. So does Howard.'

Lizzie knew that Andrew was right about Howard Dunn, her editor, but there was no certainty that the television people would be as sympathetic or obliging.

'Quite right to be cautious, my darling,' Christopher said later that night, after he'd returned from London, and they were sharing a nightcap in the drawing room. 'Though I expect they'll all be flexible. They want you happy, after all, clearly.'

The children were all in bed, and Lizzie was confident that both Edward and Sophie were sound asleep, though it was unlikely that Jack would be sleeping. He often slept badly, but coped with insomnia by having two Walkmans by his bedside, one loaded with music, the other with an audio book, so that all he had to do was stick on his headphones and press a button.

What Jack did not appreciate these days was too many night-time visits by either of his parents to check on him.

'If I have a problem,' he told them, 'I'll let you know.'

'I daresay Vicuna would prefer me to be happy,' Lizzie answered Christopher now. 'But TV people have rigid schedules, and unions, and weather conditions to consider, all of which I'm sure they'd expect me to fit into.'

'And which I'm sure you'll manage to, as you always manage most things, my love. Brilliantly.'

Christopher was nothing if not charming, had always been that,

17

and supportive, too, of Lizzie and her talents, and she had almost always been grateful for that.

Gratitude had, in fact, been a large part of the package when she had first met and fallen in love with him. A car crash in her early thirties had left Angela Piper with ugly scarring on her left breast and abdomen. The priority at the time of the accident had been to keep her alive, after which no one had seemed to understand how desperately the pretty brunette had felt about her disfigurement – not even Maurice Piper, her husband, who had frankly been too busy rejoicing at having his wife still with him and nine-year-old Lizzie. But Angela had found herself unable to cope with what she regarded as great ugliness and, ashamed for what she saw as her own ingratitude and superficiality, she had stumbled into deep, long-term clinical depression, during which time Lizzie had grown into an isolated teenager, looking forward to escaping to university.

Ten years later, Maurice had suffered a fatal heart attack, Angela had gone into free-fall and Lizzie, reading English and enjoying freedom in Sussex, had felt compelled to return home. Bleakness had spread out before her like fog; an end, she had felt, to learning and fun and friends, until Angela's psychologist, Stuart Bride, had suggested that perhaps if someone were able to improve the old scars that clearly still disturbed his patient, it might do more for her mind than years of therapy.

Christopher Wade – tall, impressive, with shaggy blond hair and piercing grey eyes behind round steel spectacles, a man who wore hats and doffed them regularly for ladies – had swept into the Pipers' world with a blast of kindness and, in the fullness of time, at least a degree of healing. And Lizzie, thirteen years younger, had been there to witness it all, the gentleness, commonsense and skill, as well as the charm, so that when the surgeon had first asked her to lunch, soon after her mother's second successful operation, she had been intensely pleased to accept.

'Be careful,' Angela had said when Lizzie had told her about it.

'It's only lunch,' Lizzie had said.

'No such thing between an attractive older man and a beautiful innocent.'

'Not quite innocent, Mum, and hardly beautiful.' Lizzie liked her blue eyes and blond hair well enough, but her nose was rather sharp and her legs, in her opinion, too short. 'Certainly not when you consider what he must be used to.'

'Damaged goods,' Angela had said, wry yet serene, 'is what he's used to.'

Lizzie and Christopher had married the following year, the bride, back at her studies, now at London University, the groom proud and happy, guiding his young wife out of St Paul's, Knightsbridge into their new life in his large garden flat in Holland Park. An almost undiluted marital joy that had lasted until first son Edward was three, baby Jack was one, they had just bought the house, and the nearest thing to an imperfection in Lizzie's world was Edward's allergy to dogs and cats.

The other – very much less attractive – side of her husband of which Lizzie would, in time, become all too aware, had manifested itself the first time in little more than a glint of darkness, like a small warning slick of brake fluid beneath a car, an alert of trouble to come.

It had happened in the summer of 1993, following an evening spent celebrating the news that, after several years of writing magazine articles, Lizzie's first book, *Fooling Around . . . In the Kitchen* had been accepted for publication by Vicuna Press.

Christopher had come home from London, drained by hours in the operating theatres at the Beauchamp Clinic (of which he was a director) and St Clare's Hospital, but bearing a bouquet of white roses, and had told Lizzie how very clever she was, how proud of her he was, and what a brilliant career she was going to have. And he'd insisted, despite his fatigue, on taking her out to dinner in Bray, and it had all been wonderful.

Until about three in the morning, when he had woken Lizzie by switching on his bedside light, pulling up her nightdress and determinedly fondling her between her thighs until he was sure she was properly conscious.

'I'm half asleep.' She'd smiled up at him but pushed away his hand.

'I don't mind,' he'd said, and put it back.

The kiss had been the first thing that had jarred because of its roughness, though in a second or two, its intensity had swept away the last of her sleepiness, arousing her, and she'd kissed him back with equal passion.

'God, Lizzie,' he had said, and then, right away, begun making love to her, and that had been uncharacteristically rough too.

'Go easy, darling,' she'd said, after a few moments.

'Be quiet,' he'd told her, and gone straight on.

Lizzie had told herself afterwards that nothing much had happened, that it had just been a blip, something to forget about as soon as possible. After all, nothing major had occurred. Just that slight – *not so slight, not really* – roughness.

And those words.

'*Be quiet.*'

Christopher never spoke to her like that.

She had broached it next morning, before breakfast.

'That was unusual,' she said. 'Last night.'

'Unusual?' he repeated.

'Not the lovemaking,' she said. 'That was lovely.'

'I thought so.'

'Except,' she said.

'Except what?' Christopher had asked.

'It was a bit rough,' she said.

'I'm sorry,' he said. 'I really am, Lizzie.'

'It's all right,' she said. 'It was just a surprise, that's all.'

Something had worked in Christopher's face for a moment. A hint of disappointment, Lizzie had thought.

'I'd hoped,' he had said, and stopped.

'What did you hope?' Lizzie had asked, curiously.

'Nothing,' he had said. 'It doesn't matter.'

Six books and another child later, while Lizzie was still trying to work through the logistics of how she could possibly accept the offer Andrew France had brought her – in view of her reluctance to leave the children for any length of time – Christopher promptly rendered it not only possible, but also almost unavoidable.

'I'll come with you,' he told her, 'with the children and Gilly.'

'How could you?' Lizzie thought about the daily demands on her husband.

'It's already as good as organized.' He saw her face. 'Only in theory, obviously. And provided you don't object, of course.'

It was a pleasant day, for March, and they were outside on the

20

stone terrace at the top of the garden, wrapped in woollen sweaters, drinking coffee.

'For one thing,' Christopher went on, 'you know that if I'm involved, no one will dare bugger you about on the special needs front.'

That was so true she could think of no comment to make.

'And, of course, it could be terrific news for the charity.' Christopher gave Lizzie a challenging look over the top of his spectacles. 'Especially if you'd consider donating some of your royalties.'

'Oh.' Lizzie was startled.

'You wouldn't mind too much, would you, darling? Dalia was very excited when I mentioned the idea to her.'

If there really were a way to get not blood, but cash, from a stone, then Dalia Weinberg, one of the mainstays at the HANDS head office in Regent Street, was the person to do it. She was in her sixties now, but no less energetic or consumed by enthusiasm than a person half her age.

'You told Dalia before me?' Lizzie asked.

'Sorry. Got carried away.' He paused. 'You don't have to say yes to the donation. It's just an idea.'

'It would be pretty churlish of me to refuse now, wouldn't it?'

'Not at all.'

'Hm.' Lizzie watched a pair of sparrows in Sophie's birdbath a few yards away.

'HANDS aside, though,' Christopher said, 'there'd be another huge plus if you were to agree to all this. Certainly from my point-of-view.'

'Which is?'

'Us,' he said.

Lizzie said nothing, though the meaning behind that single word chilled her. Because as sincere as Christopher's stated motives undoubtedly were – a chance for a family trip that would benefit HANDS – there was deceit in it too. Speaking to Dalia before tackling her, neatly cutting off any avenues of escape she might have thought of.

The fact was, she probably *would* have done just that, asked Andrew to apologize profusely to Howard Dunn and the Food and Drink people, but to tell them she simply couldn't manage it.

Too late for that now, and Lizzie decided she wouldn't be

21

surprised if Christopher hadn't already told Dalia that it was safe to leak a little something about the venture to the press, because that was his style when he really wanted something. It was what had made him such an enormous success; determination and – couched in all that charm and courtesy – a degree of ruthlessness.

So because of that, not only Dalia, but also Vicuna and the TV people would all be extra delighted because she was going to donate part of her royalties, which meant more positive press and media coverage.

And soon, too, all the children and Gilly would be bouncing with excitement, and perhaps Angela – recently engaged to William Archer, a lovely retired stockbroker – might want to join them at some stage of the journey, and Andrew would, she supposed, be trying to get them a table at The Ivy or The Caprice to celebrate.

But all Lizzie could think about – instead of the delights of the travel, and the new creative challenge, and the compliment that was being paid her by both Vicuna and the Food and Drink Channel – was the prospect of being trapped in all those hotel rooms with her husband, surrounded on all sides by family and closely scrutinizing colleagues.

And yes, it did chill her.

It was a very long time since she had felt so trapped.

6

On a sunny April afternoon in the late 90s, Joanne Patston – until recently a customer services assistant at the Chingford branch of the Savers Mutual Building Society – and her husband, Tony, a mechanic with his own one-man garage near Walthamstow, had brought their new baby daughter home for the first time to their semi-detached house in Chingford Hatch.

Her name was Irina, she was a three-month-old Romanian orphan, and her homecoming had been duly celebrated by her ecstatic adoptive parents, next-door-neighbours Paul and Nicola Georgiou, and by Irina's overjoyed new grandmother, Sandra Finch.

'Isn't she the most beautiful baby you've ever seen?' Sandra had cooed over her daughter's shoulder, as Joanne cradled Irina. 'Eyes just like black cherries.'

'Even darker than mine,' Paul Georgiou had remarked to his wife.

'Intelligent eyes,' Tony Patston said.

'Her hands are so tiny,' Joanne marvelled.

'Delicate fingers,' Tony said.

Irina kicked her bootied feet.

'Maybe she'll be a ballerina,' her new father said.

'Or a footballer.' Paul laughed.

Tony, who Joanne had once said – looking through the eyes of love – resembled Will Carling, threw his neighbour a look of mild disgust, downed the last of his champagne, went over to their Ikea sideboard and picked up a can of Fosters.

'I don't care what Irina does,' Joanne said, 'so long as she's healthy and happy.'

'Absolutely,' Nicola agreed.

'I can't believe it,' Sandra said. 'My first grandchild.' She bent to stroke Irina's dark hair. 'I'm so happy for you, Joanne.'

'What about me?' Tony asked. 'I mean, I did have something to do with this.'

'Of course you did,' his mother-in-law told him. 'I'm happy for you both.'

'How about a toast?' Paul suggested, raising his lager in the air.

'Tony?' Joanne looked at her husband.

'Give her to me.' Tony put down his beer and stooped to take the baby.

'Support her head,' Nicola said automatically.

'He knows,' Joanne said.

'Course I know,' Tony said. 'Been practising for long enough.'

'The toast,' Paul reminded him.

Tony cleared his throat. 'Our daughter.' His voice cracked with emotion.

'Is that it?' Paul said.

Tony ignored him. 'It's taken a long time, and a lot of trouble,' he went on. 'But trouble's not really the right word, is it, Jo?'

Joanne shook her head, tears rising.

'Because nothing would have been too much to get us to this moment. Being able to bring this little one home to where she belongs.' Tony paused. 'Our Irina.'

They had broken laws in their own country and in Irina's and, so far as they knew, all manner of international laws, but both Tony and Joanne had ceased caring about that a long time ago. They cared about not getting found out, and they cared about keeping and bringing up Irina as their own. And to hell with the law.

Joanne's motivations had been straightforward. Yearning for motherhood for years, thwarted by her husband's infertility, she'd become desperate enough to do almost anything. Tony's motives were not as clear-cut. Made resentful by what he saw – despite Joanne's reassurances – as his failure, he'd come to view her unhappiness as a reproach. The idea of sperm dona-tion had offended him and having, after lengthy soul-searching, agreed to adopt a baby, he'd been swiftly put off by the inten-sity and personal nature of the questions posed by the authori-ties.

24

'They'll never let us adopt,' he'd told Joanne flatly after one early meeting. 'Not once they get hold of my record.'

'But that was so long ago,' his wife had said.

'I was a drunk who hit people,' Tony had said, uncharacteristically realistic.

'You've never hit me,' Joanne had said.

'And I'd be a bloody good father,' Tony had added. 'But I've still got a record.'

'What if we just come out and tell them?' Joanne had ventured. 'Before they find out for themselves. We could say you haven't had a drink for years.'

'That'd be a lie.'

'I don't mind lying.'

'I don't, either,' Tony had said, 'except all they'd have to do is go round the Crown and Anchor and they'd know.'

They'd all but given up when, one evening some months later, they'd watched the repeat of a TV programme about Romanian orphans in the post-Ceausescu era. Even while they were still watching, Joanne had been surprised that Tony – who hated documentaries – had neither switched channels nor even got up to fetch a beer.

Till afterwards. Then he'd opened a can right away, drunk the whole thing, before sitting down again on the sofa beside Joanne, and taking her hand.

'Why not us?' he'd said.

'Us what?'

'That.' He'd nodded at the TV. 'This could be it. This could give you what you want more than anything in the world. And me.'

'But all the assessments and stuff,' Joanne reminded him. 'You hated all that.'

'This might be different. We'd be helping one of those poor little babies, wouldn't we, getting them out of one of those fucking horrible places. Maybe the people over there wouldn't be so bloody fussy.'

'I don't know, Tony.'

'Think about it, love,' he said. 'A kid of our own. We'd be helping a child.' He'd paused. 'I might even start feeling like a real man again.'

'You've always been that,' Joanne had said softly.

*

25

She'd begun researching the possibilities next lunchtime at the library near her branch of Savers Mutual, discovering – with such ease that Tony said later that it was fate, that they'd been *meant* to see that programme – the Overseas Adoption Helpline.

'Mind what you tell them, though,' Tony had cautioned. 'Tell them you just want to ask questions for now.' He paused, saw her expression. 'What?'

'Nothing,' Joanne said. 'Except you said "you", not "we".'

Tony had smiled easily. 'You're in charge of this, Jo. For now, anyway.' He'd paused. 'Not too much for you, is it?'

'Of course not,' Joanne had said quickly.

She'd taken him at his word, had begun asking questions, received more answers and assistance than she could have believed possible, though each snippet of help seemed to come wrapped in a great blanket of information.

'There's so much reading,' she told Tony one weekend.

He'd glanced at the piles of pamphlets and photocopies and printouts from the computer Joanne had taken to using in her lunch hours at an Internet café.

'I can't handle all this junk,' he'd said.

'It isn't junk. It's our path to being parents.'

He'd laughed at that, told her she sounded like she'd swallowed one of the books she'd been reading. 'Bottom line, Jo,' he said. 'That's all I'm interested in.'

So Joanne had gone on with it until all her preliminary questions had been answered, when her head was jammed with hundreds of facts about practical and ethical aspects of 'inter-country' adoption, *thousands* of facts, cautions about conflicts and pitfalls to avoid and choices to be made.

Forms to be completed.

'Oh, no.' Tony had been emphatic. 'We're not going through that again.'

'We have to, Tony.' The relief had already gone. 'Obviously.'

'The only obvious thing to me is that we'd be great parents.'

'But we still have to convince the authorities of that,' Joanne reasoned.

'And they'll find out about my record and we'll be back to sodding square one.' Tony's face had reddened. 'I thought I'd made myself clear, Jo. We're prepared to help some little no-hope kid from some God-forsaken country and that's that.'

'But it's not that simple.' Joanne had tried not to cry.

'It's got to be,' her husband had told her. 'Simple, or no kid.' He'd stood up, his face redder, his eyes harder. 'You want this, you find a way.' He was already halfway back to the kitchen door. 'Get back on the Internet. Find someone who understands what we want.' He paused. 'Tell them we'll pay, if you like.'

'Pay?' She had been startled. 'For a baby? That's horrible.'

'Not if it works.'

'We don't have enough money.' Joanne could hardly believe she'd said that.

'Find out how much it would cost.' Tony had opened the door. 'If it's not too much, I'll pay. I'm not mean, Jo.'

'I know you're not, but—'

'Find out, Joanne. Or drop it.'

She was on the verge of giving up again when, suddenly, she hit on the website that led her to the '*someone*' Tony had so airily told her to find. An adoption 'practitioner' claiming to have legitimate links with agencies on three continents, and specializing in couples feeling let down by the 'system' because of age, class or other irrelevant and often petty considerations.

Too easy, Joanne thought, trying not to get too excited as she clicked on the e-mail address offered on the site – doing no more, she promised herself, than dipping her toes in the water.

Which was warm and congenial, as it turned out, and came in the form of a middle-aged, bespectacled Scandinavian doctor named Marie Jenssen who told Joanne she was in charge of the UK 'intake' on behalf of the international operation, and who appeared to want nothing more than to help her and Tony achieve their hearts' desire and offer a new life to a child in need.

With Dr Jenssen, there were no long interviews and a minimum of forms to fill in. Just one meeting in the coffee shop of a hotel off Russell Square, a contract between themselves, and money to be found – such great, alarming wads of cash that Joanne was continually afraid Tony might call a halt.

But then their baby was located.

Irina Camelia Karolyi. Five weeks old, parentless and currently in a Bucharest orphanage. No relatives. No prospects. No hope.

'She's so beautiful,' Joanne had said softly, staring at the photograph Dr Jenssen had sent of a tiny baby girl with huge dark eyes, looking for all the world as if she really was smiling from her crib.

'She's gorgeous,' Tony had said. 'I could really love her, Jo.'

From that moment on, he had become every bit as unstoppable as Joanne. While she paved the way with Sandra, the neighbours, a few friends and the building society, preparing them for the arrival of their adopted child, keeping the real truth from them all, Tony worked like a demon at Patston Motors to build up the ever outward-flowing supply of cash – even when the exact nature of what he was paying for became less clear.

'You should have made her itemize this,' Joanne said once, after Tony had handed over yet another five hundred pounds to Marie Jenssen.

'You know she wouldn't,' Tony had told her. 'You know the score by now.'

She did, which had begun to trouble her even more than the frightening expenses. The '*score*', as Tony had put it, was illegal adoption. The money, Joanne feared, was going towards whatever it took to buy visas, bribe officials in God-alone-knew how many countries. She'd read about illegal trafficking in babies, had been sickened by the notion that anyone could be so wicked or desperate as to sell their child, let alone buy one.

'Do you think we're being wicked?' she asked Tony one night. 'Doing this?'

'No, I bloody don't.' He'd been angry at the suggestion. 'We're saving that baby, Jo. We're helping Irina.'

Any lingering doubts disappeared the instant they saw Irina being carried towards them by Marie Jenssen at King's Cross Station on the last Friday of the following April – though Joanne had experienced one final thrill of terror, imagining a horde of policemen descending the instant Marie handed the baby over.

No police.

Just a little girl, by then just over three months old. With immense dark eyes that had gazed, with intensity, up at her new mother and father.

'Hello, princess,' Tony had said softly to her.

Joanne, beyond words, had held her breath.

And Irina had smiled.

'Happy, Joanne?' Marie had asked, gently.

'Not the word for it.' Joanne's voice had sounded almost strangled.

'Tony?' Marie had looked at him.

'Same.' Tony had shaken his head. 'I can't believe it.'

'It's true,' Marie told him.

She'd taken her leave just moments later, throwing Joanne into fresh panic.

'I need to know more,' she'd said. 'Learn more about her.'

'You know all you ever will,' Marie had answered. 'You know that, Joanne. It's the way of these adoptions. Better for you all.'

'Marie's right, love,' Tony had backed Marie up. 'Irina's ours now. That's all we need to know.'

'What if she gets ill?' The baby squirmed in her arms. 'Surely we need to be able to find out her family history.' She already knew the answer, had broached the question before.

'Irina's a healthy little child, Joanne,' Marie reassured her. 'Your child now, as Tony said.'

'Stop worrying, Jo.' Tony had stroked the baby's cheek. 'Enjoy her.'

Joanne had bent her head, closed her eyes and breathed in the smell of her new baby daughter.

By the time she had raised her face again, Marie Jenssen had gone.

7

Within an hour of the body on the allotment being found, Helen Shipley, a thirty-three-year-old, currently hung-over, detective inspector with AMIT NW – having responded to her pager while picking up her dry-cleaning during her lunch hour – had been taking her first long, sickening look inside the white Incitent with her boss DCI Trevor Kirby, and not long after that the Home Office duty pathologist, Stephanie Patel, had joined them.

Less than three hours later, John Bolsover, an assistant supermarket manager who had reported his wife missing over a week earlier, had assisted with the identification. As grief-stricken and distraught for his children as he appeared, once Lynne's sister and neighbour had both declared him a first-class bully, Bolsover had rapidly become prime suspect. Depressed and under her husband's thumb as her sister had been, Pam Wakefield said, Lynne had, now and again, summoned the strength to fight back to a point where he would bellow at and frequently punch her.

'What exactly are you telling me, Pam?' Shipley had asked in the shattered woman's living room.

'Isn't it obvious?'

'I need to hear it in your words,' Shipley said.

'I'm saying I think he probably went too far.' Pam Wakefield had stared with harsh, tearful openness at the grey-eyed, cropped haired policewoman. 'I'm saying that John Bolsover' – she spoke his name as if the words were poison in her mouth – 'probably bashed my sister's head in and then dumped her in that place and threw sacks onto her.'

Probably. The rub.

'Nail this one smartish,' DCI Kirby, a stout, grey-haired bachelor from Wolverhampton, had told Shipley.

Easier said, Shipley felt, with not the slightest sign of wavering by Bolsover, let alone confession, after three long interviews at AMIT NW's temporary housing in a drab brick building a mile from Claris Green (temporary, like the unit itself, for more than a year now, but feeling increasingly like home), and the insistence of the suspect's solicitor that his client should now either be charged or allowed to go home and grieve with his family.

'We're still nowhere,' Shipley told the team, five days into the enquiry, assembled in the incident room. 'I've got a brief telling me to shit or get off the pot, and not a bloody shred of real evidence. No witness, no forensics, no murder weapon, not a damned thing.'

Three massive blows had been struck in the fatal attack, but Dr Patel had informed Shipley that the first blow inflicted had been sufficiently violent to have caused death, suggesting that the two subsequent blows might perhaps have been struck in rage or frenzy. The murder weapon, the pathologist felt, had probably been a small rock picked out of a garden or park in an area of London clay, perhaps not too far from where the victim had been found, but the fingertip search at the crime scene had found nothing but a handful of broken beer bottles – smudged prints only – a litter of empty, kicked-about soft drink cans – likewise – crumpled crisp wrappers, a couple of discarded syringes and no usable prints from shoes or boots.

That was the hell of it. As strong a suspect as Bolsover was, that search and those of his house, his Honda and his desk and locker at work had all proven fruitless. And so much time having passed between Lynne's death and the discovery of her body, the chances of retrieving any potentially damning evidence from Bolsover's clothing or person had of course been long gone by the time Shipley and her team had first spoken to him.

'Nothing yet on door-to-door,' said DS Geoff Gregory now.

'And still no one to disprove that Bolsover was home,' said Ally King, a pretty black detective constable on loan from CID.

At the time of Lynne's murder – a Tuesday, while the children had been at school – her husband, off work because of a bad back, claimed to have been snoozing in front of the TV at home, and even Valerie Golding, who admitted that she'd have liked nothing

31

better than to be able to discredit her neighbour's tale, had said she'd been out at Brent Cross herself for much of that day.

Shipley sighed and looked, for the hundredth time, at the white-board with its dearth of alternative suspects. No lovers – either John's or Lynne's – unearthed. No one with a bitter grudge against Lynne. No scraps with other parents at the children's school, no complaints of being stalked, no recent robberies at the house.

Not even any report of an argument heard that day between husband and wife. Though even if the neighbours had heard yelling or screaming, it would not have been conclusive proof that John Bolsover had killed her.

Lynne's face smiled at Shipley from one photograph.

Another face, dreadful in its bloody death mask, but still hers.

Lynne Frances Bolsover. Twenty-nine years old. Mother of two young kiddies.

Wiped out by person or persons unknown.

'We do know it was him, though, don't we?' DC King said.

'We know sod all, Ally,' Shipley said.

DS Gregory, middle-aged and overweight, stood up. 'Better get back out there, then, find something to nail the bastard with.'

'Sooner the better,' Shipley said.

8

For the first month after her new parents had brought her home, Irina had smiled an amazing amount of the time, hardly ever crying. But then, as if she had perhaps not previously comprehended her power to demand anything from life, the baby had begun not just to cry, but to scream, piercingly, whenever she wanted either milk or a clean nappy or to be held or to be put down.

'Can't you stop her doing that?' Tony had asked his wife.

'Of course I can't stop her,' Joanne had said distractedly. 'If I could, she wouldn't still be crying, would she?' She'd looked at Irina's bright red cheeks. 'I'm getting worried about her, Tony. We're going to have to take her to a doctor.'

'I thought we were going to wait,' her husband had said.

They had agreed that, with the exception of normal check-ups and vaccination visits at their local GP's surgery, they would, if the need arose, go to a private paediatrician rather than take any potential risks with the NHS. One more bill or two, Tony had said blithely at the time, wouldn't make much difference with all he'd forked out already.

Now that the moment was here, he wasn't quite so convinced.

'No point overreacting, Jo.'

'We don't want to take chances, though, do we?'

'You said she hasn't got a temperature.'

'She's very warm.'

'You'd be warm if you were bawling like that.'

'She isn't just bawling,' Joanne had said. 'Something's upsetting her.'

'Maybe it's you?'

'Me?'

Tony looked at his wife's appalled, anxious eyes.

'Yeah,' he said. 'Okay.'

'Take her privately?' Joanne had looked at him expectantly.

'Yeah, why not?' He'd paused. 'Just this once, Jo, okay?'

'Of course.' She would have agreed to anything at that moment, with the awful sound of her baby's crying reverberating in her head, and the feel of her warm little body stiffening with each wail, and she knew that Tony didn't mean it, that if Irina ever needed to see a paediatrician again he wouldn't mind a bit, not if their daughter's health was at stake.

Their daughter's health, according to Dr Anna Mellor in Wimpole Street, was excellent.

'She's a lovely little girl,' the doctor had declared after a thorough examination, during most of which Irina had demonstrated her talent for screaming. 'Very vocal, I agree.' She had beamed at Joanne and Tony. 'But clearly, that's simply her nature.'

'You mean she's going to go on like this?' Tony had asked.

Anna Mellor had twinkled at Joanne. 'Bit of a shock to the system for father.'

'It's just that she was so quiet until a few weeks ago,' Joanne said loyally.

'Maybe she hadn't discovered her voice,' the doctor said. 'Anyway—' she went on briskly '—I certainly can't see any nasty underlying problems, which is surely what you were both so concerned about. That's the main thing.'

'That's wonderful,' Joanne had said, hugely relieved.

As if on cue, Irina had begun crying again.

'She will grow out of it, won't she, doctor?' Tony asked.

'Of course she will,' the older woman told him, 'eventually.' She stood up, smiled again at Irina. 'Clearly you have a little girl with a good, strong character.'

'Great,' Tony said.

'Cheer up, Mr Patston. You'll get used to it.'

Bolstered by Dr Mellor's reassurances, Joanne had begun to take Irina's shrieking in her stride. It was, after all, what motherhood was all about, an integral part of what she had hungered after for so long.

'I can't stand it,' Tony said, coming into the nursery two weeks after their visit to Wimpole Street.

'She'll stop soon.' Joanne was sitting in the nursing chair her mother had bought them, rocking.

'No, I mean it, Jo. I really can't stand this *bloody* racket a second longer.'

Joanne had looked up in surprise. 'Take it easy, Tony.'

'She's doing my head in, Jo.' He put both hands up to his temples, began pacing. 'I've never heard a baby like this. It's not normal.'

'Of course she's normal.' Joanne felt defensive. 'And you've only not heard it because you've never lived with a baby before.'

'I'm beginning to wish I wasn't living with one now,' Tony said, stomping out.

That was just the start of it. Irina's wailing, her father claimed, went right through him and made his head bang, so as the weeks went on, as soon as the baby began to cry Tony left her almost entirely to her mother. If Irina cried at night, he stuffed cotton wool in his ears, pulled a pillow over his head and yelled at Joanne to shut the kid up. If the baby screamed in the evenings or at weekends, he went out into the garden, or next door to see Paul, or, failing that, to the Crown and Anchor.

'You can't just walk out every time your daughter cries,' Joanne told him.

'Watch me,' he said, and did just that.

One Sunday morning at the end of August, when Irina had been with them for four months, Joanne had just got into the bath when she heard Irina begin crying.

'Joanne!' Tony yelled from downstairs.

She started to stand, then changed her mind, sat back down and leaned back instead, shutting her eyes. *He's her father*, she told herself. Maybe she was making a mistake running to Irina each time she cried, maybe she ought to give Tony a real chance to take care of his daughter.

Irina was still crying.

'Joanne!'

She opened her eyes. 'I'm in the bath,' she called.

'Bloody hell!'

Irina's crying grew louder. Joanne heard Tony's tread on the staircase, picked up the bar of soap and tried to relax.

35

The crying became shrieking.

Joanne put down the soap. 'Tony?'

The shrieking grew louder, like hysteria.

'Oh, my God.' Joanne lurched from the bath, sending water cascading over the side, grabbed her towel and ran to the nursery.

Tony was inside, holding the baby.

Shaking the baby.

'*Tony*!' She ran to him, let the towel fall, grabbed Irina from him, saw that his face was red with anger. 'What are you *doing*?' She held the baby close, felt her small body clenching, vibrating with distress, little arms slippery against her own wet body. 'What were you *thinking* of?'

'Shutting her up,' he said. 'That's what I was thinking of.'

'You were *shaking* her – it's *dangerous* to do that, you *know* that!'

'You didn't come,' he said. 'I had to do something.'

From then on, the more impatient Tony became with Irina, the more she wailed when he so much as came near her. Aggrieved, he either ignored her altogether or picked her up in a challenging manner which fuelled her distress. Disappointment and irritation turned into resentment.

'She's not nearly as pretty as she was,' he told Joanne.

'I think she's beautiful.'

'Not as bright, either.'

'Just because she cries doesn't mean she isn't bright.'

'I hope that bloody Jenssen woman didn't land us with a dud.'

'She's not a used car, Tony,' Joanne protested. 'She's our daughter. And if she ever did have problems, I'd only love her more.'

'You're such a romantic,' he ridiculed.

'I'm a mother,' she said.

'Not a real one,' Tony said.

Joanne's greatest fear, all through that first year of motherhood, had been that Tony might decide he wanted to get rid of Irina, but, consoling herself with the knowledge that that would hardly be feasible, she had determined to take the best possible care of the baby without provoking her husband or leaving him alone with her. If Irina so much as whimpered, Joanne flew to her side. If she

36

had to go somewhere without Irina, she took her to her mother's house in Edmonton.

While Tony was at Patston Motors, Joanne's time with Irina passed contentedly, and then, of course, there were several more hours of peace most evenings when he was at the Crown and Anchor. Except that because alcohol had always tended to feed Tony's aggressive side, Joanne had begun to dread his return from the pub, and her own tension had transmitted itself to Irina, so that invariably, when the front door banged on his arrival, Irina was already crying.

The first time Tony actually hit Irina (three days after her first birthday, a day on which he'd bought presents and fussed around her like any doting daddy) he wept afterwards with mortification, swore he'd never do such a terrible thing again, but the baby's screams heightened soon after, and his anger returned.

'If you ever, *ever* hit her again,' Joanne warned, 'I swear I'll report you.'

'Oh, yeah?' he jeered. 'Who to?'

'The police, social services, whoever.'

'And then what?' he said. 'Even if you don't care about getting into trouble, the first thing they'll do is take her away, and you'll never see her again – which quite frankly wouldn't bother me all that much.'

'It'll bother you all right—' Joanne's voice trembled '—if you end up inside and they get to find out what you've done.'

'Shut up, Joanne!' Tony yelled.

She stood her ground for once. 'Everyone knows what happens in prison to men who hurt little kids,' she said.

He'd settled down a bit after that. 'No need to blow everything out of proportion.'

'You *hit* our daughter.'

'It was just a little smack.'

'She's a *baby*.'

'I know,' he'd said. 'And I'm sorry, and it won't happen again.'

'Better not,' Joanne had told him.

'It's down to you too,' Tony had said. 'You keep her under better control, and I'll do the same with my temper.'

Joanne had wanted to believe him.

9

One night in the sixth year of their marriage, while Lizzie and Christopher had been making love in the bedroom of their Holland Park flat, Christopher had ducked his head suddenly, and bitten her left breast, bitten it so violently that Lizzie had cried out in shock as well as pain.

'My God, Christopher!' She put out both her hands and pushed him away, shoved him so hard that he almost fell off the bed. 'What the hell do you think you're *doing*?'

It was two or so hours since they had left the Groucho Club where Vicuna Books had thrown a launch party to celebrate the publication of *Fooling Around . . . In the Kitchen*, an evening during which Christopher had stayed modestly in the background, stepping forward only to speak of his great pride in his beautiful, clever wife.

'I'm sorry,' he said, on his knees, panting a little, his eyes not a bit apologetic.

Lizzie stared down at her breast, and even in the dimmish light from her bedside lamp, she could see the red marks. 'Have you gone mad?'

Christopher crawled tentatively towards her. 'I got a bit carried away, and I . . .'

'And you what?' She grasped the edge of the duvet, tugged it up over herself, covering her breasts, feeling suddenly cold.

'I thought you'd like it,' he said.

'Why on earth should you imagine I'd like being *bitten*?'

'Just a little love bite, Lizzie.'

'It was a full-blown, anything-*but*-love bite,' she erupted, intensely relieved that the boys were both in Marlow with Gilly

38

Spence, the part-time nanny from Maidenhead they'd found when Lizzie had begun writing the second draft of her book. 'And it bloody well *hurt*, you idiot.'

Disappointment of the kind she'd seen once before, eight months ago, when he'd startled her with the unexpected roughness of his lovemaking, flicked across his handsome face.

'I'm sorry,' he said again, a little coldly.

'You were cold that night too,' Lizzie said abruptly.

'What night?' he asked. 'What are you talking about?'

'Just remembering that the last time you decided I might fancy rough sex was the night we celebrated the Vicuna offer.'

'Rough sex?' His eyes were amused. 'Hardly.'

'I'm not laughing.' Lizzie's upset was growing by the second. 'Just wondering why my getting published should be some sort of catalyst for something like this.'

'That's absurd.' His amusement was gone. 'Utterly absurd, Lizzie, and not a little offensive when you know how proud I am of you.'

She felt, instantly, ashamed, pushed away the notion that his untypical behaviour might have been rooted in some semi-subconscious power thing, a need to re-establish his dominance in their relationship.

'Yes,' she said. 'I do know that.'

'Well then?' He made a move towards her, then stopped. 'See? I'm nervous to come near you now.'

'Don't be silly.'

'Idiotic and silly,' he said. 'A man could develop a complex.'

'I'm sorry,' Lizzie said.

'No.' Christopher shook his head. 'My fault. I shouldn't have done that.'

'No,' she said. 'You shouldn't.'

'May I see?' he asked, softly.

She hesitated, the duvet still pulled over both breasts.

'Please, Lizzie,' he said. 'I didn't mean to hurt you.'

Still she made no move, but Christopher reached for the cover and pulled it slowly away, his hands and expression very gentle now.

'Dear God,' he said, still very quietly, seeing the marks. 'Did I do that?'

Lizzie didn't speak.

39

'May I kiss it?' he said.

'Kissing it better?' Lizzie's irony was soft, too. Old memories of Angela passed across her mind, before the accident, long before her breakdown, kissing away her scraped knees and bumped heads.

Christopher touched his lips, with great gentleness, to the breast, then looked up at her. 'You know I love you far too much to want to make you cry.'

'Glad to hear it,' Lizzie said.

His expression was almost boyish now. 'Am I forgiven?'

'Yes, of course,' she said. 'So long as you never do it again.'

'I won't,' Christopher said.

'I'd have thought,' she said, 'that you'd know me well enough not to imagine, even for a moment, that I might enjoy any kind of roughness.'

'You're right,' he said. 'Of course.'

'Though then again,' Lizzie went on, 'I thought I knew you too.'

'And so you do,' he said, then hesitated.

'What?' she asked.

'Just, perhaps,' he said, 'not quite all of me.'

It had, of course, happened again. Christopher was incapable, as Lizzie now knew, from the vantage point of several more years' experience, of *not* letting it happen again.

The next time was during that same summer.

July the eighteenth. Another night in London without the boys, because Lizzie had attended meetings with Andrew France and with Howard Dunn at Vicuna to discuss her second book, and Christopher had been in surgery for much of the day.

They'd dined at l'Escargot in Greek Street, and afterwards, leaving the restaurant, a man had come up to Lizzie and asked for her autograph, and she had been both embarrassed and delighted, and Christopher had teased her about it in the taxi on their way back to the flat, and the teasing had continued, gently enough, most of the way to bed, and almost immediately, after that, they'd begun making love.

'My very own celeb,' he told her, planting kisses on her belly.

'You're still the star of this family,' Lizzie told him, running the palms of her hands over his shoulders.

40

'I've always wanted to fuck a star,' he said, parting her thighs.

The word alone seemed to sound in the air like a warning, for Christopher never used it with her, certainly never during sex.

'Don't,' she said.

'Don't what, star?'

'Talk like that.'

'Like what, fuck-a-star?'

'Christopher, please.' Lizzie wriggled away from beneath him.

'Where are you going, fuck-a-star?'

'I'm getting,' she said, 'out of bed.'

'Oh, no,' he said. 'Oh, no, you don't, my little fuck-a-celeb.'

He leaned down heavily to one side, stopping her getting out that way, and then, as she began to turn the other way, he made a sudden grab for both her arms, pinning her down.

'Not funny,' she said, glaring up at him. 'Let me go.'

'Oh, God,' Christopher said. 'Oh, my God, Lizzie, you look so wonderful.'

'Let me *go*, Christopher.' She began to struggle.

'Oh, yes,' he said, and straddled her. 'Oh, *yes*, my Lizzie.'

He bent his head, tried to kiss her, but she turned her face away. He bit her neck.

'Jesus,' Lizzie exclaimed, and kicked at him, saw that he was smiling, and kicked out again, harder, but that only seemed to inflame him, for he began to push her thighs apart again with one knee. 'If you don't let me go—'

'What'll you do, fuck-a-star?'

Swiftly, smoothly, he released her left arm, lowered his upper body over her, trapping her more effectively, put one hand around her throat and squeezed.

She stared up at him, struggling to stay calm, sudden rage just managing to keep down her fright. 'I will wait till you've finished,' she said tightly, 'and then I will call the police and have you arrested.' It was hard to breathe. 'Let go of me *now*, Christopher.'

For another long moment, his fingers remained on her neck, half choking her, and then, abruptly, he released her and sat back on his haunches. 'Better?'

She took a deep, trembling breath. 'Now get out,' she said, quietly.

'No need for such a drama,' he said. 'Just a game.'

41

Lizzie went on looking into his face, not moving.

'Get out of this room, Christopher,' she said.

'You need to learn to loosen up a bit,' he said.

She took another, deeper breath.

'Get *out*,' she said.

He got off the bed, walked naked to the door, opened it, and left.

Lizzie waited for about ten seconds.

And then she began to cry.

10

Helen Shipley had just emerged from DCI Kirby's office on the top floor of the AMIT NW building, still smarting from her govenor's remarks about their lack of progress in the Bolsover murder case – three weeks now since the discovery of Lynne's body – when Geoff Gregory let her know that Pam Wakefield, the victim's sister, was waiting to see her.

'Someone else to apologize to,' Shipley sighed, heading down the stairs with Gregory. She'd woken up that morning with a headache, which her boss's haranguing hadn't done much to cure. Another encounter with a still deeply shocked and understandably angry relative wasn't going to help.

'I don't think she's here to have a go,' said Gregory.

'Can't imagine why not.'

They reached the first floor, turned left along the corridor, and Gregory, an old-fashioned man, stepped ahead of Shipley and opened the door of the interview room for her. 'Here's the Detective Inspector for you, Mrs Wakefield.'

'Mrs Wakefield.' Shipley walked in, shook the other woman's hand.

'I hope this is all right,' Pam Wakefield said, nervously.

'Of course it is,' Shipley said. 'I told you, any time.'

'Coffee?' Geoff Gregory asked.

'Not for me,' Mrs Wakefield said.

'Me neither, thanks, Geoff,' Shipley said.

DS Gregory closed the door softly behind him.

At thirty-three, the victim's sister was the same age as Shipley, but looking at her now, she might have passed for forty-five. Bereavement in the natural sense was often damaging enough, but this kind of devastation often took a more dramatic physical as well as emotional toll. Pam Wakefield's brown hair was greyer than it had been when Shipley had first seen her, her eyes, dark brown, as Lynne's had been, were deeply shadowed and had a haunted look, and her mouth was pinched.

'I found something,' she said now.

Helen Shipley's pulse skipped as she sat down opposite her.

'It was in a bag of Lynne's.' Pam Wakefield laid a small, white-backed card in the centre of the table.

'May I?' Shipley asked.

'Of course. That's why I brought it.'

Shipley stood, leaned over to take a better look, taking care not to touch.

'It's all right,' Mrs Wakefield said. 'It's not evidence or anything.'

It was a business card belonging to a Michael Novak of a firm named Novak Investigations with an address in New Smithfield, E.1.

'Any idea who Michael Novak is?'

'None. Like I said, I found it in a bag of Lynne's – actually, not really hers, it was one she borrowed from me a long time ago.'

Shipley sat down again. 'Take your time, Mrs Wakefield.'

Pam Wakefield shook her head. 'Nothing else to say. I lent Lynne this canvas shopper ages ago – months, I think, I'm not sure – and I've used it since she gave it back, but I can't ever have emptied it out properly till last night, and that was in it, right at the bottom, wedged in the seam in a corner.' She paused. 'I phoned Novak Investigations, and it is a detective agency, which is obvious, I suppose. The woman I talked to asked why I wanted to know, how I knew about them, but I put the phone down. I shouldn't have done that.'

'No reason why not,' Shipley said easily. 'If you didn't feel like talking.'

'I don't like people who do that when they've dialled the wrong number. I usually say I'm sorry for bothering them, then hang up.'

'Do you have any idea why Lynne might have been in touch with a private detective?' Shipley asked.

'No idea at all. Except the obvious, I mean.'

'What's that?' Shipley wanted it to come from her.

44

'Maybe Lynne was checking up on John.'

'But you've said you didn't think she was suspicious of John in that way?'

'If she was, she never told me.' Pam Wakefield paused. 'Then again, she never really told me about John hitting her, not in so many words. I just knew.'

'Yes,' Shipley said, and waited.

'Maybe someone just gave her this card. Maybe she never called them.'

'Maybe,' Shipley said. 'I'll certainly be trying to find out.'

'So this could be useful?'

Shipley saw the naked appeal in the older woman's eyes.

'You never know,' she said carefully, not wishing to arouse false hope. 'The small things sometimes are.'

In an area in which so much striking new development had taken place, New Smithfield, a narrow, dark little cobbled cul-de-sac of disused warehouses, felt to Shipley forgotten and almost decrepit.

There it was. Number twenty-nine, with, to the right of its front door, a rusted brass plate bearing six push-bell buttons, and a small plaque beside that – well-polished by comparison – bearing the name **Novak Investigations Ltd.**

Shipley rang the bell, heard no buzz, and pushed at the door, which opened at her touch, heavily and creakily. The entryway was poorly lit and dingy, with a wide, aged-looking lift that had once, presumably, carried freight and passengers, but now bore only an Out of Service sign and large padlock on its iron gate.

'Fifth floor.' A voice, female, clear and lightly Scots, rang out from above. 'Sorry about the stairs.'

'That's okay.'

Shipley regretted, as she regularly did starting up arduous stair-cases, having let her gym membership lapse two years ago. Only a block and a half from her flat in Finsbury Park, it could hardly have been more convenient, but Shipley, struggling for excuses at the time, had said that what she actually needed was a club near work, since she spent most of her life there.

'All right?' the voice called as she reached the third floor.

'Bit dark, isn't it?' Shipley said, already breathless.

'Sorry.' The woman sounded cheery. 'We keep meaning to brighten it up.'

Shipley was on the final approach. 'Isn't that the landlord's job?'

'Huh,' came the reply.

Shipley reached the top floor, was met by almost dazzling brightness in the shape of three working light-bulbs and a warm, welcoming smile from a woman with jaw-length curly red hair.

'Clare Novak.' The woman extended her hand, shook Shipley's firmly. 'DI Shipley, I presume?'

Shipley, who had telephoned a little more than an hour earlier, took out her warrant card and showed it to Clare Novak, who took a moment over checking it before stepping aside to show Shipley into the office.

'Not much, but we like it.'

It was one room, large enough for two desks, a wall-long run of filing cabinets, a tall, fully-laden book-case, a biscuit-coloured couch and a cheap coffee table. One of the desks was densely cluttered with papers and folders stacked on three sides of the computer and keyboard, a telephone barely visible in the jumble; the second desk the antithesis, perfectly organized, paperwork divided in trays. The whole room, even the messy part, looked and felt clean.

Clare Novak invited Shipley to sit and offered her coffee. 'We make quite decent stuff, so you might want to say yes.'

'You sound like you've tasted ours.'

'No, but I worked in hospitals for a while.'

'Even worse,' Shipley said. 'I'd love some. Black, no sugar.'

The red-haired woman opened a door just beyond the cabinets, vanished for a few moments, then reappeared holding two blue pottery mugs which she set on the table before sitting beside Shipley on the couch. Her movements, the detective observed, were lithe, her legs slim and long. Shipley had gained more than breathlessness when she'd stopped going to the gym; the semi-sedentary nature of her work, too many doughnuts on the run and pints with the lads at the end of the working day had added a stone to her weight. She was far from fat, had her dad's fair hair – cut very short, but in no way mannish – and her mum's nice grey eyes, but there was something about the nature of her job, about always feeling a need

46

to be tough, physically and mentally, that she sometimes felt might have taken more than the edge off her femininity.

Clare Novak was feminine, bordering on ethereal, clearly highly efficient and, at first meeting, probably nice into the bargain.

'I'm really sorry Mike hasn't made it back yet,' she said. 'He's on a matrimonial job somewhere around Bayswater, but if there's anything I can't help you with, he's on his mobile.'

The coffee, Shipley found, sipping it as she gave the other woman a minimal explanation for her visit, was as good as promised. She watched Clare's hazel eyes dull with dismay at the news of the Bolsover murder, then clear again as she resolved to be of assistance.

'I certainly remember the name,' she said, already up on her feet, heading for the computer on the more organized desk. 'Not much else, I'm afraid.'

'But your husband did have dealings with her?'

'We'll soon see.' Clare sat down, keyed in the name and waited. 'Yes, he did.' She scanned the entry on her monitor. 'Briefly, last summer.'

Shipley stood up. 'May I see?'

'By all means.' Clare got up again to make room. 'Would you like me to print out what there is?'

'Please.' Shipley did not sit, just stooped to read the entry. 'Not much.'

The printer was already humming, the single page print-out emerging. Clare handed it to Shipley. 'Do you want me to try Mike?'

'Please,' Shipley said again. 'Soon as possible.'

They met in a café in Queensway, close to Novak's job, ordered two mineral waters, and Shipley sat, for a moment, sizing up the private detective. Informally dressed in jeans, open-necked blue shirt and leather jacket, he was nice looking, gentle, she thought, despite the slightly roughed-up nose.

'I wish I'd known about this,' Novak said. 'I'd have been in touch, obviously.'

'Obviously,' Shipley said.

He noted her dryness. 'Was it reported?'

'Only in the local press,' Shipley allowed. 'And there was a mention in one of the south-east TV news round-ups, but that was before the identification.'

'Makes me feel a bit less guilty,' Novak said.

'Why should you feel guilty at all?'

'Because I know how important it is to get as many facts as possible at the start of an enquiry like this.' He shook his head, smiled slightly. 'No other reason.'

'Make up for it now,' Shipley said.

'Any way I can,' Novak said.

He'd been asked, he told her, the previous summer, by a regular client of his to contact Lynne Bolsover on his behalf and to offer his assistance if she wanted it.

'What kind of assistance?' Shipley asked.

'I can't tell you that,' Novak said.

'This is a murder enquiry, Mr Novak.'

'I can't tell you, because I don't know.' He paused: 'My client is a solicitor, but I don't know if this was official business. All I can tell you is that I did contact the lady back then, arranged to meet her in Asda in Southgate – it's a big barn of a place, very anonymous, which was how she wanted it.'

'And?'

'And very little,' Novak said. 'I told her I understood she had some problems and that if she wanted any assistance, my client thought he might be able to help her. She was very jittery about us being seen together – I remember her glancing around before she'd even take my card. She called a few days later, said that even if she did want help, she had no money for fees. I said that as far as I knew, that wouldn't be an issue. Then, after a moment, she said that if she were to talk to my client, it was vital her husband never find out.'

Shipley waited a second. 'And?' she said again.

'I told her that was understood and gave her my client's number. So far as I know, she did meet with him once, but nothing more came of it.' Novak sipped his water, gazed out of the window for a second, then back at Shipley. 'I remember her as seeming a nice, very nervous person, with a big bruise that she'd tried to cover with make-up, on the left side of her face and neck.'

'Did you ask her about it?'

'No.'

'So what kind of solicitor's this client of yours? Divorce lawyer?'

'Yes.'

'Does he have a name?'

Novak smiled. 'Robin Allbeury.' He paused. 'I called him before you got here. He's in Brussels right now, but he said to tell you whatever I could and that he'll be glad to answer any questions himself when he gets back.'

'When's that?' Irritation kicked in.

'End of the week.' Novak preempted her next question. 'He said he'd appreciate your waiting till then, because he might need to refer to his notes.'

'Does Mr Allbeury make a habit of offering unofficial "help" to strangers in trouble? Or is it only to women?'

Mike Novak smiled. 'As a matter of fact, he does.'

11

Lizzie had spent the rest of the night – after Christopher had bitten and half-choked her in the name of sexual pleasure – sleepless, fully dressed in a tracksuit lying on the bed, debating whether or not to leave, unsure if he'd gone to his dressing room and left the flat, or if he was waiting for her, and neither the prospect of that kind of encounter, nor of driving aimlessly around or maybe checking into a hotel, had appealed to her.

She certainly couldn't have driven to Marlow at that hour without risking questions from the children or Gilly.

At seven, she'd found him in the kitchen, wearing navy cords and a white T-shirt, a cafetière and mug on the table, unread folded newspapers beside them. He'd risen as she'd come in, had offered her coffee, which she had refused, before filling the jug kettle at the sink to make her own.

Say something.

She'd returned the kettle to its base and switched it on.

Now.

'I can't live with this.'

Christopher sat down. 'Oh, God.'

'You've given me no choice,' Lizzie said.

'Oh, *God.*' His eyes filled.

'You can "oh, God" me all you like.' She felt strengthened by his weakness. 'And you can cry your eyes out, but it won't change what you did to me.'

'What did I do?' He took off his spectacles, dropped them on the table, his eyes now aghast. 'Lizzie, darling, what did I do to you?'

'You know exactly what you did.'

'No.' He shook his head, gripped the edge of the table with both hands. '*No*.'

Lizzie's fear altered, grew to different levels, for the children as well as herself, and she sat down opposite him. 'Are you claiming not to remember what you did to me less than six hours ago?'

He waited before answering. 'Not exactly.'

'So you do remember?' Disgust filled her, and she began to rise.

'No, wait, Lizzie. Please. You don't understand.'

'No,' she had agreed. 'I don't.'

'I don't always, *entirely*, know what happens when I feel that way.' He shook his head again. 'I don't mean black-outs, just . . . details.'

'Like putting your hand around my neck and—'

'But I stopped.' Christopher fumbled with his spectacles, put them on again.

'Only after I threatened to call the police.' Lizzie felt sick at the memory. 'It was *assault*, Christopher. You hurt me, and you frightened me.'

'What can I say,' he said helplessly, 'except that I'm truly sorry?'

'Sorry won't cut it,' she said, 'not this time.' She took a breath. 'Nor will lying about not remembering *details*.'

'You don't understand,' he said again. 'How can you? And you can't begin to understand that, in a way, my coming to you like that is a kind of compliment.'

'*Compliment*?' Outrage made Lizzie feel quite dizzy. 'You must be mad.'

'I know,' he said. 'I know it's hard to see what I mean. I don't suppose you'll accept it even after I try to explain.'

Lizzie had ceased to speak then, had sat there silently at their kitchen table, saved just a little, she decided later, by a sense of being somehow outside herself, as if none of it was entirely real.

It was a compliment, Christopher said, because it meant that at long last he was doing what he had always wanted to do: trusting her with his deepest secrets.

'I thought, you see,' he said, 'that I might never be able to do that, that I had no alternative but to keep on taking that side of myself – those needs – to strangers.'

'Strangers?' Lizzie echoed softly.

51

'Prostitutes.' He saw the devastation in her face. 'Lizzie, it was just as repugnant to me.'

'I doubt that very much.' Her voice shook.

'How could you imagine otherwise?'

'I don't want to imagine it at all.'

Christopher reached across to try and take her hand, but she snatched it away, staring at him as if she'd never really seen him before.

'I've tried so hard,' he said, 'ever since I first met you, done everything in my power to help make your life as happy and fulfilled as possible.' He shrugged, as if what he was telling her was normal, commonplace. 'I suppose I've just begun thinking that maybe you might be willing to try and do the same for me.'

'How?' Suddenly Lizzie sounded almost shrill. 'By fulfilling these *needs* of yours? By taking the place of these other poor bloody women, these *strangers*?'

'I made a mistake,' Christopher said, bleakly. 'A terrible mistake.'

'And that's supposed to stop me leaving you?'

'*Leaving* me?' He was horrified. 'You can't leave me, Lizzie.'

'I can't stay with you. I can't live with a man so out of control he can assault me when the *need* strikes him. If it weren't so appalling, I think I'd laugh.'

'Please don't laugh at me, Lizzie.' Christopher was on his feet again, beseeching her. 'Or rather, *do* laugh at me, do whatever you feel like. Just don't talk about leaving me.'

'Why would I stay? How *can* I stay?'

'To help your husband,' he said. 'The father of your children.'

He had sat down again, had told her that he loved them all utterly and completely, that they were everything to him. He said that he couldn't face life without her, and when she told him, in disgust, that he was being pathetic, he admitted that he supposed he was exactly that, that he was both ridiculous and very weak.

'That's a hard thing for a man like myself to admit, Lizzie.'

She didn't speak.

'I've had these needs,' Christopher had gone on, 'for more years than I can remember. I've tried stopping, believe me, but that never lasts for long.' He'd paused. 'It's a form of addiction.'

'Is that a diagnosis?' Lizzie asked wryly.

'It is.'

'You've seen someone about it?' She was very cool.

'Once,' he answered. 'A long time ago.'

'Why only once?'

'It was too humiliating for me.'

'I see.'

'No, you don't,' he said. 'How could you? All the years of guilt and shame, trying to find ways to hide it, hide *from* it so that I could carry on with the rest of my life – the worthwhile part. I told myself, when it all got too much, that at least on balance the good I was doing might outweigh my weakness.'

'And did you believe that?'

'Yes, I did,' he replied. 'I do believe that, on the whole, Lizzie, I am – if not a good man – not a bad one either.' He paused. 'I think I'm a good father – at least I hope I am.'

'Yes,' she said. 'Of course you are.'

She had realized later that she had still been in a state of shock at that point, that, as she'd sat there listening to him that morning, a part of her had been horribly fascinated by the self-abasement of a man who'd always seemed so controlled and dignified.

'I need you, Lizzie,' he told her. 'I need you so badly. If I still have you, I can go on with my work, caring for my patients, helping the charity.'

'And if I leave you, all that stops? Is that what you'd have me believe?'

'If you leave me,' Christopher answered quietly, 'then yes, I do think all the rest might have to stop.' He paused. 'I honestly don't think I could go on without you. Believe me or don't, but it's the truth.'

She had said nothing for a long time.

'If I stay,' she said at last, 'will you agree to be treated?'

'Anything.'

'I don't want *anything*,' Lizzie had said quite violently. 'I want your word that you will seek treatment – now, right away – and that you will never, ever abuse me or any *other* woman in any way again. Because otherwise, I shall most certainly leave you and take our sons, and nothing you say or do will stop me.'

She stopped, and he waited for a moment.

'Well?' she said.

'Is that all?' he asked.

'Yes. That's all.'

'You have my word,' he said.

She stood up at last, her legs weak, looked down at him. 'I'm doing this for Edward and Jack,' she said. 'Giving you this chance. Because you're right about that, at least. You are – have been – a good father.'

'Thank you.' Christopher reached out and caught her hand, held it, his own fingers cold. 'You won't regret it.'

'I hope not.' Lizzie had paused. 'Now please let go of me.'

He let her hand go. 'I thought—'

'I don't want you touching me,' she said. 'Not when we're alone. Not till I know I can trust you again. Which may never happen, Christopher.'

A little of the gratitude had left his eyes then, pushed out by an unmistakable tinge of resentment. 'I didn't know you had such a hard side, Lizzie.'

'Then apparently,' she had said, 'neither of us has ever known the other as well as we thought we did.'

When Lizzie had realized, soon after, that she was pregnant again, she had done her best to try to contemplate termination, but had found it simply impossible.

Another brother, or a sister, for Edward and Jack.

Joy had kicked in, ousting dismay.

And so the marriage had gone on, Lizzie still wary of Christopher, grieving for the end of her trust in him but relieved that he at least seemed, judging by his restraint with her, to be doing as she had asked. She asked him from time to time if he was still receiving treatment, and, when he said that he was being counselled, asked no more, for she had no wish to know more, and she supposed it might be healthier for what was left of their marriage if she could leave him at least a vestige of self-respect.

And she had her boys and her unborn child to focus on.

Sophie had come into their world the following spring. A dainty, sweet-tempered daughter, golden-haired with dark-blue eyes, born into the outward ideal that was the Wade family. Christopher had been ecstatic, had continued – Lizzie had never had the slightest doubt that this side of him was utterly genuine – to be a loving, giving, well-balanced father.

That September, six months after Sophie's birth, having obtained a prescription from Dr Hilda Kapur, their GP in Marlow, for the Pill, Lizzie had let Christopher make love to her again. It was very tentative and almost sad, in view of what they had shared in her ignorant, more innocent past, but Christopher seemed so glad of the breakthrough, so grateful and filled with optimism that Lizzie decided that forgiveness *had* been the right thing, for all their sakes, that happiness, albeit of a diluted kind, might once again be in reach.

And then, five months later, the Wade family's world fell apart.

12

The promise of self-control Tony Patston had made to Joanne after Irina's first birthday had proven empty. On the contrary, he'd begun drinking more, his growing alcohol dependence equating, so far as he was concerned, with what he had begun to see as the source of all his troubles: the little cuckoo in his semi-detached nest. Without drink, Tony felt increasingly tetchy, unable to cope with his money problems and with the cuckoo's incessant squawking; with a few pints sunk, he felt better, more capable of magnanimity, but *in*capable of stopping at those few, and soon after that the better feelings drained away and the reddening mists of anger began to overwhelm him.

He hit the child regularly. 'Just a smack', he maintained. 'Not with a belt, like my dad used on me.'

Small mercy so far as Irina and her mother were concerned. The sound and sight of his slaps against Irina's skin made Joanne's stomach clench with rage, made her want to lash out at him, screaming out her feelings, but on the two occasions she had done that, Tony had turned back to the child and actually punched her.

'Your punishment,' he told his wife as Irina wailed.

'You bastard,' Joanne wept. 'You filthy *bastard*.'

He'd raised his right hand. 'Want me to give her another one?'

'*No*!' she'd screamed. 'If you need to hit someone, for God's sake hit *me*!'

Tony had dropped his hand. 'I don't want to hit you,' he had said.

Joanne had longed to report him, or at least tell someone, either

her mum or Nicki next door, but she knew she couldn't, knew as well as Tony that she would never, *could* never, do that, because then the truth would come out and they would take her little girl away.

Maybe, she wondered sometimes, that might be better for Irina.

No, she answered herself each time, it would not, because Irina loved her, because she was her mother.

Not her real mother.

Real enough, she told the voice in her head, fiercely. Real enough to love her, passionately, desperately.

Enough for both parents.

It was not enough. Far too much of Irina's development between the ages of one and three had been influenced by tension, fear and pain. Joanne knew it, shared it, but felt ever more helpless and inadequate as she observed Irina reverting, in one way, to how she had been when she'd first come to them.

Soon after her second birthday, she had stopped crying.

'Bloody hell,' Tony said, after three or so evenings of peace. 'This is great.'

'Yes,' Joanne had said quietly.

'About fucking time,' he'd added.

Joanne had said nothing after that, because the silence was making her feel sick, because she realized what had created it. Like an animal submitting to a whip, Irina, feisty little girl that she had been, had finally learned that it was better, infinitely less painful, not to cry.

'Good, strong character,' Joanne remembered Dr Mellor saying.

She'd wondered, shuddering, what the paediatrician might say now.

The peace hadn't lasted. Irina's new introversion and lack of responsiveness had begun to irk Tony almost as much as the crying had.

'All I asked for was a loving child,' he had told Joanne.

'She is loving,' Joanne had said, fearfully.

'With you, not me.'

'Maybe if you—' She stopped.

'What? Maybe if I *what*, Joanne?'

'Nothing,' she'd said, quietly. 'I know you try.'

57

'Bloody right, I try,' Tony had said. 'I sweat blood for her, and what do I get for it – an ungrateful kid who hates my guts.'

'She doesn't hate you,' Joanne had protested. 'You wanted her quiet, so that's what she's given you.'

And Tony, as usual, had gone to the pub.

13

Jack's tendency to stumble had been sufficiently apparent, when he was only two, for Lizzie to have mentioned it to Dr Anna Mellor during his annual check-up, but the paediatrician – married to Peter Szell, a cardiologist and a close friend of Christopher's – had been reassuring, had pointed out, after her examination, that falling was perfectly usual in new walkers.

Lizzie had put it, if not completely out of her mind, at least to the back.

'He's so gorgeous,' grandmother Angela had said, *everyone* had said, for Jack, with his beautiful grey eyes and golden hair and happy disposition, was decidedly gorgeous.

Edward adored his little brother, but teased him frequently as they grew.

'You're so slow,' he complained when they played together.

'He's only little,' Christopher had reminded him. 'You have to be patient.'

'I am,' Edward had said, 'but he's so clumsy.'

'Can't all be natural athletes like you, Ed.'

'What's an athlete, Dad?'

'People who run races and do high-jump, that sort of thing.'

'Jack can't jump,' Edward had said.

'Of course he can,' Christopher had said.

When Sophie had come along, three-year-old Jack had revelled in his opportunity to be a big brother, cuddling his baby sister every chance he was given, liking to watch her being bathed and changed, taking pleasure in stroking her soft cheeks.

A gentle boy.

A boisterous, inquisitive, even-tempered, loving boy.

59

'I don't think I've ever known a more easy-going child,' Gilly said.

'I know,' Lizzie agreed. 'We're so lucky.'

And then, in the space of a few hours, on a February morning three months after Jack had turned four, everything changed forever, when Christine Connor, the head of Jack's nursery school, asked Lizzie, just dropping her son off, if she might have a private word.

'I'm a bit worried about Jack,' she said.

'Why?'

Lizzie spoke the word lightly, like the woman she had, till that second, gone on pretending to be, the blessed, untroubled wife and mother of three. But in her mind, in her already recoiling body and clenching heart, all the lightness had already gone.

'I think,' Mrs Connor said, 'he may have a problem.'

'What sort of a problem?'

Don't listen, Lizzie.

'For one thing,' the other woman said, 'I don't think he can jump.'

'I doubt he'll ever be a gymnast,' Lizzie said.

'No, Mrs Wade,' Christine Connor said. 'I mean I don't believe that Jack *can* jump. At all. I've been watching him. It's as if, when he tries, his feet stay glued to the ground.' She paused. 'Haven't you noticed?'

No. No. Go on hiding.

'Yes,' Lizzie said quietly. 'I have.'

'Something else too,' the teacher went on.

Lizzie felt, *thought* perhaps that she felt the way a prisoner in the dock might have felt in hanging days, waiting for the judge to pass sentence. She wanted to tell Christine Connor to stop, not to say another word, to stop watching Jack, because he was Lizzie's child, not hers, and he was *fine*.

'It's the way he gets up when he's been sitting on the floor.'

Bottom first, hands on his legs, straightening.

'Yes,' Lizzie said again.

'You've noticed that as well then, Mrs Wade?'

'I have.'

She knew that the woman was waiting for her to say more, to ask a question perhaps, or to volunteer a suggestion, to be an effective parent. But she seemed, for the moment, incapable of that.

'It may all be nothing, of course,' Christine Connor said.

No hiding place.

'But you don't think so,' Lizzie said.

'I think, perhaps, a word with your doctor?'

The fear, having been allowed to surface that morning, had never gone away.

Lizzie had gone straight home and spoken to Gilly.

'I hoped it was just me,' Gilly had said.

'A lot of that about,' Lizzie had said, and gone to telephone Christopher, who had dropped everything, just as she had known he would, handing over two operations to another surgeon, postponing a HANDS meeting, jumping into his big, powerful BMW and driving too slowly, because of traffic, on the A40, and then too fast on the M40.

For twenty-four hours after Jack was picked up from nursery school, all his waking moments – and many of his sleeping, too – had been surveyed with a growing sense of creeping dread by both his parents.

'Why are you doing that?' Edward had asked, once.

'Doing what, darling?' Lizzie had said.

'Looking at Jack like that,' the six-year-old, dark-haired and – dark-eyed, like his maternal grandmother, had said.

'We're not, sweetheart,' his mother had lied.

'We're looking at him like this,' his father had said, with the natural, one-on-one, matter-of-fact approach that he felt most children preferred, and which made him, as Lizzie had always had to admit, such an especially gifted parent, 'because we think Jack might be ill.'

'Like a cold, you mean?' Edward asked.

'Something like that,' Christopher had answered, seeing no reason, honesty notwithstanding, why the older child should have to be made afraid for what might – he was still praying, silently, frantically – be no reason.

'Okay,' Edward had said, losing interest.

That had been the last thing Lizzie remembered going well for a very long time. For first their own observations, and then an unusually sombre Anna Mellor's in her London consulting rooms, had shown that Jack's thigh muscles were weaker than they ought to have been, and that he was also displaying weakness around both his pelvis and shoulders.

'What do you think?' Lizzie had asked the paediatrician after her examination, while Jack was playing in the room next door with the nurse.

'I think,' Anna Mellor said, 'Jack should see a specialist.'

'Why?' Lizzie asked. 'What do you think's wrong with him?'

Christopher had given her a look then, a look of such pity and such personal despair, that she had felt as if her blood were freezing.

'Best just to wait and see, darling,' he had said, gently.

And Lizzie realized then that even Christopher, a man able to cut through skin and bone and immerse his hands in the blood of strangers, was, at that moment, no different from herself.

Hanging on to ignorance with all his might.

It was a blur after that, several days of phone calls from the London flat, of trying to keep Jack occupied and reassured, of doctors' and hospital waiting rooms with out-of-date magazines and well-mannered, wretched patients and families. Of consulting rooms and X-ray departments and laboratories, with poor, uncomplaining Jack being poked and prodded and asked to walk and sit and stand – to *perform*, Lizzie felt, with impotent rage – by a series of men and women in suits and white coats. They saw a paediatric neurologist and an orthopaedic consultant and a geneticist, and Lizzie and Christopher were quizzed, their own questions responded to, dozens of facts and statistics and advice presented to them.

And, somewhere amidst all that, the diagnosis, handed down like the sentence Lizzie had been waiting for since Christine Connor had asked her into her office.

Duchenne muscular dystrophy. Bestowed on Jack by a faulty gene carried on the X-chromosome. The female chromosome.

Given to him, in other words, by his mother.

'I don't understand,' Lizzie had said, much later that last endless day-into-night, back in Marlow. 'How can it *be*? There's no family history. Is there?'

She had thrown the last question at her mother, who had driven from London earlier to help Gilly with Edward and Sophie.

'Not as far as I know,' Angela said, feeling – not inaccurately – under attack.

All three children were asleep upstairs, Jack through sheer exhaustion, and Gilly had gone home a while ago to her flat in Maidenhead, and the other adults were in the drawing room, slumped in front of the log fire which crackled and glowed as usual, but seemed, just then, to give off none of its normal warmth or comfort.

'What about your brother?' Lizzie asked.

She had known, for as long as she could remember, that there had been an uncle named James who had died very young, but Angela had told Lizzie years ago that she'd never known exactly what her brother had died of, because her parents – both gone now too – had never seemed to want to talk to her about it.

'Could it have been this?' Lizzie pressed.

'I don't know.' Angela was white-faced. 'I suppose it could.'

'Please find out.' Lizzie knew she sounded harsh, could not help herself.

'Really?' Angela asked.

'Of course, really.'

'Will it make a difference?' Angela asked. 'Knowing that?'

'No.' It was Christopher who answered. 'No difference. Not to Jack.'

Lizzie looked at him, wildness in her eyes. 'But maybe they're wrong,' she said. 'Maybe what James died of was something *like* this, but not *actually* it. It might be something they've found a cure for since then.'

'They're not wrong, Lizzie,' Christopher told her, very gently. 'And though there very well may be a cure in time, there isn't one yet.'

For a long moment, just then, Lizzie had hated him with all her might.

As she had, earlier, found herself filled with hatred for Anna Mellor.

'I went to her two *years* ago,' she'd said to Christopher, in the geneticist's waiting room. 'I *asked* her if he was all right, and she said he was fine, that it was nothing to worry about.'

Christopher had told her that he'd telephoned Anna a little while ago, while Lizzie had been in the loo with Jack, to ask her that very question, and Anna had said she'd thought of DMD right

63

away and had examined Jack's calves for the enlargement that was often an early warning sign in toddlers.

'She said his legs seemed normal,' Christopher had told Lizzie, 'which was a great relief.'

'I'm glad Anna was relieved,' Lizzie had said with venom.

'She's very upset for us all,' Christopher had told her, and then added, with quiet but vast pain: 'I didn't see it either, Lizzie, or if I did, I chose not to.'

'*Did* you?' she had asked him, quickly, violently. 'Did you see?'

'I saw our beautiful little boy, who wasn't as athletic as his older brother.' Christopher had striven for honesty. 'I knew that he'd begun walking later than some, I saw his difficulty with kicking balls and running fast and jumping, and I saw that he was sometimes a little clumsy-looking, but I told myself it didn't matter, so long as he was happy and healthy.'

'Me, too,' Lizzie had said.

'But I'm supposed to be a healer.'

'You're a plastic surgeon,' Lizzie had told him, being kind.

But her hating stage had begun, being aimed in all directions, at Anna Mellor for not realizing till now, at the paediatric neurologist *for* realizing, at all the parents in those waiting rooms whose sons did not have DMD, at Christopher – whatever she'd told him to the contrary – for not recognizing the signs, and then at Angela, for not making her parents tell her about James, not finding out that she was a carrier.

But then she had remembered that if there was hating to be done now, if there was *blaming* to be done, then it ought surely to be Christopher directing it at *her*.

Her faulty gene, after all.

Yet he did not do that, neither that night, nor at any time after, had remained, even through their darker hours, as Jack's nightmare-to-be had begun unfolding, the most tender of husbands. Comprehending the irrational, yet perhaps inevitable, guilt that Lizzie was suffering, Christopher's kindness had known no bounds, his care and love for Jack and Edward and Sophie wondrously all-enveloping.

And the only thing that had changed, that had insinuated itself back between them – though on different terms now – had been that three months after Jack's diagnosis, Christopher had come to her again, quite openly, with the more perverse sexual needs that he had, for so long, been managing to suppress.

'The counselling,' he told her, 'has rather shifted emphasis, as you might expect, isn't really helping me much any more. And I don't ever want to go to anyone else but you, Lizzie, and I've been trying to hang on, but I'm not as strong as you, and I do, shameful as it is, seem to need this, and so I've been praying that you'll try and understand how it is for me.'

She did understand. Which was, in a way, one of the stranger features of what had happened inside herself – everything altered, innocence gone, priorities radically dislocated. She could not begin to comprehend her husband's urges, but she was sufficiently imaginative to see that this might be something he now genuinely needed to help him cope with their sorrowful new world; a dark channel through which he might release at least a little of his pent-up anguish and pain.

So she had agreed to try. And she had almost forgotten, had managed to blot out, how he could be, how ugly, how utterly unlike the other Christopher. Yet she saw how much he hated, even in the midst of it, the thought of hurting her badly, and that helped a little, and anyway, the pain, she found now, was nothing by comparison to her heartbreak over her son. And besides, perhaps this was another part of her punishment for what she had brought to Jack.

She felt contempt for herself, sometimes, lying in bed with her husband driving at her, doing things to her that she had sworn never to allow him again. But then she made herself think about what lay ahead for their child, and, like the pain, the self-hate became nothing.

I don't count, she told herself. *Not any more.*

And in the light of day, knowing precisely what she was doing, Lizzie had consigned memories of the night, of her pain and degradation, to her emotional bottom drawer. No longer despising Christopher, she had seen instead, over and over again, why she had fallen in love with him, seen again all his real goodness and strengths. It was, as he had told her when he had first unloaded his weakness, his own private sickness, trying to plead his case. His good qualities did, after all, outweigh his failings.

And besides, Jack adored him.

14

Though Shad Tower was probably one of the least historically respectful and, in her own eyes, least admirable structures in the riverside area around Butler's Wharf, it was also, Helen Shipley had to admit, as she gave her name to the doorman, far and away the most glamorous apartment building she had ever visited.

When Robin Allbeury had phoned the previous afternoon – the second Friday in April – to alert her to his return from Brussels and to tell her, in a deep, mellow voice, that he could see her at any time convenient to her the next day, Shipley had willingly dropped her own Saturday morning plans (Tesco, launderette and vacuuming), and headed south, first thing, to the fifteen-floor building near Tower Bridge.

No prejudices, she tried telling herself on arrival, but it was hard to shake them off in the marbled, magnificently carpeted lobby or in the quietly rising lift – complete with its own videophone system and cameras – that served just one man's home, let alone entering an apartment that smelled more like the Savoy than a private residence. Shipley's own flat was a first floor walk-up that reeked, when the wind came from the north, of rancid fish and chips, and she'd only recently got around to having the lino in the bathroom covered with a bit of pale blue cut-off she'd snapped up in a local carpet sale. Yet still, whenever she closed her front door behind her, a real sense of home, of privacy and individuality, wrapped around her.

How could anyone feel properly at home in *this*?

'Good of you to come so far.' Robin Allbeury – wearing casual slacks and a blue cotton sweater – awaited her as she emerged from the lift, his hand outstretched.

'Good of you to call so soon.' Shipley looked the millionaire – *surely, with this for his home* – in the eye, became abruptly and annoyingly aware of the comparatively inferior cut of the trouser suit in which she'd begun her day feeling smart enough, then turned her gaze deliberately back to the gorgeous flowers and stunning artwork in his entrance hall.

'This not your cup of tea,' Allbeury said astutely.

'I'd love one,' Shipley countered.

'Coming right up,' the solicitor said, then bade her sit down in his living room and went off, apparently, to make the tea himself.

'Shit,' Shipley said softly, taking a look around.

The room itself had been fascinatingly decorated and furnished, embracing a blend of Eastern and European styles, but the views of the river and beyond were clearly the star attractions, wall-to-wall glass doors opening onto a sweeping terrace, with big, handsome telescopes both inside and out. The walls themselves were plain and softly-coloured, with large, delicately painted, Chinese-looking wall-hangings; black lacquered tables, richly woven rugs on the parquet floor, and slender vases everywhere of what Shipley – who scarcely knew a daffodil from a rose – thought *might* be lilies or perhaps orchids.

'I had to use bags.' Robin Allbeury carried in a tray with a teapot, cups and saucers and a plate of biscuits, just as she was sinking into one of his comfortable armchairs. 'Hope that's all right.'

'Fine.' Shipley had anticipated something more exotic. 'Thank you.'

'I was extremely sorry to hear the news of Mrs Bolsover's death.' Allbeury poured their tea and handed Shipley her cup.

'Murder,' she amended.

'So I gather.'

Allbeury offered her the plate of biscuits, and Shipley, seeing that they were ordinary Cadbury's fingers and McVitie's digestives – both of which she loved – took one of each and waited for the solicitor to apologize for having nothing ritzier, but he just took a bite out of a digestive and leaned back in his own armchair.

'How can I help you?' he asked.

'By telling me everything you can about the victim,' Shipley said. 'Anything you can think of, whether you feel it relevant or not.'

'Right.' Allbeury crossed his legs. 'Victim, I'm afraid, was the right word for Lynne Bolsover, long before someone killed her.'

'How long ago did you meet her?' She paused. 'I gather this might have had nothing to do with your firm. "Unofficial" business, I think, Mr Novak said.'

'Something like that.' He smiled slightly. 'I met her last August, though she had come – been brought – to my attention a month earlier.' He paused. 'I'd never have known she existed, Detective Inspector, but for an anonymous letter.' He saw his guest's sceptical expression. 'I know. I felt that way the first time I received one.'

'Get them regularly, do you?' Shipley asked wryly.

'No, thank goodness. Just once before.'

'What did this one say?'

'That Lynne Bolsover was a deeply unhappy woman, whose husband, John, was in the habit of beating her. That they had two young children, that Lynne would like very much to leave their father, but that she was too bullied and too defeated to seek a way out.' Allbeury's brow creased, remembering. 'And that, in any case, because she had no money of her own, she felt she had no option but to stay.'

'Was this letter handwritten, typed?'

'Typed. Inkjet printing, Arial font, on white copier paper. No fingerprints, central London postmark – no way of tracing that I or Mike Novak could easily come up with.' He shrugged. 'Not that I was especially concerned with who'd written the letter.'

'Your concern was with Lynne,' Shipley said.

'Yes.'

'Why?'

Allbeury tilted his head slightly to one side. 'Isn't it obvious? A woman in such difficulties, unable to see her escape route.'

'Thousands just like her,' Shipley said.

'I can't help thousands.'

'But you do help some.'

'I have helped several women, yes.'

'Just women?' Shipley asked.

'I do my best to help both men and women in my capacity as a solicitor.'

68

'But we're not talking about you as a solicitor, are we, Mr Allbeury?'

'Not in this instance.' He paused. 'I have the letter in question, Detective Inspector, if you would like to see it or have it examined.'

Shipley said that she would, then asked about the first letter he'd been sent. Same format, Allbeury said, and offered to make that available to her also. Shipley asked if it, too, had concerned an unhappy woman. Allbeury said that it had, and that, after hearing what had happened to Lynne Bolsover, he'd asked Mike Novak to make some enquiries into the current status of the first woman too.

'Alive and well, I'm glad to say, and happily separated.'

'With no help from you?' Shipley checked.

'Correct,' Allbeury said. 'Just to satisfy any curiosity you might have, I did offer my assistance to that first lady, and she rejected my offer, told Mike Novak she didn't need my help.'

'Apparently true,' Shipley said.

'Yes. I'm glad to say.'

'Are you?'

'Certainly,' Allbeury replied, then went on, rather more crisply. 'You wanted to know about my meeting with Mrs Bolsover.'

'If you wouldn't mind,' Shipley said.

'As you already know,' the solicitor said, 'I asked Mr Novak to make the initial contact. Mostly because Mike's a gentle person and possesses a greater ability to blend into different surroundings.'

'More ordinary,' Shipley said, remembering the private investigator.

'I don't find Mike at all ordinary,' Allbeury said. 'But he tells me I tend to stick out like a sore thumb in some surroundings.'

'You said you met Lynne Bolsover last August.'

'In the McDonald's near Tottenham Court Road Underground station. Her choice,' he added. 'It was too crowded and noisy, so we moved to a big, rather badly lit pub nearby – I'm afraid I can't remember its name, but I don't suppose that matters.'

'Not really,' Shipley said.

'I don't have a great deal to tell you, I'm afraid,' Allbeury continued. 'Mrs Bolsover was very nervous, and I thought she seemed depressed. Not ready to trust me. Perhaps – though I had no way of knowing – not ready to trust anyone, let alone a stranger.'

'Easier, sometimes, with strangers,' Shipley commented.

'Sometimes,' Allbeury agreed. 'Not that time, unfortunately.'

'Did she tell you anything about herself? About her unhappiness with her husband?'

'Only in response to my questions,' Allbeury said. 'I asked if she was afraid of John, and she said that she was, but that it wasn't too bad, and that there was really no need for anyone else to be concerned for her.'

'Did she know about the letter?'

'Mike Novak had told her about it. I asked her if she knew who might have written it, and she seemed perplexed about it, appeared to have no idea.' He paused. 'I tried to ascertain if there might be any risk to the children in her situation, but she said there was no risk of that kind. She seemed very definite about that, though less so, I felt, about herself.'

'If she wasn't ready to trust you,' Shipley said, 'why do you think she agreed to meet you?'

'Perhaps,' Allbeury replied, 'she felt very desperate when she agreed to the meeting, then found it all too frightening. The prospect of her husband finding out, I mean, rather than our meeting itself.' He recalled something. 'She wanted a brandy, I remember, then changed to white wine in case he detected it on her breath.'

Shipley shook her head slightly.

'What is Bolsover like?' Allbeury asked quietly. 'If you feel you can tell me.'

'He's held up well in interviews, maintained his shock and grief.' She paused. 'I have no doubt he's a probably violent bully, but I don't know if he's a killer.'

'Thank you.' Allbeury paused. 'Mrs Bolsover had a little of her wine, stayed with me in the pub for no more than fifteen minutes, then told me that she didn't know why she'd come, that she was grateful for my interest, but that there was nothing I could, or needed, to do for her. And then she left.'

'You made no further attempt to contact her?'

'No,' he said. 'I had to respect her wishes, and she knew how to get hold of me again if she chose to.'

'But she never did.'

70

Allbeury shook his head.

'You've told me you found her nervous and depressed,' Shipley said. 'Anything else? Difficult, I realize, on such a brief meeting.'

'Difficult to *know* her, obviously,' Allbeury said. 'But first impressions are often dangerously easy to form, don't you find?'

Shipley wasn't sure if she saw, in the solicitor's rather warm brown eyes, the element of a tease behind those words. 'What was your impression of her?'

'I found her desolate,' he replied.

'In fear of her life?' the detective asked. 'So far as you could tell?'

'Not so far as I could tell.' Allbeury paused. 'She was ground down and afraid, certainly. But more of pain, I thought, both physical and emotional, rather than of being killed.'

Shipley declined a second cup of tea, though she did accept another finger biscuit as well as the two anonymous letters which the solicitor fetched for her, carefully enclosed in separate plastic sleeves.

'I imagine you'll want my fingerprints, for elimination,' he said. 'Will you ask them to contact me to arrange it?'

'I will,' Shipley said. 'Thank you.'

'You're welcome,' Allbeury said.

'Do you know,' Shipley asked as they walked back towards the lift, 'why this anonymous letter writer should have chosen you?'

'Hard to say, since I don't know who they are,' Allbeury said.

'Clearly someone,' Shipley said, 'who knows about your penchant for helping unhappy wives.'

Allbeury stopped about five yards from the lift. 'You're sceptical.'

'A little, yes.'

'Perhaps I ought to reassure you.'

'Can you?'

His smile was regretful. 'I can tell you that all I've actually done – for an all-too-small handful of women – is give them the benefit of my legal experience free of charge, but without the convolutions of the legal aid system.'

'And is that really all you offer them?' asked Shipley quietly.

Robin Allbeury stepped forward, pressed a button beside the lift door, and it slid open, smoothly and almost silently.

'What else could there be?' he asked, and smiled.

*

71

Shipley had already had Ally King ask for both Allbeury and Novak to be run through HOLMES, the Home Office Large Major Enquiry System, but nothing had surfaced linking either man to any known crime. One a successful man, renowned in his field, the other less remarkable, neither with convictions or even arrests to their name.

Mike Novak seemed, to Shipley, on reflection, as open a book as any private investigator was likely to be. He'd been a PC in the Met for just two years, record unblemished though bearing remarks that while Novak was eager and intelligent, he had been both overly critical of bureaucracy and, at times, overly sensitive. Which tallied with the impression Novak had given Shipley at their brief meeting: fairly open, glad to help, upset about Lynne Bolsover – lucky, with Clare as his wife, in love.

Robin Allbeury intrigued her far more. His qualifications and career were well-documented, but the rest was fuzzier. Forty-two, never married but almost certainly heterosexual; plenty of sightings – even reported in tabloids at a time in the early nineties when he'd been involved in society litigation and very much the lawyer of the hour – of him out on the town with women. No particularly glamorous females, Shipley noted, and definitely no bimbo types; all the women attractive but also either brainy or highly successful, usually independent. Aside from that, Allbeury appeared to keep himself to himself, liked his privacy and was in a position to pay through the nose for it.

'On the face of it then,' she said to Ally King on the Monday after her appointment at Shad Tower, 'just two men aware – *made* aware, which still bugs me – of this woman's miserable marriage, trying to help her and failing.' She shrugged. 'Not their fault, probably. Unusual, even odd kind of involvement, but more than likely innocent.'

'Nothing from FSU on the letters yet,' King said. 'I'll chase them up.'

'Thanks.'

The DC gone again, Shipley returned her mind to John Bolsover. Three years older than his wife, a man with hair razored so short its mousey colour was almost undetectable. A physically strong man, judging by appearance, overweight but muscled, his wife's name tattooed on his left arm and prominent veins at both temples. A man Shipley had no difficulty picturing in a state of rage; a man she knew she'd have found easy to dislike even if she had not known of his predilection for hitting and bullying his wife.

The kind of preconceptions a police detective working on a murder enquiry needed to beware of. Though that was not the only reason Shipley was still not ready to charge Bolsover. It wasn't even because, like most homicide investigators all over the world, she badly wanted a smoking gun to make her case unassailable.

It was another maddeningly, unreliably *reliable* element. Instinct.

There was something wrong about this case, Shipley felt, and a great deal more to be learned. And maybe it *was* just the absence of the smoking gun, of the piece of evidence that would enable her to push Bolsover all the way into a life sentence, or maybe it was something else entirely, but either way, she was just not ready yet to try to make *do*.

Despite what she had just said to Ally King, Robin Allbeury was still sticking right slap-bang at the forefront of her consciousness, and she hoped, with critical self-analysis, that it had nothing to do with his being an unusual and attractive man.

Christ knew her own life had been devoid of interesting men – *any* men – for so long now, and like it or not, she was only human.

Yet it wasn't that. She didn't *think* it was that.

If not though, what?

15

'How is everything, my darling?' Angela Piper asked her daughter on the telephone one Sunday afternoon near the end of April.

'Everything's lovely,' Lizzie told her, and, leaning back in her leather working chair and stretching out her legs, she realized that she was, for once, speaking the absolute truth.

'Jack not fretting too much?'

'Jack's feeling pretty good, actually.' Lizzie knew as well as her mother that in general when Christopher was away – as he currently was, lecturing in Germany – Jack did tend to mooch around, impatient for his father to get back. 'He had some physio yesterday, and it went very well.'

'Sophie's cold?'

'Better,' Lizzie replied. 'And neither of the others getting it.'

'Good,' Angela said.

'And Edward's gone out with Mark' – his best friend – 'for the day, but Gilly's here for the weekend, which means I've actually managed to get some work done on the new project.'

'I'm disturbing you,' her mother said.

'Not really,' Lizzie said. 'I'm ready for a break.'

'You do sound very content,' Angela remarked.

'I am,' Lizzie agreed. 'How about you? How's William?'

'We had a tiff last night.'

'Serious?' Lizzie hoped not. Her mother had been so happy since their engagement. Even if no date had been set – which had struck both her and Christopher as slightly odd given their ages – romance definitely agreed with Angela.

'Not a bit.' Her mother was cheery. 'We made it up at bedtime.'

'Good.'

'All thanks to Christopher,' Angela said.

'What is?' Lizzie asked.

'You know what, darling. Giving me back my life.'

'Long time ago now, Mum,' Lizzie said. 'And you got it back yourself.'

'Still down to him,' Angela insisted.

Lizzie gritted her teeth till the end of the call, but when she put down the phone, some of the loveliness had gone out of the day.

Should be used to it by now.

Lord knew she'd grown used to so many things. Like cherishing the times when her husband had to travel (Jack's concerns notwithstanding), and the awareness that she often nowadays used her own work to block out her problems rather than for its own pleasure.

'The Lizzie Piper Roadshow', as the forthcoming project had now been named, was, however, starting to thoroughly absorb her. Once the contracts had all been signed, Lizzie had begun feeling better about it. Both Howard Dunn and the television series producer, Richard Arden, had voiced their thoughts as to how she might deal with the idea over a string of lunch meetings, but then they'd left it to her to come up with her own outline, which was the way Lizzie preferred it. She'd toyed with a number of concepts, some conventional, others more inventive and complex, but then, during a meeting at the Vicuna offices in Chancery Lane, Howard Dunn had persuaded her to return to the precept she usually worked by: simplicity was best, whenever and wherever possible.

The fact was, she was being given virtual *carte blanche* to pick and choose seven locations, provided they were colourful, European, and would inspire her, her readers and viewers.

'You don't actually need a gimmick, Lizzie,' Dunn told her in his office, a charmingly crooked room with sloping ceiling and beams.

'Not a gimmick as such,' she'd agreed, 'but I thought a hook of some sort to hang it all on, to drag in the audience.'

'You're the hook, darling,' her editor said. 'Why else do you imagine they're prepared to put so much money into this thing?'

'Really?' She was dubious.

'Of course, really.'

'But why? I'm not dependable like Delia, or dishy like Jamie, and I'm certainly not gorgeous like Nigella.'

'You're gorgeous like Lizzie,' Howard Dunn pointed out.

'Don't be silly.'

'Don't be coy.' Dunn smiled. 'Anyway, it's not just your looks, it's your personality.'

'I'm just me,' Lizzie had said.

'Which is precisely what we and the TV people are paying you to be. Just Lizzie Piper.'

Even the research was fun after that, wandering through travel books and histories and browsing her atlas in search of places that would most pleasurably tickle her own tastebuds.

'I feel a bit of a fraud,' she'd told Christopher one evening. 'This should be harder, less fun.'

'Give it time,' he'd said astutely.

'I suppose you're right.'

She had smiled at him, knowing that he was, of course, absolutely right, that as the book ran its course she would become subject to panics, become fed up with it and with herself and her lack of talent or inspiration or application. And Christopher would listen to her, let her take her mood swings out on him and would seldom object, though he would often, calmly and rationally, set her back on track. And at times like that, Lizzie would see again exactly why she had married him, and part of the reason she had stayed with him, and if only it could have been like that all the time.

If only.

More than six years had passed since Jack's diagnosis and her subsequent decision to put up with Christopher's 'other' side, and the shock that had enabled Lizzie to accept his behaviour had long since faded, natural repugnance soon returning with a vengeance.

Not that it had made any real difference. She had begun to object again, to protest or even threaten him when it all became too much, but the threats were empty and Christopher knew it. The man who found fulfilment through using violence against his wife while he fucked her, who used foul language *while* fucking her – and that *was* what it was, that was how Lizzie thought of it, for it had nothing whatsoever to do with lovemaking – who regularly still bit and hurt her and frightened her, the bites and other marks always now in places no one else would see, and he had

76

enough self-control for *that*, Lizzie, in distress and anger, had pointed out more than once. That man, *that* Christopher Wade, knew she would not leave him, or take the children, or report him.

'Anyway,' he had said to her one night at the flat, 'you like it.'

'I *hate* it. It disgusts me.'

'You're a strong woman,' Christopher said. 'If you hated it so much, you wouldn't be here.'

'You know why I'm here.'

'You're here,' he said, 'because of our children, but not only because of them. You're here because you still love me, and this is a part of me.'

'Yes,' Lizzie said. 'That's true enough. But it's the part I loathe.'

'Yet you're party to it, you *acquiesce* to it.'

'Yes,' she had said. 'And I despise myself for it, and I wish you had the strength to do what you once swore you would, and fight it.'

'That was before,' he said.

'I don't understand,' Lizzie said. 'I can't comprehend why a man with so much goodness, a man with such a *mind* and so much strength, can give in to this . . .'

'This what?' he asked, softly. 'Depravity?'

She had said nothing.

'It's my curse, Lizzie.'

'Not only yours.'

'No,' he said.

If only.

She played that game again now, after her mother's phone call. If only life could always be as it had been this week, with Christopher away and just herself and Gilly managing the children and the household, then she could be more or less the Lizzie Piper that the outside world believed in.

Reality was the game she always needed to play next, to counteract the first. The reality was that Jack was only feeling comparatively good because his pain levels had been temporarily reduced and because his beloved daddy was only away on a short trip. The reality was that if Christopher were to move out permanently, the misery of the wheelchair-trapped ten-year-old boy and his brother and sister, would be vast and unbearable.

The reality was that there was no such person as 'Just Lizzie'.

There was a mother, and a daughter, and a woman who wrote reasonably well, and who cooked extremely well.

And, whether she always liked it or not, a wife.

A wife who, come the end of July, all preliminary meetings over, all plans completed, her outline, hopefully, transformed into a television running order and some kind of intelligible script, would set off on her travels with an as-yet unknown quantity of comparative strangers, to be joined, soon after, by her vastly respected husband and their wholly innocent, still gloriously oblivious children.

16

Business was down at Patston Motors, mostly because Tony's drinking was leading him to make too many mistakes, which meant he was losing customers, and one man had already threatened to report him for shoddy practice, which had been enough to send Tony straight to the Bell's he kept in his desk drawer.

If only, he told himself, Irina – the bottomless human pit into which he'd had to chuck all that hard-earned cash – would show him a *little* love and gratitude, things might have been more tolerable. And Joanne, for whom he'd *done* it all, was no better these days, always giving him little sideways glances that said she thought he was some kind of monster, conveniently forgetting that if anyone was to blame for all this, it was her. Her hormones, her needs, her fucking insensitivity about his failure to give her a *real* baby, and now, more than anything, her complete inability to teach Irina how to behave.

'What's wrong with you?' Paul Georgiou asked him as they were propping up the bar in the Crown and Anchor one evening in May.

'Nothing.' Tony wished to Christ, for the hundredth time, that he could share some of his problems.

'Something's wrong,' Paul insisted. 'You've got a face on you like a wet kipper. You've been like it for months, mate.'

'Business is crap.' At least that was no lie.

'Is that all?'

'It's bloody well enough,' Tony said. 'I've got bills coming out my ears, one customer threatening to take me to court or have me beaten up—'

'What did you do to him?' Paul looked impressed.

'Nothing. He had an accident after I serviced his Merc.'

'Bad accident?' Paul asked.

'Not that bad, but he's making a meal of it.'

'So that's it?'

'That's what?'

'That's what you've been so pissed off about?'

'Yeah,' Tony said. 'It's enough, I can tell you.'

'Only . . .' Paul stopped.

'What?'

Paul looked uncomfortable. 'It's just that Nicki and I – we can't help hearing, mate, the walls are so fucking thin, aren't they?'

'So?' Tony's still handsome but thickening face took on its tight, belligerent look. 'What do you and Nicki hear?'

His neighbour's discomfiture grew. 'Nothing. Just you and Joanne rowing.'

'So we row,' Tony said. 'Who doesn't?'

'No one. Me and Nicki fight all the time.'

'Well then,' Tony said. 'No big deal, right? We're human, okay?'

'Sure,' Paul said. 'I didn't mean to stick my nose in, mate.'

'Good,' Tony said.

Joanne lived with fear now almost every day of her life.

The slaps that Tony administered to Irina, now four, driving her mother half out of her mind with misery and rage, were bad enough, but it was the punches that really frightened Joanne. First, *most*, she was terrified that one day her little girl might really be hurt, that Tony would lose all control and hit Irina on her head or her body rather than on her arms or legs as he did now. But then again, the fact that the child's limbs were so often dark with bruises led to the second great fear that soon, very soon, someone was going to find out.

'Are you sure,' Sandra had asked her a few weeks earlier, 'about not sending her to nursery school?'

'Quite sure,' Joanne had said.

'It's just that, well, I've said it before . . .'

'You have, Mum.'

'I know you want the best for Irina, but staying so close to you *every* minute might not necessarily be the best.'

'She gets nervous,' Joanne had told her.

80

'And she'll stay that way the longer you let her,' Sandra had said.

'I know what I'm doing,' Joanne had said, and her mother – who'd surmised by now that Tony was not quite the angel she had once believed – had backed off.

Sandra wouldn't back off when it came to real school. And she'd already hinted more than once that she felt Joanne was deliberately keeping Irina from her.

'I don't know why you insist on changing every nappy yourself when you have a perfectly good granny on hand who's happy to do it,' Sandra had said in the past.

'She gets upset when anyone else changes her,' Joanne had lied.

'But I'm not anyone else,' her mother had said.

No difference, of course, when potty-training had arrived and Sandra had told Joanne she'd bought a nice cheery one so that Irina could spend time at her house.

'She only seems to like her own,' Joanne had said.

'Then bring hers with you,' Sandra had reasoned patiently.

If she knew the truth, Joanne thought, if she knew a *quarter* of the truth, she wasn't sure that her mother would ever speak to her again. And she'd be right, of course, because the fact was that Joanne was the worst mother in the world, because however great her love for Irina, however vast her terror that her daughter would be taken from her, she was nothing short of *wicked* letting this go on, letting *him* go on.

Yet still she said nothing, just prayed to God to make it stop.

Make *him* stop.

One evening in June, Tony came home in what he later claimed had been a 'really good mood' which Joanne had spoiled by asking him not to wake Irina, who'd been fretful all day and had only just gone off to sleep.

'I only want to look in on her,' he said.

'Do it quietly,' she said.

'Of course I'll do it quietly,' he said. 'I'm not a complete fucking moron, whatever you might think.'

'I don't think anything of the kind,' she said. 'I'm just tired, and I don't need Irina being woken up again.'

'Because it's always me who does that, is it?'

'No, of course not.' She knew, already, what was going to

happen, could have strangled herself for not keeping her mouth shut.

'Because it's always me and *only* me who upsets her, isn't it?'

'Don't start, Tony,' Joanne said, quietly. 'Please.'

'I haven't started anything,' he said. 'All I've done is come home in a halfway decent mood for once in my fucking mess of a life.'

He was at the staircase by then, foot on the first tread, and Joanne knew it was too late to stop him, not that she *could* have stopped him anyway, except maybe by chucking something really heavy, like a lamp, at his head, and dear God, she'd thought about it more than once in the last few years, she really had.

'Please,' was all she said.

It was the worst yet. The first time Joanne had known that she had no alternative but to wrap her little girl in a blanket and drive her straight to hospital in order to be sure that Tony had not seriously injured her.

'You're a monster,' she told him, quite quietly, just before they left.

'I couldn't help it,' he said, white-faced, swaying slightly, leaning against the wall near the front door. 'She woke up, took one look at me and started, and—'

'Shut up, Tony.' Joanne opened the door. 'I don't want to hear.'

'She hates me, Jo. I've told you.'

'Come on, sweetheart,' Joanne said gently to Irina, heavy and now frighteningly quiet in her arms.

'I'm sorry,' he said, to his wife's departing back. 'So sorry.'

'Go to hell, Tony,' she said over her shoulder.

'How are you feeling now, my love?' Joanne asked her daughter as she drove her Fiesta with great care towards Waltham General Hospital.

'All right, Mummy.' Small, sad, scared, brave voice.

'I'm so sorry, Irina,' Joanne said. 'I love you so much.'

'I love you too, Mummy.'

Joanne used her right hand to scrub away her tears, bit her lower lip hard to keep control, and concentrated on driving, looking for a signpost for the hospital.

'Darling,' she said, 'I need you to listen to me, okay?'

'Yes, Mummy.'

'The nurses and doctors at the hospital are probably going to ask you how you got hurt, sweetheart. Yes?'

'Yes, Mummy.'

'The thing is, baby, you mustn't say that it was anything to do with Daddy.' Irina, strapped into the child seat in the back, was silent.

'Darling? Are you all right?'

'Yes, Mummy.' Very soft again.

Joanne clenched her hands tightly around the steering wheel. 'Only if you tell them anything about Daddy—'

'He'll get cross with Rina again,' the little girl said.

Joanne swallowed more tears. 'Worse than that, my love.' She had to fight to steady her voice. 'The doctors might want to take you away from Mummy, and Mummy couldn't bear that.'

'Don't let them take Rina, Mummy.' Terrified now.

'I won't, sweetheart.' Joanne saw the sign, slowed down. 'I promise you, Irina.' She strengthened her tone. 'No one's going to take you away from me. Not ever. Just remember to tell them you fell down. Okay, baby?'

'Okay, Mummy.'

'I love you, my darling.'

'I love you, too, Mummy.'

Joanne checked the rear-view mirror then, caught sight of her own eyes, and knew that she had never hated herself more.

Until the moment inside A & E, when she was telling the first nurse about Irina's 'fall' and saw Irina's dark eyes, saw a blankness in them that made her want to scream. Or just to curl up and die.

They believed her. And, infinitely more important, Tony had done no serious physical harm. No internal injuries. No barbed questions. Just help and sympathy, for Irina and for her.

And Joanne left the Fiesta where she'd parked it, and took Irina home in a minicab so that she could cuddle her all the way, comfort her, praise her, tell her how much she loved her, try, *try*, to reassure her just a little.

And her daughter clung to her in the back of the cab, but said nothing more, not one single word for the entire journey back to the house.

And Joanne's shame was boundless.

17

Mutual admiration and warm friendship had begun developing between Lizzie and Susan Blake years ago during the very first promotional tour in the *Fooling Around* series. Now a director at Vicuna, Susan had then been a junior publicist, dispatched with orders to see that Lizzie Piper was kept calm and happy enough to fulfil the commitments on her schedule. After the first day of that tour, a day during which almost everything that could had gone wrong, it had been Lizzie who had made Susan – a twenty-two-year-old, slim, pretty brunette – sit down in the bar of their Manchester hotel and down a double malt whisky, in order to forget all about schedules and books.

'It's only a glorified cookbook,' Lizzie had said.

'It's a wonderful book,' Susan had managed to protest.

'But not exactly brain surgery,' Lizzie had said, and bought them a second drink.

'This is supposed to be on Vicuna,' Susan had said.

'This is personal,' Lizzie had told her. 'From me to you to say thank you.'

'For what?' Susan had asked. 'Everything went wrong.'

'I'd have been a gibbering wreck without you,' Lizzie had said.

'I *have* been gibbering,' Susan had confessed.

'Didn't show,' Lizzie had assured her, then sat back to enjoy her own second malt. 'Face it, we were both amazing.'

'Troupers.' Susan had raised her glass. 'You're a star, Lizzie Piper.'

'Thank you.' Lizzie had suddenly felt terribly happy. 'Next drink's on Vicuna.'

'Better remember to have dinner,' Susan had said. 'One of my duties is not letting authors get totally smashed.'

'That's okay,' Lizzie had said. 'I'm starving anyway.'

'You really do love food, don't you?'

'Isn't that what I'm being paid to do?'

'I met a gardening writer last year who said he couldn't wait to move to a flat so he didn't have to mow grass or weed ever again.'

Lizzie had thought about that for a moment. 'You can live without cutting grass or pruning roses. You can't live without food.'

Lizzie's serious relationship with food had begun with simple comfort eating in her schooldays in the early period of her mother's depression, developing – in her all-too-brief time at Sussex – into something a little more intense. She'd been at some risk of turning into a blimp when she'd met Denis Cain, a very desirable fellow reader of English who believed in taking care of his body. Through Denis, Lizzie began realizing how much real pleasure could be derived from preparation and the slower tease of cooking itself. Shopping with him in markets and, when she could afford it, at some of the better shops in Rottingdean and Brighton, Lizzie had learned how the quality of ingredients could affect ultimate tastes and textures of dishes. Even more so when she began to use her own imagination and, becoming gradually bolder, started to deviate from recipes in books and magazines.

Before long, she was hooked, though the downside was that the better her cooking became, the more she noticed Denis showing more passion for the meals she served him than for her. The sexual part of their relationship had fizzled out long before she was forced, after Maurice Piper's death, to come home and care for Angela, but for some years, until he moved to California, Denis Kane had continued periodically to invite himself to dinner wherever Lizzie was living.

'You should open a restaurant,' he had said.

'I'd have to get up in the middle of the night to go to markets.'

'You could be a chef,' he'd said.

'I'd have to start at the bottom and get yelled at.'

'You should at least get your recipes published,' Denis had persisted.

'They aren't really recipes—'Lizzie had gone on in the same negative vein '—just me fooling around in the kitchen. And anyway, I'm going to be a journalist, not write cookbooks.'

'Nothing wrong with good cookbooks,' Denis had said. 'And they make money. That Delia woman's rich as Croesus.'

'Money isn't everything,' Lizzie had said.

'Of course it isn't,' Denis had agreed. 'But it doesn't hurt.' He'd paused, poking one of his slender fingers into her Belgian chocolate and vanilla mousse. 'And you are the most spectacular cook.'

It had taken a few years of rather basic journalistic effort for Lizzie to remember that conversation, at a time when she had been finding it increasingly difficult to pay bills. Maurice had left Angela well provided for, but nothing, Lizzie had learned, deflated a financial cushion more swiftly than the treatment of chronic illness.

She had begun by phoning Denis in Venice Beach, telling him that she was rather belatedly taking his advice and asking if, by chance, he remembered any of the dishes he'd enjoyed most in the old days.

'All of them,' he'd said.

'Seriously,' Lizzie had told him. 'I need a kick start. I told you I never wrote anything down, that I was only messing about.'

'Fooling around, you said,' Denis recalled. 'Good title, by the way.'

She hadn't got round to using it for a long while. She'd gone on writing articles for publication while playing with various concepts for the book that would, hopefully, finally make it, but originality, whenever she thought she'd stumbled upon it, seemed to kill off the simplicity and freshness of her basic ideas.

And then, by the time she'd got it right, content, style, structure and title, Christopher Wade had blown into her life and changed everything forever.

'That's the way of things, isn't it?' Lizzie had told Susan Blake that first night over their rather (despite Susan's best intentions) drunken dinner. 'At exactly the time when I no longer desperately needed to get a book accepted, when I had enough money, not to mention two children, along came Vicuna.'

'But you're glad it – we – did, aren't you?' Susan had asked her.

'God, yes,' Lizzie had answered.

*

Now, years later, over lunch at Isola in Knightsbridge, Susan and Lizzie had been talking over the plans for the Roadshow tour.

'You all right?' Susan asked Lizzie as they waited for coffee after she'd demolished Italian cheesecake with wild berry sauce and Lizzie had toyed with her own dessert.

'Fine,' Lizzie said. 'Too full to eat any more.'

'You just seem a bit . . .' The publicist went on peering at her. 'Down.'

Lizzie picked up her wine glass and glanced around the busy and unashamedly opulent restaurant. 'Not down at all,' she said. 'Just a little nervous about the plans, I suppose.'

'I can understand that,' Susan said.

'Can you?'

'Sure. It's a pretty huge undertaking.' Susan paused. 'You're not worried about how the children are going to cope with it, are you? Not with Christopher organizing things for them?'

'Of course not,' Lizzie said quietly.

Susan smiled. 'He's just so extraordinary.'

'Isn't he,' Lizzie said.

'What's the matter, Mum?' Jack asked her later, as she prepared toad-in-the-hole.

'Nothing's the matter, darling,' she told him.

Edward was in his room doing homework, Sophie was in bed, and Christopher, due to operate at the Beauchamp first thing, was spending the night in Holland Park. Gilly, who'd waited for Lizzie to get back, had gone off now for three days, which was fine with Lizzie, because frankly there was nothing she wanted just now more than a few days of normality with the children.

'You've been a bit funny,' Jack said.

Lizzie looked over at him. At her beloved middle child, so like his father to look at, with hair the identical colour to Christopher's, eyes the same grey, yet much less sharp, far softer than his dad's. Even his smile almost the same. And Jack did smile a great deal, despite his sufferings.

Nothing yet, by comparison to what was, almost certainly, to come. Jack had already endured, and been forced to discard, braces and crutches, and in time he would no longer be able to manage his manually operated wheelchair and would graduate to electric. He knew about that, managed to joke about it, boasted to

Edward – who adored his younger brother and would, had Lizzie and Christopher not been watchful, have become his willing slave – that he'd be breaking speed limits long before Edward ever drove his first car.

He knew other things, too, more, much more than his parents – yearning to protect him for as long as possible – wanted him to; Jack had learned those things through his PC, as Lizzie herself had supplemented her own knowledge. Those things, facts, details, that gave her nightmares, sleeping and waking, the things that tortured and tormented her.

She wondered, sometimes, how it might have been if her maternal grandparents had not chosen to bury the nature of the disease along with Angela's brother, if she had grown up knowing the chances and had been tested. Might there have been no Edward or Sophie – both healthy and strong, thank God?

No Jack?

Could that possibly have been better? The question Lizzie and Christopher and Angela all asked themselves over and over again, pointless and agonizing as it was.

Not better for me. Lizzie's response, every time, guilty, anguished, but absolute. For how else could she answer, knowing her beloved boy? The disease was not Jack. It was an alien invader, an enemy, robbing him of dystrophin, that one crucial muscle protein, in its conspiracy to hide the real Jack Wade, to trap and lock away the bold, energetic, beautiful, strong-limbed potential of him.

His limbs might be weakening, but it had not yet succeeded in locking away any of those other things, and it had never touched his intelligence or humour. Or the lovely smile that linked him so inextricably to his family's hearts.

Yet, oh, dear Lord, the things that lay ahead. Operations, treatments. Pain and numbing fatigue. Frustrations no able-bodied person could imagine. Fear of the need for spinal surgery. Dread of the struggle to breathe, of tracheotomy and tubes, of carers to suction and irrigate the tubes, to feed and wash.

'Not yet,' Christopher would remind Lizzie now and again. 'Not now. Look at our boy *now*.' And he would take her hand and squeeze it tightly and make her look at Jack, and she'd see that he was right, that their son was playing some game with Edward, or stroking Sophie's hair, which he loved to do, or reading Harry

Potter, or watching a video, or listening to a CD, or doing his homework.

Not yet. Please, God, not ever.

'You've been a bit funny,' Jack said, now.

Jack Wade, over whose eyes it was not possible to pull even the finest strands of wool.

So pull yourself together, Lizzie Piper.

'I've had a bit of a headache,' she lied. 'Nothing too bad.'

'Sure that's all?'

'Absolutely sure,' she said, and carried on with her toad-in-the-hole.

'Loads of Bisto, please,' Jack said.

'But of course, Mr Gourmet.' Lizzie smiled, then paused. 'Are you quite happy about us all going away this summer, Jack?'

'Course I am.' The smile was there like a flash. 'It's going to be wicked.' He hesitated. 'Is *that* why you've been weird, Mum? Worrying about me and the travel and stuff?'

Lizzie grasped at the excuse. 'I suppose so,' she said. 'A little.'

'No need to worry,' Jack said. 'Not with Dad taking care of it.'

She smiled at him, turned back to supper, tried for a moment to remember exactly when 'Mummy' had given way to the more grown-up, more independent 'Mum'.

'Of course not,' she said.

18

Regularly, in the course of Joanne's ongoing struggle to keep Irina safe, she pored over her options, wondering if she might have overlooked something, *anything*, that she could do to salvage her and her child's future. Divorce was impossible. Tony had told her, loudly and clearly, that he would never let them go. Joanne had tried telling him that it would surely be the easiest solution for him: peace and quiet, no more ungrateful daughter or wife.

'Tempting,' Tony had said. 'But not quite tempting enough, with all I've forked out over the years.'

'We're not an investment,' Joanne had reminded him.

'Pity,' he'd countered. 'If you were, at least I could cash you in, get something back out of it.'

She'd left it, of course. She always did, knowing that every reproach, every murmur about separation carried with it the threat of another punch, his anger always, still, directed at Irina. Still punishing Joanne through the little girl.

'Is Irina all right?' Sandra Finch had asked her daughter, just last week.

'Fine,' Joanne answered, her stomach clenching. She had begun to dread taking Irina anywhere these days, even on the swiftest visit to her grandmother.

And, of course, Irina was far from all right. She knew that. Irina seemed, to Joanne's increasingly fearful eyes, to be fading. Like an unvarnished painting that had at first been vivid and bright, and gradually, over time, had dulled.

'Don't you see what you're doing?' Joanne had asked Tony a day or two before that visit to her mother. 'Not just to her, but to yourself?'

It had been morning, breakfast-time, the safest time of day for daring any kind of challenge, the least drunken time.

'Of course I see it,' Tony had answered, flatly.

Joanne had stared at him, not sure if she'd heard properly.

'Think I don't know I'm a monster?'

She'd looked at him. 'Then why?'

'Can't help it,' he'd said, stood up and gone to work.

Two Saturdays later, while Joanne was in the lavatory upstairs and Tony was watching Channel Four Racing, Irina got up from the corner where she'd been quietly looking at one of her library picture books, walked over to where she'd earlier left her favourite purple and white stuffed dog, and tripped over the too-long aerial cable near the television.

'Look where you're going, for God's sake!' Tony shouted from his chair.

'Sorry, Daddy.' The little girl began to get up, but one of her Start-Rite shoes was caught beneath the cable and in trying to disentangle herself she pulled too hard, dislodging the aerial connection from its wall socket.

'Jesus!' Tony jumped up. 'Can't you do anything right?'

'Rina *sorry*!' the child cried with fright.

'Let me do it,' her father yelled.

She saw him coming, struggled again to pull her foot free. The cable snaked to one side, the small metal plug at its end lashed through the air and hit the TV screen.

'I said *leave* it!' Tony bellowed.

Upstairs, Joanne heard him, froze, opened the door.

'Tony?' she called.

And heard her daughter's screams.

This time, in A&E, she knew, with sickening certainty, that it wasn't her imagination that the questions were being more carefully posed, that the receptionist and the nurse and then the doctor and then the X-ray woman were all looking at her and at Irina differently.

'She tripped over some wires and hit herself on the table and wall.'

And her father kicked her in the ribs.

'Rina fell down.'

The cover story, faithfully supported by her poor, frightened little girl.

Please, God, let her be all right.

'Rina foot got stuck.'

If she's all right this time, God, I'll find a way to stop him.

'It's all my fault, doctor. I've been meaning to get those wires sorted.'

If they believe me, God, I swear I'll find a way.

'Just waiting for the X-rays, Mrs Patston.'

Please, please, God.

She almost didn't take Irina home that night, almost grabbed at that blessed moment when the child was given the all-clear and ran with it, almost drove off with her into the night, never to return, *almost* turned the car towards the road that led to the M25 – and *any* motorway would have worked for Joanne that night, so long as it led away from the man who kicked his daughter and said he couldn't help it.

Almost.

God had listened, but Joanne wasn't sure if He'd done her that great a favour, after all. Definitely not sure if He'd done much to help Irina.

Free will, Joanne.

Not up to God, not really.

Up to you.

To help her daughter.

No motorway. No point. Not without enough cash and somewhere to go. She had a credit card, and a cash card, but Tony controlled them both, would stop them both, and even if she went to a hole-in-the-wall now and took the maximum, how long would that last?

She actually pulled over then, stopped the Fiesta at the side of the road, to rummage in her handbag.

'Mummy?'

Sleepy voice from the back.

'It's all right, baby. Go back to sleep.'

She'd left her cards at home.

So no cash. No motorway.

Home.

*

92

She began to fantasize. About escaping, about safe places to hide with Irina, faraway places where Tony would never find them. She began keeping Irina by her side every single minute of every day, even when she went to the loo, even if Tony was out, in case he came back suddenly, without warning.

'Can I come over?' Sandra asked one morning on the phone.

'We're just going out.'

'Maybe I could meet you?'

'It's just a bit of shopping.'

'I could come when you get back.' Sandra paused. 'Since I know you won't bring her to me, even though I've no idea why.'

'I'll bring her soon, Mum.'

'You're hurting me, Joanne, and I don't understand.'

'There's nothing *to* understand. It's just been so busy lately.'

'Of course,' Sandra said coolly.

'I love you, Mum.'

'And I love you,' her mother said. 'And I love my grand-daughter, too.'

'I know you do.'

Joanne knew she was hurting her mother, but it couldn't be helped, because she was too afraid that one of these days Sandra would worm the truth out of Irina, and she couldn't take that chance – she was taking enough chances just *staying* with Tony, and she wasn't sure she could bear any more tension, and one day, one day when she'd found a way out of the nightmare, she'd explain it all to her mother.

No more fantasy, she told herself. *Do something.*

She took Irina to South Chingford Library in Hall Lane, sat her down at a table by the window with a book, kept her eyes on her and tried to find out from the leaflets around the library – not asking anyone, she couldn't actually come out and *ask* – about shelters, refuges for people like her. She took the number of a twenty-four hour crisis line to a phone box two streets away and spoke to a lovely, sensible woman while Irina nestled between her legs. But even while the woman at the other end of the phone talked to her of help and places of safety and injunctions and legal aid, Joanne knew that none of these things were for her and Irina, because she was, when it came down to it, a criminal, because she had illegally brought her little girl into the country, had aided and abetted her husband in *paying* for their daughter.

Nothing compared to standing by while he slapped her.

Kicked her.

No hiding places for her. All just fantasy.

Hopeless.

19

'You never get used to it, do you?' Maureen Donnelly said to her friend, Clare Novak, over dinner at one of the small Greek restaurants off Charlotte Street.

'I never did.' Clare dipped a small piece of pitta into taramasalata, looked at it, then put it down.

'Sorry,' Maureen said. 'I shouldn't be talking about it.'

'Yes, you should,' Clare told her. 'It's on your mind. Better to unload.'

'You're right, about it being on my mind.' Maureen drank some retsina. 'This one's really bugging me. There was nothing definite, you know. It really could have been what she said – injuries commensurate with what they both said happened. And God knows kiddies do fall over all the time.'

'But you didn't believe it.'

'Not really, no,' Maureen said. 'But it was strange, in a way. I usually only care about the children – don't give a damn about the mothers who let it go on, you know.'

'Not this one though?' Clare's soft hazel eyes were intent.

'She was *so* tormented.'

'Guilty.'

'God, yes.'

'Not her doing, then?'

'Definitely not.' Maureen shook her head. 'God, that kiddie tore at me, Clare.' She paused. 'And the mother, too.'

'Do you think,' Clare asked Novak later that night, as they were going to bed, 'that you could maybe take a look at these people?'

'To what end?' Novak touched their duvet cover. 'This is nice.'

'Bought it in the John Lewis sale.' Clare turned out her bedside lamp. 'Mike, do you think you could do that?'

'Why?' He snuggled down, put his right arm around her, drew her close.

'In case you think it might be a case for Robin.'

'You hate Robin.' Novak was surprised.

'I've never said I hated him, just that I don't necessarily trust him.' Clare paused. 'Or at least his motives.' She pulled away slightly, leaned on her left elbow, looked at him in the dark. 'I need you to take me seriously about this, Mike.'

'I always take you seriously.'

She lay down again, tried to relax. 'So?'

'I thought Maureen said there was no real proof it wasn't a fall.'

'Not this time, no. Which is exactly why someone should try to help.'

'Before there's a next time.'

'Exactly.'

Novak stared into the dark, picturing a small girl with dark, haunted eyes and bruises on her body. 'I love you.'

Clare felt for his hand. 'I love you too.' She paused. 'So will you?'

'I'm not sure.' Novak hated disappointing her. 'She hasn't asked for help.'

'The mother, you mean,' his wife said. 'The child hasn't, either.'

'She can't, can she.'

'Exactly,' Clare said again.

They fell asleep after that, but Novak had woken again to hear Clare moaning in the midst of a bad dream, and when he switched on his lamp he saw tears on her cheeks, which disturbed the hell out of him.

'Are you okay?' he asked next morning, while they were getting dressed.

'Fine,' she said. 'Now I know you're going to try to help that little girl.'

'I said I wasn't sure,' Novak said, zipping up his trousers.

'I can't see how it could hurt.' Clare dabbed on a little grey eyeshadow. 'Just checking out the Patston family.'

He looked at her. 'Isn't this what you got away from when you left A&E?'

96

Clare sat on the edge of the bed. 'She's already in my mind, Mike. So it's too late, isn't it? If we don't at least try to help, I'll just worry more.'

'What if I find out it's very bad, and we still can't help?'

'That's what Robin's about, though, isn't it?'

Novak sat down beside her, looked into her challenging eyes.

'Isn't that exactly what he says he does?' she persisted. 'Takes care of women who can't get help any other way?'

'Even Robin can't help everyone,' Novak said.

'But at least he could try.' Clare paused. 'Just take a look, Mike. Please.'

Novak went on looking at her. Nothing fragile about her now.

'Please?'

He smiled. 'Give me the details.'

20

The *Lizzie Piper Roadshow* assembled in its entirety for the first time on Sunday, the twenty-eighth of July, in Vienne, south of Lyon. Lizzie and Susan had flown from London to Lyon, from where they had driven, in a hired Peugeot, to a house that had been rented by the Food and Drink Channel on the outskirts of town. Richard Arden, the producer, and Gina Baum, his PA, having travelled by Eurostar two days earlier, arrived – with smug smiles that spoke volumes of the two nights they'd spent in Paris – in a rented Citroën on the same day as Lizzie and Susan. The crew – a horde, it seemed to Lizzie, feeling panicky – came later that evening, in a minibus and lorry, out of which they unloaded tons of equipment.

'Who *are* they all?' Lizzie whispered to Susan.

'Not the foggiest.'

'I thought Richard said this was going to feel "intimate".'

'Maybe it will,' Susan said doubtfully. 'Maybe some of them are just here to help with the unpacking.'

Lizzie phoned Marlow an hour later and spoke first to Gilly, who reported that she and the children (due to follow, in less than a week, with Christopher, meeting the Roadshow in San Remo) were all well and excited.

'Christopher's here,' Gilly said. 'Hang on.'

'How's my star?' He sounded hearty.

'Petrified.' Lizzie lowered her voice. 'I'm not at all sure this is going to be a good idea for the children. What if it's all too much?'

'Jack's totally gung-ho.'

'It's not just Jack I'm worried about. Sophie's still very young.'

'Sophie's seven and very adaptable, like all our children.'

Christopher was in one of his cheerful, rational moods. 'You're worrying unnecessarily, darling.'

'All I'm saying is you need to be prepared to cancel if we have to.'

'We shan't have to cancel anything,' Christopher said. 'Worst case, I'll keep the children in the hotel and we'll have a straight-forward holiday while you slave.'

'That's all very well.' Lizzie's panic had scarcely subsided. 'But the fact is, I'm not at all sure that *I'm* going to be able to handle this.'

'Codswallop,' Christopher said. 'You could do it standing on your head.'

'I'm glad you think so.'

'I do.'

She did handle it. In fact, once the TV people had sorted them-selves out, some disappearing, as Susan had suggested they might, the others mostly melting into the background, and once Lizzie, Susan, Arden and Bill Wilson, the director (who'd arrived after the crew, astride a motorbike, clad in black leather), had got to work sorting out exactly what Lizzie was going to be doing over the next several days, she found herself much happier.

'Half a day,' Arden decreed, 'to get the feel of the place.'

'Not much time to see the excavations,' Susan said.

'Thank God for that,' Gina Baum said. 'I loathe ruins.'

'I'll keep that in mind,' Arden, who was at least twenty years her senior, said, and Bill Wilson sniggered a bit.

The fact that Vienne was one of the most extraordinary repositories of ancient Roman buildings in France had only partially figured in Lizzie's selection of it as their primary location; she had originally hoped to be able to set up her first kitchen – attempting to cook with ancient (at least ancient-looking) vessels in one of the residential town houses that had been excavated in the Saint-Roman-en-Gal district – until it had transpired that the insurance aspects, even if permission had been forthcoming, would have been terrifying.

Magnificent nearby locations for filming aside, Lizzie's other reasons for choosing Vienne had been its proximity to Lyon, thought of by many as the gastronomic capital of the world, and its claim to fame as the site of La Pyramide, home to the late Fernand Point, the legendary chef and restaurateur whose philosophies of cooking had gone on to dominate and inspire legions of chefs for decades.

'Not enough time,' Lizzie said to Susan at the end of the first of the three days they had been allocated for the shoot. 'I don't see how we can possibly manage in that time.'

'Don't start panicking again,' Susan told her, and poured her a cognac from the generous supply that Arden had laid in. 'You know you'll all manage.'

'But all we've done is look at the markets and equip the kitchen.'

'Which probably means that if push came to shove, you could probably shoot the whole thing in one go tomorrow.'

'Maybe if we were doing it all live, heaven forbid,' Lizzie said. 'But if today was anything to go by, every pepper pod I grind's going to turn into a major production.'

Susan laughed, having been in the *place du marché* early that morning when Wilson, trying to get a head-start with a small mobile unit, had insisted on Lizzie buying the same peach no less than five times before he was satisfied.

'Think of it this way, Lizzie. When it comes to writing the daily diary, the things that go wrong will be much more fun than the stuff that sails along.'

'I'm not sure if Richard will be as happy if everything's a disaster.' Lizzie had already heard two lectures from Arden on the subject of daylight-wasting and budgets.

'Everything *won't* be a disaster,' Susan said. 'Drink your cognac.'

'The Susan Blake remedy for everything,' Lizzie said. 'Alcohol.'

The house in which they were billeted, would, in normal conditions, have felt spacious and airy, but with so many people milling around, plus all the equipment and hot lights, it soon became claustrophobic. Having become almost relaxed about the outside location scenes in which she'd simply chosen produce and become a virtual tourist, Lizzie's nerves sprang instantly to jangling point when it was time for her to perform her pre-cooking spiel in the big kitchen-cum-studio.

'Fernand Point believed that *these* were the stars of both kitchen and table.'

She looked away from the camera's unflinching eye and down at the large, very naked and, by now, too-warm chicken, and the two baskets of vegetables assembled on the stone counter before her.

'If his ingredients were as he wanted them – of the finest quality and freshness – he felt it criminal to use the art of cooking to disguise their essential flavours and textures. Everything Monsieur Point included in a dish had to have—'

Somewhere in the house, a telephone began to ring.

'Fuck,' said Bill Wilson.

'Cut,' said someone else.

The phone stopped ringing, and Lizzie waited for the direction to go again.

'Action.'

'Everything Monsieur Point included—'

'Cut,' said Wilson.

Lizzie shaded her eyes against the lighting. 'What did I do?'

'You're a bit shiny, darling,' the director said. 'Someone take the shine off her nose,' he said, loudly, then, to her again, more gently: 'All right, Lizzie?'

'Bit warm,' she said.

'Part and parcel,' he said.

'I know.' A young man with a powder puff dabbed away at her, then vanished back into the blackness behind the lights. 'I'm fine, Bill,' she said.

'From the top, I think,' he said.

'Oh,' she said. 'From "Fernand Point believed"?'

'From the top, please.'

Lizzie looked down at the chicken, praying that her hands, when it came to actually doing some cooking, wouldn't be so slippery with sweat that she'd drop the bird on the floor, and began again.

'You were wonderful, darling,' Wilson told her an hour or – so it felt to Lizzie – twenty later, kissing her hot, damp cheek. 'And doesn't that chicken look fabulous.'

'Very Piperesque,' Richard Arden said, and kissed her too.

'Don't anyone try eating it,' Lizzie said, as the hot lights went out, temporarily blinding her.

'Why not?' Susan's face loomed into focus. 'It smells divine.'

'Because I don't think it was all that fresh to begin with, and then it was hanging around for much too long in the heat, and when it did finally make it into the oven, it wasn't for nearly long enough, and I don't think an outbreak of salmonella would do too much for the Roadshow.'

'It still smells gorgeous,' Susan said.

'Then clearly smells lie,' Lizzie said, 'and all I can say is that Fernand Point must be spinning in his grave.'

The first segment under their belts, Lizzie, Susan and Arden flew from Lyon to Nice, picked up another car and drove across the border to San Remo, while Bill and Gina caught another train or two, and the rest of the crew pounded down a series of *autoroutes* towards Nice, Ventimiglia and their second destination.

'*Il Dottore*' – as everyone in reception at the Palazzo Grande Hotel (the hotel selected by Christopher for the excellence of its facilities for wheelchair-users) referred to Christopher when Lizzie checked in – had already arrived with Signorina Spence and the *ragazzi* and was awaiting her in one of the two suites he had reserved. One, he'd made a point of telling her when he'd made the arrangements, for their sole use, and the other a three-room suite for Gilly to share with Jack, Edward and Sophie.

'More privacy for us,' he had said at the time.

And Lizzie had felt her insides recoil.

His sexual restraint, in the run-up to the tour, had made her no less apprehensive, had, on the contrary, made her more jittery, more certain that he was just biding his time, waiting for more atmospheric settings.

'You okay?' Susan asked now, as they headed for the lift.

'Bit tired,' Lizzie said, and reminded herself for the dozent time to be careful.

'Two whole days off.' Susan was glowing at the prospect. 'The pool's seawater, apparently, and the food's meant to be divine. Bliss.'

'So long as I don't have to cook it,' Lizzie said.

Every trace of disquiet disappeared the instant she neared one of the suites and heard the sound of her children's voices, all raised in excitement.

'Mummy!' Sophie, barefoot and gorgeous in a pale blue sundress, saw her first and came running into her arms.

'Hi, Mum.' Edward, preferring, from his twelve-year-old status, to be more laid-back, sauntered towards Lizzie, his brand new Canon Sureshot dangling from his neck.

Lizzie shut her eyes for an instant, drinking in the warm, vibrant armfuls of her oldest and youngest, then opened them again to look for Jack.

He was by the balcony doors, back to the view, his face partly in shadow, but Lizzie saw, with a great pang of relief, that he was smiling what she thought of as his Number One Smile; the one that lit every millimetre of his face, the one that meant he was truly happy, rather than his all-too-frequently used Number Two Smile, which meant that he was almost certainly in discomfort or even pain, but didn't want anyone else knowing about it.

'Hi, Mum,' he said. 'Good trip?'

Lizzie gave Sophie one more big kiss, ruffled Edward's dark hair, and made her way across the large and beautiful sitting room to where Jack, looking cool in a striped T-shirt and denim shorts, sat in his chair.

'Great trip.' She bent and hugged him. 'You?'

'Not bad,' he said. 'Except when Sophie threw up on the plane.'

'Did she?' Lizzie turned around to look at her daughter just as Gilly came in from one of the bedrooms, a towel over one arm. 'Hi, Gilly. You all right?'

'Fine, thanks.' Gilly grinned at Jack. 'Been telling you war stories?'

'I hate flying,' Sophie said.

'But you're better now, are you, my darling?' Lizzie could see, from her daughter's glowing cheeks, that she was.

'Amazing rooms.' Gilly joined Jack by the balcony, laid a hand easily on his shoulder. 'And such a view.'

'It's brilliant,' Jack said.

'Everyone happy, I see,' Christopher's voice said. 'Hello, star.'

Lizzie turned to see her husband framed in the doorway, wearing jeans and a short-sleeved white T-shirt, impressive as always to look at, and wished, in that instant, as she so often did, that she could find a way to block out his flaw and focus only on the goodness of the man.

'Hello, Christopher.' She went to him, kissed his cheek as he

103

bent his head towards her. 'We're all very happy, I think. You've really spoiled us this time.'

'Where are the others?' He put an arm around her.

'Susan's two floors down.' Lizzie slipped discreetly away, sat on the sofa, looked at Sophie, who was examining the room service menu. 'Come and tell me about your journey, Sophie.' Her daughter ignored her, and she looked back at Christopher. 'Richard's staying here, too – and I think Bill Wilson, the director, and Gina – that's his PA – are coming, but I'm not sure.'

'What about the rest of the crew?' asked Edward, who had been mugging up on TV production ever since learning of the trip.

'They're staying at another hotel,' Lizzie told him, trying to remember.

'Hotel Paradiso,' Christopher supplied.

'Why not here?' Edward was disappointed, had been harbouring fantasies about hobnobbing with cameramen.

'Too much dosh,' Jack told his brother.

'I'm hungry,' Sophie said.

'I'm starving,' Edward agreed.

Sophie came over with the menu. 'Daddy says you're going to be more famous than ever now.'

'I'm certainly not famous yet,' Lizzie said.

'You are a bit famous, Mum,' Edward said.

'Not as famous as Dad,' Jack said.

From their location in a cream-coloured villa that had once, Gina Baum said, belonged to a Russian aristocrat, Lizzie and the Roadshow crew painstakingly assembled the second portion of the series. Lizzie was filmed shopping for produce – vegetables from the *mercato* in La Pigna, the old town, full of picturesque lanes and steep steps up and down which Bill Wilson asked Lizzie to haul her baskets of tomatoes, artichokes, mushrooms, aubergines and fresh herbs; fish from the prettily yellow and cream village of Cervo; and the local wine, *Rossese*, from the vineyards around Dolceacqua. Still out and about, the crew visited various places selected by Lizzie over the past few months, filming mini-segments, many of which, she knew, would probably bite the dust at the editing stage: the castle of Doria, supposedly haunted; a Russian Orthodox church housing tombs of blue-blooded *emigrés*; a town destroyed by an earthquake more than a

104

century before; the rose and carnation gardens of Ventimiglia; and in San Remo itself, the Municipal Casino.

'Having fun now, aren't you?' Christopher observed at the end of day two, over a couple of cognacs in the piano bar, alone together for once.

'Yes, I am,' Lizzie admitted, despite her exhaustion. 'I think I was so busy being nervous in Vienne that I forgot what a once-in-a-lifetime privilege this is.'

'Might not be,' Christopher said. 'A one-off, I mean.'

'Oh, I should think it will be, and even if it isn't, first times are usually the most thrilling, aren't they?'

'I'm glad,' he said. 'I could see you building up tensions in the run-up.'

'Have I been very difficult to live with?'

Christopher drank some cognac. 'If you had been, which you weren't,' he said, quietly, 'I'd hardly have had the right to complain, would I?'

'I don't know,' she said.

'I knew I was one of the reasons you felt so tense.' Christopher glanced around. 'Hijacking your tour, turning it into a family holiday—'

'Having the children along is wonderful,' Lizzie said quickly.

'But me, too,' he said. 'Banging on about how romantic it was going to be.'

'It is romantic,' she said, quite touched by his candour, then swiftly added: 'If having people filming your every move can possibly be construed as romantic.'

'It's all right, Lizzie,' he said. 'Don't fret. I know how important this is to you.'

'Christopher,' she said, feeling guilty. 'I don't—'

'I said it's all right,' he cut in gently. 'I'm not going to spoil it.'

She thought, after that, with a quiet, but profound sense of relief, that maybe it was, after all, going to be all right; that she might, if luck held, manage to do a competent, even entertaining, job of work and that – more important – Edward, Jack and Sophie might be able to experience a truly happy, fun holiday with neither parent having to put too much effort into feigning contentment.

Day three came and went.

'Going great guns,' Arden, a fairly superstitious man who

105

tended on the whole to stick to faint praise until a production was in the bag, told Lizzie that evening before she went upstairs for a quiet family supper.

'Was Bill all right with it?' Lizzie had felt unsure about the director's reaction.

'More than.' The producer saw her face and grinned. 'Don't take any notice of Bill's mood swings, darling. They're a little dependent on the lovely Gina just now. Nothing to do with you.'

Supper was delicious, children and parents in fine spirits, Gilly out for the evening with Rupe, a dishy sound guy who'd quite fallen for her. Christopher was at his very best, full of fun, persuading Sophie to bed, telling Lizzie he was happy to stay up with Edward and Jack, who weren't tired enough to sleep, while she – exhausted enough by then to collapse – went to their suite and had an early night.

Well-earned rest. Sweet, undisturbed sleep.

Day four placed Lizzie in the kitchen of her Riviera dei Fiori villa, cool clay warmed with flowers and the heat from the rugged steel range that was a pleasure to cook on as she blended inspirations of Liguria and old Russia in a kind of *kulebiaka*, a golden pastry shell encasing delicately pickled local fish with a light mushroom cream sauce.

'Are we allowed to eat this one?' Susan asked, salivating.

'If Bill's finished filming it,' Lizzie said.

'Bill's finished,' the director said, 'and fit to eat a camel.'

'Never cooked camel,' Lizzie said, and felt a glow of pride as her main course was fallen on and picked clean.

Next morning – a designated rest day – she woke to find Christopher gone and a note on his pillow: *Take your time, star. I'll be with the children by the pool.*

She hated it when he called her that, tried not to show it to others, who thought it fond and flattering, but inside she cringed each time, heard in her head his *other* way of saying it to her, while he was abusing her. *Fuck-a-star*. One of his favourite terms of endearment.

Just a note, of course, this morning, nothing meant by the word. *Don't spoil the day, Lizzie.*

She thought of lazing for a while, maybe breakfasting in bed, but found that all she really wanted to do was be with the children, so she showered quickly, found a swimsuit, sundress and sandals, looked in the mirror, saw that, despite all the hours of filming indoors, she was becoming quite tanned, and went down to the pool.

She saw Christopher first, sitting astride a lounger, wearing navy blue trunks, sunglasses and his wide-brimmed straw hat. He had maintained his liking for hats, refrained from wearing a panama in summer because Lizzie disliked them, but still often wore a fedora in town, a slouch hat for country walks and regularly, from October till March, wore or carried his favourite, a now fairly battered tweed number that made him feel a bit like Rex Harrison.

He caught sight of her, took off the hat and waved it first at her, then towards the pool, to draw her attention to Edward, just taking a dive.

Lizzie waited a moment, watching her oldest son, then headed over to where Christopher was sitting, only now seeing that Jack was sitting just beyond his father, in his chair, wearing a white T-shirt, shorts and the pair of very cool Italian designer shades he'd bought with Lizzie in London before the trip.

'Hello, everyone,' she said, approaching.

Sophie, sitting under an umbrella two loungers away, chatting to another girl of approximately the same age, saw her mother and waved at her. She looked, Lizzie thought, her heart contracting with love, adorable in a pink bikini and baseball cap.

'Hi, Mum.' Jack made his chair give a languid wiggle of greeting.

'Hello, darling,' Christopher said. 'Why aren't you still sleeping?'

'Wanted to be with you lot.'

Lizzie dumped her bag on the table between her husband and son, gave Jack a swift kiss and looked back at the pool, where Edward was now laughing with a group of boys and girls.

'Daddy said you were staying in bed.' Sophie materialized beside her.

'Hello, gorgeous.' Lizzie gave her a hug. 'Got enough suncream on?'

'Course.'

'She looks nice.' Lizzie looked towards the girl Sophie had been talking to.

'Daniela. She's Italian, but she speaks great English.'

'Ed's diving again,' Jack said. 'Look, Mum.'

Lizzie looked, too late – just a spray of splash marking her older son's point of entry, and his slim, tanned body already sleeking away beneath the surface. She turned, looked at Jack, saw not a trace of envy and marvelled at his generosity.

'I'm going for a swim, Mummy,' Sophie said. 'Want to come?'

'Mummy probably wants to relax,' Christopher said.

'I'd love to have a swim.' With a quick movement, Lizzie pulled her sundress up over her head, and kicked off her sandals. 'How about Daniela?'

'She doesn't like swimming,' Sophie said. 'Come on.'

Mother and daughter emerged fifteen minutes later, heading straight to the shower to wash off the salt from the pool, then passing Edward on their way back to the loungers.

'I'm going to get Cokes,' he told them. 'Anyone want anything?'

'Ice cream,' Sophie said. '*Gelato.*'

'It's a bit early for ice cream,' Lizzie said.

'Oh, Mummy.'

'Their OJ's good,' Edward suggested. 'Fresh squeezed.'

'Mm,' Lizzie said. 'Would you get me one, please, darling?'

'Ice cream for me, please – chocolate,' Sophie said and ran on ahead, the soles of her still wet feet slapping the ground.

'Have you got enough money?' Lizzie asked Edward.

'Dad said to sign for stuff,' he said, and was gone.

Lizzie looked ahead towards the loungers, where Christopher was on his feet and drying Sophie with a towel. She was laughing, and it looked, from a distance as if her father was tickling her.

Something in Lizzie's mind went snap.

'*No*,' she said, so violently that several people turned to see what had happened.

Lizzie didn't care. Five strides, and she was there, grabbing her startled daughter by the hand and pulling her away from Christopher.

'What?' Sophie demanded. 'Mummy, what are you *doing*?'

Lizzie let her go, felt her cheeks burning, knew she'd taken a foolish, desperately clumsy nosedive into territory she'd sworn not to, and struggled to cover before it was too late.

'You were making a show of yourself,' she said.

Sophie stared at her. 'I was laughing.' She looked at her father for back-up. 'Daddy was making me *laugh* – what's wrong with that?'

Lizzie felt Christopher's eyes on her but couldn't bring herself to look at him, knew she had no viable alternative but to continue.

'This is a nice hotel,' she told her daughter, loathing herself. 'You were disturbing people.'

'I *wasn't*.' Sophie's eyes filled with tears. 'Why're you being so horrible?'

She didn't wait for Lizzie's answer, just bent to scoop up her sundress and beach bag, stuck her feet into her sandals and ran.

'That was nice,' Christopher's voice said, coolly.

Lizzie did look at him then, saw that he was holding his sunglasses in one hand, and that his eyes, anything *but* cool, were appalled. That he knew what had just happened in her mind. She looked back in the other direction, saw Sophie running past Edward, carrying the drinks and her *gelat*, saw Gilly, in a striking red bikini and cover-up, long dark hair pinned up, trying to speak to Sophie but failing.

'I'm going after her,' Lizzie said, and picked up her own things.

'Good idea,' Christopher said, very quietly.

'What's up with Sophie?' Gilly asked, arriving hastily, all set to turn around again. 'She looked upset.'

'I upset her,' Lizzie said.

'Oh,' Gilly said, knowingly. 'Who'd be seven?' She smiled. 'Who'd be a mum?'

Lizzie forced down her own sudden urge to burst into tears. 'Me,' she said.

'She'll be fine,' Gilly said, sympathetically.

'Hopefully,' Lizzie said. 'Once I've apologized.'

'She's a lucky girl,' Gilly said. 'Having a mum prepared to do that.'

'I don't believe you could even *contemplate* such a thing.'

Christopher had waited down by the pool until after Sophie had returned, and then he'd left her and the boys with Gilly and come up to the suite to find Lizzie. His suntan looked suddenly odd, as if the colour were make-up and he was chalk-white beneath, and his hands were clenched fists.

'I know.' Lizzie turned away, walked towards the balcony.

'Is this something you've always been afraid of?'

'I've never thought of it before,' she said.

It was the truth. It had never entered her mind before. Not only because it was too repellent, too horrific to consider, but because she had known – *thought* she'd known – that whatever Christopher might have done, might still do to her someday, he would never do anything to harm the children.

'Don't you know,' he said now, 'that I would never, ever, hurt a hair on their heads?'

Lizzie turned back to face him. 'When I first knew you,' she said, quite evenly, 'if someone had said that you might want to hurt me physically—'

'I never do,' he burst, passionately. 'Not intentionally.'

'You've hurt me repeatedly.' She was quite calm now, was unsure how it was possible to feel so calm at a moment like this.

'Then why have you stayed with me?' he asked, quieter now, too.

'You know why,' Lizzie said.

'I thought . . .' Christopher stopped, walked over to the sofa, sank down heavily onto it.

'What did you think?'

'You sometimes give the impression, to me, not just others, that you still love me. Not just as the father of our children.'

Lizzie began to feel sick. 'Please don't pretend you don't know how I feel about the things you do to me, Christopher.'

'But this isn't about that, is it?' He stared up at her. 'And even if it were, you can't deny how restrained I've been for the longest time now, because I knew how anxious you were about this tour.'

Lizzie sat down too, in one of the armchairs.

'And even here,' he went on. 'You were so sure I was going to let you down on this trip, but I haven't laid a finger on you, have I?'

'No,' Lizzie said. *Not yet.*

'Because I respect you, Lizzie,' he said. 'I respect what you do, who you are. And I know, I accept that I've lost the right to expect the same from you – I do know that – but couldn't you have just a little faith?'

'I do have faith,' she said, 'in the rest of you.'

'No,' Christopher said. 'Clearly not. Or you would never have done what you did down there.'

'I overreacted,' Lizzie said. 'I'm sorry.'

'You all but accused me of—' His colour was back, deepening with freshly mounting distress. 'I can hardly bring myself to say it, Lizzie.'

'It wasn't an accusation, it was a *thought*, seeing you drying Sophie, tickling her, our beautiful little girl—'

'Our *daughter*,' he cried. 'My own child.'

'I couldn't help it, Christopher. I saw you with her, and suddenly, this terror struck me of what might happen one day, and was that really so unreasonable, would you say, given your history?'

'Forget unreasonable,' he said, louder now. 'It's *monstrous* that you could dream up such a notion, when the one thing you've always granted me is that I'm a good father.'

Shame began to flow through her, yet still she could not seem to take back what she'd begun. 'Maybe you've abused me once too often.'

'I haven't touched you.'

'Not for a while, perhaps—'

'Not for *months*!'

'For which I'm meant to be grateful?' Lizzie was back on her feet, her own anger growing, and she couldn't wholly understand why it was all boiling over now, of all times, when nothing at all *had* actually happened. 'Give myself a convenient lobotomy? Obliterate everything you've done before?'

'Things I couldn't *help*, Lizzie.'

'You've just told me how you've managed to restrain yourself,' she lashed back. 'Can't have it both ways, Christopher. Either you *can* help yourself, or you can't – make up your mind.'

'But all this has nothing to do with what just happened – *didn't* happen – down by the pool.'

'Of *course* it has,' she yelled back at him. 'It's all about trust, can't you see that? It's all about the same thing.'

'Yes,' Christopher said. 'I suppose it is.'

Lizzie sank down again into the chair.

'It does all come down to the same thing.' He was quieter again now. 'To something I've never really understood, which is why, after all we've been through together, my simple *need* for you, my wife, should seem so very terrible.' He paused. 'And even if it does seem so dreadful, Lizzie, if it's the one awful thing you have to put up with from me, once in a while, surely you don't have that much cause for complaint?'

'Because of this, you mean?' She looked around the beautiful room. 'Or because of our lovely homes, perhaps?'

'I just think that perhaps, if you were a little more broad-minded, a little less prudish, less *frigid*,' Christopher said, 'you might realize how much you actually have to be thankful for, instead of dreaming up odious, entirely *groundless*, accusations.'

'I've already told you, I didn't accuse you,' she said coldly. 'I just reacted, instinctively, to the sight of the man who's abused me repeatedly over the years tickling my half-naked, seven-year-old daughter.'

'*Our* daughter,' he said, almost shrilly. 'Whom I love totally.'

'I know you do,' Lizzie said. 'And I do apologize for over-reacting, especially in public. Most of all, in front of Sophie.'

'And Jack,' Christopher added.

'I don't, though, apologize for my instincts.'

'Heaven forbid you should ever be entirely in the wrong.'

'I daresay I'm in the wrong a great deal of the time,' Lizzie said.

'Staying with me, you mean.'

She saw then how completely pointless the conversation was, and how dreadful, and realized that the children and Gilly would be starting to wonder where they were, decided abruptly that she'd rather it was she who returned to them before Christopher, and began to walk towards the door.

'Had enough?' he asked.

'More than enough.' She turned back to face him. 'But just in case, just in the – please, God, unlikely – event that my instincts were not wholly groundless, you should know one thing, Christopher.'

'And what's that?' He sounded very bitter.

'Simply that if you did, ever, in any way, harm Sophie or any of our children, I truly believe that I would kill you.'

21

Novak had gone along with Clare's troubled instincts. There had been no question, of course, that he would, right from the first night she'd told him about little Irina, because if he'd had to name the one thing he loved most about his wife, it would have had to be her sensitivity.

So he'd done some checking, taken some time to observe the Patstons.

The husband, Tony, good-looking man with one conviction for actual bodily harm, now working solo at Patston Motors in an alleyway off the North Circular near Walthamstow, going to the pub for liquid lunches, downing too many pints for a man working with potentially dangerous machinery, knocking off at about six-thirty, going home to the semi in Chingford Hatch for an hour, two at most, then heading out again to his local, sometimes alone, sometimes with his neighbour, for a longer session.

Joanne Patston, nice-looking too, but manifestly beleaguered, seeming to scurry everywhere, never leaving the house without the little girl, the child for whom Clare and Maureen Donnelly were both so fearful.

And Irina herself, gorgeous little kid, no outward evidence of ill-treatment, no visible bruises – though Novak knew, of course, that they existed – but always clinging to her mother's hand without any of the natural, healthy eagerness to be free that characterized most four-year-olds.

Adopted. He'd learned that much without difficulty, but then he'd struck a dead end more swiftly than he might have expected, and, just as swiftly, he had withdrawn his enquiry lest he make waves.

*

'So what do you think?' he asked Robin Allbeury in the second week of August, sitting on the solicitor's terrace with its extraordinary views over the Thames and beyond, drinking a cold beer while the other man finished reading his report. 'Anything you could do?'

'Tough call,' Allbeury mused. 'Presumably this question mark over the kiddy's adoption could be enough to stop the lady leaving or divorcing him, even if it were what she wanted.' He paused. 'I'd be concerned that any of my efforts within legal goalposts could end up getting Irina taken away from Mrs Patston, not just the father.'

'More misery all round.'

'Could be.'

'I've never asked much before,' Novak said, slowly, 'never wanted to know too much about your methods for making certain things happen.'

Allbeury smiled. 'What are you asking now, Mike? That I move outside those legal goalposts?'

'Just asking you to try and help,' Novak answered simply. 'Just telling you that my instincts seem to be siding with Clare's and Maureen Donnelly's.' He shook his head. 'Nothing much more to go on than that. I haven't seen Patston shout at his daughter, let alone hurt her.'

'Then again—' Allbeury glanced down at the notes '—you haven't actually seen him out with her, even at weekends, which is a little off, in itself.'

'Definitely,' Novak agreed.

'And clearly what we're all concerned about,' Allbeury said, more grimly now, 'is that the two visits to Waltham General may only be the thin end of the wedge.'

'Mrs Patston scared of her husband *and*, maybe, losing the child.'

'Too anxious, perhaps, to take Irina back to A&E, even if she's really hurt.'

'Robin's going to make some enquiries of his own,' Novak told Clare later on her mobile, it being one of her evenings in Wood Green with Nick Parry, her private patient.

'Is that good news?' Clare asked, while the young man with gaunt cheeks and merry eyes that often hid his inner frustrations

114

and bleaker moods – who had, until a few moments before been playing Internet poker with a woman in Fiji – zipped back and forth in his wheelchair, making coffee. 'Or does he usually do that?'

'He said no promises,' Novak said. 'But I could tell he was concerned.'

'I just hope he doesn't waste too much time,' Clare said.

'He's a careful man, my love. And he knows what he's doing.'

'Good,' she said. 'Thanks for trying.'

'I don't see we have a choice,' Novak said.

'Coffee's ready,' Nick Parry announced from the doorway as Clare put her phone back into her bag. 'Though you look like you could use something stronger.'

Clare grinned at him. 'I'm fine.'

'No, you're not.' He waited till they both had their mugs. 'Go on,' he said. 'Tell me what's up. You know you always feel better when you tell me.'

She smiled again. Parry had once told Clare that he was better than most shrinks because he'd been there himself – pretty much all the way *down* there, he'd said – for a good long while after his accident, and it hadn't been therapists who'd got him through, but other things entirely: the welcome discovery that he could still, albeit more seldom than before, get hammered with some of his old mates; the better of his carers; and his still-developing love affair with his computer and the Internet.

'Listening to other people's problems is up there too,' Parry had confessed, candidly. 'Helps put all this—' he'd motioned towards his legs'—in perspective.' And then he'd grimaced. 'Sometimes.'

Case No. 6/201074

PATSTON, J.

Study/Review ✓

Pending

Action

Resolved

22

'Christopher rejoining us tomorrow, I gather?' Arden said to Lizzie at the end of their first day's filming on Kefalonia, while the crew packed up and Wilson and Gina went over notes. 'Nice for you, darling.'

'Lovely,' Lizzie said.

'You all right, Lizzie?' Susan asked just moments later.

Always Susan – most often, Susan – detecting her troubled soul.

Careful, Lizzie.

They'd been out on location in Argostoli, the capital, with Lizzie seeking out fresh local produce or specialities as usual, chatting to traders, buying several bottles of Gentillini wine and a locally-produced honey, and checking out ingredients for the dishes she would prepare in the following days.

'Sure you won't have dinner with us, darling?' Arden asked.

Most of the crew were eating together that night at the Hotel Boulevard Pyllaros half an hour or so away – where Arden, Wilson, Gina and Susan were also staying – but since the hotel had been unable to offer suitable facilities for Jack's needs, Christopher had rented a house closer to Sami in the north of the island, more convenient in any case for much of the scheduled filming.

'I really want to get back before dark, if possible,' Lizzie told him.

'Good idea,' Susan said, 'with those alarming roads.'

Lizzie smiled at her. 'The driver I had this morning was pretty sane, and he said he'd pick me up.' She glanced at her watch. 'He's probably waiting.'

117

Arden waited till she'd vanished from sight. 'Do you know what's wrong with her?' he asked Susan quietly.

'Nothing,' Susan said, 'so far as I know.'

'Hm,' Arden said.

'What's that mean?' Susan asked.

The producer shrugged. 'Hubby back tomorrow. Wife glowing till she found out. Trouble in paradise, I'd say.'

'So long as you *don't* say,' Susan said.

'Think the same, then, do you?' Arden said.

'Not at all,' Susan said, slightly too sharply. 'Not remotely.'

Arden raised both eyebrows, then shrugged. 'Jolly good,' he said.

Gilly opened the door the instant Lizzie's taxi rattled to a halt outside the villa, a red-roofed, pink stone house with creamy shutters and jasmine and other heavenly-scented flowers in the surrounding gardens.

'You look shattered.'

'I am.' Lizzie dumped her bag on the cool stone floor, handed the two large flattish boxes she'd been carrying to Gilly and raised a finger to her lips.

'The boys are playing one of their awful computer games and Sophie's in bed.'

'She all right?' Sophie seldom willingly went to bed early.

'Absolutely fine,' Gilly reassured her. 'But she swam for quite a while, and then she played volleyball with the boys for ages, so she was exhausted.'

'Jack okay?'

'Very happy, I'd say.' Gilly smiled. 'Excited about his dad coming back.'

Sophie's room was on the upper floor, her parents on one side, Gilly on the other, while Jack and Edward were sharing the bedroom-cum-sitting room and bathroom on the ground floor.

'I'll just nip up first,' Lizzie said.

She tiptoed in, found Sophie asleep, watched her for a few moments, as she loved to do most nights wherever they were, then kissed her golden hair very gently and crept back out.

Jack and Edward were in the sitting room.

'Starving, Mum,' Edward told her the instant she appeared.

'No food tonight,' Lizzie said. 'Sorry.'

118

'Yeah, sure,' Jack said.

She went over to plant a kiss on his cheek.

'Gilly said we had to wait,' Edward said plaintively.

'No real food, anyway,' his mother said.

'What's that mean?' her older son asked.

Jack wrinkled his nose. 'Wow.' He sniffed, to double-check. 'Pizza?'

'You're kidding,' Edward said. 'I thought you'd be doing that mousse thing.'

'Moussaka,' Lizzie said. 'Why would I make that when I know you don't like it?'

'Pizza,' Jack said again. 'Wicked.'

'It's rather a dull island on the mythological front,' Christopher said the next evening over dinner on the terrace at the back of the house.

The cover explanation for his sudden return to London had been a hospital emergency, but the truth was that after the ugliness in San Remo, Lizzie had asked him – guiltily, but resolutely – if he'd mind giving her a short breathing space, and he had told her that he did mind very much, but had still given in, leaving her, the children and Gilly to travel with the Roadshow to Palermo and, from there, to the largest of the Ionian islands for the next segment.

He'd arrived that afternoon and promptly – to Lizzie's surprise and discomfiture – invited Arden and Susan, Bill and Gina to join them for dinner.

'No cooking,' he'd said, seeing her expression. 'All arranged with one of the better fish restaurants in town. They're driving it over later.'

'What about the children? They were expecting to have you to themselves.'

'All sorted too,' he'd replied, equably. 'Gilly's making supper with something light for you and I – a sort of appetizer, if you like.'

'I don't think I do like,' Lizzie had said. 'It all sounds very tiring.'

'I think it sounds sociable,' Christopher had said crisply, 'and good PR, frankly, given that everyone's been made to think I ran out on them. Anyway, our guests won't be here till getting on for ten. Most people dine late in this part of the world.'

119

'Most people don't have to get up early and be filmed all day.'

'My,' Christopher had said. 'Aren't we starting to sound like a film star?'

'I fancied shooting this segment,' Bill Wilson said now, several hours later, after the children had gone to their rooms, 'on one of the more Dionysian islands like Naxos, so that Lizzie could focus on wine.'

'Kefalonia has some of the best wine in Greece,' Lizzie said, prodding the rather limp grilled fish that the restaurant had delivered.

'But no scope for orgies,' Christopher said.

'Sad little story,' Gina said, 'about that lake we're scheduled to visit.'

'Lake Melissani,' Arden said.

'Where Melissanthe, the Nymph, drowned herself when the great god Pan rejected her,' Christopher said. 'Though some would have it she was just a shepherdess looking for some sheep who'd fallen in.'

'You've done your homework,' Susan said, impressed.

'Always liked Greek myths,' he said.

'Crammed with sex,' Bill said to Gina.

'Pan's father, Hermes,' Christopher said to the table in general, 'is said to have raped his mother Penelope in the guise of a goat.'

'So that's why Pan's painted half-man, half-goat, is it?' Gilly said.

'His grandmother,' Christopher said, 'was called Maia.'

'The fire goddess,' Arden said.

Christopher looked directly at Lizzie. 'Also known as the goddess of sexual heat,' he said. 'As Bill said, crammed with sex, these myths.'

'Was that strictly necessary?' Lizzie asked later, when the visitors had gone and Gilly was in the kitchen.

'What precisely?'

'The one-track conversation.'

'You picked Kefalonia,' Christopher said. 'Hardly my fault Pan sowed some of his wild oats here.'

She looked at him for a moment, then turned away. 'I'm going to help Gilly, and then I'm going to bed.'

'Am I permitted to join you?' he asked, quietly.

'Of course,' she said, and then added, unable to help herself: 'No real alternative, anyway, with no spare room.'

The visit to Melissani, the subterranean lake within a cave, was on the agenda for the last day on the island, but before that the plan was for Lizzie to bring her latest recipes to life on a barbecue to be set up somewhere in another cave just a few kilometres from Sami.

Drogarati, said by locals once to have been a dragon's lair, was, according to experts, a hundred and fifty million years old, a truly remarkable, vast cavern filled with thousands of multicoloured stalagmites and stalactites.

'It's so big,' Lizzie had told the children during the journey from Palermo, 'that there's a concert room at the back where they can seat a thousand people.'

'Wicked,' Jack had said.

'Can I come?' Edward had asked.

'I don't know,' Lizzie said.

'You promised I could come to a shoot,' her oldest said.

'It depends,' she said.

Arden thought it a fine idea, though not just for Edward. A barbecue in a cave, he told Lizzie, was precisely the right setting for the family-oriented segment he'd had in mind all along.

'Though the company might need you and Christopher to sign an insurance waiver.' He saw Lizzie's expression. 'Problem?'

'Not with that,' she'd said. 'You said family-oriented, Richard, but Jack couldn't possibly come to Drogarati, not with all those steps. I shouldn't think he could even get close.'

'Of course not,' Arden said. 'Stupid of me.'

'Not in the least,' Lizzie hastened. 'It was a lovely idea.'

'Would Jack mind missing out, if we went ahead without him?' The producer shook his head. 'He always seems very laid-back about his limitations.'

'He is,' Lizzie confirmed. 'I just hate leaving him out of things.'

Less than two hours later, Arden called from his hotel to tell Lizzie that the company had shot down the whole plan.

'Not because of family involvement,' he explained. 'It's the whole shebang – cooking in that place – too dangerous, apparently.' He paused. 'But it's not all bad news, Lizzie, because we've found another cave.'

'As good as Drogarati?'

'On the contrary,' he said. 'A very ordinary, dull-as-ditchwater cave.'

'Why's that so good?'

'Because we can still shoot footage in the original place, but since it's Lizzie Piper and her food the viewers are most interested in, the cave's fairly irrelevant. So now you're going to do your barbecue thing at this other little cave – or rather, just *outside* the cave on a charming little beach which even happens to have a decent enough path for Jack's wheels.'

'Richard, how lovely.' Lizzie was touched. 'How did you find this place?'

'I didn't,' Arden said. 'Gina went off location hunting yesterday, and your pal Susan went with her.'

Down to Susan then, Lizzie decided, unable, perhaps unfairly, to picture Gina caring too much about anything so unglamorous as DMD.

It was all delightful – the most enjoyable shoot of the trip so far, from Lizzie's point-of-view – until disaster struck.

'Action,' Bill Wilson said.

'Mummy!'

Sophie, impeccably behaved till then, but spotting a rather large lizard just feet away, became unnerved and made a sudden dash for her mother, grabbing hold of Lizzie's T-shirt and distracting her at precisely the instant that an unexpected gust of wind blew off the Ionian Sea.

The flames on the big stone barbecue flared startlingly high, making Sophie shriek and back into Edward, who stumbled side-ways, knocking a rack of white-hot shellfish, octopus and oil over his bare right arm and leg.

'Oh, my *God*!' Lizzie pushed Sophie out of the way.

'Water!' Jack spun his chair and started for the bucket behind his mother, but Christopher got there first.

As Edward began screaming.

122

23

Joanne was in the back garden hanging a pile of Tony's shirts on the clothes line – he liked his shirts hung out to dry rather than put in the tumble drier because he claimed they smelled better – when Irina, playing on their small rectangle of lawn, stopped bouncing her red ball, ran to her mother and grasped at her jeans.

'Man,' Irina said.

Joanne looked first down at her daughter, then up towards where she was pointing, and her heart began to pound, for there was indeed a man standing on the far side of the brick wall that separated their property from the common land beyond.

'Mrs Patston,' the man said, 'please don't be alarmed.'

'Go inside,' Joanne told Irina. 'Go on, darling, quickly.'

'Mummy come too,' Irina said.

'Mrs Patston, my name is Michael Novak, and I'm here to offer you help.'

Joanne stared at him. His head and shoulders – all she could see of him above the wall – looked respectable enough. Which meant, she knew, nothing.

'Please go away,' she told him.

'I will,' Novak told her, 'as soon as I've passed on a message.'

'Mummy *come*.' Irina tugged at Joanne's jeans again.

'Irina, go inside,' Joanne said again. 'I'll come in a minute.'

'But Mummy—'

'Now!'

The child, startled at being spoken to so sharply by her mother, ran through the kitchen door into the house. Joanne waited a moment, then took two steps closer to the wall. The man was breaking no laws she could think of and, for reasons she didn't

123

quite understand, she found she was not sufficiently disturbed by him to consider phoning the police.

'My card.' Slowly and deliberately, anxious not to scare her off, Novak laid his business card on top of the wall.

'I'll take it when you've gone,' Joanne said.

'Good idea,' Novak said. 'Better safe than sorry.'

'What do you want?' Joanne looked back at the house, saw Irina at the kitchen window, gazing out. 'Please tell me quickly,' she said, and fixed her eyes on the man again. 'I don't like leaving my daughter alone for long.'

'Of course not,' Novak said. 'I'm a private investigator, Mrs Patston.'

'What do you want with me?' Joanne felt confused, hot and bothered, as if she'd had too much sun, though it was in fact a cloudy day.

'A client of mine, a solicitor who knows a little about your predicament—'

'What predicament? Who says I need a solicitor?'

'No one.' Novak went straight on, slowly, clearly. 'My client would very much like to meet you to discuss the possibility of helping you break away from your problems.'

'Break away?' The hot, confused feelings intensified.

'If that's what you would like. It's your call.'

'Who *are* you? I don't understand how you know anything about me?' The word 'solicitor' scrabbled its way to the forefront of her mind, made her scared. 'Who is this solicitor? Why didn't you – he, she – just phone me, or write?'

'He thought this might be better for you,' Novak said. 'He thought you might prefer it if your husband wasn't involved.' He paused. 'This help,' he said slowly, carefully, 'is for you and Irina, not your husband.'

Joanne said nothing, just stood very still.

'Take my card, Mrs Patston, and think about it.' Novak's smile was gentle. 'I realize this is an unusual approach, and you're quite right to be wary, but this whole thing really would be in your hands.'

'What thing?'

'A way out,' Novak replied.

Joanne looked back, saw Irina still waiting, watching. 'I have to go inside.'

'Right,' Novak said. 'If you want to get in touch, we'll be waiting to hear. If not, we won't trouble you again. Like I said, it's your call.' He nodded towards the card on the top of the wall. 'Might be better not to leave that lying around, don't you think?'

Swiftly, gingerly, like a wild animal snatching at a piece of food, Joanne stepped forward and grabbed the card, then backed off again.

'Great,' Novak said. 'I'll be going now.'

It came to her, suddenly, like a punch in the stomach. 'Was it the hospital? Is that how you know?'

Novak read the terror behind her eyes. 'This isn't official, Mrs Patston. You don't have to worry about that, not from us.'

'So what *is* it then?' Joanne asked desperately.

'Just help,' Novak said.

24

In the days following the accident, from the chaos of casualty in Argostoli to the Athens hospital where Edward spent one night before being flown home to the Beauchamp, Lizzie saw Christopher yet again at his very best. While she feared and fretted over her son and, riddled with all kinds of guilt, forced Richard Arden to accept that she had no intention of returning to the Roadshow for the foreseeable future, her husband operated on Edward's burns, eased his pain and comforted him, still making time to console Sophie and Jack.

Observing Christopher, Lizzie felt in awe, thankful, and ashamed.

This was, just as he had told her, what really counted. That other, single aspect of their life together was minor by comparison. This was not just a *good* father she was seeing; this was a remarkable, brilliant, valuable man, a man capable of taking care of the most important people in her life.

So now, Lizzie did what mothers always did when their children were ill or in trouble: she made pacts. If only Edward would recover completely, be swiftly out of pain, be not badly scarred – if only Sophie didn't feel guilty about her part in the accident – if only Jack's condition wasn't affected by his shock and distress, Lizzie swore she'd try not to care what Christopher was occasionally driven to do to her in bed. Never complain again.

Never again threaten to leave.

25

On the first day of September, a Sunday afternoon, while her father was off somewhere with friends, and her aunt was taking care of her and her brother, Kylie Bolsover was looking for a spanner in the garage with which she hoped to be able to fix one of the wheels on her skateboard, when she found something that she did not understand.

At least, she understood *what* it was.

A rock, wrapped in a large rag stained with oil and something else; something that was not oil, but was almost, not quite, blackish.

She tried, for a few moments, to unwrap the rock completely, but some of the rag, where it was dirtiest, was stiff, reminded her of what her daddy's shirts had felt like when her mother had sprayed starch on them when she was ironing, and those stained bits were stuck to the rock.

What Kylie did *not* understand was how the rock and rag were making her feel.

Sick. Scared.

She went to find her aunt.

26

Clare took the call.

'Is Michael Novak there, please?'

An unfamiliar female voice, apprehensive, even secretive. Clare knew, with a rush of intuition, who it was. 'Mrs Patston?'

Silence.

Mistake.

'I'm sorry,' Clare said, trying to sound calm. 'Mike's—'

'It is Mrs Patston,' the woman said.

'I don't know why I thought it might be,' Clare said. *Friendly, easy, don't scare her off.* 'Mike's just out getting our lunch, but he'll be back any second. If you don't mind holding on—'

'All right.'

In the background, Clare heard a child's voice, calling. '*Mummy*,' clear enough, then something else she couldn't catch.

'Is that your little girl?' Still easily, wanting to hold her.

'Yes. How long will he be?'

Novak strolled through the front door of the office with a brown paper bag in one hand and a *Standard* in the other.

'Joanne Patston for you, Mike,' Clare said, clearly enough for the woman at the other end to hear.

'Great.' He dumped the bag and paper on her desk and took the phone.

'Mrs Patston, I'm glad to hear from you.'

27

'We've got him.'

DC Pete Jackson's voice rang with triumph as he came into the almost empty incident room, then stopped as he saw Shipley on the phone.

She ended her call. 'What?'

'Doctor Patel just called,' Jackson said. 'She couldn't hold.' The ginger-haired DC's cheeks were almost as ruddy with excitement as his hair. 'Fax'll be through shortly.'

'Come on, Pete,' Shipley said. 'Don't make a meal of it.'

'All there. The blood's Lynne's and the rag's got a good print, stupid bastard.'

'Okay,' Shipley said.

'Is that it?' Jackson was put out by her lack of enthusiasm.

'No.' Shipley frowned into her open desk drawer. 'It's great news.'

'But?'

She looked back up at him. 'In his own garage?'

The DC shrugged. 'Like I said, stupid bastard.'

'No one's that stupid, Pete.' Shipley paused. '*We're* not that stupid, for fuck's sake. That garage was searched.'

'I know.' Jackson's pleasure was already fizzling out. 'It was the first thing Mrs Wakefield said.'

Except her attitude had been accusing, not sceptical. '*I thought your people had searched the place.*' Understandable. Smoking gun right under their noses and missed. Head-rolling stuff, if it was true.

DCI Kirby – when Shipley went to see him – felt it *was* true, though he far preferred an alternative scenario in which Bolsover had kept the rock and rag hidden elsewhere until after the police search.

'But he could have just chucked them,' Shipley said. 'Stuck them in a wheelie somewhere miles away or buried them, or burned the rag and washed the rock and thrown it on someone's rockery.'

'Or hidden it where we'd finished looking.' Kirby was steady. 'People do strange and foolish things, Helen, as we know.' He paused. 'Especially panicky men who've smashed their wives' heads in and hardly know where to hide themselves let alone their murder weapon.'

'I don't know, sir,' Shipley said. 'It reeks a bit to me.'

'You're getting paranoid,' Kirby said. 'We've known from the start it was Bolsover, and now we've got the rope to hang him with.'

Thankfully not literally, Shipley thought, with a slightly sick feeling. Though Trevor Kirby was, of course, right. The rock and rag were precisely what they had been seeking. The perfect way to tie up ends, present to the CPS, ensure a charge of murder, suspect behind bars, trial and, almost certainly, conviction.

That was not to say that anyone was filled with jubilation.

'Whichever way we tart it up,' Kirby said, later, in his office, after John Bolsover had been picked up again, charged and removed to Belmarsh, 'this is still going to haunt us. A six-year-old doing our job.'

'But are we quite sure we're doing it now?' Shipley tried again.

'I'm quite sure I don't believe your theory about someone else planting the bloody evidence,' Kirby said, almost savagely. 'I mean, for Christ's sake, who? And why?'

The names Allbeury and Novak sprang straight into her mind, but she'd raised them before, had been told to forget them – especially the solicitor's, who'd done nothing but co-operate as fully as he could.

She kept quiet now.

'Quite,' Kirby said coldly.

'So.' Shipley felt tired. 'Done and dusted, sir.'

'By a child,' the DCI said.

28

'Everyone's been so kind,' Lizzie said to Christopher after dinner on the evening of the first Friday in September.

The children were all in bed, it was Gilly's weekend off, and husband and wife were drinking coffee in the drawing room at Marlow, a beautiful, comfortable room decorated in dove-grey with the warmth of terracotta on the walls surrounding the stone fireplace and tall, cluttered bookshelves. With the exception of the handsome nineteenth-century landscape over the mantle – which had been bought along with the house because Christopher had felt its removal would have diminished the atmosphere of the room – all the paintings were contemporary French works, mostly hailing from the south, seeming to spill soft sunlight and the colours of Provence and the Côte d'Azur into the air on even the darkest winter days.

'Andrew says Vicuna really are fine about moving the publication schedules around to help me out.'

'I should hope so,' Christopher said.

'But he's not convinced that the TV people are quite as laid-back as they're appearing to be.'

'Arden was understanding.'

'Very.' Lizzie shrugged. 'If anyone's actually angry, they haven't let on to me or even Andrew. But I did run out on them—'

'As any decent parent would have,' Christopher pointed out.

'No one's said otherwise. But it's clearly not going to be all that straightforward getting the Roadshow restarted, at least not before winter.'

'Do you mind very much?'

'Not a bit,' Lizzie said. 'More coffee?'

It was true that she didn't mind. God having kept His side of their pact (Edward was looking forward to getting back to school and showing off his war wounds, which had enabled Sophie to get over her guilt, and Jack had shown no ill-effects), Lizzie was more or less keeping her side too.

She was not, of course, quite certain how she would react the next time Christopher lost control, so, as often happened, one pact had led to another, with slightly moderated terms on her side. If Christopher could manage to *temper* his needs a bit, she really would do her best to focus on her gratitude for his many highly admirable qualities.

If.

29

'This is Robin Allbeury.'

It was ten-thirty the following Monday, and Allbeury, sitting facing the river in the study at the eastern end of his apartment, had been awaiting the call.

'This is Joanne Patston.'

Tentative, as Novak had led him to expect.

Allbeury had two studies at home, one right next to his bedroom to wander in and out of at night or first thing, and this, a more imposing room decorated in a strong violet-blue with black-upholstered and walnut furniture, a fine collection of antique law books and a custom-built black granite desk.

'Mrs Patston, I've been expecting your call,' he said warmly.

'Mr Novak says you'd like to meet me.'

'Only if that's what you want, Mrs Patston,' Allbeury said. 'You're in charge.'

A brief silence.

'I can't come far.'

'That shouldn't present a problem.'

'I'm usually home most of the time, you see, apart from shopping and the usual things,' she went on nervously. 'And my husband sometimes comes back when I'm not expecting him, so . . .'

'I understand, Mrs Patston.'

'On the other hand, if we meet too near home, someone might see us – people always seem to notice Irina, but she will have to come along.'

'I think I can make this a little easier.' Allbeury had anticipated this problem. 'Once we've made an arrangement, Mrs Patston, I

133

believe I could arrange for your husband to be detained on business for a few hours on whichever day you choose.'

'Oh.' Joanne Patston was clearly impressed, though a further problem instantly presented itself to her. 'We'd have to choose somewhere ordinary, because Irina sometimes tells her grandmother about her day.'

'Are there any places you often take Irina to?' He already knew the answers, Novak having logged all the Patstons' regular haunts, but this was all part of wanting Joanne to feel in control and also, more significantly, not scaring her off.

'The library,' Joanne said. 'In Hall Lane. South Chingford Library, it's called.'

'All right,' Allbeury said.

'It's near Sainsbury's,' Joanne added. 'Not that that helps much, but—'

'I'll find it, Mrs Patston, don't worry about that.'

'We often go there, you see. It has quite a good children's section.'

'So Irina could be happily occupied,' the solicitor said. 'Good idea.'

'Next Monday,' Joanne said, quite abruptly, as if she needed to get it said, make the arrangement swiftly, before she changed her mind. 'Would that be possible, Mr Allbeury, do you think? Only Tony's always quite busy on Mondays.'

'I'm not sure, Mrs Patston.' Allbeury glanced at his diary. 'I'll have to check a few arrangements of my own, but I think there should be no problem.'

'What did you mean by "detained"?' Joanne asked suddenly. 'No one's going to hurt Tony, are they?'

'I meant detained on business, Mrs Patston. Nothing more.'

'And you're sure he won't be angry when he does get home?'

'On the contrary,' Allbeury said. 'We'll see to it that whatever keeps your husband occupied on the day of our meeting is very agreeable to him.' He paused. 'All right with you so far, Mrs Patston?'

'Yes,' she said. 'Thank you very much, Mr Allbeury.'

'Let's just hope we can find a way to help you,' he said.

30

Helen Shipley hated going to court at the best of times. Even when she knew, verdict notwithstanding, without a shadow of doubt, that right was on the side of the police, that the man or woman on trial deserved what was coming to them, her stomach still churned and goose flesh crawled down her back when she saw them in the dock.

'For a copper,' Graham Shipley, her father and full-time critic, had once told her, 'you're a bit of a shirker when it comes to seeing justice done.'

'She's sorry for them,' Patricia, her mother, had said, jeering rather than defending her.

Shipley was not on the whole, she thought, sorry for them. Yet there was a streak of something in her – humanity, she hoped – that did at least give her pause to ask those two perpetually vexing and, to her still frightening, questions: Why? How?

John Bolsover's first appearance at Hendon Magistrates Court was, from her strictly personal point-of-view, worse than most. She wasn't testifying, knew Bolsover would be refused bail as a matter of course, given the charge, and, observing him in the dock, she found him just as thoroughly unpleasant a character as she had from the outset, but . . .

That was the problem.

That still-lingering, in her mind, if no one else's: *But*.

31

With Christopher's birthday falling this year on a Saturday and being his forty-fifth, Lizzie had determined to make it a special occasion. The day was to be for the whole family, with Angela and William coming for lunch and sport – weather permitting – in the garden at Holland Park.

'I'm afraid I'll be booting you out before the evening,' Lizzie had told her mother when she'd first issued the invitation. 'Though you really won't mind when you hear where we're going.'

'Opera,' Angela had said, instantly, for she loathed ballet and classical concerts of all kinds, but opera most of all. 'What does Christopher want to see, or is it hear? I'm never sure.'

'He doesn't know about it,' Lizzie had said.

'Surprise. How lovely.' Her mother had paused. 'And no, I don't mind a bit.'

Lizzie had kept the whole evening secret, inviting only four of Christopher's favourite people – Guy Wade, his brother, a cellist, and his violinist wife, Moira, and Anna Mellor and her cardiologist husband Peter Szell – and reserving a box at Covent Garden for *Ariadne auf Naxos* followed by dinner at Le Gavroche. Not Lizzie's idea of the best possible London evening, but very much Christopher's.

'That'll stretch the kitty a bit,' Angela had said when she'd heard. 'But still, Christopher's worth it, if anyone is.'

Lizzie remembered Edward screaming, Sophie crying, Jack's stricken face. Their father taking care of them all, mending Edward, bringing them all home.

'Yes, he is,' she said.

And meant it.

All the celebrations were a great success, Christopher in fine, convivial form right through from breakfast to the very end of the evening back in Holland Park with their guests for nightcaps in the living room, while the children and Gilly slept at the far end of the flat.

'Remind me to order minicabs for you,' Lizzie said, watching Christopher pouring the second round of drinks from the very old and special Calvados that Peter and Anna had brought for him. They'd left their cars outside the flat at the start of the evening, and Lizzie vaguely remembered both Anna and Moira saying – back in the Champagne Bar before the first act – that they'd be designated drivers, but by the interval they'd already weakened, and then the wine list at Gavroche had smashed any remaining resolve to smithereens.

'Unless you'd like to stay,' Christopher added.

'Only one spare room,' Lizzie reminded him.

'I've two patients to call in on tomorrow afternoon,' Peter said. 'Think I'll need the morning at home for sobering up purposes.'

'And Moira's got rehearsals,' Guy said. 'Haven't you, darling?'

Moira was already starting to nod, which Lizzie saw as the right moment to phone the local cab company, and half an hour later – a little after two-fifteen – she and Christopher were standing on the doorstep, his arm around her, waving them all off.

He closed the door, took his arm away.

'I can hardly tell you, Lizzie, how much this evening – this whole day – has meant to me.' His eyes were a little pink from weariness and too much alcohol, but there could be no doubting the love in them. 'It's been very, very special, and I'm extremely grateful to you.'

'It's been my pleasure,' she said quietly.

'You look tired.'

'I am,' she agreed, 'but in a good way, you know?'

'Very much so,' he said.

Lizzie looked towards the living room. 'Think I'll leave the glasses for morning, go straight to bed.'

'I'll take care of the glasses,' Christopher said. 'And I'll check on the children, then have one more quiet drink before I turn in.' He smiled. 'I'm off duty for the next thirty-six hours.'

137

'Happy Birthday again, Christopher,' Lizzie said.

And went sleepily to bed.

The squeak of the door hinges lifted her from deep sleep to something lighter; the creak of a floorboard near the bed brought her closer still to consciousness.

His weight on the bed itself woke her.

The smell, the *heat* of him.

'What—?'

The hand on her mouth cut off any more, and then the weight of his body on hers, his free hand on her, finding her breasts, grabbing at them, pinching her nipples, his knee seeking the space between her thighs.

'Let's fuck, star,' he said, raised his right hand and slapped her. 'Fuck-a-star time.'

She began to struggle, to try to kick, to push him off, but he hit her again, and it was hopeless, and even as she felt him begin, iron hard, to ram into her, part of Lizzie's mind was already shutting down, her thoughts and feelings concentrating on the children, asleep in their rooms just along the corridor. And there was no real need for his hand over her mouth to stop her screaming, because through every second of the nightmare she was icily aware that there could only be one thing worse than what was happening to her, and that would be for any of them to know, let alone *see*, what their father was capable of doing to their mother.

But, oh, *God*, her mind was screaming now, as he went on pounding into her, and she was dry inside, and he was *ramming*, and she knew he was hurting her, really hurting her badly.

And one of the last things Lizzie thought, with a bizarre kind of detachment, just before she lost consciousness, was that he must have taken something, some kind of drug, because after the amount of alcohol he had consumed all through that day, from lunchtime onwards, it wasn't possible, surely, for any man to be able to sustain such a powerful, brutal *onslaught* without the aid of something.

'You're okay.'

His voice.

She came to with a terrible jolt – shock first, then pain, *bad* pain.

138

It was light in the room, and she could see him, wearing his black silk dressing gown, his eyes concerned, no hint of violence in them, just fear now, being brought under control with a great effort.

'You're going to be all right, Lizzie.'

Husband again now. Doctor. *Not rapist.*

'Get out.' Her voice had no strength. She tried to move, found it hurt too much, and she moaned. Something else, too, something very wrong.

Bleeding.

'Oh, my God.'

'I'm going to take care of that, Lizzie. Don't be scared, darling.'

Darling.

She wanted to scream, wanted to call Gilly, beg her to make him get away from her, get the children out of the flat, get her a doctor, *another* doctor, but the boys and Sophie would hear, too, and anyway, she couldn't scream, couldn't do anything, was much too weak, and she was fading out again.

The next time Lizzie woke, she was lying in a bright, harsh, strange-smelling room, and Christopher was bending over her, wearing a green gown and mask, telling her again that she was going to be just fine, and her throat was sore now, and her mouth too dry, and she couldn't get any words out.

'I've stopped the bleeding, found the problem and fixed it, so you can stop worrying, Lizzie, all right?'

You're the problem, she said in her mind.

A nurse was standing nearby.

He's the problem, Lizzie said to her, in her mind.

'The children know you've been poorly, but you're going to be fine now, so you don't need to worry about them either. All you have to do now is rest.' Christopher kissed her forehead. 'Sleep, darling.'

She did.

She woke again, in a bedroom this time, in a hospital bed, a needle in the back of her hand, a tube running from it to something hanging from a contraption nearby, and more tubes from further down.

Pain.

'Hurts,' Lizzie said.

'It will,' a female voice said, 'for just a bit.'

Lizzie turned her head, saw a nurse sitting on the other side of her bed – the same young woman she'd seen earlier in the recovery room, brown-haired and pretty and smiling reassuringly, blandly.

'Where is this?' Lizzie asked fuzzily.

'The Beauchamp, Mrs Wade.' The nurse reached for her needle-free hand and patted it kindly. 'You had an operation.'

'Blood,' Lizzie said.

'Your husband did the surgery himself,' the other woman said, 'so you have absolutely nothing to worry about.'

'DIY,' Lizzie said, faintly.

There was a tiny pause as the nurse tried to make sense of that, and failed. 'Anyway, Mrs Wade, if the pain gets too much for you and if you're alone, all you have to do is adjust your on-demand drip feed or press your call button, and I'll be with you right away because Mr Wade has asked me to take the greatest possible care of you.'

'Has he?'

'Oh, yes,' the nurse said.

And Lizzie, still trapped by the remnants of anaesthesia and surgery, could only imagine how the other woman's face would change were she to ask her to telephone the police so that she could have her husband arrested.

Do it, she told herself.

But of course she wouldn't, couldn't do that to Edward or Sophie, certainly not to Jack – not to any of them, not this.

And anyway, this young woman with her bland smile – and Lizzie hadn't seen anyone else, had she? – was probably one of Saint Christopher's disciples, and this was his clinic, after all, his territory.

And she didn't think she could face not being believed.

140

32

On Monday morning, Tony Patston, in the midst of working on a motor bike at the garage, went to answer a phone call from a man named Eddie Black in Chigwell who said he owned a small fleet of BMWs and had been told that Tony was reliable and no cowboy. And that if Tony was prepared to drop everything and come over to his house to fix one of his cars that same morning, he'd have a line of profitable, legitimate business more or less guaranteed for the foreseeable future.

'If you do a good job, that is,' Black said. 'Obviously.'

'It might take me an hour or so,' Tony said.

'An hour, tops,' Eddie Black told him.

'You got it, mate,' Tony said.

'This is Patston Motors. We can't get to the phone right now, but leave a message, and we'll get back to you soon as we can.'

Joanne waited another few seconds, then put down the phone, pleased with herself for remembering to dial 141 so he wouldn't know it had been her who'd tried the garage three times now.

Funny the things you learned when you had to.

'Come on, my darling,' she said to Irina, who was sitting at the kitchen table eating a banana. 'We're going to the library.'

'Libaree.' Irina looked pleased. 'Going for books.'

'Exactly,' Joanne said. 'My clever girl.'

Within a minute of getting Irina settled at the table by the window with a little pile of books, Joanne saw the man browsing among paperbacks near the computer desks, and knew it had to be him. He was dressed casually, nothing like a solicitor, in beige cotton trousers with a navy blue sweater, but he still looked somehow out of place.

Rich.

Joanne threw one more look at Irina, happy for now with her books, then walked slowly towards him, stopping about a yard away.

'Mrs Patston?' Allbeury asked quietly.

'Yes.'

He smiled at her. 'Where would you like to talk?'

There was a table with three chairs near the entrance, empty at present, but too exposed for Joanne's liking, so she moved, without speaking, to a spot between two stands from where she and Irina would still be able to see one another.

'Is this all right?' she asked.

Allbeury glanced at the titles – pet reptiles to his left, romances to his right – and smiled again. 'Perfect.' He paused. 'I need you to understand,' he said, 'to really believe that you're under no pressure from me, Mrs Patston, that the whole point of this is to help you regain any control of your life you may feel you've lost.'

'How do you know about me? Was it the hospital?' Joanne had to know that before she went on. 'I asked Mr Novak, but he didn't really answer me.'

'One of the nurses, a friend, was worried about Irina and you,' Allbeury said.

'Oh, God,' she said. 'Oh, *God.*'

'It's all right. She didn't make it official.' He paused. 'Is your fear somehow linked to Irina's adoption?'

'Why do you say that?' Joanne asked warily.

'Because Mike Novak was trying to find out a little more about you, and when it came to the adoption, there seemed to be a few blanks.' He paused. 'Please don't worry. Mike's very good at what he does – he didn't make any waves.'

Joanne took another moment, half of her wanting to grab Irina and run away.

You have to trust someone.

'It wasn't legal,' she said, and felt as if she'd jumped off a bridge.

The library remaining quiet, hardly anyone around except the librarians – all engrossed in work, exchanging the odd bit of

142

chatter and displaying no interest in Joanne or Allbeury – they moved, after a while, to the table, opened books and newspapers and spoke in very low voices. Allbeury, Joanne found, was a good listener. She supposed that in his job he had to be.

'I know I should hate Tony,' she said. 'But I've never been able to, not *really*, because he did it all for me, getting Irina the way we did, spending all that money, taking all those risks.' She cast another swift look at the child, went on very quickly. 'I don't think he can help the drinking any more, and the violence happens because of it, and maybe because she reminds him about not being a *real* father. That's how he's always seen it, you see. And it makes him angry.'

'What do you think,' Allbeury asked, 'might happen if you stay with Tony?'

'I don't know.' Tears sprang to her eyes, and she rubbed them away.

'You're very afraid, aren't you?' Allbeury said.

'Yes.'

'What are you most afraid of, Joanne?'

'Irina getting badly hurt,' she said.

'And losing her to the authorities?' he asked.

'That's not just me being selfish,' she said, desperately, and over by the fiction hardbacks, a woman looked up at her. 'She needs me too—' Joanne lowered her voice again '—just as much.'

'Of course she does.' Allbeury paused. 'If you could find a safe place for yourself and Irina to move to, Joanne, a place where neither your husband nor the authorities could find you—'

'I haven't got any money,' she said quickly.

'What I'm offering wouldn't cost you a penny,' Allbeury said. 'You'd be safe in a whole new environment with new identities. And in time, with Irina in school, you could get another job, if you wanted to, become independent.'

'Isn't that what they sometimes do with witnesses?'

'It would be something like that,' Allbeury agreed. 'Except no one would be asking you to bear witness against Tony, because we accept there'd be a real risk of your losing Irina if you did.'

Over by the window, Irina got off her chair.

'I have to talk to her,' Joanne said.

'Go on,' Allbeury said. 'I'll wait.'

He watched her go to the child, talk to her for a moment, saw the little girl's sweet, earnest expression as she absorbed what her mother was telling her, saw her go with her over to the children's shelves, then back to the table with another small pile of books, and sit down with them again.

A good, unusually patient child. It was hard even thinking about what had made her so exceptionally well-behaved.

'I'm sorry,' Joanne said, sitting down again. 'I can't be much longer.'

'I can see that,' he said. 'You must have questions.'

'Why?' she asked. 'Why do you want to do this for me?'

'Because I can,' he replied simply. 'Because you and your daughter need help, and I think I can help you.'

'How do I know I can trust you?' Joanne asked.

'I don't suppose you can know that,' Allbeury answered. 'But then again, do you have any real alternative?' She didn't answer. 'I know I can't begin to imagine what being faced with this kind of choice must be like,' he went on. 'And as I told you at the beginning, it is all down to you. You're in control.'

'But that's not really true, is it? If I say yes to this, I won't be in charge of anything, will I?'

'Not to begin with, no.' Allbeury paused. 'But later.'

'Maybe.' She thought of something. 'What about my mother?'

He'd been ready for that, of course. 'Unless you want your mother to come with you – which is not impossible, though it would, obviously, add some complications – then no, you wouldn't be able to see her, at least not for the forseeable future.'

'I don't know,' Joanne said.

'Of course not,' he said.

'Could we meet again? Talk some more?'

'We could, of course,' Allbeury said. 'Though we'd have to see that Tony was occupied again, and we don't want to make him suspicious.'

'But if Irina and I just vanished,' Joanne said, 'he'd get terribly angry. He'd come looking for us.'

'He wouldn't find you.'

Joanne looked again at Irina, who had turned around in her chair and was now watching them. 'She and my mum really love each other.'

'I know it's hard,' Allbeury said. 'But nothing about a situation

144

like this can possibly be perfect.' He paused. 'Safer, Joanne, if no one else knows. For Irina.'

'Oh, God,' she said, close to tears again.

'Careful,' Allbeury cautioned.

'I know.' She bit her lip, brought herself under control.

'Well done,' he said.

'I'll have to do a lot of thinking,' Joanne said.

'You certainly will.'

'What happens next?'

'If you decide against,' he said, 'then you don't have to do anything. If you have more questions, or the answer's yes, then all you have to do is phone Mike Novak again and tell him.'

'And if it's yes?' Joanne asked, her eyes on his.

'Then the arrangements will be made,' Allbeury said.

33

'Just a little vaginal tear,' Christopher had told her soon after her surgery. 'Be fine again soon, you'll see.'

That's all right then, Lizzie had thought, ironic but still dazed, and after that he'd been so tender with her, first there in the clinic and then, a few days later, taking her home to Marlow, just as he'd been with Edward after his accident, the way he'd been all those years ago with her mother – the way he always was with Jack. And it was a little like being mad, she felt, because it would have been so very much easier to believe him, *in* him.

Except that she was not mad.

Wound and stitches still sore, but strength returning, she made herself confront reality. She no longer had any choice but to tackle Christopher head on. If she did not find the nerve now, she realized, she would end up like too many battered wives, too defeated to stand up for herself.

She planned time alone with him. No trickery, no messing about, simply asking him to come back to Marlow mid-week at a time when the children were at school and Gilly was occupied elsewhere.

It was Wednesday, September the eighteenth, just ten days after her surgery, ten days and several hours since Christopher had raped her, but it felt – a cliché, but nonetheless true – like a lifetime.

She chose her study for the confrontation, her territory rather than his or the whole family's, asked him to sit down in the leather chair on the opposite side of her writing desk.

'I feel,' he said, 'like an interviewee.'

'It's been a long time,' Lizzie began, her mouth dry, 'since I threatened to leave you. But what you did to me on the night of your birthday, what you have since done to me, has made me see that I owe it to our children as well as myself to—'

'You must know—' Christopher interrupted with passionate distress'—you must surely *know* I never meant you to be hurt. I would never, deliberately, have done such a thing, and dear Christ, if I could take back what I did that night, I would.'

'Rape is what you did. Hitting me and raping me. Brutally enough to injure me. And you can't ever take it back.' Lizzie made sure her tone was practical. 'But at least getting over the operation gave me some time to think. I've decided a number of things, Christopher.'

'Don't,' he said.

'I'm still prepared to stay with you, for Jack's sake. Not Edward's or Sophie's, I don't think, not any more, because I think they'd both get over it in time. But I'm really not sure that Jack would.' She took a breath. 'Even so, I'll only be staying if you agree to certain conditions.'

'Anything.'

'You say that so easily,' Lizzie said dryly. 'But we've been here before, remember? Before we found out I was expecting Sophie. You said "anything" then too.'

'Yes.' He removed his glasses, rubbed the bridge of his nose, shut his eyes, then opened them again and looked at her. 'Your conditions.'

'You will never come near me again in any way more intimate than a kiss on the cheek or a hug, and those only in the presence of others.'

Christopher was silent now, grim-faced.

'I have written a letter detailing your various assaults and my injuries, minor and otherwise, as well as your recent gross abuse of your profession—'

'God, Lizzie.'

'I've sealed it and given it to a solicitor – not David Lerman or anyone there.' Lerman was a partner at Allbeury, Lerman, Wren, who'd acted for Christopher and HANDS for years. 'But you can relax in the knowledge that it will remain sealed unless I personally direct it to be opened, or if something happens to prevent me from speaking for myself.'

147

'That's not just melodramatic,' Christopher cut in angrily, slamming his glasses back onto his nose, 'it's outrageous to imply that I'd *think* of stopping you telling anyone in such a way.'

'After what you've done to me—' Lizzie was trembling, but still in control'—after the sheer atrocity of that whole charade in the clinic, let alone what went before, *nothing* seems impossible to me any more.'

'Lizzie, please—'

'I'm aware I might not be instantly believed, but the contents of that letter would certainly be more than enough to encourage my solicitor and my mother to make every effort to have the children taken away from you.'

'I don't believe you'd do that to Jack.'

'It's the last thing in the world I'd ever want to do,' Lizzie agreed. 'But if you don't go along with these conditions now, Christopher, I will have no choices left, so I suggest you do believe me.'

'What else?' he asked quietly.

'Same as before, more or less. You seek psychiatric help.' She had an urge to stand up, walk around, but she was still in some pain, and the last thing she wanted to show right now was weakness.

'And?'

'Are you on drugs, Christopher?'

He blinked, twice, said nothing.

'I strongly suspect that you were on something the night you raped me, and I want you to know that I've included that suspicion in my letter.'

'Don't do things by halves, do you, Lizzie?' The anger was back.

'If I'm right,' she went on, 'and if by any chance you've ever treated any other patient, let alone operated on them, while under the influence of anything like that, then unless you swear to stop immediately and seek treatment for drug dependency too, I will report you without delay.'

'I'm not an addict,' Christopher said.

'Did you take in what I just said?' she asked sharply.

'Yes,' he said. 'I'll deal with it.'

'Swear it,' she said.

'If you believe I'm an addict,' he said, 'then you know better

148

than to take my word for anything.' She said nothing, just waited. 'Very well. I swear it. On our children's lives.'

'Don't,' she said, violently. 'Don't ever say that.'

'I'm sorry.' Christopher took off his glasses again. 'I'm sorry, I'm sorry, I'm so bloody sorry for everything.' His eyes were suddenly full of tears. 'What I did to you that night, what I've done before – *everything*.' He buried his face in his hands for a moment, then lifted it again. 'Just please, please don't tell the children – don't destroy their belief in me, please don't do that, Lizzie.'

'I've already told you I'm staying,' she said.

'Thank you.' It was a whisper.

'One last thing,' she said.

'Anything,' he said again.

'Separate rooms. Here and in the flat, and anywhere we stay. Don't worry, I'll come up with reasons, tell the children and Gilly I'm having trouble sleeping and keeping you awake. Sophie will like having two rooms to invade.'

Christopher took a moment, letting it all sink in.

'Do you think,' he asked at last, 'that you'll ever be able to trust me again?'

'No,' Lizzie answered. 'I don't think I can imagine that.'

34

Clare was in the office alone at nine forty-five on Thursday morning – manning the phones, updating records on the computer, tidying Mike's chaos and generally taking advantage of his being out for the day on a dull, but profitable corporate job in Dagenham – when Joanne Patston telephoned.

'Oh, no,' she said, hearing that Novak was out of the office.

'It's okay, Joanne,' Clare said, gently. 'You don't mind if I call you Joanne?'

'Of course not.'

'And I'm Clare, okay?' She didn't wait for a response, was aware that in the other woman's precariously balanced world every second might count. 'Listen, Joanne, I know you probably don't want Mike to call you, so which would you prefer? You can call him now on his mobile – but he might not be alone – or I can arrange for him to be on his own somewhere private in, say, half an hour?'

There was a pause.

'The second, please. Half an hour.'

Joanne washed up the breakfast things, dropped a cup on the floor, burst into tears, then quickly stopped when Irina started to cry too, and then, once every last fragment had been safely disposed of, she sat down with Irina on the living room sofa and read to her from *Mole and the Baby Bird*, her eyes misting every few minutes, absurdly touched by the tale, though infinitely more so by her daughter's rapt expression.

At ten minutes past ten, Joanne stopped reading.

'Mummy, read more.'

'In a little while, darling,' Joanne said.

'Now, Mummy,' Irina said.

Joanne eased herself up from the sofa, laid the book on the little girl's lap. 'You look at the pictures, sweetheart. Mummy won't be long.'

In a Dagenham car park, Novak was checking the signal on his mobile when it rang.

'Mike Novak,' he answered.

'It's Joanne Patston.'

'Yes, Joanne.' He could almost feel her tension transmitting over the line. 'Clare told me you'd be phoning. What can I do for you?'

'Mr Allbeury said I should give you my answer,' she said.

'That's right.' He paused. 'Or ask me any questions.'

'It's yes,' she said.

Novak felt a kick of excitement. 'Okay,' he said. 'That's great.'

'Is it?' Joanne asked.

'I think so, yes.' He paused. 'Are you sure?'

'As Mr Allbeury said, I don't really have much choice.'

'And is this just for you and Irina?' Novak asked. 'Or your mum too?'

'Just us.' Her voice was very quiet now. 'I know if I tell her, she'll try and talk me out of it, and she doesn't know about . . .'

'Irina,' Novak finished for her. 'I understand.'

'But she won't,' Joanne said.

The sorrow in her voice made him want to cry. Sad women often set him off. Clare called him her big softie, but he knew she loved that side of him. It worked both ways.

'What happens next?' Joanne asked.

'Nothing for a while,' he said, 'which is going to be tough on you, I'm afraid, having to sit tight and act normally while Robin makes the arrangements. He'll be moving as quickly as possible, but these things take time.'

'How much time?'

'Could be as long as a fortnight,' Novak told her. 'Maybe less.'

'Oh, God,' Joanne said.

'How are things at home?'

'Not so bad.' She hesitated. 'He's been in a better mood.'

It was true that Tony had been easier to live with since Allbeury

151

had created his promised 'diversion'. More work on Eddie Black's BMWs, more cash, less time to booze. Except it wouldn't last, Joanne knew that without any real shadow of doubt. On the contrary, if and when the work dried up which, given its source, it would, Tony would be fed up, angry, maybe worse than before.

'It's really vital,' Novak told her, 'that you act just the way you always do till you hear from me. Above all, you mustn't, repeat, you really must *not* talk to anyone about the plan.'

'Since I don't know what the plan is,' Joanne said, 'that's about the only thing that shouldn't be too hard.'

35

The run-up to Christmas aside, October was one of the most active months for Christopher with regard to the charity. First, the winding-up of the financial end-of-year, closely followed by HANDS' largest fundraising dinner at the Savoy, a period during which, as a matter of course, Christopher tended to spend almost as much time in meetings with Dalia Weinberg and the charity's accountants and lawyers, as he did in operating theatres or consulting rooms.

Presenting the united front that Lizzie had tacitly agreed to was proving a strain on them both. Around the children, whom they both loved with equal passion, it was less hard, and in a way, of course, Lizzie had already had years of practice at pretending – as much to herself as others – that all in her marital garden was well. But her declaration of intent had shifted the seat of power in the marriage, and as humble as Christopher was trying to be in private with Lizzie, real humility sat uneasily on his shoulders.

'Will you be coming to the Savoy this year?' he asked her in the kitchen at the house eight days after their confrontation.

'Have you seen a psychiatrist yet?' It was late evening, but she was in the midst of baking, rolling out dough for a pie.

'Appointment next week.' He glanced towards the door.

'Who with?' Lizzie sprinkled a little flour onto her rolling pin. 'It's all right, the children are all in bed and Gilly's taking a bath.'

'It's just for a preliminary chat and referral.'

'Even so,' she said quietly, 'I'd like a name.'

'Going to check up on me?' His cheeks flushed.

'I don't expect so.'

'Duncan Campbell,' Christopher said. 'Tuesday at eight pm.'

He paused. 'He's seeing me out of hours as a professional courtesy.'

'Good,' Lizzie said. 'That's nice of him.'

'I'm sorry,' Christopher said, 'for making you drag it out of me. I know it's part of our deal.'

'It's okay.' Lizzie stopped rolling dough. 'I have no wish to embarrass you.'

'You'd be entitled,' he said.

'I will come,' she said, abruptly, 'to the HANDS dinner.'

'Thank you.' He paused. 'I'm afraid I've another favour to ask you.'

'What's that?' She fetched a pie tin from one of the cupboards, took some softened butter from a large pat, and began to grease the tin.

'You know David Lerman's just had a hip replacement?'

'Of course I know. We sent flowers.'

'I've been dealing with the senior partner, Robin Allbeury.'

'Problems?' Lizzie transferred dough from the board to the tin, pressed it evenly down, then deftly snipped around the edge.

'On the contrary. He's actually a matrimonial expert, but he's doing this as a special favour, and he's extremely able. He's also, as it turns out, something of a fan of yours.'

'That's nice.' She looked at him. 'So what's the favour?'

'I'd like to give him dinner one evening, if you don't mind too much.'

'You want me to come?' she asked.

'What I was really hoping,' Christopher said, 'was that you'd cook.'

'Depends when,' Lizzie said.

'But in principle you're willing?' he asked.

'In principle,' she answered.

'Thank you,' he said again.

36

A week had already passed, and the waiting was pure agony.

Already filled with doubts, guilt and a vast fear of the unknown that she was about to carry her child into, Joanne was now further tormented by the fact that Tony was still behaving like a normal father to Irina. No model, but no monster either.

We could stay.

If she could only know what lay ahead, know just a little more about how her and her daughter's disappearance was going to be arranged, perhaps she might have been less terrified.

Or more?

She had entrusted her own and, far more important, Irina's future, to strangers, to a private detective with a nice face, and to a rich and presumably powerful man who knew – *said* he knew – how to make things happen.

But how did he do that? How could anyone whisk a woman and child out of one world and into another, allegedly happier, safer one? With huge sums of money, obviously, and – surely in some respect – by breaking the law.

And why on earth – this above all the questions going round and round in Joanne's mind as she waited and tried to be normal – should Robin Allbeury, this high-powered solicitor to whom she was nobody, *want* to do all that for her and Irina, to spend all that money on them? Presumably part of the reason had to be that he had so much he wouldn't miss it. Yet that still didn't explain why, not really.

Why? And *when*?

Because if took too much longer, she was going to lose her nerve.

37

'Michael Novak called for you,' Ally King told Shipley when she returned from having lunch with her sister, Laura, down from Manchester (where she lived with husband Gary and their children) for one day. 'I've just stuck a Post-it on your desk.'

Shipley was surprised. 'What did he want?'

'He said he was in the area and wanted to know how the Bolsovers are doing.' DC King was aware that despite the team's present involvement in a new drugs case, Shipley's dissatisfaction with the murder case still lingered. 'Seemed concerned about how the kids are coping.'

'Did he?'

King heard the dryness, and a frown puckered her pretty forehead. 'I know you still think there's something off about him and Allbeury, but you surely don't actually suspect them?'

'Of murder?' Shipley shook her head. 'After all, we've got our killer.'

'Seriously,' the DC persevered. 'I mean, if you've got some reason—'

'I haven't,' Shipley said swiftly.

King knew when a subject was closed. 'Nice lunch?'

'Not really.'

King gave up and went back to work, and Shipley headed back to her desk. Lunch with her sister had been a pain, since all Laura had wanted to do was talk about the new house she and Gary were buying, and how much the kids loved it, and how terrific a husband Gary was, and how much Shipley was missing out on.

'Honestly, Helen, you've no idea,' she'd said, not for the first time.

'I know,' Shipley had said, and tried to focus on her spaghetti.

'I mean, all this is okay,' Laura had said, her tone implying that all *this* was some sort of aberration, 'but if you don't start thinking about the really important side of life soon—'

'It'll be too late,' Shipley had finished for her.

'Exactly,' Laura had said.

Shipley wondered what Laura might think if she'd seen Lynne Bolsover's body on the allotment, the hideous state of it, the ghastly incongruity of decomposition still dressed in a Next jumper and jeans. Definitely not Laura's version of the 'important' side of life, but pretty bloody consequential to Lynne's family.

And to her.

No stone unturned, they used to say, yet one bloodstained rock and rag unearthed by Kylie Bolsover – *child's play* – and the law said whoopee and rolled over onto its proverbial back.

No, of course she didn't suspect Novak of murdering Lynne Bolsover. Nor Allbeury. At least, she didn't *think* so. But whether or not the odd couple had anything whatsoever to do with the killing, Shipley still felt there was a disturbing, ambulance-chasing quality about Allbeury's self-confessed private work.

Unpaid work, she reminded herself yet again. Which made it either more laudable or weirder, depending on how jaded one's outlook. And Lord knew hers was pretty bloody jaded.

Novak phoning her meant nothing.

Except it was a well-documented fact that some killers felt compelled to stay as close as possible to the investigation into their crimes.

Overreacting, Shipley.

She looked at the message King had left, picked up the phone and dialled the number for Novak Investigations.

Novak wasn't there, just his wife, who knew nothing about any specific reasons for his getting in touch.

'Would you like me to ask Mike to call you again?' Clare Novak asked.

'If he wants to,' Shipley said. 'Though I've no news for him, other than what I'm sure he already knows.'

'That John Bolsover's been charged,' Clare said.

'That's it,' Shipley said. 'And the family are coping as well as they can.'

And went back to work.

157

38

'I've said I'm sorry,' Christopher told Lizzie in the kitchen at Holland Park on Sunday afternoon while she strained freshly made chicken stock and tried not to let her irritation get the better of her. 'You're usually so relaxed about dinners I thought you wouldn't mind – and you'd already said I could ask him—'

'I expected more than forty-eight hours' notice.'

'I know, and I apologize. Again.'

'I don't like being away from the children at weekends.'

Christopher's jaw tensed and his eyes narrowed, but then he shook his head very slightly, and took a breath. 'What can I do to help?'

'Nothing,' Lizzie said, still shortly. 'Except phone Gilly and apologize.'

'I thought you already had.'

'I think it might be nice coming from you,' she said.

'Since it's all my fault.'

'Quite,' Lizzie said.

She'd been more than irritated for much of the day, mostly because on Friday – less than twelve hours after broaching the topic with her – Christopher had issued their dinner invitation to Robin Allbeury, and the solicitor had happened to mention that his weekend plans had gone awry, and Christopher had *assumed* that Lizzie wouldn't object, and had said he should come to them on Sunday evening. Dinner on Sunday meant shopping on Saturday, and Lizzie had been hoping to get back to some writing that weekend, and Gilly had been going to have Sunday off, *and* Sophie had started a cold, and Lizzie hated being separated from any of the children when they weren't well. So all in all, she'd been going to tell Christopher to postpone, but then he'd explained to her how remarkably generous Allbeury had been with his time.

'And rather than charging us at his normal rate – almost double David's – he's going to bill us at the usual rate, which is *bloody* good of the man.' Christopher had paused. 'Which was why I thought, when he told me about his cancelled weekend . . .'

'All right, Christopher,' Lizzie had given in.

'Are you quite sure?'

'Yes, of course.'

He'd been very grateful, brought her roses from Moyses Stevens, sent a bouquet to Gilly for messing her about, had even sent a little bouquet of miniature pink roses to Sophie because of her cold. Lizzie hated the fact that those gestures no longer worked on her, but still, she supposed Gilly and their daughter would both be happy, and she had to think of HANDS, and it would have been churlish to make him cancel.

Though their dining room in Marlow was more splendid, Lizzie liked this more intimate room, all pale cream and green, set off tonight by the tall lilies she'd bought that morning in Holland Park Avenue. At the house, any gathering of less than six had to be brought to the big oak table in the kitchen, but here, even with just two guests, there was no sense of being dwarfed.

The suggestion to invite Susan had been Christopher's, one that Lizzie had gladly agreed to, provided the solicitor was not led to believe there was any matchmaking attached, and indeed, sitting drinking her crayfish *bisque* and observing Robin Allbeury as he listened to Susan (more loquacious than usual due to the huge gin and tonic Christopher had poured her before dinner and the very good Montrachet they were all drinking now) talking about her last disastrous romance, Lizzie had to agree that he did seem every bit as delightful as Christopher had described – though charm, which Allbeury had in abundance, was a commodity she'd learned to distrust over the years.

'I should never have agreed to go out with him,' Susan ended her tale.

'He doesn't sound like your usual good taste,' Lizzie agreed.

'He sounds like a prize pillock,' Robin Allbeury said, and grinned. 'If you don't mind my saying so.'

159

'I don't mind a bit,' Susan said. 'It's exactly right.'

'Poor you,' Christopher said.

'I don't know,' Susan said. 'A ghastly evening like that makes you incredibly grateful to get home.'

'Like escaping in an interval of a Wagner opera,' Allbeury said.

'God, yes,' Lizzie agreed fervently.

'You always say you don't mind Wagner,' Christopher said.

'I lie out of kindness,' Lizzie said.

'You're fond of Wagner, are you, Christopher?' Allbeury asked.

'Extremely,' Christopher replied. 'And Richard Strauss.'

Lizzie threw him a very swift, very cold glance, then smiled at Allbeury. 'We went to see *Ariadne auf Naxos* a few weeks ago. My birthday present to Christopher.'

'Gruesome,' Allbeury said.

Memories of the night that had followed the opera flashed through Lizzie's mind.

'Indeed,' she said.

'That soup was unbelievable, Lizzie,' Susan said.

'This is my "homage to Escoffier" night,' Lizzie told her. 'I'm glad you liked it, though I'm not sure he'd have approved. I based it on his *bisque de crevettes*, but I made ordinary chicken stock instead of a real *fonds blanc*.'

'Why did you do that?' Robin Allbeury asked severely.

'Because it was easier,' Lizzie said.

'Shameful,' he said, then grinned again. 'Bet I liked your soup more than I'd have liked Escoffier's.'

'Actually,' Susan said, 'he was all for people adapting his recipes.'

'I'm very impressed,' Christopher said, 'that anyone other than an obsessive cook should have the slightest idea what Escoffier was all for.'

'Do you enjoy cooking, Susan?' Allbeury asked.

'Not really,' Susan said. 'But Lizzie's books have turned me on to cookery reading. I lie in bed late at night and salivate.'

'Sounds interesting,' Christopher said.

'Time to clear the soup plates,' Lizzie said, and stood up.

*

The phone rang while she was in the kitchen, Gilly reporting – because of their agreement about passing on important information regarding the children, no matter what Lizzie or Christopher were in the midst of – that Edward now had Sophie's cold, and that both were running temperatures.

'How high?' Lizzie asked, ready to shed her apron and run.

'Thirty-eight point four,' Gilly said. 'Nothing to get upset about.' She paused, knowing Lizzie well. 'Definitely nothing to make you drop everything and come roaring out of town for, either.'

'Can I speak to them?'

'Both sleeping,' Gilly said. 'Slight headaches and scratchy throats, but no sickness, *no* stiff necks and no rashes. Just feverish colds.'

'And Jack's all right?' Always the question that shot right to the front of her mind, occasionally, she realized, at the expense of the other two.

'So far, so good,' Gilly said. 'But I'll keep checking on him too, even if it does annoy him.'

'Bless you, Gilly,' Lizzie told her.

She told Christopher, asked him for his opinion, felt she had to agree with him that kicking out their guests because of a pair of colds would be a massive overreaction, and prepared to serve *filet de boeuf Saint-Germain*.

The atmosphere was strained after that. Lizzie felt it, knew it was her fault, but could not seem to lift herself sufficiently to overcome it. The food, at least, was, she had to admit, very good, and she noticed real pleasure in Allbeury's dark eyes as he ate, but still her mind kept returning to the children, and, pointlessly now, to the fact that if it weren't for Christopher, she would have been with them now.

Allbeury's eyes, in fact, and the rest of the man, too, were the only aspects of the evening after Gilly's call that really made any impact on Lizzie. Christopher had said how generous he'd been to HANDS, but he had not mentioned how attractive the solicitor was, or how warm and interested those melted-chocolate eyes.

In me, Lizzie thought, unexpectedly, and grew a little warmer.

It was true, though, she realized. Easy-going and attentive to everyone, Allbeury seemed, she thought, just a little gentler with her, as if he knew that her heart was no longer in the evening, but

161

took not the least offence.

'It's been wonderful,' he said, later, at the front door, having insisted on driving the by-now decidedly tipsy Susan home. 'What a very lucky man you are, Christopher.'

'I know,' Christopher said, and put his left arm around Lizzie, who found it a considerable effort not to pull away, and who thought – though it might have been her imagination – that Robin Allbeury had noticed her discomfort.

Nothing much, she decided, escaped that man's notice.

'Did you and Lizzie know each other pre-Vicuna?' Allbeury asked Susan as he drove his Jaguar XK8 towards Battersea Bridge. 'Only you seem more friends than colleagues.'

'If I had to choose,' Susan answered warmly, 'I'd say our friendship's been one of the very nicest things to happen to me in publishing.'

'She does seem lovely,' he said.

'Oh, she is,' Susan confirmed.

'The call about the children clearly upset her.'

'It would. Lizzie's not one to overreact, but she can't help worrying – about them all, obviously, but mostly about Jack catching bugs.'

'Why Jack in particular?' Allbeury asked.

Since Jack's DMD was no secret, Susan saw no reason not to tell him about it, and after that it seemed only natural to talk about the run of far more minor bad luck – comparatively – that the Wades had run into lately: first with Edward's nasty accident and the abandonment of the *Lizzie Piper Roadshow*, and then, more recently, Lizzie's illness.

'Though Christopher dropped everything to look after her at home, so I suppose you'd have to class that as quite good luck,' Susan added.

'What was wrong?' Allbeury asked.

'I'm not sure,' Susan said. 'She was really vague about it.'

Allbeury felt his curiosity unaccountably piqued.

'Probably just a touch of flu,' he encouraged.

'Actually I think it was a bit more than that. Gilly let slip one day when I called that she was in the Beauchamp, but when I phoned they said she wasn't there.'

162

'Odd,' Allbeury said, lightly.

'Oh, dear.' Susan felt suddenly embarrassed. 'I'm not sure she'd want me to have told you that.' *Bloody booze*. 'Not that I've really told you anything.'

'Nothing at all,' Allbeury said, and smiled at her.

39

On Monday morning, a little later than usual, Tony was just finishing his morning fry-up when the phone rang.

'I'll get it,' Joanne said from the sink.

'If it's Eddie Black, I'm here,' Tony said. 'Anyone else, I've gone.'

Joanne dried her hands and picked up the phone from the wall near the oven. 'Hello?'

From above, in Irina's room, Tony heard a series of small thuds.

'Yes.' Joanne tilted her face, listening too, in case her child was in trouble.

Who is it? Tony mouthed at her.

'It could be a bit difficult,' Joanne said.

Tony heard another thump from above, shrugged, picked up his last bit of bacon and put it in his mouth.

'Okay,' Joanne said. 'Bye.'

She put the phone back on its hook. 'Was that Irina?'

'Who else?' He swallowed the remains of his coffee. 'Who was that?'

'Do you want another cup?' Joanne asked.

'No.' Tony looked at her. 'You all right, Jo?'

She turned back to the sink. 'Course.'

'Who was on the phone?'

'Just this woman I met at the library.'

Library. Joanne stared into the sink, biting her lip, wishing she hadn't said that, but it was the first, the *only*, thing that had popped into her mind.

Doesn't matter, she told herself. *He never listens anyway.*

'What did she want?' Tony asked.

164

'She wanted to get together this morning, have a coffee.'

'Why should that be difficult?'

'Difficult?' she echoed.

'You said it might be difficult.' He sounded quite genial.

Does listen sometimes.

She ran the hot tap, struggled not to sound flustered. 'I've got ironing to do, and shopping.'

Tony stood up, picked up his plate, brought it over and put it into the sink. 'Might do you good to get out and meet a friend for a change.' He put out his hand and stroked her hair. 'You've been a bit wound up lately, Jo.'

Blood rushed to her face in a guilty flush.

'PMS,' she said.

There was another thump from upstairs.

'Better see to her,' Tony said.

40

Shortly after nine-fifteen, Lizzie was already well on her way to Marlow in the sporty Japanese coupé she enjoyed driving when she wasn't using the family's wheelchair-modified Range Rover, when her mobile rang.

'It's Susan. Okay to talk?'

'Fine,' Lizzie said. 'On the road, but hands-free.'

'Gorgeous dinner,' Susan said, 'though I drank much too much. How are the children?'

'Not too bad, Gilly says.' Lizzie paused. 'How was your drive home?'

'*Very* nice man,' Susan said. 'Dishy, too, even if he only had eyes for you.'

'Don't be daft,' Lizzie said.

'Robin certainly didn't want to talk about anyone *but* you all the way to Clapham.' Susan sounded merry enough about it. 'No need to sound so surprised about another bloke fancying you.'

'Robin Allbeury does not fancy me.' It was starting to rain, and Lizzie switched on her windscreen wipers.

'You honestly don't realize how attractive you are, do you?'

'Get real, Susan.' Lizzie laughed. 'This is a miserable Monday morning. I didn't get enough sleep last night, and I feel about as attractive as a pair of wet boots.'

'Join the club,' Susan said. 'If you don't believe me about Robin, just ask your husband.'

'What do you mean?'

'Just that I'll bet he noticed.'

'Rubbish,' Lizzie said briskly.

'Nice man, though, you'd have to agree with that,' Susan said.

'I suppose he was,' Lizzie said.

166

41

Shipley attended Hendon Magistrates Court to hear John Bolsover being remanded in custody for a second month not because she had to, but because she felt compelled to see him again.

She wanted to look at the man and *feel* he was guilty.

Which did not happen.

She had also made a point of being there because Mike Novak had made contact again, and she'd agreed to have a drink with him after the hearing.

They found a corner table in The Harp, where the private detective bought her an orange juice and a half of draught for himself. For a matter of about five or so minutes, Shipley relaxed, glad, like Novak, to be away from the oppressive atmosphere of the court, but then her tensions returned.

'So what can I do for you, Mr Novak? First time you called, you said you were in my area. Then you were just returning my call back.'

'Both true.'

'So where did you *happen* to be going this morning? Sailing on the Welsh Harp?'

Novak said nothing for a moment. 'I'm just . . .' He stopped, started again. 'I feel connected to the case.' He shrugged. 'Responsible, in a way.'

'Because?'

'Because I failed Lynne Bolsover, I suppose.'

'Not you, surely?' Shipley said. 'If anyone failed her on that score, I'd guess it was Mr Allbeury.' She paused. 'Is he as concerned as you?'

'We haven't discussed it lately.'

'Out of mind then,' Shipley said.

167

Novak leaned forward, then shook his head and leaned back again.

'What?' Shipley asked,

'Nothing.'

'You looked angry.'

'Not angry, Detective Inspector.' Novak paused. 'I was going to say that, for a person in your position, you make a lot of assumptions.'

It was Shipley's turn to shrug. 'I try not to, on the whole.'

'You've assumed things about Robin Allbeury.'

'Have I?'

They were silent for a moment or two.

'You're not sure it was Bolsover, are you?' Novak's eyes were intent.

'He's been charged.'

'Off the record?'

Shipley drained her juice and glanced at her watch. 'Time I was going.'

'We know he hit her. You found the weapon.'

'No secret.' Shipley stood up. 'Thanks for the drink, Mr Novak.'

He was staring up at her. 'But you still really aren't sure, are you?'

'Goodbye, Mr Novak.'

Novak thought about Helen Shipley as he joined the traffic at Staples Corner, his old Clio chugging a bit. Allbeury had once offered to buy him a new car, and Novak had been sorely tempted, but Clare had frowned when she'd heard about the offer, had thought that a step too far in a direction she'd never been keen on.

'He only suggested it because he wants me to have a reliable car when I'm working for him,' Novak had told her.

'Then let him lend you one *when* you're working for him,' Clare had said.

'He's not interested in owning me,' Novak had gone on, still defensively.

'You're such an idealist,' his wife had told him.

She was right about that, of course, he reflected now, entering the tunnel. His idealism had been a big problem in the police. It was okay, just about, to be that way when you joined, but after that you had to drop most of it and join the cynics, or go on floundering about at the bottom. DI Shipley was a case in point. An intelligent, highly motivated, he guessed, woman who had, Novak was now certain, some strong doubts about John Bolsover's guilt – of murder, at least – but had no real alternative but to toe the line.

Novak would have been hopeless in the same circumstances. As, he thought – surprisingly for such a sophisticated man in such a cynical profession – Allbeury would be too.

Though like Helen Shipley, he realized, Clare would probably not believe that about Robin. Even now, after asking for the lawyer's help on the Patstons' behalf, she still harboured doubts about him.

Then again, he mused, still crawling along, life was filled with doubts for everyone, wasn't it?

Most things, most people.

42

Lizzie was squeezing oranges back in her Marlow kitchen when Allbeury phoned to thank her for the evening.

'Just one snag,' he added. 'Now that I've tasted the real thing, I don't think I'll ever dare try out my Lizzie Piper recipes.'

His voice, Lizzie decided, was mellow and warm. A good voice. 'Christopher mentioned you had one of my books,' she said.

'I have three.' Allbeury paused. 'I look forward to the Roadshow book.'

'On hold, I'm afraid.' Lizzie threw orange peel into her rubbish bin.

'Susan mentioned something about that on the way home.'

'Did she?' Lizzie poured juice into a glass jug. 'I'm glad you enjoyed the evening. I think I was a bit distracted after Gilly rang.'

'Understandable,' Allbeury said. 'How are the young ones today?'

'Not too bad, thanks.'

'Happy to have their mum back, I daresay, and who can blame them?'

'I'm sure they'll be back on form very soon.'

'I know you must have your hands full,' Allbeury said, 'so I won't keep you now, but as and when you and Christopher have a free evening, I really would very much like to return the favour. Or we could do lunch, one Sunday?'

'Sounds lovely,' Lizzie said.

The solicitor thanked her again. 'I really did feel very guilty for keeping you away from your children when they were poorly.'

'Just colds,' Lizzie said, quite briskly.

'But you'd like to have seen that for yourself right away, wouldn't you?'

'Yes,' Lizzie said. 'I suppose I would.'

She thought, making her way upstairs with the juice and glasses, that Susan might be right about him. He really did seem quite genuinely nice.

Case No. 6/201074

PATSTON, J.

Study/Review

Pending

Action

Resolved ✓

43

Shortly before five o'clock that afternoon, Sandra Finch, starting to become anxious about her daughter, telephoned her son-in-law at his garage to ask if he knew where Joanne might have got to.

'Isn't she home?' Tony, who'd had heartburn since breakfast, had just decided he'd done enough work for the day, and was in the midst of cleaning himself up for the pub.

'No, she isn't.' Sandra managed not to add 'obviously'. 'It's just that she brought Irina over to me this morning.'

'So you've had her all day?' He felt annoyed.

'Joanne said she'd be back for her at around lunchtime, but I haven't heard a word from her since, and I'm starting to get quite worried. I've tried her mobile, but it's turned off.'

'It's probably at home – she's always forgetting it.' Tony tucked his phone under his chin and rubbed Swarfega into his hands. 'Why didn't you tell me before, Sandra?'

'I didn't like to worry you.'

'I'm not worried.'

'Do you think your neighbour, Nicki, might know where she is?'

'The Georgious are in Cyprus.' Tony went to the sink, turned on the tap. 'She's probably out shopping or something. If I were you, I'd be pissed off with her for leaving Irina with you all day.'

'I don't mind that at all,' Sandra said quickly. 'I love having her here.'

Tony rinsed off the worst of the grease and squeezed washing up liquid onto his palms. 'It's still taking advantage, isn't it? Of you *and* me, come to that – it was me who told Jo to go out with her friend in the first place.'

'What friend?' Sandra asked.

'Don't know.' Tony's thoughts turned to his need for a drink. 'D'you mind keeping Irina for now?'

'Of course not,' Sandra said. 'But can you please remember to phone me as soon as you hear from Joanne?'

'Yeah, sure,' Tony said. 'Though you'll probably hear first, won't you.'

'I hope so,' Sandra said.

44

Absorbed as he ought to have been by other matters on a Monday afternoon in Bedford Row, Allbeury had found himself unexpectedly preoccupied for a great deal of the time with Lizzie Piper and her husband.

He had expected, he reflected now, pouring himself a modest-sized Scotch from a decanter in his comfortable office, to step into an interesting household, an arena rife, perhaps, with a degree of healthy conflict; with two such high-achievers – one in perhaps the most arrogant profession of all *and* a high-profile philanthropist to boot – it could hardly be otherwise.

Allbeury had learned over many years to set very little store by outward appearance, knew better than many how bruised, even bloody, decent-seeming marriages sometimes were on the inside, how tarnished even the most glittering twosomes could become. And from the outset of yesterday evening, for all the welcoming warmth and courtesy of Lizzie's hospitality and Wade's geniality, he'd had a sense of something being very wrong.

Not just the children.

The call from Marlow, he remembered, had come after the first micro-clash. That thing about the opera. No more than an instant or two, but Lizzie, lovely, warm woman that she seemed, had exuded a real chill in that moment, and his curiosity had been awakened. Then of course she'd heard about the kids' colds – and he hadn't known at the time about the son with muscular dystrophy, poor boy, and that had to be an ever-present source of grief and fear for them all, especially when there were viruses floating around the family.

Poor Lizzie.

But it was the hug at the end of the evening that had really spiked his curiosity and concern – not that he had any business *being* concerned. Christopher had put his arm around Lizzie, and she had let him, had not pushed him away, had stood there beside him on the doorstep, smiling as he and Susan left.

Body language interpretation was, in his opinion, usually over-rated, but there were occasions when it was almost impossible to overlook, and that moment between the Wades had been one of those times. Lizzie might not have actually rejected her husband, but Allbeury was damned sure she hadn't *wanted* his arm around her either, and what he couldn't seem to help wondering was why not? Especially as everything he'd ever read about the Piper-Wade union had all but yelled 'golden couple'.

Busy as he had been at the office, busy as he would continue to be after he got home, dealing with Joanne Patston's predicament, Robin Allbeury just could not get Lizzie Piper out of his mind.

And it troubled him.

Because if Mrs Wade did have the kind of significant problems he suspected she might, then he knew, already, that he might feel tempted to help her.

He had never before decided to *help* a woman to whom he was drawn.

Seriously drawn.

45

Christopher returned to the Beauchamp Clinic shortly before six-thirty after three hours' of intricate surgery at St Clare's on a car accident victim, to learn from Jane Meredith, his PA, that Lizzie had called to say that Jack was now showing symptoms of the viral cold that Edward and Sophie had.

He went swiftly into his office and phoned the house. 'How is he?'

'Not bad,' Lizzie told him. 'Temperature just a little up.'

'Has Hilda been?'

'An hour ago. She was very reassuring.'

'Good.' Christopher paused. 'Shall I come?'

'If you can, I'd appreciate it,' Lizzie admitted.

'Ten to fifteen catching up with Jane,' Christopher said, 'and I'll be on my way.'

'Drive carefully,' Lizzie said. 'He really is all right.'

She felt better already, just knowing that he'd be home by around eight. The other two were already shaking off the worst of their own colds with the ease of healthy youngsters, and it was more than likely that, treated and monitored carefully, Jack would follow suit, but Lizzie and Christopher both knew that in a boy with DMD, where there was, ultimately, every probability of heart and lung involvement, any kind of respiratory infection had some potential for risk. Lizzie had every faith in Hilda Kapur, but Gilly was off now, and even if she had been here for moral support, it was at times like these when, still, after all this time, Lizzie most valued Christopher's presence.

177

'Did you speak to Dad?' Jack asked as soon as she went back into his room.

'I did.' Lizzie laid a palm on his forehead, which felt too warm. 'He's finishing up at the clinic and then he's coming home.'

'I don't want him to come specially, Mum.' Jack hated what he called 'the whole rigmarole' that happened whenever he sneezed a few times or ran even the lowest of fevers. 'Call him back and tell him I'm fine.'

'He was coming anyway,' Lizzie lied.

'Bet he wasn't.'

Jack coughed, and Lizzie tensed.

'Overreacting, Mum,' he said, seeing her expression. 'It's just a tickle.'

'I know,' she said.

He coughed again.

'All right?' she asked.

Jack nodded, but went on coughing.

'How about some soup?'

He shook his head.

'Tea?'

He nodded. 'Please.'

'Anything to get rid of me, right?' Lizzie said.

'Yup.' He lay back against his pillows.

As she left the room, he was coughing again.

46

Tony was drunk when he got home, but not so much as not to notice that his house was still empty and pitch dark, and *definitely* not too drunk not to be bloody narked by the fact.

He turned on the lights, shut the front door behind him, swayed into the living room, picked up the cordless phone, tried and failed to remember his mother-in-law's number, then remembered that Joanne had it on a memory button, keyed it and sank down onto the sofa.

'Hello?' Sandra sounded agitated.

'She's not here,' Tony said. 'Is she with you?'

'Tony, where have you *been*?'

She sounded more than agitated. She sounded *accusing*, and obviously that was because he hadn't got in touch with her or, more likely, because he was slurring his words a bit, but with no wife or kid or dinner at home, why shouldn't he have a few drinks?

'Is she there?' he asked, more belligerently than he meant to.

'*No*, and I haven't heard a word, and obviously you haven't, and I'm getting really scared now, Tony. I think you should phone the police.'

'That's a bit over the top, isn't it?'

'I don't think so,' Sandra said.

He shifted on the sofa and tried to think of something helpful to say, because his mother-in-law really did sound frightened, and now he came to think of it, he couldn't remember a single time in the whole of their marriage when Joanne had gone off and not phoned or left a message.

179

'I'll have a scout round – make sure she hasn't put a note in some daft place.'

'Okay,' Sandra said. 'Thank you, Tony.'

He stood up with an effort, wandered around the room, then went back into the hall, into the kitchen, turning on more lights as he went.

'There's nothing,' he told his mother-in-law.

'Call the police,' she said.

He aimed himself back into the living room. 'Hang on a minute, Sandra. Tell me what Jo said when she dropped Irina off this morning.' He sat down again with relief. 'She okay, by the way?'

'Fine. No problems. She's having a nap in my bed.'

'Lovely,' he said. 'So didn't Jo tell you who she was meeting?'

'She was in a rush. I told you, she just said she'd be back around lunchtime.' Sandra paused. 'Tony, you said something about a friend.'

'Just this woman who phoned at breakfast time,' Tony said.

'Didn't she tell you her name?'

'No.' He thought back, as well as he could in his beer and whisky fog. 'No, she didn't.' He paused again. 'She was a bit funny about going, I remember that, said she had ironing to do. I told her it would do her good to get out. This is what I get for trying to help her lighten up.'

'She must have said something about the woman,' Sandra persisted.

He searched his memory again, anything to put an end to this so he could get some bloody *sleep*. 'The library,' he said. 'That's what she said. Some woman she'd met at the library – she's always taking Irina to the library.'

'But no name,' Sandra said.

'For crying out loud,' Tony said, losing patience. 'How many more times? If I'd known then she was planning to dump our daughter and piss off for the whole day and half the night—'

'Tony, something might have happened to her.' Sandra was angry.

'Like what? If she'd had an accident, we'd have heard.'

'You haven't been home,' Sandra pointed out. 'At least call the hospital.'

'Which one?' He grew kinder again. 'Sandra, love, I've been at

180

work and you've been home, so if anything bad had happened, someone would have got hold of one of us.'

'I suppose so.' She paused. 'What about Irina?'

'I don't know,' Tony said. 'I don't think we should disturb her, do you?'

'Definitely not.'

'And will you be okay to keep her tomorrow? Only I've got a backlog at work.'

'What about the police?' Sandra asked.

'Not yet,' Tony said, decisively. 'Honestly, love, she'll probably turn up any minute, and we'll both yell at her and then have a good laugh about it.'

'Do you really think so?' She sounded as if she wanted to be convinced.

'Yeah, of course.' He was definite.

'It's getting so *late*,' Sandra said.

'And we're both on the phone,' Tony said. 'And we haven't got Call Waiting, so we'd better stop in case she's trying.'

'Call me if you hear anything. Anything, *any* time.' She paused. 'And first thing, if she isn't back, will you call the police?'

'She'll be back, Sandra. I know she will.'

'I hope so.'

In her house in Edmonton, Sandra Finch put down the phone and went immediately upstairs to check on her granddaughter.

Irina stirred as she came into the room.

'It's all right, darling.' Sandra went to the bed, sat down carefully on the edge, stroked the little girl's warm, soft cheek. 'Go back to sleep.'

'Is my Mummy here yet?' The voice was snuffly and dreamy.

'Not yet, darling, but soon. Go back to sleep.'

Irina opened her black cherry eyes more fully, and looked up into her grandmother's face. 'Is Daddy coming?'

'No, darling. Daddy's not coming tonight, but he sent you a big kiss and said you should stay here with me, if that's all right with you. Is it all right, sweetheart?'

The child didn't answer, was already drifting back off into sleep, but before the eyes were quite shut, they and her whole face had lit up into a beautiful smile.

Sandra had seen Irina smile like that all too seldom. She was

181

not at all sure, suddenly, that she wanted to know the reason for that, but it was lovely, *more* than lovely, to have the little girl here with her.

If only she knew where Joanne was, knew that she was safe, she could have simply lain down beside Irina, stroked her soft, dark hair, and taken purest pleasure from this night.

But she did not know where her daughter was.

Call the hospitals, she told herself, *and you'll feel better.*

More than forty-five minutes later, having established that no one of Joanne's name or description had been brought into A&E at either Whipps Cross or Waltham General, Sandra sat in an armchair with a cup of strong, sweet tea and waited to feel better.

All she felt was sick.

Sick and old and afraid.

More than afraid.

47

Jack's temperature was up to a hundred and two.

'Feeling wretched, aren't you?' Christopher said, holding his son's hand lightly. 'Fevers are buggers, even if they are protection mechanisms.'

Jack knew that people shivered to raise heat and perspired to create heat loss, had learned about things like that because his dad believed anxiety often came from the unknown, and fretting about feeling lousy only made you feel worse.

He really did feel lousy.

'I'm okay,' he said.

'Good boy,' Christopher said.

'Glad you're here,' Jack said softly.

'I'll always be here when you need me,' Christopher said. 'If I can.'

'I know,' Jack said. 'Mum gets in a tizz when I'm ill.'

'Does she?'

'She tries to hide it, but I see it in her eyes.' Jack took a slightly wheezy breath, swallowed and grimaced a bit because his throat was sore. 'She's better when you're here too.'

'I'm glad,' Christopher said.

Jack looked at him for a moment. 'You okay, Dad?'

'Me? I'm fine, Jack.'

'This is just a bad cold, you know. Dr Kapur told me when Mum was out of the room, and she's always straight with me. Lots of fluids – the usual – and I'll be fine.'

'He's getting a bit chesty,' Christopher said to Lizzie in the kitchen, where she was making him a sandwich. 'If he's no better in the morning, I might have a word with the Centre.'

There were only three specialist centres in the country funded by the Muscular Dystrophy Campaign, staffed by experts in neuromuscular conditions, and the Wades were fortunate enough to be in easy reach of two of them, one based at the Radcliffe Infirmary in Oxford, the other at Hammersmith Hospital.

'Do you think we should ask Hilda to get him admitted?'

Christopher saw the fear in her eyes. 'No need for that at present.' He looked down at the thick-cut granary bread on which she'd laid several slices of rare roast beef, with his favourite gherkins inserted between them. 'That looks wonderful.'

'Mustard?' Lizzie shook her head. 'Of course mustard.'

Christopher watched her add hot English mustard, lay the covering slice on top, flatten slightly, cut the sandwich into two and set it on a plate. 'Thank you, Lizzie.'

'You're welcome.'

Edward wandered in, wearing one of the baggy T-shirts and shorts sets he preferred to pyjamas. 'Is Jack okay?'

'Not so famous right now,' Christopher told him.

'Why aren't you asleep?' Lizzie asked. 'And where are your slippers? You've still got a cold too, darling.'

'I'm heaps better, Mum.' Edward sat on one of the chairs around the table. 'Sophie's awake too. She wanted to go in and sit with him, but I told her no.'

'Probably wise,' his father said, 'though she's not likely to catch it back.'

'Is Sophie all right?' Lizzie asked.

'Worrying about Jack,' Edward said, nasally.

'No need for her to worry,' Lizzie said. 'Either of you.'

'I suppose you and Dad are cool about it then?' He was wry.

'We're vigilant,' Christopher said. 'That's all.'

'Just commonsense,' Lizzie added.

'Okay,' Edward said. 'I think Sophie's upset because she started the cold.'

'I hope you told her that's nonsense,' Christopher said.

'I told her she didn't start it,' Edward said. 'I told her the same cold just goes round and round the country, and it's just bad luck which person gets it next.'

'Not strictly true, I don't think,' his father said.

'I don't think that's what matters, is it?' Lizzie came and sat between them. 'You both know very well that we all feel a bit like

184

Sophie when we catch any bug and bring it home. We're always scared Jack will catch what we've got, and that it might make him worse, and that's what's nonsense, because it just can't be helped.'

'Doesn't stop us feeling that way though, does it?' Edward said.

Christopher put out his hand and ruffled his son's dark hair. 'Want some of my sandwich?'

'No, thanks, Dad.'

Lizzie got up. 'Think I'll have a quick chat with Sophie, and look in on Jack.'

'He's probably sleeping,' Christopher said.

'I won't wake him,' she said.

'I know you won't.' He looked at her in the doorway. 'If Sophie can't get off, tell her to come down for a bit.'

Sophie, apparently sufficiently consoled by Edward, at least for the present, had fallen asleep, snoring a little, rather sweetly, from the remains of her own cold. Lizzie stroked her hair, smiling at Edward's image of the nation's single cold doing circuits of the country, picking up victims the way the Circle Line did passengers.

She left Sophie, moved to Jack's room, opening the door very quietly and staying in the doorway, going no further because sometimes, if he was restless, a creaking floorboard was enough to disturb him. Christopher was right; he was sleeping. She stood there for another few moments, watching, listening to her son's breathing. There was a slight chestiness, but nothing worse than Edward's when she'd returned to the house on Monday morning.

Only yesterday, she realized. It seemed longer ago.

Jack stirred, cleared his throat a little, shifted restlessly, then lay still again.

Lizzie waited a little longer in case he woke.

'Please God,' she said, very softly.

48

'Mike, it's Robin.'

Just after seven-thirty on Tuesday morning, and Allbeury was on his terrace, drinking coffee and eating a croissant – no butter needed, perfect as it was.

'What's up?' Novak, too, was still at home, but quite accustomed to hearing from his number one client early in the day.

'Everything's in place for Joanne and Irina,' Allbeury said. 'So I need you to get final confirmation from her that she's ready so we can set things up to keep Mr Patston busy on the day.'

'Do you have a day in mind?' Novak asked.

'Thursday,' Allbeury said. 'If she needs more time, Friday's possible, but try to discourage it. Every day that passes, she'll be more tempted to tell someone.'

'Or bottle out.'

'If she's not certain, Mike, I don't want her going through with it.'

'I'll call soon as Patston's gone,' Novak said. 'He leaves by eight most days.'

'Careful where you call from.'

'I know,' Novak said.

'Of course you do,' Allbeury said, and put down the phone.

'She'll be scared,' Clare said, after he told her.

'Yes,' Novak said.

They were in their small kitchen, sitting on stools at the counter that doubled as a worktop. Ordinarily Clare enjoyed breakfast, but this morning she seemed to have little appetite, nibbling round the edges of a slice of toast.

'You okay?' he asked.

'Fine.'

Novak drained his coffee, got to his feet. 'Got to go.' He kissed her on the nape of her neck.

'Mike, how do we know Robin's really going to take care of Joanne and Irina long-term?'

'If the job's done properly,' he said, putting his cup in the sink, 'then I suppose we never will know that for sure.' He saw her suddenly bleak expression. 'No perfect answers, sweetheart.'

'No,' she said.

The bleakness unsettled him. 'You feeling down?'

'Not really.' She smiled. 'Bit tired.'

'Doing too much?' Novak often thought she put too much pressure on herself, working at the agency *and* helping out Nick Parry – giving more time to him lately because another of his carers had left London, and Clare always gave her all, was wholly incapable of doing anything by half.

'Not at all.' She craned her head to see the oven clock. 'Time you were gone.'

It was eight-thirty before Novak had found a pay phone inside King's Cross Station that accepted coins *and* worked.

He put in a pound coin and dialled.

'Hello?'

The male voice – brusque, presumably Patston's – caught Novak off-balance. 'Sorry, mate,' he said, quickly. 'Must have misdialled.'

'Watch what you're doing then,' the voice said, and put down the phone.

Novak stepped away from the pay phone, pulled his mobile from his jacket, keyed Allbeury's home number and filled him in.

'Hopefully he's just late,' he said. 'Maybe got a hangover.'

'Should be used to those,' Allbeury said.

'Maybe he just overslept,' Novak said. 'Or maybe he's got flu.'

'Maybes aren't much use to me right now,' Allbeury said.

'I don't think I should call again just yet. Want me to go take a look?'

'Soon as you can,' Allbeury said. 'I don't want this on hold any longer than necessary.'

49

At five minutes to nine o'clock, a woman cyclist named Phyllis Eder who regularly cycled through Epping Forest with Dirk, her energetic, but placidly-natured springer spaniel, on a long lead attached to her bike, was taking a pleasurable morning ride, thoroughly enjoying the sights and smells of autumn, when the dog took off unexpectedly and yanked so hard on his lead that Phyllis swerved, crashed into an oak tree, and fell off.

'Dirk!'

Finding, after a moment or two, that she was not really hurt, she got shakily up, brushing leaves and dirt off her tracksuit, and looked over at her dog, still attached to the lead, barking loudly, digging at something, tail wagging.

'Dirk!' she called again. 'Stop that and *come*.'

He took no notice, went on barking, scrabbling away at what looked like nothing more than a small, leaf-covered hummock.

Phyllis bent to pick up the bike, and went to take a look for herself.

'What is it, Dirk?'

The spaniel stopped digging and looked at her expectantly.

Phyllis Eder bent halfway, then froze.

Not a hummock.

No mistaking what it was.

The partially leaf- and branch-covered body of a woman.

50

'He's much better.'

The first words Lizzie heard when she woke at nine-fifteen – much later than she'd intended to sleep – spoken by Christopher. Very briefly it occurred to her that he hadn't knocked, as he generally did these days, or that if he had, she hadn't heard.

Not that it mattered right now.

She got out of bed, put on her dressing gown, looked at Christopher, already fully dressed in suit and tie. 'No temperature?'

'Just a touch,' he said.

'Could go up again,' Lizzie said.

'Or down.' He smiled at her. 'He's on the mend, Lizzie.'

Real relief struck her almost like a small blow and, temporarily weakened, she sat down on the edge of the bed. 'Sorry,' she said.

'I was the same,' Christopher said gently.

Lizzie looked up into his face. 'We always are, aren't we?'

'Always will be,' he said.

However long *always* might be, she thought, knew she didn't need to say. It was always the same for them whenever Jack became unwell and then recovered, always that same immense weight lifting for a moment, then descending again almost immediately in a kind of superstitious fear that seemed to grow, Lizzie thought, each time Jack went through any kind of crisis, however minor. Each recovery a small miracle for which they were both – all – vastly grateful. Each, they could not seem to help fearing, signalling another slip closer to the brink.

'They've all had breakfast,' Christopher said.

'Goodness,' Lizzie said. 'Thank you.'

189

'It was a pleasure.' He smiled again. 'Edward and Sophie have both got their appetites back, but even Jack managed one pancake.'

'Goodness,' Lizzie said again. 'Pancakes.'

'Special request by Edward,' Christopher explained. 'I could hardly refuse.'

'Maple syrup?'

'What else?'

Lizzie stood up, suddenly hungry too. 'Don't suppose there are any left?'

'I saved you a few,' Christopher said.

It was at moments like that that Lizzie almost forgot their troubles.

Almost.

51

The uniforms had come first, then CID – just as the weather had changed, bringing rain; the surrounding area had been cordoned off and, soon after, the team from the Major Investigation Section at Theydon Bois had arrived, its leader Detective Superintendent Ann McGraw attending the scene together with the detective inspector whose job it would be to investigate the crime, Jim Keenan.

'Very nasty,' McGraw said as they stood inside the Incitent, waiting for Simon Collins, the ME – running late after a hit-and-run – to arrive, pronounce 'life extinct' and conduct a preliminary examination.

Keenan, older than McGraw by at least a decade, with pepper-and-salt hair and a lined, thin face, looked down at the dead woman, at the nightmare of wounds in her chest and abdomen and – bloodiest of all – her neck; looked at the face, ghastly in both colour and contortion, and though he knew, after more than a year of working under Ann McGraw, that she preferred self-control at all times, he found it very hard not to give way to the sick, sad rage burning its way up through him.

'I'll leave her in your hands then, Jim,' McGraw said.

'Thank you, ma'am.'

They both emerged – moving as carefully as they'd entered – out of the tent into the rain, removed their paper suits and plastic overshoes, bagged them as evidence, and then Keenan waited until his team head had vanished from sight before taking a couple of minutes to walk around the perimeter of the cordoned-off area, glad of the opportunity to get his head and stomach together. Collins would be with them shortly, and after that it would be the

191

mortuary, leaving the crime scene to the fingertip search team, so what Keenan wanted right now was a few gulps of decent air in which the only scent of decay came, sweetly and naturally, from the layers of old dead leaves under his feet. Jim Keenan liked forests, their sounds and shadiness as well as their smells; they reminded him of nature rambles with his school as a young boy living just outside Croydon.

'Sir?'

Too good to last. He turned around. The young, already rain-bedraggled, PC, whose job it presently was to log people in and out of the crime scene, was shifting from foot to foot.

'Sorry, sir, but Dr Collins is here.'

'Right you are,' Keenan said.

And snapped back to the present, in all its ugliness.

Simon Collins, crisp-looking despite the weather and circumstances, told Keenan little more than he had already seen for himself, namely that the deceased had been stabbed four times, that, judging by the heavily blood-spattered surroundings and the appearance of the body and clothing, the attack had taken place at that location, and, finally – though that would have to be confirmed later – that she had died about twenty-four hours earlier.

'One piece of luck,' Collins said, gently raising one red-stained hand.

'Skin under her nails?' Keenan asked.

'A little,' the ME said.

Keenan knew there was no point speculating now. The stuff under the woman's nails might be her own, if she'd clawed at her own wounds, but if they were lucky, they might perhaps have something to play with.

Don't hold your breath, Jim.

He went for another walk, this time with senses on full alert, hoping against hope that his eyes might just fall on some perfect piece of evidence, preferably the murder weapon dropped in a panic, *and* with a full set of prints on it.

Even seasoned detectives could dream.

52

'What did the police say?'

The first time Sandra had called Tony at the garage that morning to ask him that, he'd fobbed her off by telling her he was with a customer, but he knew now that he was going to have to come clean.

'I haven't called them yet.'

'Why not?' Sandra was horrified. 'Tony, Joanne's been out all night. You have to report her as missing.'

'It's hardly been twenty-four hours,' Tony said.

'I don't care,' his mother-in-law said. 'My daughter's missing, and if you don't tell the police, I will.'

'They'll only think we've had a row.'

'Have you?' Sandra asked. 'Did you have a row?'

'No, of course not.'

'Then why don't you want to phone them?'

'Because you've already phoned the hospitals, so we know she hasn't—'

'I only phoned Waltham General and Whipps Cross.'

'How many other hospitals are there round here who *take* bloody casualties, Sandra?' Tony demanded. 'You think of any, I'll phone them.'

'I don't understand you,' she said, 'I really don't. If Joanne was all right, she'd have phoned to check on Irina, wouldn't she?' Her son-in-law didn't answer. 'Even if you two did have some kind of row, and you don't feel like telling me—'

'We didn't have a fucking *row*, okay?'

'No, it's not okay.'

'Well, that's just too bad, isn't it, because I'm not going to

193

phone the fucking police because my wife's gone off in a strop.'

'Could you stop swearing, please,' Sandra asked, quite softly.

'Yeah. Okay. Sorry.' Tony paused. 'I'm just upset.'

'So am I.'

'I know.'

'So are you going to phone the police now, or am I?'

Tony took a breath. 'I will.'

'Promise?'

'Sandra, if I said I will, then I will.'

'I don't know how you can bear to work,' Sandra said. 'I don't know why you're at the garage. Why aren't you at home, or out looking for Joanne?'

'Jo expects me to work, Sandra. We have bills to pay, remember?'

'But you are going to phone now, aren't you?'

'Sandra, you're really starting to wind me up.'

'Good,' she said, and put the phone down.

53

'Still nothing,' Novak told Allbeury at five to twelve, sitting in the Clio a few hundred yards down the road from the Patston house.

It was the fourth time he'd phoned in that day, and Allbeury had long since informed his contacts that a delay was likely in the effort to remove Joanne and Irina Patston from their situation.

'No one home here,' Novak said. 'No sign of Joanne's Fiesta, all windows still closed, front and back, no visible movement.'

'Irina still with the grandmother?'

'In Edmonton, yes. And last time I looked, Patston was working on an old Sierra at the garage.' Novak paused. 'I hope I'm over-reacting, Robin, but I don't like the feeling I'm getting.'

'Do you mind sticking around a while longer?'

'Not at all,' Novak said.

Allbeury put down the phone and leaned back in his chair, returning his mind to his other current preoccupation, Lizzie Piper Wade.

His then – and now – state-of-the-art home computer system had been set up five years earlier by Adam Lerman, his partner's son, a student back then with a flair for computer technology and a passion for the Internet. Alas, Lerman Jr had since gone to live in Los Angeles, and obliging as he was about being e-mailed by Allbeury at all times of day and night with queries about add-ons and up-to-date software and above-average difficulties, it was not nearly as satisfactory as having Adam able to come and sit at the two terminals in the penthouse.

Nevertheless, Allbeury had not spent all that time with Adam and post-Adam without learning a good deal about PCs and the Internet and how to make full use of them for his own purposes.

195

For the most part, when it came to research, he tended to save himself time and effort by using Novak Investigations, but Mike was otherwise occupied and in any event, this was one piece of work he felt more inclined to tackle personally.

54

At Patston Motors, Tony had his head – thumping despite the second dose of paracetamol he'd swallowed with a Becks for lunch ten minutes earlier – back under the bonnet of the Sierra that Novak had seen him working on earlier, when a blue Mondeo pulled up in the forecourt and two men got out.

He knew, instantly, they were police.

'Mr Patston?' The older of the two men fished in his pocket.

'Yes.'

The man produced his warrant card. 'I'm Detective Inspector Keenan, and this is Detective Sergeant Reed. We're from the Major Investigation Section based at Theydon Bois.'

The word 'major' gave Tony a hollow, sick feeling in his stomach. 'Is this about my wife?' He wiped his hands nervously on his overalls, looked from one man to the other. 'Only she went missing yesterday, and I was . . .'

'Could we go inside, Mr Patston?' Keenan interrupted him gently.

'Can't we talk here?'

'Might be better if you had a seat, sir,' Terry Reed, a stockily-built man with a sharp, almost bird-like face, suggested.

'God,' Tony said, and began to sweat. 'What?'

'I'm afraid I have some very bad news for you,' Keenan said, gently.

'Oh, God.' Tony felt his legs begin to shake. 'Oh, Christ, what's happened?'

'Sir, let's go inside,' DS Reed said.

'Tell me here,' Tony said. 'For God's sake, tell me what's happened to Jo.'

'This morning,' Jim Keenan said, 'just before nine o'clock, the body of a woman was found in Epping Forest. I'm afraid we believe her to be your wife.'

'Epping Forest?' Tony's voice was pitched suddenly higher, ringing with disbelief. 'Why would Jo be in Epping Forest?' He shook his head, managed a smile at both men. 'You've made a mistake. It couldn't be Joanne.'

'Unfortunately, Mr Patston,' Keenan said, 'we don't believe it is a mistake.'

'We need you to come with us, sir.' Reed started towards the one-storey building that housed Patston Motors' office. 'To identify her.'

Tony stayed put. 'If you need me to do that, then you're not sure it's her.' He stared at Keenan. 'Her bag, is it? Oh, God.'

'I'm sorry to say that a handbag has been found close by,' the detective inspector confirmed.

'Oh, Christ,' Tony said. 'Oh, Jesus Christ.'

'You'll want to lock up, I should think, sir, won't you?' Reed said. 'Or is there someone else to look after the place while you're gone?'

Tony leaned against the Sierra, visibly shaking. 'My little girl,' he said. 'She's with her grandmother.' His eyes filled. 'Oh, God, Jo's mum.'

'I really am very sorry, Mr Patston.' Keenan's lined face creased even further with sympathy. 'But in the circumstances, I'm afraid we really do need you to come with us now.'

'Oh, God,' Tony said again. 'Oh, Christ.'

Mike Novak, just cruising past Patston Motors for another look, saw Tony Patston getting into a dark blue Mondeo with two men he was almost certain were CID.

He pulled up at the corner, held up an *A-Z* to mask the fact he was watching them, saw the car pull away, waited for another two cars for cover, and then followed.

55

At half past one, Mike Novak called Allbeury again.

'Bad news, Robin,' Novak said. 'The worst, it looks like.'

'Tell me.'

'The police have picked up Patston, and taken him to Waltham Forest.'

'Hospital?' Allbeury asked.

'Mortuary,' Novak said. 'They went in a few minutes ago. I'm outside.'

Allbeury was silent.

'I presume you don't want me to go in?' Novak asked.

'Definitely not. But stick around if you can.'

'I'll get back to you when I know something.'

'Right,' Allbeury said. 'Be careful, Mike. I'm really not keen for the police to know about my involvement.'

'Goes without saying,' Novak said.

Inside the mortuary, Jim Keenan waited patiently while Tony Patston, to all intents and purposes in a state of deep shock, sat with his head down between his legs. The newly-bereaved man's hands were shaking, and when Patston looked up, his eyes were wet and glassy, staring out of a chalky-white face.

'I can't believe it,' Patston said. 'I can't take this in.'

'I'm very sorry,' Keenan told him.

'Do you know . . .?'

Keenan waited again while the other man controlled himself.

'Do you know who did that to her?' Tony asked, finally.

'Not yet,' Keenan said. 'But we will.'

DS Reed appeared with a cup of tea, but Tony shook his head.

199

'Sir?' Reed offered it to Keenan.

'Mr Patston.' Keenan ignored the tea. 'Whenever you're ready, I'm afraid I'm going to have to ask you a few questions.'

'All right.' Tony looked up at him. 'But can we do that at home? I want to see my daughter.'

'Of course you do,' Keenan said. 'We've already sent an officer to your mother-in-law's house. Probably best you and Irina stay there for now anyway.'

'I don't want to stay there,' Tony said.

'We'll be needing to search your house,' Keenan told him, 'as a matter of routine. So it really would be easier for everyone, especially your little girl, if you stay away while that's happening.'

'Right,' Tony said, then shook his head in bewilderment. 'Why do you want to search our house?'

'As I said,' Keenan replied, 'it's routine.'

'Right,' Tony said again, and stood up.

He felt numb – *not numb enough* – about what he'd just been shown.

Joanne. His wife, but *not* his wife at all.

What was shaking him though, almost as much, at this instant, really startling him, was that what he'd just said to the policeman was true. He wanted, quite desperately, more than *anything*, to see Irina, to feel her in his arms.

Jo would love that, he thought.

Again his eyes filled with tears.

Novak watched them emerge from the mortuary, saw Patston's ashen face, resisted the impulse to call Allbeury again and followed instead from a safe distance as they drove to Edmonton. To the semi-detached house, outside which a marked police car already stood.

He parked well away, just close enough to see comings and goings. He saw the door being opened by a female constable for Patston and the two plainclothes officers – who might, he thought, be AMIT or, if something had happened to Joanne further out than Waltham Forest, MIS from either Theydon Bois or Harlow.

He didn't see either the grandmother or the little girl.

They were there though, inside the house. He could almost feel it.

Almost feel the pain.

*

'Oh, God,' Tony Patston said when he saw Sandra and his daughter both sitting on the couch in his mother-in-law's living room. 'Oh, God, Sandra, it's so—'

He stopped speaking when he saw her right index finger fly to her lips.

Silencing him.

Irina doesn't know.

He managed it somehow, dragged himself together, put out his arms.

'Hello, my love,' he said to Irina.

The little girl didn't move, neither closer to her grandmother, nor towards him.

Tony went to her, knelt on the carpet before the sofa, took her small hand in both of his and did his best not to cry.

'All right, Irina,' he said, gently. 'All right, my darling. Daddy's here.'

'Where's my Mummy?' Irina asked Sandra.

'It's all right,' Tony said again. 'Daddy's here.'

Behind him, in the doorway, DI Jim Keenan looked at Karen Dean, the slim, attractive dark-haired DC who'd been sitting with Sandra Finch since she'd been brought the news, and saw that the child's lack of response to her father had not escaped her. He was glad to have Dean on the case, knew that she was excellent with little kids.

He, for the most part, did better with grandmothers.

56

At three-thirty, in Marlow, Christopher received a phone call from Jane Meredith telling him of an urgent case coming in to the Beauchamp that evening.

'I'm not sure,' he told her, then noticed Lizzie gesturing. 'Hold on, could you, Jane? My wife's telling me something.'

'Just telling you to go, if you're needed,' Lizzie said. 'Jack's so much better.'

'I'd be happier if the fever were right down,' Christopher said.

'If Jack hears you turning down a patient,' Lizzie said, 'he'll have a fit.'

Christopher smiled, lifted the phone back to his ear. 'On my way, Jane.'

The next call, just after Christopher had driven away, was from Susan Blake.

'Is it all right to talk shop?' she asked after they'd chatted about family and Jack's cold in particular. 'Only we really need to discuss publicity for *Pure Bliss*.'

'Goodness,' Lizzie said. 'Is it that time already?'

'We definitely want to tour you again,' Susan said now. 'The subs are looking excellent, and it's the right moment to boost the Roadshow people's appetites.'

'When will you need me?' Lizzie asked.

'Thursday week. Please say that's okay.'

Lizzie panicked silently, then told her it would be. 'Subject to all the usual things,' she added quickly.

'I know,' Susan said. 'Children first, books last.'

'I wouldn't put it quite like that,' Lizzie said.

'Yes, you would. So, all things being equal, I thought we'd start in Oxford.'

'Lovely,' Lizzie said.

57

Novak had just finished talking to Allbeury on his mobile, and was keying the #1 speed-dial to let Clare know what was going on, when he became abruptly aware that the front door of the Patston house had opened and that a man – the younger of the two plainclothes officers who'd earlier gone in with Tony Patston – was now bearing down, rather rapidly, on the Clio.

'Mike?' Clare's voice.

'Call you back,' Novak said and slid the phone back onto its hands-free kit.

The policeman tapped on the window, motioned to Novak to wind it down, and then, as the man in the car hesitated, took out his warrant card and slapped it against the glass.

Novak wound it down.

The officer bent to look at him, his face and expression sharp. 'Detective Sergeant Reed, sir,' he said. 'Would you mind telling me who you are, and what you're doing?'

'Stopped to make a phone call,' Novak said. 'Name's Michael Novak.'

'Long call, Mr Novak,' Reed said.

Novak said nothing, thinking primarily that Allbeury was going to be less than thrilled. *Loss of concentration.* Bloody idiot, he castigated himself.

'Would you mind getting out of the car, sir?'

'What for?' Novak asked, not being bolshy, just *asking.*

'We've had a report of a man fitting your description, driving a car fitting this car's description, loitering in this area.'

Novak hesitated, wondering if he wanted to ask permission to

204

phone Clare, or if he'd rather she didn't have to worry about him 'helping' the police out.

The latter, definitely.

He got out of the car.

'Mind bringing your phone, sir?' Reed asked.

'If you like.' Novak leaned back into the car, took the mobile off its cradle.

'Keys, too,' Reed said.

'Why?'

'Because we'd like a word with you at the station, if you've no objection, and I'm sure you'd rather lock your car.'

Novak looked at the sharp, beady eyes.

'No objection,' he said, 'but I'd certainly appreciate a good reason.'

'Murder good enough for you?' DS Reed said.

Inside the house, Tony and Sandra had just got Irina – who'd refused any tea, far too upset now by her mother's continuing absence, the strangers in her grandmother's home and, not least, the painful atmosphere – to bed for a nap.

'Daddy?' It was the first time the child had spoken to him since he'd got back. 'Why isn't Mummy here?'

Sandra glanced at Tony, saw that he was barely managing to hold back his tears, swallowed hard to contain her own, and came to his aid.

'She can't be here, my darling,' she said, gently, 'but she wants you to have a nice sleep and dream sweet things.'

'What things?' Irina asked.

'How about Wibbly Pig?' Sandra remembered one of the child's favourite books.

Irina chuckled softly. 'Reena likes Wibbly Pig.'

The awareness that this might be the last moment of pleasure the little girl might know for a long time almost wrecked both adults.

'Love you, darling,' Sandra managed, and kissed her.

'Daddy loves you too,' Tony said, throatily.

Down in the living room, they seemed, Tony thought, to have settled themselves down rather too firmly for his liking.

'DC Dean's in the kitchen making some tea,' DI Keenan said,

apologetically. 'I hope that's all right, Mrs Finch?'

'Yes.' Sandra sat down heavily in an armchair.

'I know you said you don't need a doctor, but—'

'No,' Sandra said, quickly. 'No doctors. I'm all right.'

'With respect,' Keenan said, gently, 'you're not all right at all.'

'No,' she said.

'I think you should get someone,' Tony said, thinking he'd never seen her look so old. 'You might need something to help you sleep.' He knew he would, though what he thought he really wanted, *needed*, now, more than anything, was a bloody massive drink, preferably a whole row of drinks, anything to block out what he'd seen in that place.

Don't think about it.

Karen Dean, in a navy suit and white blouse, her long dark hair fastened in a thick plait, looked in to ask if they wanted their tea brought in. Keenan thanked her, then contrived, with her help, to get Sandra Finch out of the living room and into the kitchen while he remained with Patston.

'All right now, sir, if we get these questions out of the way?'

'Of course,' Tony said. 'Anything I can tell you to help.'

'Thank you.' Keenan glanced down at the tray on the table. 'Don't forget your tea. I'm sure you could use a cup.'

'I'm all right.' Tony didn't like to ask for a drink.

'If you change your mind, just tell me.'

'If I change my mind,' Tony couldn't help saying, 'I'll help myself.'

'Of course,' Keenan said.

As the questions got underway, however sympathetic his tone, there was no mistaking the thinking behind them. Jim Keenan wanted to know as much about the last time Tony had seen Joanne as he could tell him, and he clearly found it strange that Tony could not remember the name of the friend his wife was going to meet.

'I never heard it,' Tony explained for the second time. 'She just said it was a woman she'd met at the library who wanted to meet her for a cup of coffee.'

'And she'd never mentioned her to you before?'

'No.' Tony shrugged. 'I'm not the kind of husband who's got to know every last thing his wife gets up to.'

'Gets up to?' Keenan echoed.

'I don't mean like that,' Tony said.

'Like what?'

'Nothing.' He shook his head. 'I can't do this, not now. It's too much.'

'All right, sir.' Keenan was soothing. 'Just a few more questions and then we'll let you have some peace.' He paused. 'Still sure about that cuppa?'

'Couldn't face it,' Tony said. 'Wouldn't say no to something stronger though.' He gave a grimace of a smile. 'If that's allowed?'

'Why shouldn't it be?' Keenan said. 'You're not the one on duty.'

'I wish I was,' Tony said.

There was no whisky in Sandra's cabinet, but there was a bottle of brandy, and Tony's first swallow, drunk deliberately rapidly, designed to burn, did just that and released a few tears. He wiped them roughly away, drank the rest of what was in his glass, poured a little more and sat down again.

'Which library did your wife go to?' Keenan asked.

'I don't know,' Tony said. 'One near here, I suppose.' He nodded towards the kitchen. 'Her mum might know which one.'

The DI paused. 'Were you still at home yesterday morning when Joanne left to meet her friend?'

'No,' Tony answered. 'I'd gone to work.'

'How was she when you left her?'

'Fine. She was fine.'

'Your mother-in-law told DC Dean you said you had to encourage her to go.'

'Yeah.' Tony nodded. 'I told her it would do her good.'

'Why did you say that? Wasn't she well?'

'No, she was fine. I told you.'

'Only "do her good" seems to imply that she might have been under the weather in some way,' Keenan went on.

Tony shook his head, then shrugged. 'PMS. I remember now that's what she said. I told her she'd been a bit wound up, and she said she had PMS.'

'Get that badly, did she?'

'Not too bad.'

'My wife used to get it,' the older man said confidentially, and

207

pulled a face. 'I love her, but she could drive me round the twist.'

'Joanne wasn't that bad,' Tony said.

'So she wasn't exactly upset before you left for work that morning?'

'She wasn't upset at all. I told you, she was fine.'

'But you said she had PMS.'

'I said *she* said she had it.'

'Why would she have said it if it wasn't true?' Keenan asked.

'I don't know,' Tony said exasperatedly. 'Maybe she did, how should I know? I just said she wasn't upset, just fussing about not being able to go out because she had ironing to do. I told her it would do her good to get out. End of story.'

'Unfortunately not.' Keenan saw Patston's tears coming again, a few escaping down his cheeks, one into a crack in the corner of his mouth. 'So you didn't have a row?'

'A row?' Tony was startled. 'No, of course not.'

'Why of course not? People have rows all the time.'

'We didn't, not that morning.'

'But you did row, sometimes?'

'Of course. Who doesn't? Like you said.'

'But not that morning? No harsh words?' Keenan didn't wait for another answer. 'Nothing you know of – not necessarily anything to do with you – that might have led to Joanne going out and not coming back?'

'But that's not what happened, is it?' Tony said bitterly.

'Wasn't it?'

'Obviously not,' Tony said. 'Now you've *found* her.' This time he made no effort to contain the tears, just let them come, put down his drink on the floor beside his chair, covered his face with both hands and sobbed noisily into them. 'Oh, God,' he wept. 'Oh, Jo.'

'All right,' Keenan said.

'But it's *not* bloody all right, is it?' Tony's hands left his face, his cheeks red. 'And what I don't understand is why you're sitting here asking me these *stupid* questions instead of getting out there trying to find the scum who did that to her.'

'There are plenty of people out there,' Keenan said reassuringly, 'all doing their very best to do exactly that, Mr Patston. And I'm very sorry for what may seem like stupid questions to you at this minute – and I can understand that they must seem that way, and cruel too, probably.'

Tony nodded at that, was unable, for a moment, to speak.

'But this is a vital part of our enquiry, sir. Even the tiniest details can make a huge difference. We need to know how Joanne was feeling when you last saw her, the kind of mood she was in, because it might have made a difference to where she went, who she saw, what she did.' Keenan paused. 'If, say, she'd had a headache and no pills in the house, she might have gone to a chemist. If she'd been bored and fed up, she might have gone to, say, a hairdresser, or to buy a new dress.'

'She went to meet a friend,' Tony said, very wearily. 'The friend who phoned her.' He sighed, picked up his glass, drank some more brandy.

The door opened, and Karen Dean looked in.

'Sorry, sir,' she said. 'There's a call for you.'

Keenan stood up. 'You'll excuse me?'

Tony nodded, said nothing, leaned back in his chair, closed his eyes.

Keenan went out into the hall.

'Mrs Patston's car's been found in Hall Lane Car Park,' Dean told him quietly. 'That's the shoppers' car park next to Sainsbury's in Chingford.'

'Near the library?'

'Practically opposite,' Dean said. 'Nothing at first glance in or around the car, sir.' She paused. 'And no joy yet from fingertip search on a weapon.'

Keenan nodded, started to turn away, then stopped. 'I'm going to ask you to act as family liaison on this one, Karen, if you've no objection.'

'I'd like to keep working on the enquiry too, sir, if that's possible.'

Keenan nodded again. 'We'll get a uniform to stay around the Patston house when you're out in the field, but I do want you as liaison.'

Dean's eyes, dark, slightly slanted and sharp, betrayed fleeting disappointment, mixed with a dread Keenan readily sympathized with.

'Of course,' she said.

58

At ten past five, Clare telephoned Allbeury to see if he knew where Novak was.

'He did call me a while back,' she said, 'then had to go suddenly and said he'd phone back, but he hasn't, which isn't like him, and now he's turned his phone off, and he usually keeps it on silent.'

'I'm afraid I can't help you, Clare,' Allbeury said. 'I'm waiting to hear too.'

'If you do hear first,' she said, 'please ask him to call me.'

'Of course,' he said.

'You said murder,' Mike Novak said to DS Reed when he finally came back into the interview room at MIS headquarters in Theydon Bois, carrying two polystyrene cups of coffee. 'Who's been murdered?'

'What were you doing hanging around that road?' Reed set down Novak's coffee in front of him, took the lid off his own. 'You said black, no sugar, didn't you?'

Novak knew there was no point now in prevaricating.

Not too much anyway.

'Is it Joanne Patston?' he asked.

'Do you know Mrs Patston?' Reed asked.

'I've met her once,' Novak answered. 'Briefly.'

'Why were you sitting outside her mother's house, Mr Novak?'

'Has Joanne Patston been murdered?' Novak persisted.

DS Reed stared at him for a long moment.

'Yes,' he said at last.

'Christ.' He remembered the nervous woman hanging her

210

husband's shirts on the line in her back garden while her child played with a red ball. 'Oh, dear Christ.'

Was it the husband? That was what he wanted to ask, come right out with, no time-wasting. But unless it became unavoidable, Allbeury didn't want the police knowing about his involvement.

'I need to make a call,' he said. 'To my client.'

'Client?' the policeman queried.

'I'm a private investigator.' Novak paused. 'I was there on a job.'

'Who's your client?'

Novak disliked getting stroppy with the police, but he had no choice. 'I'm not under arrest for anything, am I?'

'Should you be?' Reed asked.

'No,' Novak said, 'so I'd appreciate a couple of minutes to make the call.'

'Be my guest.'

Novak took out his phone, turned it on. 'Alone?' he said to Reed.

'Don't push it,' the other man said, but stood up.

Novak waited till he'd left the room, saw there were several missed calls, ignored them and dialled Allbeury's mobile.

He picked up right away. 'What's happening, Mike?'

Novak gave him the news.

'Murdered?' Allbeury's shock was audible. 'Christ almighty, Mike.'

'I know.' Novak hesitated, hoping for direction. 'Thing is . . .'

'What have you told them?'

'Nothing. That I'm an investigator and that I had to phone my client.' Novak heard the silence. 'I didn't have much choice, Robin, I'm sorry.'

'Don't worry about that now.' Allbeury was already regrouping. 'Mike, don't get yourself in difficulties on my account. Tell the truth.' He paused, choosing his words carefully. 'Namely that Mrs Patston was in an unhappy marriage and had asked me for help, hence your surveillance. The usual – I'm a divorce lawyer, but this was off-the-record.'

'And if they want more?'

'You don't have any more.' Allbeury paused. 'If they need to speak to me, I will, of course, get in touch right away.'

The door opened and Reed came back in.

'DS Reed's just come back,' Novak said.

'Take it easy, Mike,' Allbeury said, 'and find out what you can.'

'I will,' Novak said. 'And Robin, could you tell Clare I'm okay?'

He ended the call, turned the phone off again and told Reed – already sitting down again opposite him – what Allbeury had asked him to pass on.

'So it was Mrs Patston you've been watching?'

'Not so much watching,' Novak said. 'Looking for. At her home and her mother's.'

'Was Mrs Patston wanting a divorce then?' Reed asked.

'I don't know any details,' Novak said.

'But your client is a divorce lawyer?'

'He is, but he takes other cases too, sometimes, I think.'

'You think.' Reed paused. 'You said Mrs Patston had asked for help.'

'That's what Mr Allbeury told me.'

'And when you met her?' Reed asked.

'That was just to arrange a meeting,' Novak said.

'Why not just phone?'

Novak shrugged. 'I was in the neighbourhood. It seemed easier. Friendlier.'

'And did you just see Mrs Patston? Or was her husband there?'

'Just her. And her little girl. Poor kid.'

'Yes,' Reed agreed. 'So you don't know why the lady was unhappy? You did use that word, didn't you?'

Novak was about to claim ignorance, but then the memory came back again. She'd looked so nice, so vulnerable, pegging up those shirts, and then the little girl had run to her, huddled close to her mummy. And now her mother was gone, forever, and they were going to find out about Tony Patston anyway, and if he didn't at least *start* them off on the right track . . .

'All I know,' he said, abruptly, 'is that there was some question of possible violence – unproven, so far as I know – in the family.'

'Against Mrs Patston?' The beady eyes were sharper.

'Against the daughter,' Novak said.

He tensed against further questions, for Clare's sake, and Maureen Donnelly's, too, as the source of the information; didn't relish getting a well-meaning nurse into trouble because of his flapping mouth.

212

Not to mention Robin. Because this wasn't the first time a client of his had been murdered, was it? And Novak didn't know what, if anything, he was supposed to make of that. All he wanted, right now, was to get this interview sorted and to get the hell out of here as quickly as possible.

'And who is alleged to be using violence against Irina Patston?' DS Reed asked.

'Her father. The husband,' Novak answered. 'That's why I've been hanging around. Keeping a bit of an eye on the situation.'

'Have you been inside the Patstons' house?'

'Never.'

'How long has this surveillance been going on?'

'Not really surveillance,' Novak said.

'What would you call it?'

'Keeping an eye, like I said.'

'How long?' Reed repeated.

'Yesterday morning,' Novak answered.

'Why then?'

'Because my client wanted to get in touch with Mrs Patston, and she didn't seem to be home.' Novak paused. 'Because he was concerned about her.'

'And the child?'

'Yes.'

'Have you reported this alleged violence to anyone?' Reed asked.

'Not yet.'

'Has your client—' Reed glanced at his notes '—Mr Allbeury – reported it?'

'I don't know,' Novak said. 'It might all have been nothing.'

'That doesn't seem very likely now, does it?' Reed said.

Novak didn't answer, picturing Joanne Patston again.

'Who brought this allegation of violence to your client's attention, Mr Novak?'

'I don't know,' Novak said, conscious that it was the first outright lie he'd told.

'Are you sure about that, Mr Novak?' Reed asked.

'Yes,' he said. 'Sorry.'

Case No. 6/220770

PIPER-WADE, E.

Study/Review   ✓

Pending

Action

Resolved

59

'How are you doing?'

Jim Keenan, having been called out of the living room by Karen Dean to report a call from DS Reed, had gone back in to see that Patston had gone out into the garden, so, feeling it an appropriate moment for a break in the questioning, he'd come into the kitchen where Sandra Finch was sitting at the table.

The window, he saw, overlooked the small garden, the light from within cast right across it so that even in the dusk, in the unlikely event that Patston tried to leg it over the back fence, he or Dean would certainly notice.

'I know what a foolish question that is, Mrs Finch,' he said, with sincerity. 'I don't think any of us ever learns the right things to say at a time like this.'

'It can't be easy,' Sandra said, kindly.

She was very pale, but quite composed. It wasn't real composure, of course, Keenan knew that. It was in place partly because the truth had probably not yet fully penetrated, but mostly, he thought, because of the child.

'When you feel,' he ventured carefully, 'the time has come to tell Irina about her mother, and if you need a little support, I know Karen – DC Dean – might be a good person to have around.'

Karen Dean left the kettle she'd been filling, came closer to the table. 'I won't intrude, Mrs Finch,' she said, 'unless you want me to.'

'Sandra,' the bereaved woman said. 'If you don't mind.'

'Not at all,' Dean said.

'Do you mind if I sit down?' Keenan asked. 'Talk for a bit?'

'Why would I mind?' Sandra said. 'I want to help, don't I?'

215

Keenan glanced towards the ceiling. 'Is Irina a good sleeper?'

'I'm not sure,' the grandmother answered. 'Usually, I think.'

'She's a very beautiful little girl,' Keenan said.

The woman smiled, tears springing into her eyes. 'She was adopted, you know. When she was three months old. She was an orphan, from Romania.'

'Irina,' Keenan said, understanding the exotic name and almost black eyes.

'What a wonderful thing to do,' Karen Dean said.

Sandra nodded, struggled against tears, failed, and pressed an already sodden tissue to her eyes. 'Joanne waited such a long time to have Irina,' she said after a moment, wiping her face, then clenching the tissue in her right fist. 'She was desperate to have a baby, but they couldn't.'

'Adoption's a big decision for most couples,' Keenan said. 'I know it can be tough for some dads, bringing up another man's child.'

Karen Dean strolled back towards the kettle, closer to the window.

'I wouldn't say my—' Sandra stopped.

'What wouldn't you say, Mrs Finch?' Keenan asked benignly.

Her voice was lower. 'I was going to say that I never thought of my son-in-law as a very paternal man, but he was completely behind Joanne about the adoption.' She shook her head, remembering. 'They saw one of those programmes about the orphans over there, you know, and after that, it was all they wanted to do.'

'Can't have been easy.' Dean dropped tea bags into the blue and white pot.

'It wasn't,' Sandra said. 'Joanne wouldn't talk about it much – she was superstitious, afraid if she said too much it wouldn't happen – but she was always telling me how Tony just wouldn't give up.' She paused. 'Four and a half years since they brought Irina home.' Her voice caught. 'It made Joanne so happy – she was such a wonderful mother.'

For the first time, she broke down, her sobs deep and bereft, her face in her hands, as Patston's had been earlier, shoulders heaving.

From upstairs, as if her grandmother's pain might have woken her, they heard the sound of Irina crying too.

Sandra lifted her head, got quickly to her feet, tugged a couple of tissues from the box on the table and dried her eyes. 'I'd better go to her.' She blew her nose, went across to throw them into the pedal bin and saw Tony outside, kicking disconsolately at a grass verge. 'He gets very upset when Irina cries.'

'Really?' Keenan asked. 'All children cry, after all.'

'Of course.' Sandra paused to listen, but there was no sound now from above. 'Joanne never said much about it, but it was obvious all the same because she was always making sure Irina wasn't left to cry for more than a minute. She was always giving her an extra bottle when she was little, or picking her up when it might have been fine to leave her for just a bit, you know?'

'Does Tony get angry when she cries?' Keenan asked, casually.

'I don't know about angry,' Sandra said, awkward suddenly. 'I'd better go up.'

'You mustn't worry,' Keenan said, 'about saying the wrong thing.'

'I'm not,' Sandra said, still uncomfortable.

'All that matters now,' Keenan pressed on, 'is telling us anything at all that might help us find out what happened to Joanne, and why.'

Sandra Finch's face visibly changed, went even paler, her eyes widening in new shock. 'You're surely not suggesting that Tony . . .'

'No one's suggesting anything, Mrs Finch. These are just routine questions, to help us get to the bottom—'

'How can you use words like that?' Sandra exclaimed. 'My daughter – that little girl's mother—' she glanced up at the ceiling '—has just been *murdered*. How can anything be *routine*?'

217

60

Clare was already up on her feet as Novak came through the door of their flat shortly after seven, and he saw instantly from her face that she knew.

'Robin told me,' she said. 'He phoned to give me your message, and I could hear from his voice that something was wrong.'

'I wanted to be the one to tell you,' Novak said.

'He tried not to tell me, but I got it out of him.'

'You're good at that.' Novak went to put his arms around her.

'Poor woman.' She burst into tears. 'And that *poor* little girl.'

'She'll be okay,' Novak said, knowing that was a lie.

'But she's not *safe*.' Clare's voice was muffled against his jacket. 'Not while she's living with that monster.'

'The grandmother's been looking after her,' Novak said soothingly, 'so it stands to reason she'll probably move in with Patston now.' He drew back, looked into his wife's face. 'And after what I just told one rather sharp DS, it's pretty likely they'll be looking at Tony Patston very hard indeed.'

'What did you say?' Clare wiped her eyes.

'Just enough.' Novak fished in his pocket for a handkerchief, dabbed at her face, then handed it to her. 'I didn't mention you or Maureen or the hospital. But I did say that Joanne had been very unhappy, and that there was a suspicion that Patston had been violent against the child.'

'Good.' Clare blew her nose. 'If it weren't for Maureen, I'd go to the police myself, this minute.'

'No need, sweetheart,' Novak said. 'They'll get there without you.'

*

Both Tony Patston and Sandra Finch had been fingerprinted, and Tony had elected to give a hair rather than a mouth swab for DNA – all strictly for purposes of elimination, Keenan had assured them. But after that, the awareness that just a few miles away a police team was searching his own house began to weigh on Patston heavily.

'I want to go home,' he said to Keenan in the kitchen while Sandra was upstairs checking on Irina. 'Isn't this all terrible enough without being made to stay away while strangers make Christ knows what kind of a mess in my house?'

'I can assure you—' Keenan remained gentle '—that no one will be treating your property with anything but respect. As I've told you, it's all simply part of the routine.'

'It's routine to suspect husbands, isn't it?' Tony said. 'You always read it, don't you, but it's different when it happens to you.'

'It's true to say that in all such cases, it's normal procedure to try to rule out close relatives and colleagues.'

'Jo didn't have any colleagues,' Tony said. 'And you wouldn't think her mum killed her, so that's just me left, isn't it?' He began to weep again. 'Oh, God,' he said. 'Oh, my God, this is *unbelievable*. I've just lost my wife, and instead of leaving me in peace so I can grieve, I have to put up with this *shit*.'

'I'm sorry, Mr Patston,' Keenan said, immovably. 'I can assure you that the last thing we want to do is harass an innocent man who's—'

'But you don't think I'm innocent,' Tony interrupted, distraught, 'do you?'

'Why don't you sit down for a bit?' Keenan suggested. 'Have a cup of tea.'

Tony sank down onto one of the kitchen chairs and stared up at the detective inspector. 'You think I did it, don't you? You think I killed my own *wife*.'

61

Shortly after eight-thirty on Wednesday morning, as Helen Shipley was eating a doughnut at her desk prior to seeing Trevor Kirby before he left for a meeting in Victoria, Geoff Gregory came into her office.

'I've just heard something that might interest you.'

Mouth still full, Shipley licked sugar off her fingers and raised her eyebrows in response.

'About the Epping Forest murder,' Gregory said.

'What about it?'

'Word is they're looking hard at the husband, but—'

'But what?'

'But another bloke got hauled into Theydon Bois yesterday for keeping watch on the victim's house.'

'For God's sake, Geoff.'

'Private investigator,' Gregory said. 'Name of Novak.'

'Jesus,' Shipley said.

In the blue study at the eastern end of Allbeury's apartment, sitting in one of the plush black leather armchairs, Novak decided that he'd never seen the lawyer look as grim as he did now.

'I know it was my fault for getting myself picked up,' Novak said, 'but Clare's really wound up about the little girl now her mother's gone, and—'

'You'd like her kept out,' Allbeury finished for him.

'Obviously, I want to help them nail the scum who did this, whether it's the husband or not, but all Clare did was pass on some information, and—'

'I get the picture, Mike,' Allbeury cut in again. 'And I can't see

220

any good being served by involving either Clare or her friend, and the police are already checking Irina's hospital records as we speak, so . . .' He picked up a gold pen, rolled it between his fingers. 'The only shred of good news in this bloody awful mess is that at least now they know the child's at risk, they're bound to bring Patston in quite quickly.'

'What if it isn't him?' Novak said. 'What if his violence against Irina's a red herring, and because of what I said, the police don't bother looking for anyone else?'

'They're not fools, Mike,' Allbeury said. 'You know that better than most.'

'They're human,' Novak said. 'They like results.'

'With a bit of luck,' the solicitor said, 'Patston will break down and confess.'

Novak looked morose and said nothing.

'Anyway,' Allbeury added, 'probably not the world's greatest injustice if they do set their sights for a while on a man who hits his four-year-old daughter.' He stood up, went over to the picture window behind the granite desk, gazed out at the river. 'To be honest, I've my own reasons for hoping they prove Patston's their man, and swiftly. I don't want or need too many questions about how I might have been planning to help Joanne.'

'My damned fault if they do ask questions.' Novak was bleak.

'You weren't to know you'd parked your car slap bang in the middle of a murder enquiry.' Allbeury turned back, sat down again. 'It's not just me, Mike. There are others involved in these operations.'

'I appreciate that,' Novak said.

'I'm not telling you what to say if MIS comes knocking – it's your choice – but I can tell you that if they come to me, I'll be keeping it simple. When I met Joanne, she was unsure of what to do, scared of divorce, and, as you said, I was concerned not to be able to reach her and asked you to take a look.'

Novak came, finally, to what was most on his mind.

'What if they remember your link to Lynne Bolsover?'

The thought had not escaped Allbeury.

'If – when – the time comes,' he said, 'I'll deal with that.'

Shipley, her eye on the clock on the wall, was on the phone to DC Pat Hughes at Theydon Bois, raising the possibility of a link between the Epping Forest murder and the Lynne Bolsover killing.

'Two unhappy marriages and a private detective working for a divorce lawyer,' DC Hughes summed up. 'Sounds more like a coincidence to me.'

'All the same—' Shipley stood her ground '—I'd appreciate your raising it with your DI.' She paused. 'Please tell him my reason for raising it is because certain elements in the Bolsover case have troubled me from the outset.'

'I thought the husband had been charged,' Hughes said.

'Exactly,' Shipley said.

62

'I'm feeling better, Mother.'

When Jack called her that, Lizzie knew he meant business.

'I'd like to go back to school.'

'Maybe tomorrow,' she said.

'I'm fine today,' Jack said. 'Ed and Sophie have gone back.'

'They started their colds earlier than you.'

'So you do agree it was just a cold.'

Lizzie looked at him. 'You're turning into a real point-scorer.'

'But do you get it?' he asked. 'My point.'

'Tomorrow,' Lizzie said.

Jack sighed.

Christopher, who'd spent the night alone in Holland Park, arrived at the clinic at nine-fifteen to find that Jane hadn't come in yet, but that Alicia Morgan, his head of administration, was hovering in the corridor outside his office.

'Morning, Alicia.' Christopher took off his battered tweed Rex Harrison hat. 'Waiting for me?'

'I'm afraid so.' Alicia looked very nervous.

'Something wrong?' He opened the door, let her go ahead of him, caught a whiff of discreet perfume, put down his briefcase and looked at her expectantly.

'There's been a minor security breach,' Alicia said, 'in the computer system.'

Christopher frowned. 'Surely that's your province?' He took off his Burberry.

'Yes, of course.' The anxious look was still there, a crease between her finely-plucked eyebrows. 'And I've followed all the appropriate procedures, naturally, but . . .'

The pause irritated Christopher, who'd been hoping for a quiet cup of coffee and a call home to Jack before his first rhinoplasty. 'Get on with it, Alicia.'

Alicia Morgan, unaccustomed to being spoken to that way by Wade, lifted her chin. 'My reason for troubling you with it,' she went on, 'is that one of the files accessed without authority was Mrs Wade's patient file.'

'Lizzie's file?' Christopher was taken aback. 'Are you sure?'

'I'm afraid so.' Alicia forged on. 'I've taken all measures within reason to ensure that nothing like this can ever happen again—'

'Within reason?' Christopher's eyes were sharp with annoyance.

'I simply mean that in the very unlikely event of one of these horribly sophisticated hackers – not that there could be any reason for them wanting to access our files, not unless we had, say, a huge pop star or a footballer—'

'I don't know about footballers,' Christopher said crisply, 'but the Beauchamp's certainly had more than its share of big names. And in case you've forgotten, Alicia, my wife is quite well-known herself.'

'That's why I thought you might want to bring in a security firm,' Alicia said. 'Someone to make sure we've got the very best protection.'

Christopher made his way slowly round to the other side of his elegant mahogany desk and sat down. 'How many other patient files were accessed?'

'None.' Alicia grew a little pink. 'That's what's so odd. All the files appear to have been linked to the departments involved with Mrs Wade's stay.'

'Departments?' His irritation was growing by the second.

'Anaesthesia,' she explained. 'Recovery, nursing—'

'Yes, all right,' he snapped. 'I get the picture.'

'I was wondering,' Alicia ventured, 'if you might want to call in the police?'

'Good God, no,' Christopher said.

She looked surprised. 'I just thought, it seemed so personal, such an invasion of privacy. In the old days, if they'd broken in and got into the filing cabinets . . .'

224

'Yes,' he said. 'I see your point.'

'What would you like me to do, Christopher?'

'Let me think about getting in these security people.'

'Not the police?'

'No.' He paused. 'I'm thinking of Lizzie. She's only just got over all that, and I believe this might upset her.' He managed a smile. 'She's got a new book out any minute, and one of these publicity tours – more than enough on her plate.'

'Yes, of course.' Alicia considered. 'Do you think it might have been some scurrilous journalist? Scouting for something for a slack news day?' She shook her well-coiffed head. 'In which case, they'd have been disappointed, I suppose.'

'Yes, I see what you mean,' Christopher said. 'Much too dull.'

'Thank goodness,' Alicia said.

'Indeed,' Christopher agreed.

63

The night had been unbearable for Sandra.

She had finally gone to bed, relieved to have some time alone, to know that Irina was sound asleep so that she could cease the grotesque parody of semi-normality she'd been forced into. But exhausted as she was, rest was out of the question, and lying in bed, truths descending on her with such agonizing weight that she felt torn into pieces, she had hardly slept, and when she had, it had been a shallow, dreadful kind of twilight sleep from which she'd woken with a jerking horror, her heart pounding.

Reality clamping down again.

Joanne was not here, would never be here again.

With the search at the house in Chingford Hatch apparently concluded, they had all returned at lunchtime.

Irina had been happy to be back, had run through the house as soon as they'd arrived, and Sandra and Tony had both known, with shared flashes of pain – and all the pain was worse now, in Joanne's house, *much* worse – that the pleasure would be brief, because the person for whom the child was searching was not there. And for once, Tony was ready for his daughter's tears, ready to give consolation, but when Irina came back to them in the sitting room, it was her grandmother to whom she went for comfort.

'We're going to have to tell her,' Tony had said, earlier, still in Edmonton.

'I know,' Sandra had said.

'Is it all right, d'you think,' he'd asked, almost like a kid himself needing adult approval, 'if we leave it a bit longer?'

The longer the better, Sandra had thought. *Ten, twenty years, if possible.*

'I don't see why not,' she had said.

The moment would come soon enough. She'd lain in bed the previous night imagining it, trying to think of the best way to tell Irina, but there were no good ways to tell a four-year-old that her mother had died, let alone been murdered.

'I don't want her to know *that*,' she had said to Karen Dean some time before that, during Tuesday evening. 'I don't want her to know about how her mummy died till there's absolutely no choice left.'

'I can see that,' the attractive officer had said gently. 'Except one day, someone else might say something to her, or just in earshot, maybe at school, and that would be much worse for her.'

Sandra had sat for a moment, then said: 'She doesn't go to school yet.'

'I meant nursery school.'

'Not that either.'

'Really?' Dean's slightly slanted, dark eyes had shown surprise.

'I know,' Sandra had agreed. 'I didn't understand myself, but Joanne wanted to keep Irina close for as long as possible.' The ever-present tears had threatened again. 'Maybe . . .' She'd turned her head away for a moment, brought herself back under control. 'Maybe she had some instinct.'

'I don't suppose she did,' Dean had said. 'But anyway, it'll be nice, later on, for Irina to know how much her mum loved her.'

'If she remembers her.' It was one of the multitude of dreads that had begun plaguing Sandra. 'How much do you remember from when you were her age?'

'I'm not sure,' Dean had said. 'Quite a bit, I think.'

'I don't seem to be able to remember much of anything,' Sandra had said.

'Anyway,' the younger woman had said, gently, 'you'll keep Joanne's memory alive for her, won't you? You and her daddy.'

'Yes,' Sandra said wearily. 'But it's not supposed to be like that, is it?'

'Nothing useful from the victim's handbag, sir,' DS Reed told Jim Keenan during their first morning briefing in the incident room at Theydon Bois. 'Outside wiped clean, and the only prints on the inside – on the purse, powder compact and lipstick – were Joanne's and a set of really tiny smudged prints that have to be the little girl's.'

'Nothing in the diary?'

'Nothing helpful.'

'We're contacting all numbers and addresses, sir,' Karen Dean said.

'Nothing on door-to-door,' Reed said. 'The neighbours they're supposed to be friends with aren't due back from Cyprus for a month, and no one seems to know exactly where they are. Do you want them located?'

'They weren't here at the time in question,' Keenan said, 'so let's hold off on that.' He looked at Dean. 'CRIS, CRIMINT and Community Support all checked?'

'No results,' Dean answered. 'And nothing on Patston since the ABH.'

'One thing,' Reed said. 'She had her passport with her.'

'Someone checking airlines, travel agencies, the usual?' Keenan asked.

'I'm onto that, sir,' DC Pat Hughes, an earnest young woman who never wore make-up and kept her rather wispy fair hair pinned up in something close to an old-fashioned bun, said. 'Nothing yet.'

'Just her passport?' Keenan asked Reed. 'Not Irina's?'

'No,' Reed said. 'And we didn't find one for her at the house.'

'I'll check applications, sir.' Hughes paused to make a note. 'Apparently it's going to be a while before they get round to the Fiesta.'

Keenan shook his head. 'CCTV footage yet from the library?'

'Problems with that, sir, I'm afraid,' Hughes said. 'Breakdown inside, vandalism outside.'

'Great.' Keenan shook his head again.

'I'm going to Waltham General after this,' Dean said. 'Try and check out Irina's and Joanne's records, have a chat.' She paused. 'They're not known to social services, by the way, sir.'

Reed was going through a small sheaf of papers. 'We've completed data protection and applied to BT for details at the house and Patston Motors.'

Keenan turned to the pathology report. 'Dr Collins says Joanne died where she was found. Four stab wounds, the first to the

228

external jugular . . .' He glanced around the room. 'That's buried quite deep in the neck, for anyone who doesn't know, which implies considerable force behind the stabbing, or, possibly, anatomical know-how.' He looked back at the report. 'It also means the first wound was enough to kill, so if death was the only aim, the other three were gratuitous.'

'So we're looking at crazed?' Reed said.

'Or enraged,' Dean said.

'Don't people sometimes carry on stabbing,' Pat Hughes ventured, 'because they're too scared to stop?'

'Joanne Patston must have been pumping arterial blood all over the shop,' Reed said scathingly. 'Not much to be frightened of.'

'Could have been terrified of what they were doing,' Keenan said, and gave Hughes a nod. 'Too terrified, or just too far gone to stop.'

'But they did hit the jackpot first time.' Reed felt in need of another point over the young DC. 'And most frenzied attackers strike out blindly.'

'Doesn't make the jackpot impossible, Terry,' Keenan said, then held up the report in his right hand to cut off the now aimless speculation. 'Toxicology.' He paused. 'Mrs Patston had enough benzodiazepine in her system to have made her very sleepy, though probably *not* unconscious. So someone please get on to the GP.'

'Will do.' Reed rummaged through his notes. 'No tranks in the bathroom cabinet at home, sir.'

'I'll raise it with Mr Patston in our next chat.' Keenan looked at DC Dean. 'Witnesses, Karen?'

'No one credible yet, sir,' she told him.

'There's still this call outstanding,' Pat Hughes reminded Keenan. 'From DI Shipley at AMIT NW.'

'Shipley's going to come with me this afternoon,' Keenan told Reed forty minutes later in his office, a drab slab of a room slightly humanized by family photographs and three small pots of red geraniums on the window sill, 'for a chat with Robin Allbeury.'

'When are you going to talk to Patston again?' Reed asked.

'I'm going to let him steam for a bit,' Keenan said, 'then drop by later.'

'Not ready to bring him in then, sir, do I take it?'

'Not till you give me something halfway solid.'

'We already know he's a brute,' Reed said.

'We know sod all,' Keenan disagreed.

'One for ABH.'

'Long time ago,' Keenan said.

'But drink-related,' Reed said. 'And we know he still drinks.'

'Not nearly enough. If Karen's lucky at Waltham General, that'll go some way, but if anything had been that cut and dried, social services would probably know.' Keenan scratched his left ear. 'As it is right now, we haven't even got enough to hold him for hitting the child, let alone murdering his wife.'

'It is him though, isn't it?' Reed tried doggedly to sort it in his head. 'There's the passport. Maybe Patston's story's half true; maybe she did say she was going to meet a friend, and maybe he saw her take the passport, found out she was leaving him, killed her in a rage.' He grimaced. 'Except she died in bloody Epping Forest.'

'And full of pills,' Keenan reminded.

'He could have got them into her first, then taken her out there.'

'Doesn't strike me as much of a schemer,' Keenan said. 'More the type to lash out, then shed crocodile tears.' He paused. 'Anyway, we're both ignoring the fact that Joanne *did* go out that morning just as he said, and left Irina with Sandra Finch.'

'She still might have been planning to leave Patston,' Reed said. 'Just not that morning. Unless she was leaving the child.'

'With him?' Keenan said. 'Not for a minute.'

'Maybe she always kept her passport with her,' Reed pondered. 'Always ready to run, or just scared he might not let her have it.' He paused again. 'Do you think Joanne might have decided to shop him for child abuse?'

'It's more likely than the rest,' Keenan said, then shook his head again. 'Mrs Finch said she thought Patston got – gets – upset when Irina cries, which is probably when he loses it with her. But he must have known that with Joanne dead, he'd be stuck full-time with the child.'

'No logic in passion,' Reed persevered. 'Or jealousy, or plain old rage.'

'Giving her the tranquillizers points away from anything that hot-blooded.'

'Maybe not the long, brewing kind,' Reed said.

'Not enough,' Keenan said.

The two men were silent for a moment. Outside, beyond the closed windows, traffic rumbled back and forth, a lorry braked sharply, an impatient driver hooted.

'What about getting in CPT so we can talk to Irina?' Reed asked.

'Not yet.' The creases in Keenan's face deepened. 'I'd rather keep a careful eye on her for now, keep on digging around her. Kiddie's still in the dark about what happened to her mum, and I don't want us to be the ones to change that. I certainly haven't had any sense from her that she saw or heard anything upsetting.'

'I suppose,' Reed said, 'so far as protecting her from Patston goes, we don't have to worry too much as long as grandma stays and we're in and out.'

'When Karen's done at the hospital, I want her back at the house as much as possible,' Keenan said. 'And someone posted outside for protection when she's off duty.'

'Done,' Reed said.

64

Lizzie's e-mail, when she got around to checking it just before lunchtime, included her proposed schedule for the *Pure Bliss* tour, and a message from Andrew France.

She called Susan first. 'This is great, but a bit daunting.'

'It's only Edinburgh and back,' Susan said, 'not quite what you're used to now.'

The barbecue on Kefalonia flashed into Lizzie's mind, and she pushed it swiftly away. 'It's terrific, Susan,' she said. 'So long as you're coming with me.'

'Wouldn't miss it,' Susan said. 'Obviously the schedule's subject to any number of changes, since it's a whole week away, but you're happy in principle?'

Lizzie looked over the pages she'd printed out. 'Starting in Oxford – lovely.'

'You'll see there's a gap in the middle for you to spend some time at home.'

Lizzie did see that, told Susan she was a darling and that she was delighted, then chatted for a few moments before ending the call and ringing Andrew back on his direct line.

'Glad I caught you,' she said when he picked up. 'Thought you might be lunching.'

'Sandwich at my desk today,' he said. 'Family okay?'

'Fine,' Lizzie said, not bothering with details. 'What's up, Andrew?'

'Time to start talking about Part Two of the *Roadshow*.'

'Oh, God,' she said.

'Vicuna have been fine, as you know, about postponing, but the Food and Drink people are now insisting you sign an addendum to your contract.'

'What sort of addendum?' Lizzie felt herself tensing.

'They want a guarantee that, barring natural disasters and other major unforeseeable difficulties, you'll complete recording.'

'What does *major* mean?' she asked, already prickly.

'Let's not even go there, Lizzie,' Andrew said.

'I think we should,' she disagreed. 'What's major to me, I suspect, might be very minor to them.' She paused. 'Is this Richard Arden's doing?'

'Don't think so for a minute,' Andrew said. 'Their legal people, I expect, but I don't think we need be too concerned.'

'You might not need to be, but I do.' Lizzie was perplexed and annoyed. 'They know about my commitments, they have since the outset. Richard seemed to understand perfectly after the accident that I had to go.'

'And of course he did understand that.' Andrew was beginning to sound soothing. 'But now the lawyers are saying that he and, more to the point, his masters, did rather expect you to go back as soon as the initial crisis was over.'

'Richard knew that wasn't going to happen.'

'Hard to prove, darling,' the agent said. 'And no need to do so, anyway, since no one's threatening to sue or even get nasty.'

'I should hope not.'

'Their implication seems to be that with Christopher at Edward's bedside, there was no need—'

'So is that what they're after now?' Lizzie cut in. 'My guarantee that I cease being a mother for the duration of the *Roadshow*? Because if that *is* what they want, I'll be saying no to the rest of it.'

'Lizzie, don't get so upset.'

'And if they want their advance back, they can have it.'

'You need to think about this, darling,' Andrew said.

'No, I don't,' Lizzie told him.

'I frankly don't think turning them down flat's the best long-term move.

'Too bad,' Lizzie said.

'Lizzie, are you unwell?'

'Never better,' she said.

65

'Maybe,' Sandra said to Karen Dean, currently making sandwiches for their lunch – ham for the adults, peanut butter for Irina, 'we should go on TV, the way people do, to ask for witnesses?'

'They do that when kids go missing, don't they?' Tony said, sitting beside his mother-in-law at the kitchen table.

'And for . . .' Sandra didn't finish the sentence.

Irina, who had been helping Dean spread her peanut butter, held up her hands, palms up, for her grandmother to see. 'Reena dirty, Grandma,' she said.

'You're too old for baby-talk,' her father told her.

Sandra threw him a look. 'Come on, darling.' She stood up and extended her own right hand to the child. 'Let's wash all that off.'

At the sink, she helped Irina stand on the red plastic step that Joanne had bought for the purpose, turned the taps for her, squirted Fairy Liquid onto her palms and watched her rub them into a lather.

'Surely,' she went on quietly, speaking to the constable, 'anything that might help's worth trying.'

'Maybe,' Dean said, 'when DI Keenan gets back, you should raise it with him.'

'We could talk about all the love that went into finding this little one.'

'Adoption', like 'murder' or 'killing', was another word they had all tacitly agreed to ban in Irina's presence.

'I wouldn't want to talk about that,' Tony said. 'It's private.'

'Finished,' Irina announced.

Sandra helped her down, pulled the tea towel from its holder and watched her granddaughter dry her hands. 'I'll do it if you won't,' she told Tony sharply. 'I'll do anything if it helps get whoever did this to us. I should have thought you'd feel the same way.'

Tony, still at the table, began to weep, not burying his face in his hands now, just letting the tears flow from his eyes down his face into his stubbled chin.

'For God's sake,' Sandra hissed. 'If I can control myself, why can't you?'

'Why's Daddy crying?' Irina asked.

'Because he's a bit sad, darling,' Sandra told her gently, and glanced helplessly at Dean. 'We're all sad, Irina.'

'Cos Mummy's not here?' Irina asked.

'That's right, my darling,' Sandra said, and her own eyes filled.

'I want my mummy,' her granddaughter said.

As Karen Dean watched tears begin to well up in the child's big dark eyes, it was all she could do not to join in.

66

'Everything all right there?' Christopher asked on the phone shortly after two.

'Fine,' Lizzie said, 'unless you count my behaving like an unprofessional idiot with the Food and Drink people.'

She told him, briefly, what had happened.

'You were absolutely right,' Christopher said. 'Bullying you.'

'I'm not so sure. I think I rather startled Andrew,' Lizzie said. 'I bet he doesn't pass on what I said without calling me again.'

'I think he should tell them exactly what you said.'

'You just think I should be home with the children,' Lizzie said coolly.

'That's a ridiculous thing to say,' Christopher told her, equally coolly.

'Yes,' Lizzie admitted. 'I suppose it is.'

'I may have my faults,' he said, 'but—'

'May?'

'I *do* have my faults,' he amended. 'Huge, unforgivable, monstrous faults, as I know only too well.'

'I'm not in the mood for sarcasm,' Lizzie said sharply.

'And I'm not in the mood for being got at,' Christopher said.

'Tough,' Lizzie said, and put down the phone.

67

'Robin called,' Novak told Clare when she got back to the agency at four o'clock, after a few hours in Wood Green with Nick Parry. 'Jim Keenan, the DI from Theydon Bois, is coming to see him at five.'

'Doesn't he want to see you?' She hung up her raincoat on the pine coat stand.

'Not yet,' Novak said.

He followed her into their tiny kitchen, moved behind her as she filled the kettle, kissed the back of her neck. Generally, if he did something like that, even at work, Clare responded with warmth, but today she just plugged the kettle in.

'You all right?' Novak asked.

'Bit tired.' She took the top off the tea jar, tossed a bag into a mug. 'Didn't sleep too well last night.'

'It's okay to be upset,' Novak said gently. 'And I know you're afraid for the little girl.'

'Aren't you?' Clare turned so sharply that her curly hair bounced.

'Of course.' Novak was startled by the accusation in her eyes, put a hand on her arm. 'You're trembling, sweetheart.'

'I'm not.'

'Come and sit down.'

'I'm making tea.'

'I'll do that in a minute.' He steered her back into the office towards the couch. 'Now sit down and tell me what's going on.'

She sat. 'Nothing's going on.'

'Nick okay?'

'Fine.'

Novak heard the kettle boiling, went to make the tea, brought it back and sat down beside her. 'I've put a bit of sugar in.'

She smiled for the first time. 'I don't need sugar.'

'You need energy,' he said. 'You've been looking tired for a while now, so I know it's not all to do with the Patstons. And I thought we had a deal about sharing feelings.'

'Okay,' she said.

'Okay, what?'

'I'll share.'

Her voice was soft, but so tense that he felt suddenly fearful. 'What is it?'

'I'm pregnant,' Clare said.

Novak felt as if his mind had split into two, one part blazing fireworks, the other groping in dark bewilderment.

'But that's *wonderful*,' he said.

'Is it?' Clare asked.

And instantly he realized – already angry, *furious*, with himself for his denseness, his insensitivity – that of course any joy she might be feeling was being cloaked by the memories of last time.

'Oh, God, I'm sorry,' he said.

Clare looked at him. 'Do you see?' Her voice was very tentative.

'Of course I see.' Novak put out his arms, relieved when she came into them, leaned against him. 'Of *course* I see. I know how you felt, know how *I* felt, for God's sake, and I'll never forget it for the rest of my life.'

'Oh, Mike, I'm sorry.'

He drew back a little way, saw tears in her eyes. 'Don't say that,' he told her. 'You have nothing to be sorry for.' He drew back further, laid his right hand against her flat stomach. 'A baby,' he said, quietly.

'You're happy,' she said.

'Christ, yes.'

'I'm frightened,' she told him.

'I know,' he said.

'Tell me it's going to be all right,' she said.

'Of course it's going to be all right,' he said.

'You don't know that,' Clare said.

'I do,' he told her. 'I honestly believe that I do.'

'From your mouth to God's ear,' she whispered.

238

Amen, he thought, but didn't say, because he'd just told her he was certain, and anything less now would feel like hedging his bets, and if there was one thing Clare needed right this minute, it was his confidence.

And the dark bewilderment had already fallen from his mind, and the other side, the soaring rockets, the *hope*, was taking over.

'Our baby,' he said.

68

If Robin Allbeury was less than pleased to see Helen Shipley
again when she arrived (having persuaded DCI Kirby to give her
time out from the drugs case and her pile of overdue paperwork)
at his apartment with Jim Keenan, he didn't let it show.

'Not surprised to see me?' she asked as the solicitor, wearing a
grey cashmere sweater over charcoal wool trousers, showed them
both into the living room with its fabulous view.

'Sadly, not very,' Allbeury said. 'In view of the link between
these two women and myself, I was anticipating a visit.'

'Do you have an explanation for this link, sir?' Keenan
asked.

'Please,' Allbeury said, indicating the sofa and armchairs,
'make yourselves comfortable.'

Shipley wandered across to the big telescope just inside the
glass doors.

'Feel free to use that,' Allbeury told her.

She turned around. 'No, thanks.'

Keenan sat down as invited, on the sofa. 'The link, sir?'

'No explanation,' Allbeury said. 'Though I assure you that if I
thought for an instant that this was more than a coincidence or that
my connection had any relevance to these two deaths, I'd be even
more wretched about them than I already am.'

Shipley came to sit in the armchair closest to Keenan, noticed,
with mild irritation as she crossed her legs, that her tights had
snagged in two places, wished she'd worn a trouser suit.

'Can I get you both some coffee?' Allbeury asked. 'Though you
prefer tea, don't you, DI Shipley?'

'Nothing for me, thanks,' she said.

240

'Nor me.' Keenan waited as the solicitor sat too. 'What makes you so sure your connection has no relevance?'

'I've thought about it long and hard, naturally,' Allbeury answered. 'And yes, I suppose it is remotely feasible that both women's husbands found out that their wives were in contact with a solicitor, and became enraged enough to kill them.'

'Maybe that's exactly what did happen,' Shipley said.

'Unlikely, at least in *both* cases, surely?' Allbeury was sceptical.

Shipley said nothing.

Allbeury regarded her for a moment longer, then turned to Keenan. 'So how exactly can I help you, Detective Inspector Keenan?'

'First,' Keenan said, 'by remembering where you were at the times of both deaths. Second, by telling us precisely what your involvement was with the victims.'

'I'll need to consult the diary on my computer for the first,' Allbeury said. 'As to the second, I've already told DI Shipley about my one encounter with Lynne Bolsover.'

Again, Shipley made no response.

'As I recall,' Keenan said, 'you told DI Shipley that you offered Mrs Bolsover some sort of legal advice gratis, but outside the legal aid system.'

'Correct,' Allbeury said. 'But she didn't want my advice.'

'Probably a bit convoluted, from her point of view,' Keenan said. 'When all she had to do was go to Citizens Advice or open the Yellow Pages for one of the firms who do freebie first-times.'

'But she didn't do either of those things,' Allbeury said, unruffled. 'That's exactly the point. Mrs Bolsover was too afraid of her husband finding out, to risk that kind of visit.'

'You mentioned,' Shipley said, 'an "escape route." '

Allbeury thought for a moment. 'I believe what I said to you was that many unhappy women seem unable to see that they might *have* an escape route.'

'Because they have no money,' Keenan added.

Allbeury nodded. 'That's often the primary stumbling block.'

'So how would you have helped Lynne Bolsover to "escape?" ' Shipley asked. 'If she hadn't said no to your offer.'

'I can't answer that,' Allbeury said.

'Can't, or won't?' Shipley asked.

He smiled. 'Can't, Detective Inspector. Each case is different, and clearly, any advice or help I might have given Mrs Bolsover would have depended upon her specific circumstances or needs.'

'What about—' Jim Keenan leaned forward slightly '—Joanne Patston's needs?'

'I'm sorry to say,' Allbeury replied, 'that I can't be very much more helpful to you there either.' He paused. 'Mrs Patston and I had only one meeting, at her local library.'

'The branch in Hall Lane?' Keenan asked.

'That's right.' Allbeury paused. 'She brought her daughter, Irina, and we talked while the little girl looked at books – her mother kept an eye on her the entire time.'

'What did you talk about?' Keenan asked.

'Mrs Patston was afraid for Irina,' Allbeury said, 'because her husband had been hitting the child. We spoke about that, and about the possibility of my being able to help her find some way out of the marriage.'

'What kind of way?' Keenan asked. 'Divorce?'

'Divorce might not have been a clean enough break,' the solicitor said. 'Too long a process, too great a risk of Patston losing his temper, becoming violent, any number of times along the way.'

'She could have applied for an injunction,' Shipley said.

'Of course,' Allbeury said, 'though I'm not sure if she would have been up to coping with all that would have entailed.' Allbeury paused. 'In any case, as you know, violent men don't always heed injunctions.'

'Why didn't she report him?' Keenan asked.

'Fear,' Allbeury replied simply.

'How did you come to hear about Joanne Patston?' Shipley asked. 'Another anonymous tip-off?'

'Yes,' Allbeury replied. 'Though not a letter, this time.' He looked straight at Keenan as he told the small lie. 'A telephone call.'

'Untraceable, I suppose?' Shipley said.

'I didn't attempt to trace the source of the call,' Allbeury said. 'I was more interested in the subject.'

'Joanne Patston,' Keenan said.

'And the risk to her daughter,' Allbeury said.

'Why didn't you report that risk?' Shipley asked.

'I wanted Mrs Patston to feel she could trust me,' he answered. 'Calling social services or the police might simply have made her life, and the child's, harder.'

'And did she trust you?' Keenan asked.

'I believe she was coming round to thinking that she could.'

'Yet you never saw her again?' Shipley's question.

'No.'

'Did you speak to her?' Keenan asked.

'Not after the meeting in the library,' Allbeury said.

'What about Michael Novak?' Shipley asked.

'I believe he spoke to her twice after the meeting,' Allbeury replied.

'About?' Keenan again.

'She was making up her mind,' the solicitor said.

'What about?' Shipley asked.

'About whether she wanted me to help her leave the marriage.'

'You still haven't told us,' Keenan said, 'what *kind* of way out you were suggesting, Mr Allbeury.'

'I was waiting for her answer.'

'You must have had something in mind,' Shipley said.

'Of course,' Allbeury agreed.

'Which was?' Keenan pushed, still politely.

Allbeury was silent for a moment. 'If Mrs Patston had told me she wanted to go,' he said, at last, slowly, 'I would have done all I could to enable her to take her daughter to a place where they would have felt secure.'

'Long-term?' Keenan asked.

'Yes,' Allbeury answered. 'Nothing else would have helped her feel safe.'

'But you were still waiting for her final response?' Keenan asked.

'When Mike Novak told me she was dead,' Allbeury said.

He took them into his blue study, invited both detectives to look over his shoulder as he brought up the diary on his PC and scrolled back to the twentieth of February, the day of Lynne Bolsover's disappearance and killing.

'If essential,' Allbeury said, 'both those morning appointments could be verified.'

'Not the one in the afternoon?' Shipley asked, standing on his left side.

243

'It was with a client who appreciates confidentiality and is, at present, overseas.' He looked up at her. 'I was under the impression that John Bolsover was in Belmarsh awaiting trial for his wife's murder.'

'He is,' she said.

Allbeury returned his attention to his diary, scrolled on eight months to October, then glanced up at Keenan, standing to the right of his chair.

'Monday,' Keenan said. 'The seventh.'

'The office.' Allbeury leaned back for them to see. 'Allbeury, Lerman, Wren in Bedford Row.' He looked at Keenan again. 'If you're going to check, Detective Inspector, I would appreciate discretion.'

'Goes without saying, sir,' Keenan said.

'Were you there all day?' Shipley asked.

Allbeury looked back at her, and half smiled. 'I had a great deal to attend to on Monday. One of the juniors fetched me a sandwich – I don't know where from, but it was thick-cut ham with relish and very good.'

'You seem very lighthearted,' Shipley said, 'considering you said you were wretched about these two deaths.'

'Forgive me,' Allbeury said. 'I suppose I'm not accustomed to being asked for alibis, Detective Inspector.'

'You've been very helpful, Mr Allbeury,' Jim Keenan said.

'Is that all?'

'I think so,' Keenan said.

Allbeury stood up. 'If you do need anything further, don't hesitate to call.'

'We won't,' Shipley said.

'Thank you very much,' Keenan said.

'Not quite the whole story, obviously,' he said as they rode down in the gleaming lift.

'Lying through his teeth,' Shipley said, looking up at the camera.

'More a case of gentle evasion, I'd say,' Keenan said. 'Probably reluctance to have his affairs looked at too closely, rather than anything to do with the killings.'

'Did you like him?' Shipley sounded curious.

The doors opened, and they walked out through the marbled

lobby, past the doorman and out onto the riverside walk. A stiff, chilly wind was blowing off the river.

'I didn't *dis*like him,' Keenan replied. 'Certainly not as much as you clearly do.'

'It's not just him,' Shipley said. 'It's the whole set-up I don't trust.' She turned with him away from St Saviour's Dock and Butler's Wharf, into the side road where they'd left their cars. 'Novak out there, maybe – I don't know – *pimping* for the guy in the tower.' She shook her head. 'I certainly don't believe in coincidences.'

'Yet they do happen.' Keenan fished in his coat pocket for his keys. 'And logically, if Allbeury wanted to kill anyone, it would have been the husbands.'

'Maybe—' Shipley retrieved her keys from her shoulder bag '—he despises women he sees as too weak to stand up for themselves.'

'Maybe he does,' Keenan said.

They came to her old Mini first. 'You don't really believe that though, do you?'

'Not really.' The wind billowed his coat. 'As I've already told you, my team's money's on Patston.'

Shipley ground the heel of her right shoe into the pavement.

'Sorry,' Keenan said.

'Could I see the pathologist's report on Joanne?' she asked suddenly.

'I'll fax it to you tomorrow.'

'Not going back to your office now?'

Keenan smiled again. 'I'll fax it when I get back.'

69

Christopher, staying overnight in Holland Park again, could not get the computer incursion at the Beauchamp out of his head.

Lizzie's uncharacteristic snappishness earlier on the phone had exacerbated his anxiety. He was beginning to wonder, in fact, if Lizzie herself, or some sharp-practising lawyer, might have been behind the hacking – if that *was* the right word for it – possibly trying to gather grounds for divorce.

More grounds, he reminded himself – the thought making him no happier – since surely she already had more than enough.

All the same, the idea that she – normally so straight from the shoulder – might be doing something so underhand, was making him very upset and, indeed, quite angry.

He poured himself a very large malt whisky.

Nothing in those files to help her in a divorce, he was sure of that. Just more evidence, really, of the loving husband taking care of his wife.

And he *was* a loving, if not completely ideal, husband.

And a perfect father.

Christopher took a large swallow of whisky, and shuddered.

The notion of Lizzie even *thinking* about divorce made him ill.

70

By nine that evening, Shipley was home, eating KFC drum-
sticks and drinking Coke – she'd had a couple of beers with
Jackson and Gregory after work, and if she had any more, she
mightn't be able to make sense of the reports on the coffee
table in front of her.

Jim Keenan, true to his word, had faxed not only the pathologist's report on Joanne Patston's death, but also the scene-of-
crime report.

'For your evening's entertainment,' Shipley muttered.

She wiped her greasy hands and picked up the new report,
having pretty much committed Dr Patel's to memory.

Reading did little to boost her spirits, not that she'd expected
anything glaringly useful. A mention of the skin that had been
found beneath Joanne Patston's fingernails having been her own,
which Shipley knew must have dashed a few hopes in Theydon
Bois. And more differences than similarities between the two
killings. Joanne Patston had been full of tranquillizers, but toxicology on Lynne Bolsover had shown no drugs in her system.
Lynne's body had shown signs of past beatings; no such indica-
tions on Joanne Patston. If the rock and rag found by young Kylie
Bolsover in their garage had, as she'd always personally believed,
been planted – presumably by the killer – they hadn't, at least as
yet, delivered the same blow to Tony Patston.

'Okay,' Shipley said softly, a few minutes later.

There was, after all, one quite striking similarity.

Stephanie Patel had reported that the first blow inflicted on
Bolsover would have been enough to kill her, and according to Dr
Collins, Joanne Patston's first stab wound would have finished her

247

too. Yet in both cases, the killers had gone on striking: twice more in the first instance, three more wounds in the second.

Not exactly a pattern, but *something*.

She made a note, then mulled over the other, weaker, parallels between the cases. The husbands, obviously, both allegedly violent, though Patston's aggressions apparently directed at the child rather than his wife. No overtly sexual element to either attack.

She turned to the crime scene report, and found another possibly significant detail from the Patston crime scene report that tallied with her recollection of the older case. Both bodies had been poorly concealed.

'Which means what?' she murmured, and drained the rest of her Coke.

That the person who'd killed them had wanted them found? Or that they'd been unable to bury the bodies properly for some reason.

Or maybe that was simply another coincidence. Maybe both killers had just been nervous of passers-by happening on the scene.

No more parallels presenting themselves.

Except, of course, Allbeury and Novak.

71

Sandra had been wondering – in between the endless cups of tea, and taking care of Irina, and talking to Karen Dean, to whom, just now, she found it easier to talk than her son-in-law or any of the well-meaning friends who called – why Tony now seemed so set against talking to anyone about Irina's adoption, when he had, at the outset, been so proud of it.

It kept creeping back into her mind, she kept on brooding over it, perhaps because it was one way of trying to keep her mind off Joanne, because not thinking about her was the only way to keep sane, to keep going for Irina's sake.

And then, suddenly, Sandra *knew* why, and once she had seen it, she couldn't understand why she had never done so before.

For the longest time, when they'd first tried to adopt, Tony and Joanne hadn't been able to make the system work for them, and then, out of nowhere, they'd found a way and after that, in a matter of months, Irina had been theirs.

She waited until her granddaughter was asleep and Dean was in the kitchen making spaghetti for their dinner, to go in search of Tony.

He was in the garage, doing something under the bonnet of his car.

'Dinner ready?' he asked, seeing her coming through the side door.

'Soon.' Sandra closed the door behind her, drew a breath and plunged straight in. 'Tony, I've worked out why you've been so odd with the police and not wanting to talk about the adoption or even go on TV.'

He straightened up, his face a mask. 'I don't know what you mean.'

'It wasn't legal, was it?' Her voice was hushed. 'Getting Irina.'

'Sandra—'

'I just wish you and Joanne had told me,' she said, having to get it out. 'I'd have understood – how could you think I wouldn't? I'd have helped, done anything—'

'For Christ's sake,' Tony hissed, cutting her off, 'keep your voice down.'

'It's all right,' Sandra said. 'Karen's cooking and Irina's asleep, and I *am* keeping my voice down, and that's just what I'm trying to tell you. You can trust me, Tony. I'd never do anything to—'

'Bloody hell, Sandra, just shut *up* about it.' Tony slammed down the bonnet, cheeks red. 'If you want to help, just keep it to yourself and don't talk about it. God knows I've lived to regret the whole bloody thing.'

Sandra stared at him. 'Not having Irina, surely?'

'No, of *course* not having her, and if you'd just shut up and *listen* for once.' His eyes were desperate. 'Don't you understand, it's all going round and round in my head, and I don't know what to *do*.' He turned on the last word, slapped both hands on the roof of the car. 'I'm beginning to think it *might* be better to tell them about Irina, because it's got to be a sodding sight better getting done for illegal adoption than for *murder*, hasn't it?'

Speechless, his mother-in-law went on staring at his back, and in the silence Tony felt the stare and turned around, his own expression horrified.

'You don't think, for one second, that I did that to Joanne?'

'No,' Sandra said. 'Of course not, it isn't that.' And it was true, she didn't believe he could have done it, not *that*. 'But don't you realize that if you tell them the truth about Irina, they might take her away?'

'Of course I do,' Tony said.

'Don't you care?' Sandra asked, disbelieving.

'Won't make much difference to me, will it,' he answered, 'if I get life for killing her mother?'

The side door opened again, and Karen Dean popped her head around it.

'Pasta's ready,' she told them. 'If you are.'

72

Shipley got to Theydon Bois early on Thursday morning hoping for the chance of another chat with Keenan.

He'd got in just ten minutes after her, holding a bag containing a jam doughnut and a capuccino.

'Would have got two of each,' he said as they walked up the stairs together, 'if I'd known you were coming.'

'Sorry to land on you like this,' Shipley said.

'No, you're not,' Keenan said.

She waited till they were in his office, taking in the framed photos of a dark-haired woman she assumed to be his wife and three children photographed at various ages, none much seeming to resemble the thin, worn-looking DI, while he put the breakfast on his desk and hung up his raincoat.

'Yours?' She felt a swift, surprising prick of envy.

Keenan nodded, smiled. 'Afraid I'm not gentleman enough to give you my capuccino, but I'll fetch you a cup of machine stuff if you want it.'

'I'll pass, thanks.'

Keenan removed the plastic lid from his coffee cup, drank a little, then wiped the trace of froth from his top lip. 'You compared the reports?'

'I did.' She ran efficiently through her own analysis.

Keenan listened attentively, waited till she was finished, then compressed his lips for a second before speaking. 'I think – I hope – I'm an open-minded copper, DI Shipley.'

'Helen,' she said. 'But?'

'But everything, so far, in my case, still points to Patston.'

'With no signs of violence at the home or garage, and the crime scene being miles away? And the fact that Joanne really *did* go out when he said she did, left Irina with her grandma, also like he said?'

'Doesn't mean she didn't see Patston later,' Keenan said. 'Drop by at the garage, or meet him for lunch. She had her passport with her – maybe he said he was going to book them a holiday.'

'You're reaching,' Shipley said.

'I know,' Keenan said.

One of the phones on his desk rang and he picked up, listened for several seconds, scribbling a few notes on a pad, thanked the person at the other end and put the phone down.

'Joanne's GP prescribed diazepam for her several months ago,' he told Shipley. 'And since there are no pills at home now, she either finished them some time back, or threw them out – or maybe Patston slipped them in her morning cuppa or juice.' He glanced down at the notepad. 'We've got a librarian and another woman at South Chingford Library who both remember Joanne being there a few weeks ago talking to a man while her daughter looked at books.'

'Allbeury?' Shipley said.

'Middle-aged, well-dressed, dark hair, greying.' Keenan smiled. 'Corroborates his story.'

'I still don't trust him.'

'I've had a good look at him since yesterday afternoon, as you've undoubtedly done before me. The man's squeaky clean.'

'At the very least,' Shipley said, 'I don't trust his motivations.'

'People's motivations for all kinds of things often seem strange to others. Doesn't make them deranged, or evil killers.' Keenan shrugged. 'Maybe Robin Allbeury really does like helping women, no strings attached.'

'Maybe,' Shipley said dubiously.

Keenan unwrapped his doughnut, laid it on top of its paper bag. Shipley took the hint. 'I'll leave you in peace.'

'Mind a word of advice from a bloke who's been around a while?'

'Not at all,' she said, standing up.

'Hunches have their uses,' he said. 'I believe in them, always

252

have. But they're only useful so long as we don't let them become obsessions.'

'Think I'm obsessed with Allbeury and Novak?'

Keenan looked up, saw it was a genuine question.

'Not quite yet,' he said.

73

Nick Parry had finished the laborious business of showering and drying, most of which he could manage solo these days, though when Clare or one of his other carers was on the scene the process was unquestionably easier, and he'd got past the worst of his humiliation a long while ago – though that, too, varied depending upon exactly who was helping him. Clare Novak was his favourite, he thought, overall, partly because she was efficient and gentle, matter-of-fact but sensitive about the uglier essential procedures he still hated; partly because he always felt she genuinely liked being with him, talking to him.

And she gave far and away the best aromatherapy massages.

She was doing that now, and professionally detached and expert as she was about what she did with her hands, Parry couldn't help remembering a couple of other great massages he'd had *before*, when he'd been a normal, active, inquisitive young male. In one way, of course, those memories were acutely painful, leaving him depressed as hell, but on the other hand, he had decided a while back that having memories had to be better than never having had the experiences in the first place.

'Go on telling me about last night,' he said now.

'Relax,' Clare told him.

'I need you to talk to stop me thinking horny.'

'Nothing stops you thinking horny, Parry,' she said lightheartedly.

'Come on, Novak,' he countered. 'You know I'm a safe pair of ears.'

She had been talking until a few moments before, but then she'd stopped, quite abruptly, feeling disloyal because she'd been telling him about the previous evening's dinner with Mike, who'd wanted to take her out to celebrate. She'd chosen instead to cook a stir-fry at home, and Mike had wanted her to open up about her fears for the new pregnancy, had tried convincing her yet again that last time had not been in any way her fault, that it had been timing and fate, that if she hadn't been alone, if he'd been with her, it would have been different.

'He says it won't happen again,' she told Parry now. 'That they told us there was no reason for anything like that to ever go wrong again. He says that anyway, this time he's going to stick so close, he'll probably drive me nuts.'

'You're lucky,' Parry said.

'I know,' Clare said, and put more neroli and apricot kernel oil onto her palms. 'He thinks maybe I ought to take it easier, cut down my hours.'

'But you love working.'

'He said he wasn't saying I shouldn't work, just do less.' Clare paused, worked some oil into his left calf muscle.

'Did he want you to stop coming here?'

Clare smiled. 'He suggested it.'

'Maybe he's right,' Parry said.

'He's not right at all,' Clare said, 'which I told him.'

'Was he okay with that?'

'He was fine.' She switched to his right leg. 'Mike never tries pushing me into things I'm not happy with.'

'But?' Parry waited.

'I asked him if he wasn't scared, too.' She paused. 'He thought I meant just about the baby.'

'But you didn't mean just about that, did you?' Parry said.

Clare shook her head, stopped massaging. 'There are so many things to be scared of in this world, if you let yourself.'

'You're thinking about the little girl, aren't you?' Parry asked. 'Irina.'

'Yes,' Clare said. 'I am.'

'And her mother.'

'Of course,' Clare said.

'Poor cow,' Parry said.

74

Joanne's car having offered up nothing of interest or use, and blanks still being drawn on all other lines of enquiry, Keenan waited until Saturday morning to turn up a little more heat under Tony Patston's already agitated backside, by telephoning to ask if he'd mind coming to Theydon Bois for another chat.

'What kind of a chat?' Tony asked, defensively.

'We'd just like to clarify a few points.'

Something beneath Keenan's pleasantness chilled Tony to the marrow.

'If I wanted,' he asked, carefully, 'to bring someone with me—'

'What kind of someone, Mr Patston?'

'A lawyer,' Tony said. 'Just to keep an eye on things, you know.' He was sweating, knowing how it had to be sounding to the policeman. 'It's not what you think,' he said, quickly.

'By all means,' Keenan said smoothly, 'bring your solicitor along.' He paused. 'Would you like to make your own way to us, Mr Patston, or would you like us to pick you up?'

Tony said that he would drive.

'This isn't going to take too long, is it?' he asked about three hours later, seated in an interview room opposite Keenan and Reed.

It had taken him more than ninety minutes to find anyone – scrabbling frantically through the Yellow Pages for solicitors quoting 24-hour emergency numbers – free and willing to meet him at Theydon Bois on a Saturday morning.

The man who sat beside him now, Richard Slattery, was, if nothing else, solid, in that there was a great deal of him, but beyond that and the fact that he'd been available and, for a fat fee, prepared to come along at a moment's notice, Tony had no idea if he was any shakes at all as a lawyer.

Better than nothing. Hopefully.

'You're not under arrest, Mr Patston,' Keenan said clearly, 'and you're free to leave.'

'It's all right,' Tony said, his stomach churning. 'Only—'

'You're entitled to legal advice,' Keenan went on, 'but it's clear you've made your own arrangements.' He nodded at Slattery.

'Only,' Tony said, 'I don't want to leave Irina for too long, you see.'

'She's with your mother-in-law, isn't she?' Keenan asked.

'Yes,' Tony said, 'but she's fretting for her mum, obviously.'

There were three plastic cups of coffee on the table. Slattery was drinking his, making tiny lapping sounds as he did so, like a little cat, which Tony found odd for a man of his size. Neither Keenan or Reed had picked up their cups yet, and Tony hadn't dared touch his because he was scared his hand would shake.

'I'm now going to switch on the tape recorder,' Keenan said.

Terry Reed unwrapped two cassette tapes, inserted them into the recorder at the wall edge of the table, and Keenan reached across and turned it on.

'You love your little girl, do you?' DS Reed asked.

'Of course I do,' Tony said, thinking again about the strangeness of the fact that since Joanne's death he had been discovering that he really did love Irina much more than he'd realized.

'If you love her,' Keenan asked, quietly, 'why do you hit her?'

'I don't,' Tony said, reddening. 'Who says I do?'

'We have reason to believe,' Keenan went on, 'that Irina has been punched, or worse, on several occasions, her injuries sufficiently serious to necessitate her being taken to Waltham General hospital.'

'I wonder,' Richard Slattery said, leaning forward, his large balloon stomach rubbing the edge of the table, 'if I could have a few moments alone with my client?'

'No,' Tony said, rather loudly and abruptly.

'Mr Patston,' Slattery said.

'No,' Tony said. 'We don't need to be alone.'

He'd always prided himself on recognizing a golden opportunity when it was dangled right under his nose, and the way things

257

were looking this might be the only one for a bloody long time, and, Christ forgive him, Joanne couldn't be any more hurt than she had been.

'I've never wanted to say anything,' he said, with a show of reluctance. 'And I wouldn't be saying it now, but . . .'

'What's that, Mr Patston?' Keenan asked.

Tony could feel them all watching him. He was sweating again, and his head was starting to ache.

'It was Joanne,' he said, 'who hit Irina.'

The room went silent. Keenan glanced at Reed, while Slattery, observing the unmistakably icy distaste as keenly as he might have felt a hard slap, looked down at his hands.

'That's not,' Terry Reed said, after several seconds, 'the impression we've been getting.'

'Well,' Tony said, 'it wouldn't be, would it?'

'Word is,' Reed went on, 'your wife had to be careful not to let Irina cry too much because you didn't *like* it.' He stressed the word as if it possessed a bad smell.

'That was what she wanted people to think.' Tony could feel inspiration continuing to feed him his lines, and it *was* inspiration, because poor Jo couldn't contradict him, and no one else had ever seen him touch Irina, had they? 'Maybe,' he went on, as if it pained him to say it, 'maybe she even wanted to think it herself, because she was afraid of the truth.'

'What truth was that?' Keenan asked quietly.

'That she couldn't cope as well as she made out,' Tony replied. 'That after all we'd gone through to adopt Irina, she wasn't as good a mother as she'd thought she was going to be.'

'So what are you saying?' Keenan asked. 'That it was Joanne who got angry when Irina cried?'

'That's right,' Tony said.

'Yet Joanne went out of her way to keep your daughter with her as much as possible,' Keenan said.

'I'm not saying she didn't *love* her,' Tony said. 'Just that she couldn't cope.' He looked at his audience. 'She knew how upset I got when she hit her.' He paused again. 'You've no idea how much I hate saying this now, with poor Jo . . .' He shook his head, felt tears spring into his eyes, wasn't sure if he felt more proud or ashamed of his performance, but it was good, no doubt about that, and, more to the point, it was necessary.

258

'Take your time, Mr Patston,' Keenan said.

'I was going to keep it to myself forever,' Tony said. 'I wanted to help her get over it, you know? And I'd rather Sandra didn't have to hear about it, because it'll really do her head in, won't it? But Joanne could get very screwed up sometimes – especially when she got her PMS – I told you about that, didn't I?'

'Actually,' Keenan said, 'you said she didn't get it too badly.' He referred to his notes. 'You said, in fact, that Joanne told you she had PMS that last morning. I asked you if she suffered from it badly, and you said: "She wasn't too bad." ' Keenan smiled. 'Which was it, Mr Patston?'

A tickle of unease passed through Tony. 'It was bad,' he said, as if confessing. 'I just didn't want you to know.' His confidence returned. 'Because of what I've told you. I didn't want anyone thinking badly of her.'

'Very commendable of you,' Keenan said.

Reed leaned forward. 'You said Joanne knew how upset you got when she hit Irina.' His beady eyes had grown particularly sharp.

'Of course she knew,' Tony said. 'It used to go right through me when Irina cried, because I knew what was going to happen, and it made me feel sick.'

'Did you try to stop her?' Reed asked.

'Of course,' Tony said again.

There was another pause.

'Is that what happened that day?' Keenan asked.

'What?' Tony said, not understanding. 'When?'

'That last morning,' Keenan said. 'Before Joanne went out. Did you have to try to stop her hitting Irina then?'

'No.' The confidence disappeared, swift as water down a plughole. 'No, not that morning.'

'Was it the last straw?' Keenan asked. 'Was that when you knew you had to kill Joanne, Tony?'

Tony saw, suddenly, sickeningly, the hole he'd dug for himself.

'Hold on,' he said, looking sideways at Slattery, but the big man was just sitting there. 'That's crazy. This has got nothing to *do* with her being killed. I was just explaining about Irina getting hurt, that's all.'

'But if you did do it—' Keenan was leaning forward now, his

face intent, his tone encouraging '—what you just told us would make it almost understandable.'

'But I didn't.' Tony stared at the tapes going round and round.

'Seeing your little girl being hit—' Reed, too, leaned in '—that's more than enough to push any loving daddy over the edge.'

'You're both twisting my words.' Tony looked desperately from Keenan to Reed, then to Slattery, the useless lump at his side. 'I had nothing to do with Joanne being killed – I loved her – I never, ever, touched her, never wanted her dead, not for a *second*!'

Keenan sat back in his chair again, and his smile was merciful, almost priestlike. 'Take your time, Tony,' he said. 'Think about it. Do the right thing now, while you can.'

'Right thing?' Tony echoed incredulously. 'Christ.'

He stared at them again, looked from one to the other, and knew, with ice in his stomach, that he had no choices left.

'Okay,' he said. 'Okay.' He took a gulp of air. 'I'm going to tell you about something – something I've been trying and trying to keep secret for so long.'

He had to pause, had to rub the back of his right hand over his eyes, because suddenly he wanted to cry again, but he didn't have time to start blubbing like a kid now, he had to get this said, had to get it *out*, before everything got any more out of control.

'It's all right,' Keenan the priest said. 'Take your time, Tony.'

Tony let his hand fall back onto his knee. 'No,' he said. 'It isn't that. It's nothing to do with Jo. It's something else.'

At last, Richard Slattery reacted. 'Mr Patston,' he said. 'I think a break—'

'No,' Tony cut him off. 'No breaks. No more going round the houses.' He was sweating again, shaking.

'I really must advise—'

'*No*.' Tony sat right forward, more urgent than ever now. 'You've got to listen.' He focused on Keenan. 'Because once I tell you this, you're going to understand why I've been so messed up. Because Christ knows it's been hard enough coping with losing Jo, but I'm so scared now of losing Irina too, I'm scared to *death* of that.'

'Why should you lose Irina?' Keenan asked. 'Because you hit her?'

'No,' Tony half shouted. 'Nothing to do with that – though I didn't do that either, I swear it.' He looked into the detective's

260

thin, attentive face, sucked in another desperate breath. 'I'm scared I'm going to lose Irina,' he said, 'because of the way we adopted her.'

Keenan scanned mentally back over the facts Pat Hughes had delivered to him regarding Irina's adoption, then swiftly returned his attention to the wretched man opposite him.

'We *bought* her,' Tony said. 'We couldn't get a baby any other way, and Jo wanted to be a mum more than anything else in the world.' He was crying again. 'I did that for Joanne because I loved her so much – I'd have done anything for her, *anything*. I could never have hurt her like you think, never.' He shook his head, and his voice sank lower. 'Never.'

75

At home on Saturday afternoon, sitting in his living room at Shad Tower, leaning back comfortably in his custom-made leather recliner, flicking through satellite TV channels, Robin Allbeury located the Food and Drink Channel and the programme he'd already established was showing at that time.

There she was in her studio kitchen, looking very fetching in a white cotton shirt and snug-fitting jeans with a blue and white striped apron, working alongside a man wearing a foolish smock. Her hair seemed a little different, longer, maybe a touch blonder – though that might have been the harsh lighting. A little younger around the eyes – another clue that this was a repeat of a show recorded at least two, maybe three years earlier. Not that she looked exactly *older* now.

She laughed at something the man said.

The laugh made her extremely beautiful, Allbeury thought. Gave her, for its duration, a more truly relaxed, carefree air, before it drifted away, leaving her other face in its wake. The face that declared all was well, that Lizzie Piper Wade was doing fine, able to cope with everything life threw at her – even if she might be willing to acknowledge, if pressed, that just a *little* of what it threw at her was hard to take. The face now on the screen was the one Lizzie had presented at the Wades' dinner party last week.

The face that had so compelled him.

Was still doing so.

Allbeury pushed the mute button on his remote control, glanced at his watch, wondered if the Wades were in Marlow this weekend, or in Holland Park.

Find out.

He'd intended to wait a while longer, at least a few days, before calling again, was, as a rule, a patient man.

With a few notable exceptions.

Of which Lizzie was most definitely one.

He put down the remote, picked up his Palm Pilot, checked the Marlow number, and called it.

'Hello?'

Her voice.

'Lizzie, it's Robin Allbeury.'

'Oh, hello.' She sounded pleased. 'How nice to hear from you.'

'Good or bad moment?' he asked. 'Not that I'll keep you long.'

'Quite good actually,' Lizzie said.

He thought he heard her sitting down, imagined her settling herself comfortably, imagined her with, perhaps, a dog on her lap . . .

For God's sake.

'I'm hoping,' he said, slightly briskly, 'that you and Christopher will agree to join me for dinner one night soon. Next week, perhaps, or the week after.'

'I'm sure we'd love to,' she answered. 'Except I've got a new book out at the end of next week, and the publishers are touring me.'

'Pity.' Allbeury contained his disappointment well. 'And immediately after that, I expect you'll be exhausted.'

'Probably,' Lizzie admitted. 'I think, from memory, the tour has me in London for a couple of days in the middle of the schedule, so maybe, if by chance our free hours coincide, we could at least meet up for a cup of something.'

'Or perhaps,' he suggested, 'I can give you a nice, relaxing glass of something at the end of one of your interview days.'

In her study at the house, Lizzie told Allbeury that would be lovely, gave him her mobile number, then hung up and leaned back.

The thought of meeting up with him, possibly on her own, if that was how it happened to work out (and Christopher had already arranged to be in Marlow for the children for at least part of her tour) was quite surprisingly appealing.

Careful, Lizzie.

She thought back to their dinner, ran through the memory to see

263

if she'd felt, at any point, that the solicitor had been flirting with her, and decided that whatever Susan had said to the contrary, he had not. And she, even more so, had been far too preoccupied with the children coming down with their colds to give any impression of flirtation back to him.

Yet her memory of Robin Allbeury was of a decidedly attractive, very charming man. And rather a nice one too, she'd thought.

Susan had said she'd thought he 'fancied' her.

Lord knew that was the last complication she needed.

Careful, she told herself again.

76

Sandra was on her daughter's kitchen phone on Wednesday morning, pretending to listen to Lilian West – her next-door-neighbour in Edmonton – telling her about her husband's forthcoming prostate operation, when the doorbell rang.

'Lilian, I have to go.'

She heard movement from the living room, knew it would be DC Dean, rather than Tony, going to answer, and that was becoming almost routine, her son-in-law sitting morosely in his chair, letting other people take care of things, and Sandra knew it wasn't laziness, could read the now permanent fear in his eyes, and she understood that emotion well enough now, saw it in her own eyes each time she glanced in a mirror. She'd been so sure ever since they'd found Joanne that there was nothing left to *be* afraid of, but now that she knew the truth about the adoption – now that the police knew too – knew the endless fear that her own poor child must have endured, day in, day out, of losing Irina, Sandra too, had fallen into a permanent state of terror.

Of hearing the doorbell.

Of this moment.

She heard the voices at the door. Heard Karen Dean going back into the living room, saying something to Tony, heard him start to shout.

Sandra began to tremble as she opened the kitchen door.

The hall seemed full of strangers, two women and a man, and DI Keenan was there, too, in the background, and DC Dean coming from the living room . . .

She heard the cry then.

Irina's cry. Wordless, but shrieking.

265

'Sandra, I'm so sorry.' Dean looked distressed as she came towards her.

'What?' Sandra pushed past her, saw that a woman with orange hair had picked up Irina, was holding her tightly. 'What are you *doing*?'

'Leave it, Sandra.' Tony was behind the woman, holding a piece of paper in one hand, his face very pale, just standing, doing nothing, just *standing*, watching them take his daughter away.

'They have to take her,' Dean told her, put out a hand to touch her arm.

'No!' Sandra moved suddenly, arms out, fingers splayed, trying to grasp at Irina, but the orange-haired woman dodged sideways, and all Sandra's desperate fingers caught at was the sleeve of her coat. 'Give her to me!'

'There's nothing you can do, Sandra.' Dean's eyes were wet.

'Give her to *me*!' Sandra wailed.

She saw Irina's scared, huge eyes staring at her, and the child's mouth was open, but for that instant or two she wasn't actually crying, just open-mouthed with shock and bewilderment. And then the woman holding her turned around and began to walk out of the door, and Irina began to scream again.

'*No!*' Sandra yelled after her, and her hands, helpless, frenzied, flew to either side of her head, clutching, grabbing handfuls of her own hair. 'They *can't*! Tell them they *can't*!'

'They can,' Tony said, quietly.

The other strangers followed their colleague, faces bland, showing no feelings at all, either for the screaming child or the distraught woman who had already lost her only daughter and was now, at this very instant, also losing her only grandchild.

Sandra stared after them, then at the people left behind. Keenan, his thin face wretched; Karen Dean, tight-lipped, trying not to look at her.

And Tony, still standing, like a block of wood.

'You *bastard*!' She flung herself at him, began pounding at him with her fists, weeping as she hit him, and still he remained motionless, not looking at her, looking past her into the distance. 'You stupid, selfish *bastard*!'

'Mrs Finch,' Keenan said gently. 'Why don't we—'

'How could you let them *take* her?' The nails of Sandra's right hand caught her son-in-law's cheek, drew blood. 'How could you *do* that?'

'I didn't do anything,' Tony said, at last, though still he didn't move. 'It's the law,' he said, softly. 'We knew it was coming.'

Karen Dean came up behind Sandra, put her hands on the older woman's arms to restrain her, but there was no need. All the strength, all the fight had gone out of her now, and her own arms fell limply to her sides, hung there.

Tony Patston, arrested and bailed after his confession on Saturday, and treading water since then, hardly able to breathe, let alone function, was no longer looking past Sandra into the distance.

He was looking at Keenan–

– who now stepped forward and began to speak to Tony.

'Anthony Patston, I am . . .'

Sandra was aware of the inspector's voice, low and steady, but if she heard the words he used as her son-in-law's pale, now bloody, face grew even whiter, sicker, she was incapable of making sense of them.

All she could hear, ringing in her ears, as she thought they would forever, were the screams of her murdered daughter's only child as she was carried away.

Case No. 6/220770

PIPER-WADE, E.

Study/Review

Pending ✓

Action

Resolved

77

Lizzie's tour began at five on Thursday morning with Susan arriving, bleary-eyed, to collect her from Marlow and drive her to Oxford for her first radio interview of the day, after which there was to be a signing in Waterstones, followed by lunch with the *Oxford Mail*. Then on to Cheltenham for the *Gloucestershire Echo*, before Gloucester itself for another radio interview. Then two more signing sessions and down to Bristol for drinks with the *Western Daily Press* and dinner with the *Evening Post* at the Marriott, where they were overnighting before another early start for breakfast television.

It was Friday, after six-thirty, when she walked wearily, but with the sense of warm relief the hotel always gave her, into the Savoy and up the stairs to the American Bar, where Robin Allbeury was waiting at a corner table.

'You look tired.' He kissed her cheek, then pulled out a chair for her to sink into. 'Lovely, of course, but worn out. And possibly hungry?' He sat again too.

'Hungry, yes,' Lizzie said. 'Lovely, most definitely not.'

'You'll forgive me for disagreeing with that.' He watched her sit back and look around. 'Bit hectic, isn't it? How about just one glass of something here, and then elsewhere for a quiet dinner?' He saw her dubious expression. 'Somewhere you can just collapse and not have to watch everything you say.'

'Sounds wonderful,' Lizzie said. 'So long as it's not too late. Susan's got me up before the crack of dawn for GMTV.' She saw him frown. 'Something wrong?'

'Only that I probably should have asked Susan to join us.'

Lizzie shook her head. 'She was dying to get home. No weekend off for her either, don't forget.'

'Still,' he said, 'I should have thought.'

'Susan isn't easily offended,' Lizzie said.

They had a glass of champagne each, and then Allbeury drove her out of town to a cosy restaurant in a West Hampstead side road run by two hospitable men who'd clearly known Allbeury for years.

'You don't have to talk at all,' Allbeury told her after they'd ordered, 'unless you want to. And I can either chat away or be silent, if you'd rather.'

'I think,' Lizzie said, 'I wouldn't mind listening for a bit.'

'A barrister I know has told me how tiring performing can be.'

'Did you never want to be a barrister? I could imagine you in court.'

'In a wig and gown?' he said. 'I can't.'

'So why matrimonial?'

'It was an area that interested me.'

'But not so much any more?' Lizzie remembered him saying at their dinner party that he no longer worked full-time.

He nodded. 'There were other things I wanted more time for.'

'Intriguing,' Lizzie said.

He smiled. 'Not really.'

'I'm sorry,' she said. 'I didn't mean to pry.'

'You're just being interested,' he said. 'Which is nice.'

Their first course arrived, a creamy cauliflower soup that Lizzie found herself devouring as if she hadn't eaten for a week, and after that she was almost too busy with her melting fillet steak and *frites* to talk much, and she noticed, more than once, that Allbeury – who'd ordered a good Burgundy, but was not drinking – was sitting back watching her eat, smiling.

'Do I have mustard on my cheek?'

'Sorry,' he said. 'Was I staring?'

'I don't mind,' she said. 'This is far too good for me to mind anything.'

'Good.' He paused. 'How's Christopher?'

'Fine. Being a more-or-less house husband in Marlow while I'm off being wined and dined all over the UK.'

'Very commendable,' Allbeury said.

'Gilly's there too, of course,' Lizzie said. 'And he has patients to see in one of the local BUPA hospitals.'

'So it's not all child-minding?'

She heard the touch of irony, felt compelled to rise to Christopher's defence. 'He wouldn't mind if it was.' She smiled. 'Though Edward, our oldest, would most definitely mind hearing himself described as a child in need of minding.'

Allbeury nodded, asked about Jack and Sophie, followed that up with a few questions about DMD – intelligent queries that Lizzie found quite easy to cope with. And it was, all in all, one of the most relaxing evenings she could remember having in a long time. Allbeury told her a little more about his practice and his partners, said that he'd always made a point of trying to work, if possible, with people he liked or at least respected. He told her about a former unnamed partner he'd let go because of his preparedness to accommodate a client who'd turned out to be a thug; though even that experience, Allbeury added, smiling, had led him to one of his now favourite colleagues, a young private investigator named Novak, who ran a small agency with his wife.

'Nice people,' he said.

It was only as they neared the end of the evening, *en route* to Holland Park, that Lizzie realized how skilfully Allbeury had drawn facts, opinions and even, to a degree, feelings out of her, while telling her next to nothing of real consequence about himself.

She already had a husband who was attractive and charming.

A husband you only stay with for the children.

And Robin Allbeury, she decided again, glancing at him sideways as he drove, really was *extremely* attractive.

Careful, Lizzie.

That self-caution again.

He halted the Jaguar outside the flat and turned off the engine.

'So, back again in a few days, didn't you say?'

She felt, suddenly, absurdly, like a teenager saying goodnight after a first date outside her parents' home.

Not a date.

'Yes,' she said, quite briskly, 'but only after Manchester, Leeds,

York, Newcastle, Glasgow, Edinburgh *and* the Lakes.' She picked up her bag from the floor. 'By which time, I'll almost certainly be ready for nothing more than total collapse.'

'Then if you should happen to want a friend to collapse with,' Allbeury said, 'or if, by remote chance, you have just a sprinkling of strength left, I hope you'll remember my number.'

78

Keenan had eaten his wife's Sunday roast beef and Yorkshires, and he'd played football with his boys and cuddled his daughter, but all the while inside his mind he'd been seeing the little adopted – not *really* adopted – girl being carried out of her house by a stranger, and the thought that he might have been in any way instrumental in that made him feel sick and useless, because it was all so wrong and lousy, and he couldn't see a decent end to it.

He'd told poor Sandra Finch that he would try and help in any way he could, and he *was* going to do his damnedest, but he couldn't see himself making any difference, not about the little girl, anyway.

'At least Irina's not at risk from Patston any more,' Terry Reed had said, because Tony Patston was back home again, the only charges against him to date relating to the adoption, and they'd been trying, now, to trace the Georgious, the Patstons' neighbours, in Cyprus, in the hope that they might be able to shed some useful light on the relationship between Tony and Joanne, but nothing as yet there either.

Reed had meant well enough. They'd all meant well enough.

Didn't make it right.

Didn't stop Keenan from looking at his own children and wanting to punch a hole in his living room wall.

Shipley was beginning to accept that obsession might, after all, be the right diagnosis for what was ailing her.

The thing was, no matter how strong her hunches, she'd always been able to recognize when a case or a situation was over, even if she'd been proven wrong. Till now. She'd tried, *really* tried, dumping this or at least shoving it to the back of her mind and getting on, wholeheartedly, with the drugs case, but Lynne Bolsover and Joanne Patston just wouldn't get lost. And it made little real sense, given that both prime suspects were filth, for her to be as vexed as she was.

As *obsessed*.

Except that something she and Keenan had lightly touched on after calling on Allbeury – that Keenan had then dismissed – was back in her head now, needling, *itching* at her.

What if it *was* the men, those two scummy husbands, that Allbeury, self-styled defender of unhappy women, was after? Killing the women, maybe putting them out of their misery, in order to send the men down?

Patston hit the kid, not his wife.

Defender of unhappy women and children.

And maybe – Shipley took the line of thought further a few hours later, prodding absently at her roast beef meal-for-one, while the *Eastenders* omnibus screeched its way through early Sunday afternoon – there had been more than two shitbag husbands? More than two unhappy wives?

'Christ,' she said, and pushed away the food.

She thought again about the Bolsover murder weapon, remembered Kirby calling her paranoid when she'd told him she thought the discovery reeked.

No one was going to listen to something this wild, either. This *groundless*. And without official back-up it was going to be incredibly tough to try sifting through old wife-slaying cases searching for invisible links with Robin Allbeury.

So only one thing to do, Shipley decided, wrapping her dinner in an old Tesco plastic bag and going to get dressed.

Ask him.

'May I be frank, Mr Allbeury?'

'I'd appreciate that.'

She had phoned ahead to say she needed another word, and had thought she'd heard him sigh, but then he'd said she was welcome to return, and that was *one* thing she was determined to try to do, she'd decided on her way back to Shad Tower, try needling him out of that infuriatingly calm courtesy, maybe reach the other side of him.

274

If it existed, a cautionary voice had said.

They were on the terrace, outside the living room, which Shipley now saw ran the full length of the apartment. It was warm for mid-October, and Allbeury was sipping mineral water and wearing a black short-sleeved polo shirt and jeans.

'I don't understand you,' she said.

'Do you need to?' he asked.

'I don't much enjoy puzzles I can't solve,' Shipley said. 'You're a puzzle.'

'I find all sorts of people puzzling,' Allbeury said.

'If we weren't dealing with the murders,' she went on, 'of two very nice women, I wouldn't give a stuff about trying to work you out.'

'So how do you propose I help you to work me out?' For the first time, he showed a touch of irritation. 'I've answered all your questions – and DI Keenan's – as well as I could. You apparently suspect me of something – perhaps even something in connection with these dreadful deaths. I can do no more than assure you that you couldn't be more wrong.'

'You can do a lot more,' Shipley said. 'You can tell me what you really think – really *feel* – about Lynne Bolsover and Joanne Patston and any of the other women you've supposedly tried so hard to help.' She watched Allbeury, sitting perfectly, infuriatingly, still. 'You can tell me exactly why you claim to care about them.'

'I have my reasons.'

'Which are?'

'Private.'

Shipley shook her head.

'I'm sorry to exasperate you,' Allbeury said. 'I get no pleasure from it.'

'And what do you get out of helping those women?'

'Simply the knowledge, when I'm successful, that I am doing just that.'

'How,' she asked, 'do you measure success?'

'That depends on the individual case.'

She took her time. 'In the case of Lynne Bolsover, do you consider that you succeeded or failed?'

Allbeury frowned. 'Since you're anything but stupid, DI Shipley, you must have some reason I don't understand for asking such an absurd question.'

'Do you feel that you failed or succeeded in that case, Mr Allbeury?'

'Obviously,' he said, 'I did not succeed.'

'Yet the man who caused Lynne's misery is now in prison.'

Allbeury said nothing.

'Some might call that a result, don't you think?'

'I can't speak for anyone else,' he said, 'but I certainly would not call it that.'

'Because Lynne had to die to achieve it?'

'Obviously,' he said.

'What do you think of John Bolsover or Joanne Patston's husband?'

'I've never met either of them.'

'But you think them despicable men, surely?'

'Probably,' he admitted.

Shipley got up, walked to the telescope, turned at the parapet to face him – still sitting there so calmly, one leg crossed over the other, watching her, waiting for her next question. Behind Shipley, beyond the terrace and fifteen floors below, pedestrians on the riverside walk and traffic on the Thames flowed back and forth.

She knew that she was running out of time, had achieved nothing at all.

Last-ditch.

'I still don't know,' she said, 'if you really are an altruist or a very evil man.'

'That's it,' Allbeury said, and stood up. 'Some solicitors enjoy game playing,' he said coldly, 'but I never really have.' He paused. 'I leave that to your kind.'

'What kind's that?'

'I would not presume to guess,' he said.

'Are you going,' Shipley asked, 'to report me for harassment?'

'I wasn't planning to.'

'I think,' Shipley said, 'most men in your position might do just that.'

'Innocent men, you mean?' Allbeury said.

79

On Monday afternoon in Newcastle, Lizzie was having fun at one of the nicest events Susan had ever dreamed up, with a team of sales people from most of the bookshops in town competing against each other in the kitchen of a charming French restaurant, each cooking up their favourite recipes from *Pure Bliss*.

With nothing but good, calm news from Christopher and Gilly, and only Glasgow and Edinburgh – one of her most beloved cities – to go before they turned south again and headed for the Lake District, Lizzie was in fine spirits.

At four-thirty on Tuesday afternoon, having found himself so unable to settle to work at Bedford Row that he'd given up and come home, Allbeury was sitting at the computer in the study adjacent to his bedroom, doing something he seldom did.

Brooding.

Not about Helen Shipley's intrusive and insulting visit on Sunday. Not much he could do about her opinion of him.

He was brooding about two other matters.

The first concerned Lizzie. Or, more accurately, Christopher Wade.

If the dirt was there, Allbeury had learned, and if you dug deep enough, used the right resources, the right people, you tended to find it. So he had dug. And found.

Christopher Edward Julian Wade had a conviction, almost sixteen years old, for possession of cocaine. Two years after that, he had been arrested and cautioned for kerb crawling in King's Cross.

And now there was the second thing.

His computer had just crashed twice in a row, and, prior to that – yesterday and again first thing this morning – it had displayed a series of strange, inexplicable glitches.

Not that he actually knew exactly what made a computer glitch odd as opposed to commonplace. He might have learned a good deal from young Adam Lerman and gone on learning since, but what Allbeury truly understood about the *inner* workings of his amazing box of tricks could have been balanced on the pointed end of a pin.

He did, on the other hand, possess instincts that he had learned, over the years, to trust. And it was those instincts which were by now starting to gnaw at him in a manner he found troubling.

Troubling enough, he decided, to call Adam at his Los Angeles home, and hope that he was there.

'Not too early, I hope.'

Adam, a well-brought up young man, said, rather blearily, that it was not.

'I think someone may be hacking into my PC. I need to know if I'm right and who it is.'

'What exactly are we talking about here?' Adam asked. 'Someone snooping – gaining access just to read your files? Very hard to track, by the way.'

'Great,' Allbeury said. 'I'm not sure yet exactly what's going on, just that something is.'

'Hackers are the guys who usually do it for the challenge, remember, for fun.' Adam was waking up properly now, warming to his favourite topic. 'If their intentions are malicious, then they're called crackers.'

'Whatever you say,' Allbeury said.

'I do.' Adam paused. 'I know a guy who can help you.'

'In London?'

'Almost certainly.'

'Will you call him, or should I?' Allbeury asked.

'I'll do it,' Adam said. 'How soon do you want him, if he's free?'

'Sooner the better.'

'If you don't hear from me again,' Adam Lerman said, 'assume he'll be with you some time tomorrow.' He paused. 'This is at your place, is it, not the office?'

Allbeury told him it was, and that he was very grateful.

'This guy looks a bit weird,' Adam said, 'but believe me, he's a genius. And – though obviously it's your call – you can trust him.'

'If he's such a genius, how come you think he'll be available?'

'Because he loves me,' Adam said.

80

By noon on Wednesday, Lizzie had completed an interview with one of her favourite broadcasters, Alex Dickson at Radio Clyde, had done two rushed signings in Glasgow and then jumped with Susan onto the Edinburgh train to make her lunch appointment with John Gibson from the *Evening News*, when her mobile rang, and it was Christopher calling to tell her that Jack had come down with another bug and was rather poorly.

'Don't worry,' Susan told her as soon as she heard. 'At least not about the book side of things. We'll get you back as fast as humanly possible.'

Lizzie, sitting opposite her, stared out of the window, seeing nothing. 'I hope we get hold of John. I don't want to leave him just sitting.'

'At least he'll be sitting at the Caley,' Susan said. 'And anyway, he's much too lovely to mind when he knows the reason.'

'Yes,' Lizzie said. 'Thank you.' She could think of nothing more to say.

'I'm calling the office.' Susan's mobile was already pressed against her ear. 'Easier for them to organize flights, cancel arrangements.'

'Again.' Lizzie turned from the window. 'Running out on you all again.'

'Not your fault,' Susan said, then, raising a finger to signal that she was through to the office, she began to talk.

Lizzie leaned back in her seat and closed her eyes, knowing that Christopher would never have pushed that alarm button were he not sufficiently concerned. What worried her most was that she'd asked if Jack wanted to speak to her, and Christopher had said he was sleeping.

'Sleeping, or too poorly?' she'd asked, and he'd replied, quite sternly, that as she very well knew, honesty when it came to Jack's health was something she could trust him on.

Yet still, Lizzie also knew that being aware she was in Scotland, he might have seen no purpose in frightening her any more than he already had.

'Next available flight's at three-fifteen,' Susan said, gently. 'You're on it.'

Lizzie opened her eyes, looked at her friend. 'I'm so sorry.'

'Don't you dare apologize,' Susan said.

Lizzie reached the house to find that Angela was on the way to help Gilly and generally bolster Sophie's and Edward's spirits because Christopher and Hilda Kapur had arranged a bed for Jack in the private hospital near Windsor he'd been in several times before.

'Tell me,' Lizzie said to Christopher quietly, after she'd given Edward a hug and Sophie a cuddle and before she went upstairs to Jack.

'He's all right.' Christopher was clear, firm. 'This is just to be on the safe side. He needs fluids and antibiotics and monitoring, and Hilda's fairly certain a couple of days should see him well enough to come home.'

'You said a bug. What kind?'

'His throat's sore and he's got a fairly nasty cough.' He paused. 'A little worse than last time.'

'Did you speak to someone at the Centre?'

'I did,' he said. 'They seemed to feel we were being sensible.'

Lizzie started towards the stairs, then stopped. 'Why did you call Mum?'

'I didn't,' Christopher said. 'Angela happened to phone just after Jane had called about a serious burns case and I'd told her to pass it on.'

'But?' Lizzie was tired, frightened and irritable. 'Christopher, do you want to go, is that it?'

'Jack got wind of it, and practically ordered me to go.'

'Then *go*, for heaven's sake.'

She turned her back on him, ran up the stairs and into Jack's bedroom.

'Hi, Mum.'

'Hi, yourself.'

She bent to kiss him.

'You'll catch it,' Jack said.

'I never catch your bugs,' Lizzie said.

She sat on the edge of his bed and surveyed him. He was pale and flushed, and she could hear a slight wheeze, but he seemed fairly typically Jack.

'I really want Dad to go to the clinic, Mum.' He was earnest. 'If some poor sod needs him, he should go.'

'I think you have first claim, my darling,' Lizzie said.

'Maybe,' Jack allowed, 'if I was really ill, but this isn't anything.'

'There are other surgeons, you know. Your dad's not the only one.'

'But he is the best,' Jack said.

Lizzie looked at him, saw that he was adamant.

'Are you quite, quite sure you don't mind just having me?' she asked.

'Cross my heart,' he said, then managed a grin. 'You may not be a hot-shot surgeon, Mum, but you're not too bad – so long as you don't fuss.'

Lizzie stood up. 'I'd better go and tell him to go then.'

'Cool,' Jack said.

'And you,' Lizzie said, 'are one in ten million, Jack Wade.'

Allbeury got home to find Winston Cook – the young man so highly recommended by Adam Lerman – still working at the computer in the blue study, where he'd been ensconced since ten that morning. He was *very* young, Allbeury reckoned, a handsome black kid with spiked hair, green eye shadow and an unshakable conviction in his own ability.

'If someone's been cracking your system,' Cook had announced on his arrival, 'unless he's some kind of guru, I'll track him.'

Even if Adam hadn't already sung his praises so enthusiastically, Allbeury thought he would have believed him.

'Did you eat lunch?' he asked him now.

'Your man downstairs sent someone out for a Big Mac,' Winston told him. 'I took it out on the balcony. Hope you don't mind.'

'Not in the least,' Allbeury said. 'Though as I told you, my fridge is yours.'

'Wicked view out there,' Winston said.

'How're you doing?'

'Slow but sure,' the young man said.

'Have you at least stopped the rot?'

Cook shook his head. 'Can't track him down if I lock all the doors.' He looked at the solicitor's face, saw his frustration. 'It's like bait – we need them to keep coming back so we can track them.'

'Makes sense, I suppose,' Allbeury supposed, and looked at his watch. 'Shouldn't you be calling it a day about now?'

'Soon, maybe,' Cook said.

Allbeury left him, and went into the living room to fix himself a drink.

And thought, as was now becoming quite habitual, about Lizzie.

On her tour at present, away from home – and Wade. Which meant that a former kerb crawler and cocaine user was currently in charge of their three vulnerable children, which made Allbeury feel almost physically ill.

Lizzie seemed convinced that as a father, her husband was the greatest show on earth, so that, at least, was probably okay. *Probably*.

But the thought of Lizzie returning home after her tour and climbing back into the kerb crawler's bed made Allbeury shudder.

Not your place to shudder.

He wondered if she knew about Wade's past.

81

On Thursday afternoon, the consultant in charge of Jack's case in the hospital near Windsor told Lizzie that he thought Jack should be transferred either to the Radcliffe or to Hammersmith, for assessment and specialist treatment.

'I said Hammersmith, if they had a bed,' Lizzie told Angela on the phone, 'since Christopher's already in London.'

'How bad is he?' Angela asked.

'His breathing's a bit worse,' Lizzie said, 'but nothing he can't cope with, so don't worry too much.'

'Pot calling kettle comes to mind,' her mother said.

'Has Christopher phoned? Only he's not at the Beauchamp and Jane doesn't seem to know where he is, which is unlike her.'

'We haven't heard from him, darling, but if he calls, I'll tell him what's happening and get him to phone you right away.' Angela took a deep breath, bent on staying calm for her daughter's sake. 'When are you leaving Windsor?'

'In the next couple of hours.' Lizzie struggled to unscramble her brain. 'I may not be allowed to keep my mobile on once we leave – can you tell Christopher that too, please, Mum?'

'I'll make sure he's at Hammersmith, waiting for you.'

'Bless you, Mum,' Lizzie said. 'And kiss the others for me, please.'

'Big hugs from us,' Angela said.

Travelling in the ambulance with Jack, Lizzie felt her spurious calm shredding by the minute in the face of her son's unusually palpable nervousness and worsening wheeze. Yet after their

284

arrival at Hammersmith, with the admissions palaver dealt with and Jack tucked up in bed, he rallied – despite the absence of or any word from his father – and told her he didn't need her to stay.

'Of course I'm going to stay,' Lizzie said.

'There's no need. You can stay at the flat.'

'I know I can,' she said, 'but I'd much rather stay here.'

'I'm not bloody dying, Mum,' Jack said.

'I never said you were,' she said, feeling her insides shrivelling.

'Then why do you want everyone to think I'm a baby?'

'No one would ever think that,' Lizzie told him.

'If Dad was here, *he'd* understand how I feel,' Jack said.

She had no answer to that.

'You win,' she said. 'I'll go to the flat.'

There were no lights on as her taxi deposited her outside the flat, no signs of life at all, though at least there was no newspaper sticking out through the letter box nor any milk bottles on the step.

Lizzie sighed as she fished for her front door key and put it into the lock, too exhausted now, and too preoccupied by Jack to worry about where Christopher might have got to.

She came into the dark entrance hall, turned on the lights, shut and locked the front door behind her, and walked slowly towards the kitchen, in need, she decided as she went, of tea and chocolate biscuits, over and above anything stronger.

The sound, coming, she thought, from the living room, was faint, but enough to stop her in mid-step. She froze, listening.

It came again.

Like a soft groan.

Wide awake suddenly, feeling more bewildered than afraid, Lizzie walked to the living room door and pushed it open.

There were no lights on, but the curtains weren't drawn, and as her eyes quite quickly accustomed themselves to the dimness, a shape, on the sofa, moved.

Lizzie put up her hand and turned on the light.

'God,' she said. 'What happened to you?'

Christopher was sitting, or rather leaning, against one end of their sofa, an almost empty bottle of Johnnie Walker and another – not empty – of aspirin beside him.

'Lizzie,' he said, with difficulty.

His face was badly bruised, one eye almost panda black and

three-quarters shut, a smear of crusted blood at the right corner of his mouth.

'Christopher, what *happened*?'

'Oh, Christ,' he said, very weakly.

She knew, even before he spoke, as she was halfway to the sofa, *en route* to offering him help, that he was going to tell her something bad, that this was not the result of some ordinary accident.

She stopped, stood still. 'Tell me, please.'

'Oh, Christ, Lizzie.' He sat up a little way, wincing, sending the whisky bottle rolling off the cushions and onto the rug. 'Oh, God, that hurts.'

Still, Lizzie remained where she was.

'I could lie to you—' his voice was slurred '—tell you it was a car accident or a hit-and-run, but then you'd ask what the police were doing about it, so I might as well come clean right away.' His mouth quirked wryly. 'Clean,' he echoed.

Lizzie sat down, away from him, in one of the armchairs.

'I've been beaten up,' Christopher said, his eyes veering from hers, 'by a pimp who objected to what I was doing to one of his girls.'

Lizzie felt her head start to spin a little, felt sick.

'No more Lizzie for me.' Christopher held up both hands for a moment in a confessional kind of shrug. 'So it's back to where I was, doing it with prossies.' He got to his feet with difficulty and looked down at her. 'And what are you going to do about it now that you know? Your worst?'

She stared up at him for several seconds, then shook her head, looked away from him, into the bleak, empty fireplace.

'What I would like to do,' she said, shakily, 'is finish it all right now. Tell you to clear out and never come near me or our children again—' She halted, feeling dizzy.

'Lizzie?' He took a step towards her. 'Are you all right?'

'Don't you *dare* come near me,' she snarled suddenly. 'Of course I'm not all right, you bloody, *bloody* fool.' She looked at him again. 'Not because someone's beaten you to a pulp – I wish to God they'd done a better job.'

'You don't mean that.' Christopher sank down again, back onto the sofa.

'Jack's in hospital.'

'I know he is.'

'Not in Windsor,' Lizzie told him. 'In Hammersmith.' She stood up, went to the fireplace, put out a hand to the mantel to steady herself. 'Which you'd know, if you hadn't been . . .' She shook her head.

'Why?' Christopher's voice, behind her, was sharper. 'Why's Jack been moved? What's happened, Lizzie?'

She turned around, slowly, saw the terror on his face, chalky now around the bruising, knew that the fear, at least, was real. 'Don't panic,' she said. 'His breathing got a bit worse, but it's not too bad. They were concerned they might not be quite up to it, if he were to deteriorate, and I chose Hammersmith because you were here.'

'So why aren't you with him now?' he asked.

Anger returned in full force. 'Because Jack didn't want me to stay,' she said coldly. 'He doesn't want people thinking he's a baby.' Strength was coming back with the fury. 'He said you'd understand, if you were there.'

'Oh, Christ.' Christopher began to rise again, then stopped. 'I can't let him see me like this. Oh, my God, what have I done?' His eyes filled. 'Lizzie, what are we going to do? You can't tell him, you *can't*.'

'I have no intention of telling Jack, or Edward or Sophie – remember them?'

'Lizzie, please.'

'And clearly this isn't the moment to discuss separation or divorce.'

Christopher covered his face with his hands and began to weep.

'For God's sake,' Lizzie said in disgust. 'Your ten-year-old son's got a thousand times more courage than you have.'

Christopher's face emerged from above his hands, tear-streaked. 'I *knew* that was what you were planning,' he said, still weeping. 'I knew it as soon as Alicia told me someone had been snooping in our computer system, in my files.'

'I don't know what you're rambling about,' Lizzie said, 'and I don't care.' She took a deep breath. 'I was going to make some tea, but I think I deserve something stronger.' She looked down at the bottle on the carpet. 'If you've left anything.'

He didn't answer, and she went to the cabinet, found a bottle of Glenfiddich, poured herself a single, knowing anything more might tip her over the edge, and she needed to be capable in case the hospital phoned.

'Do you need a doctor?' she asked him abruptly, then took her first swallow, felt it brace her just a little.

'No,' he said. 'Nothing broken.'

'Then you may as well go to bed, don't you think?'

'What about Jack?' he asked, pitiful again.

'I'll telephone in a while, check on him. With a bit of luck, he'll be sleeping, so I won't have to make excuses for you not speaking to him.'

'I can speak to him, surely?' He raised his face, aggrieved.

'Not till you're sober and sounding like yourself,' Lizzie said. 'And you'd better do something about your face, patch yourself up a bit, or God knows when you'll next be fit to see him.'

'Oh, Lizzie,' Christopher said. 'I'm so sorry.'

She took another swallow of her drink and looked down at him.

'Go to hell, Christopher,' she said.

82

When Clare had told Novak, that morning, that she intended to take the day off, he had been surprised and concerned, had asked her before leaving if she was sure she was okay, if she needed a doctor or wanted him to stay with her.

'Yes, no and *no*,' she'd told him, exasperated but lighthearted. 'I just feel like taking a day off, which is what you've been on at me to do, isn't it?'

Which was true, of course, so he'd done as she asked, gone to the agency and spent most of the day paying the bills that still flowed in at a frighteningly faster and higher rate than their invoices went out, aware that now there was a baby on the way it was more vital than ever that he kept their heads above water.

He had phoned to check on her twice during the morning, but the second time she'd bitten his head off, told him he was stopping her from relaxing, and he'd backed off after that, not ringing her again till around four pm, when she'd been out.

He'd tried her mobile, but she'd switched it off, and after that he stewed for a while, picturing all kinds of emergencies, then went home, found the flat empty and went on stewing, until just after nine o'clock, when she finally came home.

'Where the hell have you *been*?' he said the instant he saw she was okay.

'At Nick's,' Clare said.

'You've been with Nick Parry?' He was incredulous.

'That's what I said.' She began to take off her coat.

'You were meant to be having a day off, not *nursing*.'

'Have you finished shouting at me?' she asked, quite mildly.

Novak leaned back against the wall, weak with relief and anger.

'Yes,' he said. 'I'm sorry for yelling, but I've been worried sick.'

'Why?' Her surprise was genuine.

'Because I didn't know where you were, and your mobile was turned off.'

'I didn't take it.' Clare walked into the kitchen. 'Nick phoned me at lunchtime, very pissed off, and I was bored, and I knew you'd be cross if I changed my mind and came to the agency, so I went to spend some time with him instead.'

Novak's anger had already dissipated, and he felt, if anything, ashamed.

'I'm sorry,' he said again. 'I know I drive you nuts sometimes.'

'Pretty much all the time just now,' she said.

'It's not my intention,' he said.

'I know.' Clare picked up the kettle, swished around the water already in it, put it down and switched it on. 'Being with Nick takes my mind off things.'

'Unlike me,' Novak said, trying not to sound hurt.

'Unlike you,' Clare agreed.

83

Christopher had been asleep in his room for a while, and Lizzie had spoken to the sister on Jack's floor, who'd assured her that he, too, was sleeping peacefully, before she remembered to check the voice mail on her mobile phone and found a message from Robin asking how the tour was going, and saying that he hoped she'd have enough strength left when she got back to London at least for a drink.

'And dinner, too,' he'd added, 'if you're up to it.'

Lizzie listened through to the end of her messages, called home again, spoke to her mother first, then Gilly, then Sophie – who was refusing to go to bed until she heard the latest about Jack – and then, finally, to Edward.

'Is Dad okay?' he asked after he'd learned about his brother.

'Dad's fine,' Lizzie told him. 'But really worn out, so he's gone to bed early.'

'Send my love,' Edward said.

'You bet,' Lizzie said.

She called Susan next, thanked her again for being such a true friend, asked her to send more apologies to Howard and all at Vicuna, said she promised faithfully to make up for this unprofessional streak, and Susan said that frankly, good as *Pure Bliss* might be, it was still only a book, and hardly to be compared with Jack's health.

Lizzie said goodnight to Susan, made herself a cup of hot chocolate, took it into the living room, found Allbeury's number and dialled it.

'What a lovely surprise,' he said, hearing her voice. 'What's wrong?'

She wondered, briefly, at his intuition, and told him what had happened, felt warmed by the intensity of his concern for Jack, and his sympathy regarding the abrupt ending of her tour.

'Shall I have a quick word with Christopher?' Allbeury asked, easily, as if they were old friends who regularly chatted.

'He's gone to bed actually,' Lizzie said.

'Nothing like kids being ill to drain you,' Allbeury said.

He made it sound almost as if he'd had first-hand experience of that, and Lizzie wondered why that might be, if, maybe, he had nephews and nieces, and realized, not for the first time, how very little she knew about him.

'I'll let you go,' he said, gently. 'If you need anything, Lizzie, please don't hesitate to call me.' He paused. 'Any time.'

She thanked him, said goodnight, put down the phone.

'Who was that?'

She looked up, saw Christopher, looking cleaner but still dreadful, standing in the doorway in a white towelling robe with CW embroidered on the breast.

'I was returning some calls,' she said. 'That was Robin Allbeury.'

'Why's Allbeury calling you?'

'He thought I was still touring, wanted to know how it was going.' Lizzie paused. 'You know we had dinner together last week.'

'Cosy,' Christopher said.

'What's that supposed to mean?' Anger returned.

'Dinner with a divorce lawyer.'

'He would have dined us both if we'd been together.' Lizzie shook her head. 'Why the hell am I explaining myself to you?'

'I'm sorry.' Christopher remained in the doorway. 'What did you tell him?'

'Just now? That Jack's unwell, obviously.'

'Nothing else?'

'Of course not,' Lizzie answered coolly.

'Thank you,' Christopher said.

'I didn't keep silent for your sake,' she said.

By morning, Jack was responding well to his new antibiotics, Christopher's bruises were purple, green and black, and he and Lizzie had settled on the cover story of a mugging, though when

Jack, on the phone, told his father that he wasn't going to believe he was *really* okay unless he could see him for himself, Christopher had come away from the call and begged Lizzie to reconsider.

'Now he thinks I've been mugged, it'll be okay – he'll probably be impressed.'

'It won't be okay,' Lizzie said. 'It'll be a lie.' She paused. 'And even if you don't care about lying to your son, as soon as you set foot inside the hospital, everyone will be asking you for the gory details and what the police are doing, and—'

'All right,' Christopher said. 'You've made your point. Jack just sounded so upset about not seeing me.'

'Whose fault is that?' Lizzie said.

84

Glad as he had been to hear from her, Lizzie's call last night had been, from Allbeury's perspective, unsatisfactory. Too brief and too disturbing.

She'd explained away the tension in her voice; Jack was in hospital and she was, naturally enough, afraid. Yet Allbeury had sensed more than that in her strain, something perhaps not greater than, but on equal footing with her fears for her son.

Wade at the root of it.

Christopher, the fine father, the one-time kerb crawler.

It had taken him a long time to get to sleep after that, and when he had, he had dreamed of *her*, an abstract dream in which nothing had been clear but her face and a soprano singing something operatic and painfully shrill.

Leaving him even more disturbed, because he was becoming more certain than ever that Lizzie Wade was a woman in need of help.

The kind of help he was in the habit of giving women.

Who, ordinarily, he did not dream about.

85

Christopher returned to Marlow on Monday with Lizzie and Jack, for his bruising was a little less horrifying to look at by then, and the mugging tale had, as he'd predicted, quite thrilled Jack once he had, finally, seen his dad for himself. And with the spectre of tracheotomy blotted out again for now, Lizzie found that she was more grateful for that gift than she was repulsed to have her husband still at her side.

'Did you fight back, Dad?' Edward wanted to know.

'I tried,' Christopher said.

'Much better not to,' Lizzie told her older son. 'Better to hand over what they want and be safe.'

'Better catch the bloody bastards,' Jack said.

'Language,' Christopher said.

'Well, they were, weren't they?'

'Bet they don't catch them,' Edward said.

'Probably not,' Christopher agreed.

'Does it hurt, Daddy?' Sophie asked.

'It did hurt, my darling,' Christopher told her. 'But it's much better now I'm here with you all.'

Lizzie *was* repulsed now, knew that this time she would not, would never be, able to forgive him. No matter how wonderful he was with the children, no matter how perfect a daddy they all believed him to be, it was, in the privacy of her heart and mind, finished for her.

'Poor Christopher,' Angela, scheduled to leave later that evening, said after she'd seen his face. 'What a dreadful thing to happen.'

'Dreadful,' Lizzie said.

'And so much worse for him than most of us,' Angela said. 'At least if any of us are ill or injured, we have Christopher to take care of us, but he has no one.' She smiled at her daughter. 'Not anyone like him, I mean.'

'Quite,' Lizzie said.

'You all right?' her mother asked, then shook her head. 'Silly question, after all you've been through.' She paused. 'Sure you want me to leave? I'd be glad to stay on a while longer.'

'No need.' Lizzie drew brightness determinedly around her. 'William's missing you, and Gilly's here to help.'

'Quite sure?' Angela laid a hand on her daughter's arm. 'I'm still your mum, Lizzie. You don't have to pretend to be strong all the time with me.'

'I know I don't,' Lizzie said.

Over the next few days, Christopher seemed, in the presence of the children, to be able to hold himself together well enough to deceive them, but when they were at school or with friends or asleep, he became, increasingly, more morose.

'I'd be grateful,' Lizzie told him on the Wednesday, 'if you could try a little harder in front of Gilly. She's no fool, and she knows something's wrong.'

'She thinks it's the mugging.'

'I'm asking you to make an effort,' Lizzie said.

'Oh, I am,' Christopher said. 'You've no idea how great an effort.'

'Am I supposed,' she asked, 'to thank you?'

On Thursday night, Hallowe'en, with Gilly out at a party and after an evening of sitting around the drawing room, decked out with pumpkins and candles, telling spooky tales, because Jack wasn't quite fit enough to go out trick-or-treating and the other two hadn't wanted to go without him, Christopher went to bed before Lizzie, giving her an hour or so of peace before she checked on the children and then went to bed herself.

It was just after midnight when she heard the knock on her door.

None of the children ever knocked, so it was either Gilly – back from her party – or Christopher.

296

She turned on her bedside lamp and drew up the covers.

'Yes?' she called, softly.

The door opened, and he was there, in his black silk dressing gown.

'What is it, Christopher?'

She saw right away it had nothing to do with the children, since then he would have banged or just come straight in, and he was wearing his new hangdog expression, and he might as well have stamped PITY ME on his forehead, only she had no pity left for him now, just contempt.

'I seem to have run out of painkillers,' he said.

'I thought you had plenty.'

'Plainly not enough.'

'All right.'

She got out of bed, pulled on her robe, walked into the bathroom, opened the cabinet and took out a pack of Nurofen.

And heard his step behind her.

She turned around, saw him in the bathroom doorway.

'I'd have brought them out.'

'No need.' He came into the bathroom, shut the door behind him.

'What are you doing?' Fear hit her hard, instantly. 'Christopher, open the door.'

'Don't be afraid.' In the bathroom's bright light, his grey eyes appeared brighter than usual against the dark bruising. 'You smell wonderful,' he said, softly.

Lizzie stepped to her right, then smartly to the door, certain, suddenly, that he was going to try and block her, but then she was gripping the handle and safely out of the bathroom again, feeling faintly foolish.

'The pills?' Christopher came back into the bedroom, held out his hand.

'Here.' Lizzie thrust the pack at him, but it fell to the floor.

Christopher looked down at it. 'I'm afraid I can't bend very well just yet.'

Lizzie said nothing, just bent to pick it up, straightened again, took his left hand and slapped the pack firmly into his palm.

'Thank you,' he said.

'You're welcome.'

He took three paces towards the door – closed now, Lizzie

noticed, and he must have done that when she'd gone ahead of him into the bathroom – and stopped again.

Turned back to face her.

'Look at me,' he said.

'Go to bed, Christopher,' Lizzie told him.

'Not at my face,' he said.

She looked, despite herself, saw what he wanted her to see.

Rage filled her.

'Get out,' she said.

'I don't want to get out,' he said.

'Get *out*.' Lizzie came at him, her right hand outstretched, shoved at his chest. 'Get out of my *room*.' She moved past him, heart pounding wildly, reached for the door handle.

'I told you.' Christopher turned, grabbed her arm, held it. 'I don't want to go.'

'Let me go,' she hissed. 'Let me go right now, or I'll scream.'

'No, you won't.' His face was contorted, half-smiling.

'Try me,' she said.

He dragged her arm downwards, towards his groin.

'Don't you *dare*.' Lizzie wrenched her arm free, shoved at him again, harder this time, and Christopher fell back against the door with a loud thud.

'Bitch,' he said, wincing with pain.

'Get out,' she said again.

'Not this time.'

He recovered, came forward, and Lizzie backed away, saw that his pupils were dilated, and the last time returned to her, and realization hit her that she'd been both mad and foolish beyond belief to imagine she could control this, go on *living* with this, even for the children.

'I need some comfort, Lizzie,' he said.

'Find it elsewhere,' she said. 'On the street, or wherever.'

'You're still my wife,' he said, and made another sudden, darting grab for her.

'Not for much longer.'

She looked around for something to pick up, use as a weapon if she had to, but there was only a book and her bedside lamp – too heavy – however angry or afraid, she knew she would never do such a thing to the children.

'It's not so much to ask,' Christopher said and came at her again.

Lizzie picked up the book and hit him with it on his shoulder.

'Bitch,' he said again.

He shoved her and she stumbled against the bedside table, then, while she was still off-balance, shoved her again, harder, in the stomach, pushing her onto the bed.

'No!' she said, in pain, still struggling not to scream. 'Christopher, *don't!*'

He pulled his robe open, wrenched it off himself, like someone burning with heat, let it drop, got onto the bed, kneeling. Lizzie tried to roll away, but he grabbed at her, pinned her with one arm, pulled up her nightdress with the other hand, thrust a knee between her thighs and raised his right hand.

'Dad, what are you *doing?*'

They both froze at the sound of Jack's voice.

Christopher let go of Lizzie's arms, scrambled off the bed, retrieved his robe.

'It's all right,' he said.

Lizzie, trembling, head spinning, still in pain, heart breaking at the sight of her middle child sitting in the doorway in his wheel-chair, eyes wide with horror, struggled to sit up and push her nightie back down.

'Jack, go back to your room.' Her voice was shaking. 'Darling, go on.'

'No,' he said, and began to wheel himself into the room. 'What were you doing?' he demanded, heading towards his father, braking sharply. 'What were you doing to my *mother?*'

'Take it easy, Jack.' The unbruised portions of Christopher's face were ashen as he fumbled with the black silk belt. 'Nothing to get excited about.'

'You pig,' Jack said. 'You disgusting *pig!*'

'It's okay.' Lizzie started to get off the bed. 'I'm okay, Jack.'

He ignored her, staring at his father.

'How could you?' he asked, quite softly. 'How could you *do* that?'

Christopher put out his right arm, his hand shaking. 'Come on, son. You don't understand, you're too young—'

The bellow that escaped from Jack as he drove the chair forward suddenly into his father's legs, was a roar of purest anguish. Christopher let out a yell of pain, shuddered with it for an instant, then stepped to his left, trying to escape.

Jack wheeled himself back several feet, then, with another of those terrible bellows, accelerated forward again, one steel front corner of the chair colliding with Christopher's right knee.

'Jack, for God's sake!' he screamed with pain, and slid down onto the floor.

'Jack, please!' Lizzie began to weep. 'Jack, darling, please stop it.'

Edward appeared in the doorway, fuzzy with sleep, then all too swiftly awake with horror and disbelief. 'Jack, what the hell are you *doing*?'

'Ask *him*!' his brother said, and reversed again.

'He's gone *mad*.' Christopher was hugging his leg in pain.

Lizzie's tears ceased instantly. 'Edward, please go and make sure Sophie stays in her room.'

'But what's *happened*?'

'Edward, go to Sophie,' Lizzie ordered. 'Now!'

Jack seemed to hover for a second, and then the chair shot forward again.

Christopher screamed again.

And Edward ran.

The hours that followed came and went in a blur of semi-control for Lizzie. As Jack had, at last, slumped in his wheelchair, shattered and totally drained, Christopher had limped from the room, dressed and made his escape from the house. Edward had emerged from Sophie's bedroom to report that, miraculously, his sister had slept through the whole nightmare.

He wavered in the doorway of his mother's room, hardly looking at Jack, who was still sitting in his chair, over by the wall, not speaking, his eyes shut. Lizzie had gone briefly to his room, pulled the blanket from his bed and brought it back, wrapped it around him, for he was still shaking badly.

'Is Jack going to be all right, Mum?' Edward asked, softly.

'I think so,' Lizzie answered, also very quietly.

Still, Edward had not come into the room, as if he feared that doing so might allow him access to whatever mystery had sparked such horrors. In time, Lizzie supposed, dully, he would begin to ask more questions, would want to know what his father had done

300

to so enrage his loving, peaceable brother, but for now he was, apparently, hoping to be spared the full truth.

'What about you?' he asked her.

'I'm all right, darling,' Lizzie said.

One more lie laid on the pile.

'Go back to bed, Edward,' she told him. 'If you can.'

'You sure?'

'Quite sure.'

He came in then, moving very swiftly, not looking to right or left, just coming quickly to his mother, planting a cold, nerve-laden kiss on her cheek, then going straight back to the door.

'If you need me, Mum,' he said.

'I'll call you, darling,' she told him. 'Goodnight.'

'Night, Jack,' Edward said.

Jack did not answer.

Gilly came home soon after, came upstairs, saw Lizzie's door open, came in, saw Lizzie sitting on the carpet beside Jack's wheelchair over by the wall, holding his hand, Jack facing the wall, not moving or responding.

'What's happened?' she asked.

Lizzie turned to look at her, her face a mask of barely-controlled despair.

'We've had a bit of an upset,' she said.

Jack stirred for the first time, opened his eyes, squeezed his mother's hand.

'I'm okay, Gilly,' he said.

'Glad to hear it,' she said.

Lizzie still held onto his hand. 'What do you want to do, my love? Get some rest? Maybe have a hot drink?'

He looked at her for the first time since he had stopped pounding into his father, and his soft eyes were still glazed over with shock. 'Rest, I think, Mum.' He paused. 'If you're okay.'

'I am,' she said. 'Want me to wheel you?'

'Please.'

Lizzie let go of his hand, got up off the floor, looked over at Gilly.

Another one lingering in the doorway, as if the room were quarantined, or giving off frightening vibrations.

'We'll be all right, Gilly.'

301

Gilly nodded, getting the message. 'I'll see you in a bit.'

Lizzie waited till the younger woman had gone downstairs and into the kitchen, and then she began to push Jack out of the bedroom and along the corridor to his own.

'Want me to stay with you, my darling?' she asked him.

'I'm all right,' he said.

She helped him out of the chair and onto his bed, covered him up.

'I think, maybe,' Jack said, 'I should have a diazepam.'

'Good idea,' Lizzie said.

'Only if I get ill again,' he went on, 'I won't be much use to you or the others.'

Hot tears stung his mother's eyes then, threatened to choke her, but she held on – *if he can, you bloody well can* – and went to get one of his pills. He was ten years old, and he knew the names of far too many damned medicines, and he was more mature than some people twice his age, and he put her to shame.

'Are you going to tell Gilly?' he asked when she came back.

'I don't know,' Lizzie said. 'What do you think?'

'It's up to you,' Jack said. 'I think . . .'

'What, my love?'

'I think, maybe, I'd rather she didn't know.'

'Then I won't tell her,' Lizzie said.

She told Gilly only that there had been a big row, and that Jack had been very upset, and that Edward knew something about it, but Sophie nothing at all, and that that was the way she wanted to keep it, if possible.

'I'll tell her that her father had to go to London again,' Lizzie said.

'She's used to that,' Gilly said.

She asked no more questions, had always possessed a gift for sensitivity and for not prying, just made Lizzie hot sweet tea and sat with her while she tried to drink it.

'I'm very tired,' Lizzie said after a while. 'I think I'll go up.'

'Right,' Gilly said. 'If you need anything – however late . . .'

'Yes,' Lizzie said. 'Thank you.'

She went into Jack's room first, found him sound asleep, and whether that was from pure exhaustion or from the tablet he'd taken, she was grateful for it.

302

Edward, too, was out of it, had, his mother supposed, escaped into sleep, and her daughter was still slumbering peacefully on, Sophie, the only one untouched so far, though that would change all too soon, would *have* to change.

A feeling of something slightly related to relief flowed through Lizzie then, because at long, long last, the worst had happened, and she would no longer have to keep on lying to her own children that all was well between her and their father.

The memory hit her, still horrifically fresh, of Jack, driving his chair at Christopher. Of his face as he'd done it, of the terrible, anguished *sounds* he had made. Of her husband, cowering on the floor.

That was what Jack would remember, what he would see over and over again whenever he shut his eyes, or even when he did not.

That, and Christopher pinning her down on the bed, *hurting* her.

The small relief was extinguished, and only shame, guilt and pain remained.

And terrible anger.

She had not intended to sleep late, had been sure she would not sleep at all, had still been lying awake in some pain and reliving it all at four o'clock, but soon after that she had drifted off, and when she awoke, with a terrible start of grinding bleakness and, still, the pain she'd gone to bed with – more discomfort now, but still there – she saw that it was after nine.

She put on her dressing gown, went into the bathroom, remembered *him* in there, washed her face with cold water, felt the ache again, wondered if, perhaps, that final shove of Christopher's had done something to the internal scarring left by his last assault and the operation.

Not now, Lizzie.

She went back through the bedroom and out into the corridor.

The house was empty, the hush heavy.

Gilly had left a note on the kitchen table: *I've taken all the children to school. Jack said he was fine and wanted to go.*

Lizzie's eyes and throat filled with tears again.

First crop of the day.

She blessed Gilly and, more, much more than that, she blessed Jack and Edward for their remarkable, staggering courage.

303

She made coffee, took it, moving slowly, feeling like an old woman, to the kitchen table and sat down. The *Daily Mail* and the *Independent* were lying neatly folded, awaiting her, but she didn't look at them.

She had to talk to someone.

Not Gilly, because she'd promised Jack. Not Angela either, who'd never got over her belief in Christopher's saintliness. She considered Guy, his brother, but she thought it might be somehow cruel to expect him to take sides.

Hilda Kapur came to mind, but was quickly dismissed again, in case some NHS mechanism were to click in once she'd confided in her, something that might compel the GP to report Christopher and magnify her children's suffering.

Lizzie drank some coffee, found the normality of ritual lent her tiny comfort.

Robin Allbeury.

He was a solicitor – not that she wanted to speak to him *as* a solicitor – but it meant he was accustomed to listening, advising and, of course, to confidentiality. Still virtually a stranger, which might make him detached – probably a good thing; yet also a friend now – and more to her than Christopher, even if he had brought them together in the first place.

Lizzie put down her cup and went to find his number.

He was at his office, took her call immediately.

She told him that she badly needed to talk, and that what she had to say was desperately private.

'Goes without saying,' Allbeury told her. 'Where are you, Lizzie?'

'Still in Marlow, but I'll come to town.'

'Are you sure?' he asked.

'I'll come to your office,' she said. 'If you don't mind.'

'I'll be waiting for you,' Allbeury said. 'Drive carefully, Lizzie.'

Case No. 6/220770

PIPER-WADE, E.

Study/Review

Pending

Action ✓

Resolved

86

Lizzie had not realized before she began her drive into London how completely drained she was, but by the time she parked the coupé in Bedford Row just before twelve, she found that she was almost too tired to stand.

Sheer will-power got her into Allbeury, Lerman, Wren's reception, helped her give her name to the young woman behind the desk, and she had barely made it to one of the leather chairs when Allbeury appeared, took one look at her and turned to the receptionist.

'I'm going out,' he told her. 'Would you please tell the others?'

'Of course,' the young woman said.

He turned back to Lizzie, bent and said, quietly: 'Can you manage the walk to my car, do you think?'

Lizzie mustered a smile. 'I've just driven from Marlow.'

'Quite,' Allbeury said.

He gripped her arm firmly, helped her out of the office, around the corner and into his Jaguar, did up her seatbelt for her, ignoring her protest, walked around to the driver's door and got in.

'Do you need a doctor?' he asked. 'And would you like to come to my flat, or would you rather go to Holland Park?'

'Your flat,' Lizzie answered unhesitatingly. 'I don't think I need a doctor.'

'If you change your mind,' he said, 'just say the word.'

She was perfectly aware that he had not asked if she wanted him to get in touch with Christopher.

Winston Cook, who had worked for less than a full day before disappearing for more than a week, and who Allbeury had

306

believed gone for good, had returned early that morning with a story about a sick sister that Allbeury had, for reasons he was not entirely certain about, chosen to believe.

He was still there now, in the blue study, intent on the PC's flat screen monitor, fingers flying over the keyboard.

'I'm really getting somewhere,' he said as Allbeury looked in, having left Lizzie sitting in his den at the far end of the flat. 'Won't be long now.'

'This is a bad time for me,' Allbeury said. 'I need you to go.'

'Can't leave now, man,' Cook said. 'I'll lose it.'

'I have someone with me who's unwell,' Allbeury said.

'That's fine,' Cook said. 'You won't know I'm here, I won't make any noise.' His expression was imploring. 'I'm nearly there.'

Allbeury smiled despite himself. 'Okay.'

He went back to Lizzie in the snug, but gorgeous, corner room, two walls filled with paintings, picture windows taking up the rest. She was sitting gazing out at the view, but he felt she was seeing nothing.

'You all right here while I make tea?' he asked. 'Very strong, lots of sugar. Good for shock, okay?'

'Fine.' She wondered how he knew she was shocked rather than ill. 'Thank you, Robin.

'Don't go away,' he said.

'I won't,' Lizzie said.

She told him everything, right from the beginning.

'I feel so ashamed,' she said. 'I feel many other things too, but I think shame is there, right at the top.'

'For not leaving?' Allbeury said.

'Yes,' Lizzie said.

'You stayed for the children.'

'Of course.'

'For Jack, mostly.'

'Yes,' she said again. 'But what has my staying achieved now?'

Allbeury thought for a moment. 'The children don't know all this, do they?'

Lizzie shook her head. 'Jack only knows what he saw last night, and Edward can't know more than what Jack's chosen to tell him.' She paused. 'And Sophie, thank God, knows nothing at all yet.'

307

'They don't have to know everything,' Allbeury said. 'Unless you want them to. Which I rather doubt, knowing you.'

'Do you?' She felt mildly curious. 'Know me, I mean?'

'I think I know enough to be sure of a very few things.'

'What are they?'

'You're a wonderful mother,' he said. 'And a much more loyal wife than your husband deserves.' He saw her eyes fill, watched her fight the urge to cry. 'And you're one of the loveliest women I've ever met.' He paused. 'Though you may not have wanted to hear me say that.'

'I don't think I know, just now,' she said, wearily, 'what I want.'

'Sleep,' Allbeury said. 'If I'm any judge, it's what you need most.'

He showed her to an ivory-coloured guest bedroom in which all the paintings were of softly-coloured flowers and gardens.

'There's a bathroom through that door. And a phone here—' he motioned to the bedside table '—if you want it. And if you happen to want me, I'll be around, so either call, or come looking, whichever you prefer.'

'You're so kind,' Lizzie said.

'Not kind at all,' Allbeury said. 'I just want you to feel safe.'

'I do,' she said.

'Sleep well,' he said, and went to the door.

The clock on the bedside table read 14.10. 'All right if I set this for four?' Lizzie asked. 'I need to speak to the children when they get home.'

'Of course,' he said.

In the blue study, Winston Cook was pacing in a state of high excitement.

'I've got it all now,' he said. 'I told you I was nearly there.'

'That's great.' Allbeury's mind was too filled with Lizzie to care. 'Do me a favour and write me a report and leave your bill and I'll settle with you tomorrow, if that's okay.'

'I don't mind sending you my bill,' Cook said. 'I trust you, man.'

'Good,' Allbeury said. 'Thank you, Winston.'

'But you still need to take a look at this now.'

'I don't have the time now to—'

'You really need to.' Cook was adamant. 'There's an IP address come up here that I think belongs to someone you know pretty well, and if I'm right – and I'm *always* right, just ask Adam – then I reckon they've been cracking your files for a long time.'

'Who?' Allbeury ran an irritated hand through his hair.

'Take a look,' Winston Cook insisted.

He paid Cook cash, twenty per cent more than he'd asked for, showed him out and then went, very quietly, to check on his guest.

Lizzie was fast asleep, on her side, her forehead puckered, looking a little, he thought, like a child in the midst of a disturbing dream.

Allbeury took a long look at her, pulled the duvet a little higher over her, and then he took a small leather-bound notepad and a pen from his pocket and wrote her a note, leaving it propped against the clock where she'd be sure to see it when she woke. And then he left the room.

He took the private lift down to the underground garage.

Where he sat, in the Jaguar, for several more moments, thinking about what Winston Cook had shown him, before taking a card from his wallet, keying one of the numbers on it into his mobile, and driving out of his space and up to street level.

'This is a message,' he said, 'for DI Shipley from Robin Allbeury.'

He went on speaking as he exited the building.

Unaware, as he spoke and drove, that just across the street, standing in a doorway, half-concealed, someone was watching him go.

87

Shipley had just emerged from a root canal session at her dentist's surgery in Chalk Farm and had got into her old Mini when she rang the office and heard from Ally King that Robin Allbeury had left a message for her.

'He said to tell you it's urgent,' King said.

Shipley's anaesthetised jaw began tingling.

'He wants you to meet him.'

'Where?'

King gave her the address. 'Do you need any back-up?'

'No, thanks.'

Shipley started the engine, slipped into gear, and put her foot down.

88

Novak was still alone at the agency at two forty-five, the ancient Bush radio on his desk switched on to a play on Radio 4, more for company than content, when the door opened and Allbeury marched in.

'Robin, hi.' Novak reached for the radio's off switch. 'I wasn't expecting—'

Without a word, Allbeury walked around Novak's desk, bent and yanked his computer's main plug out of the wall.

'What the hell?' Novak was on his feet, amazed.

Allbeury wound the cord around his wrist and fist, pushed Novak out of the way and with a single, ferocious motion, punched a hole in the monitor's screen.

'Jesus Christ, Robin! What are you *doing*?'

Allbeury unravelled the cord, let it drop to the floor, headed over to Clare's immaculate desk.

'That's enough!' Novak got between the other man and his wife's PC. 'What the hell has got *into* you?'

Allbeury's eyes were hard and very cold. 'I have just one question for you.'

'You have one for *me*?' Novak was incredulous.

'Why the fuck have you been spying on me?'

'I don't have a clue what you're *talking* about!'

The office door opened again, and Novak swung around in time to see a tall, middle-aged stranger with a vaguely familiar face that looked as if it had taken a recent beating, make straight for Allbeury, ignoring him.

'You're a bastard.' He shoved the solicitor in the chest, hard enough to send him sideways into the wall beside Clare's desk.

311

'What is going *on* here?' Novak demanded.

'Good question.' Allbeury, recovering his balance, dusted off his jacket. 'What are you doing here, Wade?'

'I'm here—' the other man's words were slurred '—to tell you to stay the fuck away from my wife.'

Novak moved away from the other two men, back to his own half-wrecked desk. 'I don't know what's happening here,' he said to Wade, whose eyes, behind his spectacles, looked wild, drunk, maybe, or drugged, 'but I'd like you to get out of my office before I call the police.'

'I don't give a *stuff* who you call,' Christopher said.

'Why don't we take this outside,' Allbeury said, cooler now, 'unless you'd like Mr Novak to know what kind of husband Lizzie really has?'

'You *scum*.' Christopher lunged at Allbeury, missing him and sending the lamp on Clare's desk flying, and this time Allbeury retaliated, grabbed his right arm and pushed him away with enough force to knock him down.

'For God's sake, Robin,' Novak yelled.

Shipley saw the Jaguar, illegally parked in the narrow cobbled road, a shiny black BMW practically on its bumper, and left her Mini ten yards behind the other two cars.

The front door was ajar, and she started up the stairs.

The sounds of fighting were audible by the second floor.

She accelerated up the next two flights, paused outside the door, heard Novak's voice yelling something, and went straight in.

A man she didn't recognize was charging at Robin Allbeury, roaring something indistinguishable as the two men collided and fell to the floor, grappling, while Novak struggled to separate them.

'Bloody hell,' Shipley said.

'Don't just stand there,' Novak said from the floor.

She swore again, wished she had some, *any* kind of a weapon to threaten the men with. 'Police,' she said, loudly, and weighed in.

The stranger with the messed-up face bellowed as she grabbed at his arms to pull him off Allbeury, then swung at her, and she saw that he was high as a kite.

'*You're* under arrest,' she said, panting.

312

'Jesus, Inspector,' Allbeury said, as Wade's weight was removed from his chest, 'your timing's improving.'

Christopher Wade, blind with rage and dope, threw another punch at Shipley, connected this time with her shoulder, making her shout with pain and anger. Novak went for him, grabbed him by the sleeve of his jacket, but Christopher jerked out of his grasp and ran to the still open door.

'No, you bloody well don't!' Shipley caught him at the top of the staircase, got hold of his right arm and yanked it behind him in a half-nelson.

'*Bitch*,' Wade yelled, and twisted away from her.

She knew it was going to happen before it did, knew he had her totally off-balance, and it *shouldn't* have been so easy for him, but she was still full of fucking novocaine or whatever they used these days, and her feet went from under her and she tried to grab hold – of *him*, first, and then the handrail, and then the iron outer cage of the lift, but nothing stopped her–

Until the hard stone floor of the landing beneath.

89

'Where's Mum?' Edward asked, joining Jack and Sophie in the Range Rover outside his school and finding Gilly at the wheel.

'In London.'

Gilly's stomach was clenched tight as she glanced first at Edward, then back at Jack's face – still registering nothing at all. He had asked the same question half-an-hour earlier when she'd collected him and Sophie at their school, and his sister had asked when Lizzie would be back, then simply accepted it, accustomed to her parents' comings-and-goings, and Jack had looked at Gilly for a second, then looked away and kept silent.

'Will she be back later?' Edward asked now.

'I'm not sure yet,' Gilly said.

'I've got homework,' Edward said, as soon as they got into the house.

'What about some tea?' Gilly asked.

'Not hungry,' he said, and went upstairs.

'Chops for supper,' Gilly called after him. 'Okay?'

'Fine,' he said. 'Thanks.'

'I've got maths,' Sophie said to Jack. 'Will you help me?'

'Later,' Jack said.

He waited while his sister carried her bag upstairs, then looked at Gilly.

'Have you talked to Mum?' he asked quietly.

'Not yet,' Gilly said. 'She was gone by the time I got back from the school run.'

'So how do you know she went to London?'

'She left a note.'

314

She went to fetch it for Jack, and to check for messages, but found none. 'I'm sure she'll call later, or maybe she's already on her way back.'

Jack's expression was closed, only his hands, clenched in fists, betraying him.

Gilly took a quick breath.

'Would you like me to try and reach your father?'

'No,' Jack said.

Gilly forced a smile. 'Cup of tea then?'

'And if he phones,' Jack added, 'I don't want to talk, okay?'

'Okay,' Gilly said.

'I'm going for a rest,' he said.

'Are you all right, Jack?'

He nodded, began to wheel himself towards the stair lift, then paused.

'I definitely want to talk to Mum,' he said, 'if she calls.'

'I promise,' Gilly said.

90

Christopher was gone, sidestepping frantically past Shipley's body, stumbling down the next two flights of steps and out into the street.

'I've called an ambulance,' Novak said from above to Allbeury, kneeling beside the fallen officer.

'I don't need an ambulance,' Shipley said. 'Just help me get up.'

'Stay where you are,' Allbeury told her. 'I think your ankle's—'

'Help me.' She began heaving herself off the ground, then cried out with pain and sank back again. 'Shit,' she said. 'Oh, bloody *shit*.'

'You'll be okay.' Gently, Allbeury took her hand.

Novak came down, holding a raincoat. 'Ought to be a blanket, but this is all I could find.' He crouched on Shipley's other side, laid it gently over her.

'Who the hell *was* that lunatic?' she asked, hating her sudden vulnerability.

'Just someone who seems not to like me,' Allbeury said. 'Which you ought, I suppose, to sympathize with.'

'You've got a point,' Shipley said.

'That's Lizzie Piper's husband, right?' Novak said to Allbeury, having realized a few moments back why Wade's face had seemed familiar. 'The surgeon?'

'Lizzie Piper, the cookery woman?' Shipley asked.

Allbeury's smile was grim. 'The very one.'

'Tell her from me,' Shipley said, 'she can do better.'

'I may do just that,' he said.

Shipley looked at him for a long moment, then turned to Novak.

316

'Could you do me a favour? Get me a cup of tea. This raincoat isn't quite doing it for me.'

'No problem,' Novak said, glad of something to do.

She waited till he'd gone, then looked back at Allbeury. 'I'm assuming,' she said, very softly, 'that your message was connected with the killings?' She moved her leg, and winced.

'Don't worry about that now,' he said.

'*Tell* me,' she hissed. 'I have been right, haven't I? There is a link?'

Allbeury's mind was travelling now, moving back and forth, putting things together, things he'd far sooner *not* have been able to put together.

'Allbeury,' Shipley said, impatiently. 'I'm not wrong, am I?'

'No,' he told her. 'I'm beginning to think you may not be.'

She stared at him, trying to read his expression, heard Novak coming out of the office above, began to mouth a question at Allbeury.

'I've made it sweet and strong.' Novak was beside them, handed the mug carefully to Shipley. 'It's very hot, mind.'

Allbeury thought about Lizzie, hoped she was still sleeping.

And abruptly, one more piece of the puzzle clicked horribly into place.

Shipley, raising the mug to her lips, caught the expression in Allbeury's eyes, then looked at Novak on her other side.

'Where's that bloody ambulance?' she said.

91

Christopher, stuck in traffic on the Embankment, knew he was in no condition to be driving, but he was also aware, as he battled the thick fuzz in his head in order to face the truth, that he'd left himself with very few choices.

He had just pushed a police officer down a flight of stairs. He had blown it – totally and irrevocably – with Lizzie. And, worst of all by far, he had forever destroyed his beloved Jack's image of him, and probably all the children knew by now, but Jack, oh, God, Jack was the one who needed him most.

Needed.

In the past. All over now.

Behind him, someone sounded their horn and, blinking to clear his vision, he saw that the cars ahead had moved on.

He lifted his right hand in apology, drove on.

Nothing ahead for him but disgrace, shame, perhaps even prison, and isolation.

Only one choice left for him to make, and that was which way to die.

Lucky for him, he supposed, in that at least he *could* choose.

Though if he didn't do it quickly, they might find him, stop him, ruin that too.

92

Lizzie was still sleeping when the sound woke her.

Buzzing.

She opened her eyes, stared around at the now semi-dark and unfamiliar room, disoriented for a moment, then, remembering everything – *everything* – she sat up and fumbled with the clock.

The buzzing continued. Not in the room, but from a distance.

'Robin?' she called.

She pushed away the duvet, saw the note propped up against the clock and reached for the switch on the bedside lamp.

I've had to go out for a while – shouldn't be too long. Help yourself to anything and everything you want. Love, Robin.

Lizzie found her shoes and went in search of the buzzing, out of the bedroom, along a corridor, turning on lights as she went, passing more beautiful paintings, into the entrance hall.

Near the lift was a videophone system, source of the buzzing.

She lifted the handset, looked at the screen, saw, in monochrome, a young woman with curly hair, pressed one of the buttons to speak to her.

'Yes?' she said.

'Are you Mrs Wade?' the woman asked in a light Scots accent.

'I am,' she said, surprised.

'Robin told me you were here.' The woman paused. 'Did I wake you?'

'It's all right,' Lizzie said. 'Come up.'

'There's no time. I need you to come with me.'

'I don't understand,' Lizzie said, bewildered.

319

'There's been an accident,' the woman said. 'Robin's been hurt.'

'My God – what kind of accident?' Lizzie hesitated. 'I'm sorry, but I don't know who you are – I can't just come without—'

'My name's Clare Novak,' the young woman said. 'I'm a friend of Robin's, and can you please, please come *now*, because Robin's asking for you.'

Lizzie's confusion mounted – she fought for commonsense. 'Where is he? Is he in hospital?'

'It isn't far,' Clare Novak said. 'Please come – it's in walking distance.'

'I don't—'

'Please,' the other woman said. 'Robin needs you.'

Lizzie thought of his kindness.

'I'll be right down.'

93

The ambulance had arrived in New Smithfield, and Shipley was being carried down the stairs by the paramedics, who wanted to know if either Allbeury or Novak would be coming to St Thomas's.

'Police'll want a word with one of you, I should think,' one of the men said.

'I am the police,' Shipley said.

'Even so, love,' the paramedic said kindly, as if he thought her delusional.

'She is,' Novak told him. 'She's a detective inspector.'

Allbeury stooped to speak softly against Shipley's ear. 'I'll come to the hospital later,' he said, 'tell you everything I can, I swear it. But right now, Mike and I have to go, really *have* to.'

Shipley looked into his face and, as forcefully as this man had exerted a hold on her suspicions over the past few months, she felt the hold twist suddenly now, flip half-circle, pushing her, compelling her to run *with* him.

'You go,' she told him.

Allbeury waited till the ambulance was out of sight and turned to Novak.

'We have to go and find Clare, Mike,' he said.

Novak stared at him, his bizarre entrance – before Wade and Shipley had hijacked the show – coming back into his mind.

'You smashed my computer,' he said. 'And then you said I'd been *spying* on you, and I want to know what the hell you were talking about.'

'Hacking,' Allbeury said, 'or rather, cracking.' He felt in his pocket for his car keys. 'It's going to have to wait till after we get to Clare.'

'If anyone's going to Clare,' Novak said, 'it's me.'

'Not without me,' Allbeury said.

'You've lost it.' Novak turned his back.

Allbeury caught hold of his arm. 'Listen to me, Mike, just *listen*.'

'Let go,' Novak said.

'Not unless you listen to me.'

'Let go of my *arm*.'

Allbeury let go. 'I think,' he said, 'in fact, I'm almost sure, that Clare's in a great deal of trouble.'

'What kind of trouble?'

'Can we just *find* her?' Allbeury said intensely. 'Because if we don't get to her very soon, Mike, I'm afraid of what might happen.'

94

Tower Bridge had been raised when Lizzie and Clare had left Shad Tower, and Lizzie had heard the tall, red-haired woman curse under her breath, but even as they hurried over the St Saviour's footbridge, around the Design Museum and into Shad Thames, trying not to slip on the cobbles, heading for the steps that led up to the bridge, the tall ship for which it had been raised had already sailed beneath, and in moments it was lowered again.

'Wouldn't it be better to take a taxi?' Lizzie asked, peering through the dusk. 'Where exactly are we going?'

'Do you see any for hire?' the other woman said, quite tersely.

Lizzie looked around, already feeling drained again, but all the black cabs had their lights turned off. 'I don't think I can go too fast,' she said. 'Sorry.'

Clare Novak took her arm. 'I'll help you.'

Lizzie didn't much care for the closeness, but she didn't argue, felt weak enough at this instant, out here in the wind, with people and traffic all around, to need support.

'Why didn't you phone,' she asked, 'instead of coming to get me?'

'Robin's machine was on,' Clare Novak said, 'and I didn't want to just leave a message in case you didn't pick it up.'

Being drawn on, Lizzie felt perplexed, was not at all sure, now, if this was a clever thing to be doing, walking *somewhere* with this forceful woman who might well be a friend of Robin's, but was still a total stranger to her – and everything was crowding in on her, Christopher and Jack, and she hadn't phoned the children.

They were over the bridge now, crossing at the lights into East Smithfield, and the street was clogged with cars and pedestrians, and Clare's hand was still on her elbow, and Lizzie, on unfamiliar territory, felt disoriented again, and crowded by the other woman's proximity.

'Is it much further?' she asked, already breathless.

'Not too much.'

'I still don't know what's happened.'

'You're worrying, aren't you?' Clare Novak said.

'Of course I'm worrying.'

'He'll be all right,' the other woman said. 'I'm a nurse, I took care of him.'

Lizzie extricated her arm, stopped walking.

'What's wrong?' Clare halted too, looked at her.

'I have to slow down for a moment.' She tried to catch her breath, felt the need to take control.

'Okay,' Clare said. 'Of course.'

'Now tell me what happened, please.'

'A fight,' Clare said, bluntly.

'A *fight*?' Lizzie blinked. 'Who with?'

'If you must know,' the other woman said, 'with my husband, Mike.'

Lizzie took another moment. She was sure she'd heard the name Mike Novak before – from Robin, she supposed – but she couldn't remember what he'd said.

'All right to go on now?' Clare asked.

A man and two women stepped around them to pass on the pavement, all chattering, their normality slightly reassuring.

'Yes,' Lizzie said. 'I'm fine.'

'Only I don't want to leave him for too long,' Clare said. 'Robin, that is.' She smiled at Lizzie, a kindly smile. 'You're not feeling great, are you? Why don't you just take my arm again?'

'I'm all right,' Lizzie said, and began walking.

'Closeness to strangers does make some people uncomfortable,' Clare said, walking beside her. 'I know, from nursing.'

She lengthened her stride a little, and Lizzie had to speed up, and this weakness was so unlike her, she usually had so much energy, though perhaps, if she thought about it, she'd never got wholly back to her old self since the surgery.

Surgery, she thought, savagely, feeling sick, and walked faster.

'I think Robin's upset as much as hurt—'

'Why were he and your husband fighting?' Lizzie interrupted.

324

'—and I know he's got a bit of a thing for you, Lizzie, which was, frankly, the *real* reason I came to get you, because I'm hoping he'll listen to you and not press charges against Mike.'

Clare turned left, moving very quickly now. Lizzie glanced at the street sign – Dock Street – and followed, caught up.

'Mike's such a good person.' Clare was still talking rapidly. 'And I need him so badly, especially now the baby's coming, that's why I want you to try to help.'

'You're pregnant?'

'Yes,' the other woman said. 'Only our last child died.'

Lizzie's heart softened, went out to the stranger. 'I'm sorry,' she said.

'So you do see?'

'A little, I suppose.' Lizzie wanted to be tactful now. 'And if there's some way I can help, I will, but I don't see why Robin should listen to me – we hardly know each other.'

'That can't be quite true,' Clare said, 'surely. Or else you wouldn't have been sleeping in his flat, would you?'

95

'Try your number again,' Allbeury said, in Kingsway's heavy traffic.

'I don't want to,' Novak said, belligerently, 'if she's sleeping.'

He hadn't wanted to come in the Jaguar either, had wanted to collect the Clio from the car park, but Allbeury's urgency had persuaded him, and now, though his anger with the solicitor still lingered, Novak's anxiety over Clare was taking over.

'For the last time,' Allbeury said, 'I'm sorry about your computer.'

'I don't give a fuck about the computer, I just want to understand why you've turned into a bloody madman and what Shipley and that other lunatic were doing in my office.'

'I'm sorry about that too.' Allbeury braked hard as a van cut in front of him, then flashed his headlights in irritation. 'And I will explain it all to you later, but I can't right now, okay?'

'Not okay,' Novak said. 'Not okay at all.'

Allbeury shook his head, detached his thoughts from his angry passenger. He'd phoned the apartment twice since leaving the agency, but of course his machine had picked up, and he'd called Lizzie's name a couple of times, in case she was awake, but she hadn't picked up, and he hadn't left a message since he was certain she wasn't the type to listen to another person's messages.

'Any short cuts from here?' he asked Novak now.

'Nothing that'll help at this time.'

Allbeury set his mind back onto a different track, trying to avoid the temptation to put two and two together and make a thousand, and even now he knew he couldn't be certain that it *hadn't* been Mike Novak poking around in his PC, and just because the guy claimed not to know what the hell was going on, and just because he *liked* Novak didn't mean anything.

He glanced at the man, sitting tight-lipped and strained beside him.

A gap in the traffic opened up just ahead to his right. Allbeury checked in his wing mirror, put his foot down and filled it.

Still going nowhere.

96

'Nearly there now,' Clare told Lizzie.

'Thank God for that,' Lizzie said, then saw the dead-end sign and the dark, narrow cobbled cul-de-sac, and hung back again.

'It's all right.' Clare smiled and pointed. 'That's where we're going.'

Lizzie peered past a straggle of parked vehicles, looking for Robin's Jaguar.

'In the car park,' Clare said, reading her mind.

They reached the building, and Lizzie saw the sign – **Novak Investigations Ltd** – and of course, *that* was where she'd heard the name; Robin had mentioned the Novaks during their dinner in West Hampstead, the private detective and his wife who ran the agency together. '*Nice people*,' she recalled him saying.

'This is your agency,' she said.

'That's right.'

'I thought you said you were a nurse.'

'Used to be. Still am, part-time.' Clare opened the outer door. 'Bit dilapidated, I'm afraid, and a bit of a hike up, so watch your step.'

She was right, Lizzie saw. Not well lit, but adequately enough to show grubby white walls, a wide, archaic-looking lift with an Out of Service sign and a padlock attached to the kind of old-style gate that concertinaed when opened.

'I'd better go ahead,' Clare said. 'You take your time.'

Lizzie, feeling ragged, didn't need telling twice.

They passed the first floor, silent, doors closed, a dusty parcel leaning against a wall beside a Yellow Pages, then the second and third floors, just as unoccupied, and by the fourth, Lizzie could scarcely catch her breath.

'Sorry about all the stairs,' Clare called down. 'You get used to it.'

'Rather you than me,' Lizzie gasped.

The top floor was brighter, the single door bearing another, smaller, agency sign. Clare stood for a moment, looking at the door.

'What's wrong?' Lizzie asked breathlessly, her legs aching.

'Nothing,' Clare said. 'I hope.'

She pushed the unlocked door open and went through.

97

'She's not here.'

Novak's statement as he returned to the living room of the small Lamb's Conduit Street flat, sent a signal of alarm through Allbeury.

'No message?' he asked. 'Note?'

'Nothing.' Novak shook his head. 'There's no reason why she should have left a note. No reason for her to have stayed in all day either, just because she didn't come into the office.'

'So where do you think she is?'

'She could be anywhere.'

'Anywhere's a little useless from the search point of view,' Allbeury said.

'That's if I wanted to search for her,' Novak said.

'Take my word for it,' Allbeury said. 'You need to find Clare.'

'For *fuck's* sake stop telling me that, and start telling me *why*.'

'All right,' Allbeury said. 'But you'd better sit down.'

'Just *tell* me.' Novak sat down anyway.

Allbeury remained standing, conscious that he was taking a chance by going with his instincts, even if those instincts were almost always pretty fine-tuned. But Winston Cook's trail had led him to Novak Investigations, and there were *two* Novaks working at the agency, and Mike was always hailing Clare as his in-house computer whiz.

'I think,' he began, very slowly, 'that – though I have no idea why she should have done such a thing – Clare may have been breaking into my computer system.' He saw the expression in the other man's eyes, the colour rising in his cheeks, went on quickly, regardless. 'Invading the files on my hard disk. Hacking.' He paused. 'Cracking.'

'You bastard.' Novak sprang to his feet. 'You lousy piece of *shit*! Telling me Clare was in trouble, scaring me half to death just so you could come here and accuse her of such unmitigated *balls*!'

Allbeury waited for Novak to take a swing at him, ready to let him have the one, at least, because he could well understand the anger – and his friend's rage, in any case, was adding to his conviction that he wasn't the one behind the hacking.

Novak threw no punch, just stood there seething.

'I'm very much afraid,' Allbeury said, quietly, 'that I do have proof, Mike. I wish to God I hadn't, but I have.'

'What proof?' Novak spat contemptuously.

'And I'm pretty sure that DI Shipley's going to be reaching a few conclusions of her own as soon as she gets her head back together.'

'What's Shipley got to do with it?' Fear and confusion were back in his eyes, mixing with the defiance.

'Do you know where Clare could be, Mike?'

'Answer *my* questions. What proof, and why should Shipley care?'

'I had an expert work over my system – a friend of Adam Lerman's. He traced the cracker to the agency.' Allbeury paused. 'Mike, do you have *any* idea where Clare is? Just so you can talk to her – so *we* can talk to her – maybe help her.'

'Because you're so *great* at helping women in trouble?' Novak said.

The images Allbeury lived with, much of the time lately, of Lynne Bolsover and Joanne Patston, loomed larger, made him shudder, but he pushed them away.

'You need to find her, Mike,' he said doggedly.

Something came into Novak's eyes then, and was promptly blanked out.

'What?' Allbeury asked. 'Mike, *what*?'

Novak took another second.

'She has a patient,' he said.

Allbeury remembered Novak mentioning him. 'The paraplegic?'

Novak nodded. 'Nick Parry.'

'Call him,' Allbeury said. 'See if she's there.' He saw

331

uncertainty in Novak's face. 'At least you'll know she's safe.'

'I'm not going to interrogate her on the phone.'

'Of course not,' Allbeury said.

Novak half turned, then stopped. 'Nick Parry plays chess and poker on the Internet.' He paused. 'Clare's told me he considers his PC a friend.'

'See if she's there, Mike.'

'Maybe this is his doing, Robin.' Hope flared.

'Or maybe he's been teaching Clare a thing or two.'

'It's probably the other way around,' Novak said agitatedly. 'Young guy trapped in his wheelchair, bored out of his mind – it makes more sense than Clare.'

'Just make the call, Mike,' Allbeury said.

98

Entering the office behind Clare Novak, Lizzie looked around, took in the lamp on the floor on one side, and, on a second desk, a smashed-up computer monitor.

A fight, it seemed, had certainly taken place.

'Where are they?' Lizzie's voice was tense, her weariness almost gone in the presence of a new clenching in her stomach that she recognized as fear.

'I don't know,' Clare said, uneasily, and walked past the desks, past the couch and coffee table to the door beyond a row of filing cabinets, opened it, shook her head. 'I don't know what's going on.'

She turned, moving slowly around the room, looking at the smashed monitor; then, passing Lizzie, a frown wrinkling her forehead, she walked back out into the stone hallway.

Lizzie heard the sound of metal scraping, screeching, and turned around.

'Oh, my God,' Clare's voice exclaimed.

'What's happened?' Lizzie went swiftly to the door.

The lift gate was open and Clare was standing beside the broad open shaft. 'You'd better see for yourself.'

Her heart starting to thump, Lizzie went out, saw the other woman's shocked face, her own fear heightening.

'Just *look*,' Clare said. 'And be careful.'

Lizzie approached the dark, gaping mouth of the lift cautiously, put out her right hand to grip the handle of the open iron gate – no padlock on it, she noticed, with a slight stir of something – and leaned slightly forward over the edge.

The shove in her back was violent and uncompromising.

333

Lizzie gave a cry, felt her legs going, felt a massive surge of terror and adrenalin kick in, hung on to the gate with both hands, feet scrabbling to stay on solid ground.

Another shove, against her shoulders.

'My *God*,' she screamed. 'What are you *doing*?'

'Helping,' Clare said, and began unhooking Lizzie's fingers from the metal gate.

'Clare, *no*!'

She twisted and grabbed at Clare's left arm, and the other woman yelped, and for a moment Lizzie felt she might win, but then Clare pulled clear, and suddenly she was heaving at the gate, dragging out the concertina, and Lizzie's right foot lost its hold first, and now only her hands, still gripping the iron, were keeping her from falling.

'Clare, for God's sake, *help* me!'

'I *told* you.' Breathless now with effort. 'I *am* helping you.'

She changed angles, heaved at the gate again, slammed the concertinaed metal tighter, trapping Lizzie's fingers, and Lizzie screamed again.

'Just one more little push,' Clare said.

And pushed.

Lizzie plunged into the dark, her wounded fingers clawing vainly at the wall, no hope of gripping now, her right leg scraping something hard, abrasive, as she fell, struck the roof of the lift two floors down, and passed out.

99

'Parry says she's not there,' Novak said, putting down the phone.

'You believe him?' Allbeury asked.

'I think so,' Novak said. 'I don't know.' He sat down on his sofa. 'You didn't answer my question about Shipley,' he said. 'About why she should care about anyone hacking into your computer.'

Allbeury's hesitation was partly for Novak's sake. Partly because something else had just struck him.

'Shipley would care,' he said slowly, 'for a number of reasons. Mostly, I'd say, she'd care because of my files on Lynne Bolsover and Joanne Patston.'

Novak was silent for an instant, and then rage flared again. 'Don't be ridiculous.'

Allbeury said nothing, his mind ticking over.

'Don't be so fucking *ridiculous*,' Novak said.

Allbeury wasn't listening, was too busy remembering.

Other files on his hard disk. On Lizzie and Christopher Wade.

Diary entries too. Logging dinner at the Wades' flat. And drinks at the Savoy with Lizzie.

And, just like Joanne Patston and Lynne Bolsover, Lizzie Piper Wade was the victim of a violent husband.

'Oh, my God,' he said.

'What now?' Novak shook his head in disgust. 'What's next, Robin? What's Clare supposed to have done now, joined the fucking Mafia?'

Allbeury took his mobile from his jacket pocket, called home again, heard the recorded message begin and cut the call.

'We have to leave,' he told Novak.

'I'm going nowhere.'

'You need to come with me,' Allbeury said. 'Right now.'

'You're not paying for my services now, Robin.'

Allbeury picked up his keys. 'Do you love Clare, Mike?'

'Don't ask such fucking stupid questions,' Novak said.

Allbeury was already at the door.

'If you love her,' he said, 'you'd better come with me now.'

100

Lizzie came round, dazed, dizzy, sick with pain.

In the dark.

Almost dark.

There was some light, from above.

And a curious sound.

It all came back to her, swiftly, terrifyingly. The other woman – *mad* – pushing her into the lift shaft. No accident – oh, dear God, *no* accident. Calculated and cold-blooded.

She heard the sound again.

She started to tilt her face towards it, up towards the light, then stopped, afraid suddenly, in case she'd injured her neck or back, in case movement worsened it.

Assess yourself, Lizzie.

Lying on her side – on a hard, cold floor – thick dark cabling near her face.

Tentatively she moved her hands, found that they hurt badly, felt swollen, and she knew why, remembered why – the madwoman slamming the iron gate on her fingers – and her left arm, twisted under the side of her ribcage, felt bad too, maybe – probably – broken.

The ache in her abdomen had gone – *broken bones'll do that every time* – and at least she could *feel* her arm and hands – and her legs and feet too. Bruised, of course, maybe cut, but not broken. Most mercifully of all, her back seemed okay.

Thank you, God.

The sound came again. A soft groaning.

Clare.

Lizzie shifted a little, managing not to yelp with pain, but then

337

the steel floor beneath her creaked and swayed a little – *not a floor, the lift roof* – and even as she froze, the terror sucked a cry out of her.

'Oh, *Jesus*.'

Not her voice.

Clare Novak's voice, from above.

Lizzie turned her face carefully upwards.

The madwoman was staring down at her, framed in the light coming through the half-open lift gate two floors up. She was on her knees, clutching at her abdomen.

'Still with us then?' Clare said, her voice strange.

Lizzie licked her dry mouth.

'Help me,' she said.

'Why would I want to do that?' Clare Novak asked, then gasped in pain. 'Oh, Jesus,' she said again, and her voice, for a moment, was strangled. 'It's the baby,' she said. 'I'm losing the baby.'

The struggle, Lizzie thought, the heaving on the heavy gate.

The effort of pushing her into the shaft.

Not the baby's fault.

'If you help me get out of here—' Lizzie couldn't believe how calm she sounded '—then I can help you, Clare.'

The other woman groaned again.

'Clare, listen to me,' Lizzie said. 'Go and phone for an ambulance.' She felt sweat break out on her forehead, felt sick, suddenly, with the pain in her hands and arm. 'Clare, please, just *listen* to me. If you phone now, get help now, the baby will probably be all right.'

Two floors up, on the edge of the lift shaft, Clare Novak began to laugh.

The sound jarred in Lizzie's head, made her feel dizzy.

'Clare, please,' she said again. 'You must get help.'

'I don't need help,' Clare said. 'And you aren't getting any. Not from me.'

'Why not?' Lizzie knew, even as she asked it, what a foolish question it was, because the other woman had pushed her, fought with her till she'd fallen. Yet it was the question she wanted answered now, almost more than anything. 'Why *not*, Clare?'

'I've killed before, you know,' Clare Novak said.

Down in the dark, more fear crawled into Lizzie's chest, lay there.

'Women like you,' Clare said.

'You don't know me,' Lizzie said.

'I know about you,' Clare said.

'*What* do you know?' Lizzie asked, bewildered.

'I know what kind of man your husband is,' Clare Novak said.

The fear in Lizzie's chest crawled higher, spread itself around. 'How do you know?' The question was out before she could stop it.

'Ask your friend,' Clare said. 'Ask Robin.'

'Why Robin?' For a moment, fresh confusion muddied the fear. 'I don't *understand*.'

'The last time,' Clare said, 'I was far more thorough, I had time to plan, time to make it right, for the children. That's why I'm doing it, you see. For the children.'

The word cut through Lizzie like an axe.

'What do you mean?' She tried to sit up, but the pain was overwhelming, made her feel faint. 'What about the *children*?'

Two floors up, Clare groaned again as another cramp hit her.

Lizzie gritted her teeth. 'Clare,' she called.

There was no answer.

'*Clare*.' Her chest was tight with fresh panic, the dizziness getting worse. 'Go and phone for *help*.' Her head began to spin. 'For your *baby*.'

'I told you,' Clare Novak said, and her voice had grown much harder. 'I don't need any help.'

101

In the Jaguar again, back in the stranglehold of Friday's late rush-hour, Allbeury looked at Novak, hunched in the passenger seat, fists clenched, face unreadable.

'Do something for me.'

'Go fuck yourself,' Novak said.

'Christ, Mike, will you grow *up*.' For the first time, Allbeury felt real anger with the other man. 'Whether you believe it or not, I'm trying to help.'

'Then tell me where the hell we're going and *why*.'

'Just do this first,' Allbeury said, 'and then I'll tell you.' He took Novak's silence as assent. 'Take my mobile and find me a number – I think it's in the memory.'

Novak took the phone off the hands-free. 'Name?'

'Shad Tower,' Allbeury said. 'I want the doorman.'

Novak went through the functions, found the phone book.

'Or it might be under Doorman,' Allbeury said.

Novak keyed his way back through the alphabetical list. 'Neither.'

'Ring 192, see if they have a listing.'

The traffic began to shift.

'Forget it,' Allbeury said. 'We'll probably be there before we ever get through.'

'I may as well try,' Novak said.

'I said *forget* it.'

Novak slammed the phone back on the hands-free. 'So now tell me,' he said, 'what's going on in your head.'

Allbeury flashed his lights, hit his horn and changed lanes.

'And why the hell,' Novak added, 'are we going to Shad Tower?'

340

102

Helen Shipley, in considerable discomfort, lying on a trolley in A&E at St Thomas's Hospital, waiting for her leg to be X-rayed, was, above everything, pissed as hell at being out of it now.

Now, of *all* times.

Should tell Keenan.

Except that Shipley had an idea – bizarre, in the circumstances, and certainly ironic – that at this precise moment Robin Allbeury might possibly be doing a better job than either she or DI Keenan had been.

She had been off-duty when all this had started, and God knew Keenan hadn't really wanted to listen to her before.

Right, wasn't he, as it happens?

Half right, anyway.

A nurse hurried past.

'Okay, love?'

'Do you think,' Shipley said, 'I could have—'

The nurse had already gone.

'—a phone?'

Pissed as *hell*.

103

Lizzie woke, out of an ugly, painful sleep that might, she supposed as she came to, have been another faint.

Clare.

She looked up quickly, saw only the rectangle of light two floors above.

No one framed in it now.

Gone.

The place felt empty, no sound anywhere, nothing.

No one.

Lizzie looked at the thick cabling nearest her, thought about leaning against it for support, then, going on instinct, edged away from it instead. The pain in her arm and hands was sickening and the lift beneath her groaned like an aged, arthritic beast.

Keep still and wait.

She wondered how long it would be before someone came – Robin, maybe. But Clare had said that he'd been hurt.

Clare pushed you down a lift shaft.

But maybe he *was* hurt, maybe she'd done something to him too.

I know what kind of man your husband is, Clare had said. And when Lizzie had asked her how she knew, she'd said: *Ask Robin.*

I've killed before.

For the children.

Jack flew into Lizzie's mind, and Edward and Sophie, and then, almost an afterthought, the shocking mess of her marriage, and Lizzie began to cry, just bawled her eyes out for a moment or two.

Until the lift groaned again.

Making her stop.

104

Christopher was in Holland Park, in his study.

The telephone had rung a few minutes earlier, but he hadn't answered it, had let the machine pick up, neither had he checked to see if he had any messages, because they would no longer matter, might only muddy his thinking, which was, at present, very clear.

He'd already assembled what he needed: a good combination, one that would take him pleasantly on his way. Better than he deserved, he supposed, but then again he had never understood why some people felt the need to torture themselves on the way to oblivion.

He had, on the other hand, decided not to do it here – in comfort, but also the place in which his wife and children would probably continue to live; did not want to inflict that kind of ineradicable connection on any of them.

Done enough – still doing – more than enough to them without that.

And besides, there was also the possibility that someone – the police or Lizzie herself, or perhaps Allbeury, now, after the appalling fiasco in that dismal office – might come here looking for him, and he had no intention of being interrupted.

He had already written letters to Edward and Sophie, and had managed a shamefully short, entirely inadequate letter of regret and love for Lizzie.

Now he had begun to write the hardest of all.

Don't think, for a single second – he wrote to Jack – *that you were in any way wrong to go for me as you did. Even while you were battering away at me, all that fury in your face, I felt so proud of you, admired you for your strength and courage, as I always have.*

I need you to go on helping the others to take care of your mother for as long as you can, and to let her take care of you when things get worse. Don't fight her too much, make things easier for her.

I know I'm being a dreadful coward, but I'm not nearly as brave as you, Jack, and I am trying to do the right thing for you all now, at the end. I have done some terrible things, over the years, very stupid things too, and if I were to stay I'd probably have to face a trial, maybe even go to prison. Knowing your loving, generous heart, there's a chance you might forgive me in time, perhaps want to come to court to support me, even visit me in prison, and I couldn't bear that, am much too selfish for that. Unlike your wonderful, magical mother, who might have seen me punished long ago, but stayed with me, put up with me, instead.

All of you, all my precious children, but you especially, my brave-hearted son, have taught me so much, and I wish with all my heart that I could stay with you always, but that just isn't possible now. I will love you forever, Jack, and I pray that you may, in time, find it possible not to think of me too badly. But if you can't forgive me, I understand that I've forfeited any right to expect otherwise.

He signed the letter, sealed the envelope, feeling a little calmer, but then the sound of a siren from the streets startled him and he dropped the letter and his pen and felt compelled to wait, frozen in suspense, until the sound had vanished into the distance.

Not for him yet, but time marching on.

He was trembling again as he went into Lizzie's study and placed all the envelopes on her desk, so that it would be she who found them, no one else.

And then he picked up his collection of drugs, his favourite photographs of Lizzie and the children, and left the flat.

105

Clare had come to the river.

She was sitting on a bench seat close to the water a few yards from one of the restaurants on Butler's Wharf.

It was colder than she had expected, and she was very tired, and the hike back across the bridge and along Shad Thames in the dark had almost finished her, but she had known roughly where she wanted to get to, where she wanted to sit and wait.

For them to find her.

Or for it to end.

Whichever came first.

She was trying to ignore the pain, breathing through it, gazing into the river, imagining the darkness beneath the surface.

She felt the blood trickling out of her. Let it go. Neither laughing now, nor weeping.

Just letting it all go.

106

'Damn it,' Allbeury said, standing in his living room at Shad Tower, 'where's she *gone*? No note, no message.'

'Always looking for notes.' Novak was wry. 'Explanations.'

Allbeury ignored him, tried to think where else he might try looking for Lizzie, had already called Holland Park and Marlow, where he'd lied to Gilly, told her it was unimportant.

He thought of Susan Blake, then dismissed that notion, and went to his house phone to speak to the doorman.

'I'm afraid,' the man told him, 'I've only just come on duty, but if it's urgent, I know where Dermot's gone.'

'It's urgent,' Allbeury said. 'Call me back.' He took a breath, trying to compose himself, saw the anger and fear still etched on Novak's normally affable face. 'Have a seat, Mike.'

Novak started to shake his head, then slouched down in an armchair, looking like a boxer without a fight.

'Drink?' Allbeury offered.

'No.'

'Coffee?'

'No.'

Allbeury looked at the house phone, glanced at his watch. Almost seven. Where the hell *was* she?

He began to pace, over by the expanse of glass doors, back and forth, looking out as he did so, gazing into the half dark at nothing in particular.

Suddenly he stopped pacing, stood very still for one more instant, then opened the doors, stepped out onto the terrace and grasped the telescope, training it down onto the walk below and then left, scanning the little electrically operated stainless steel

346

footbridge across St Saviour's Dock, moving on along the river-side walk.

There.

He fastened on a small figure, adjusted the focus.

A woman was sitting, alone, on one of the bench seats on Butler's Wharf outside the Gastrodome.

'Clare,' he said, loudly, sharply.

In the room, Novak sprang to his feet.

'Down there,' Allbeury said.

Both men ran.

107

Lizzie had managed, as well as she could with her bad arm and throbbing fingers, to get herself into a huddled position, knees drawn up, right arm around them.

She felt increasingly cold.

And scared.

She'd tried telling herself that there was no need to feel so afraid, because the worst had already happened – she'd fallen down a lift shaft and survived. It was just a matter of waiting now, for help to come. As it would.

The children.

Clare had said that she'd done it for the children.

Killed.

But her children were safe with Gilly, and Christopher – wherever he was – would not go back to Marlow, not after last night, and Clare Novak, wherever she might have gone, was surely still in London, and *ill*, perhaps having a miscarriage, so there was no reason to be afraid for Jack and Edward and Sophie now.

What if no one comes?

They would, she told herself fiercely. It was self-indulgent to allow herself to think otherwise, because Mike Novak worked in this building, and even if it was late on a Friday, the agency had been left in too much chaos for it to be abandoned for the whole weekend. Even if Novak didn't come back, or Robin – she wished it would be Robin – eventually *someone* would come: the cleaner, or maybe the police.

Or Clare.

108

Novak reached Clare first, sat down beside her in silence, put his arms around her, gently, protectively. There was a sheen of perspiration on her face, clearly visible in the lamplight, but she was shivering.

'You're cold,' he said, took off his leather jacket, put it around her.

She began to smile at him – and then a cramp distorted her face. Realization hit him.

'The baby?' he said, and fought off panic.

She didn't answer, just rocked with the pain.

Novak looked back at Allbeury, standing, waiting. 'Can you phone for an ambulance? I've left my mobile somewhere.'

'In a moment,' Allbeury said.

'Now,' Novak said. 'Go into one of the restaurants.'

'One moment.' Allbeury came around the bench seat and sat on Clare's other side. 'Where's Lizzie?' he asked her.

'Robin, she needs to get to hospital,' Novak said, holding her more tightly.

Clare smiled again.

'Where is she, Clare?' Allbeury asked.

'Leave her alone, you son-of-a-bitch,' Novak said, 'and get us some *help*.'

Clare tilted her face towards Allbeury.

'Lizzie's at the office,' she said.

'Which office?' Allbeury asked.

'Our office,' she said.

Allbeury stood up, his mobile in his right hand, keying 999.

'I'll tell them on the way to the car,' he said and began to move away.

Novak looked back towards Shad Tower, glittering in the dark, dwarfing the warehouse conversions, then glanced towards Tower Bridge, saw brake lights, motionless, cars still bumper to bumper.

'Faster walking,' he called out.

Allbeury lifted a hand in assent, turned into Curlew Street and was gone.

109

Jim Keenan had only reached St Thomas's ten minutes earlier – had been fortuitously close, inside Waterloo Station, when Shipley had called him – and she'd just got out of X-ray and what she was telling him was a wild-sounding jumble, but he was doing his best to make sense of it.

'You're going to have to slow down,' he told her. 'So far, I have someone knocking you down a flight of stairs—'

'Please pay attention,' Shipley said impatiently. 'His name is Christopher Wade, but that's not important now.'

'Assaulting a police officer's important enough,' Keenan said.

'But not *now*.'

'So you're still saying what? That Allbeury is connected to the killings, but not *directly*?'

'I'm saying that he was trying to tell me something he didn't want Novak to hear, and I'm assuming it was because he thought Novak, and maybe his wife, were involved.'

'So this is still mostly hunch, is it?' Keenan asked.

'I suppose so,' Shipley said, 'except now, apparently, it isn't just *my* hunch, it's Allbeury's too. And if you'd seen his face, you'd know that something bad was going on – something *new*, okay?'

They'd put her in a cubicle, had given her something for her pain, and her eyelids were beginning to droop.

'By "bad",' Keenan pressed before she fell asleep, 'you think someone's in danger?'

'Maybe.' Shipley nodded. 'And if it was me, if I wasn't lying here with this bloody leg, I'd be on my way to the Novaks' flat,

351

and then I'd be going back to the agency, and if those places came up empty, I'd be tracking down Allbeury again.'

Keenan took out his notebook. 'Addresses?'

Shipley's eyes were closing. 'Then again,' she said, with a smile on her lips, 'it's your call now, and this stuff is starting to give me quite a nice buzz, and—'

Keenan laid a hand on her arm.

'Give me the addresses, Helen.'

110

'We should get you inside,' Novak told Clare, 'into the warm.'

'No,' she said.

'It's too cold out here.' He began to rise, to try to draw her to her feet.

'*No*,' she said again. 'I want to stay here.'

'Okay.' He gave in, cuddled her close. 'The ambulance will be here soon,' he told her gently, 'and you'll be fine, both of you, you and our baby, and there's no need to be scared, okay, sweetheart?'

'The baby won't be all right,' she said.

'Yes, it will. You mustn't worry.'

'The baby's dying,' Clare said. 'Or maybe it's already dead. And I'm not worrying, Mike, because it's what I want.'

He thought – was sure – he had misheard. But then she laughed.

Delirium, he told himself, hung on to that thread.

The laugh was harsh, though. Brittle.

'That's right.' She glanced at his face, went on leaning against him. 'I do mean it, Mike. I meant it last time, too, when I killed our baby.'

'You didn't kill him,' Novak said. 'I've told you and told you, sweetheart, it wasn't your fault.'

'Yes, it was.' The fingers of Clare's left hand hooked around the edge of his shirt, between two buttons, grasped at the fabric as a child might, clinging on. 'Our son didn't just *die*, Mike, didn't have problems breathing – not the kind you thought, anyway—'

'Clare, darling, stop it.' He twisted around, still holding her, but trying to see up the narrow side street, looking for blue flashing lights, though he'd heard no sirens.

353

'I kept hoping and hoping,' Clare went on, 'that it would die *before*. I prayed and prayed for a miscarriage—'

All the dark chill of the river seemed to flow into him. He turned around, very slowly, faced her again.

'—but it didn't happen, so I had to take care of it myself.'

He pulled away, but her fingers still gripped his shirt.

'I'm sorry,' she said, in a voice that held no sorrow at all. 'I'm really sorry, Mike, but it's time you knew, don't you think?'

He thought, *wanted* to believe, that he'd gone mad or that this was a nightmare, or that maybe what he'd thought just moments ago was true, that she was delirious.

But he could see from her eyes – cold eyes that had nothing to do with the Clare he had known and loved for years – that she was not.

Allbeury had run along Shad Thames, past the Chef School and the sculpture gallery and Pizza Express, on past the Anchor Brewhouse, taking the steps up to the bridge three at a time, hardly slowing on Tower Bridge itself, and even on the far side there was hardly any point looking for a taxi, the traffic was so appalling. And God, East Smithfield was longer than he'd realized, though then again, he never walked from Shad Tower to the agency, and he glanced back across the river to Butler's Wharf, wondered if the ambulance was already there, wondered what had happened to Clare.

He reached Dock Street, turned left, breathless now from running.

Almost there.

'Lizzie Piper said she wanted to help me save our baby,' Clare told Novak, 'which was very nice of her, considering what I'd just done to her.'

Another, more violent, pain had just struck her, and she was laughing and crying now, and rocking, hugging herself.

'For God's sake, Clare,' Novak said, 'let me get you inside.'

'No,' she said again. 'It wasn't the way I planned it,' she went on. 'Not like the others.'

That last word seemed to hang in the cold night air for a moment, hovering somewhere just outside the frontiers of Novak's comprehension.

'Others,' he said, icy again, helpless.

'It's gone wrong,' Clare went on, still rocking, 'because there wasn't enough time to plan this one. But it's not too bad in spite of that, all working out quite *neatly*, and Robin'll find her, and he'll try to save her, but the lift's not likely to hold his weight as well as hers.'

'Lift,' Novak echoed.

'Our lift,' she said.

'Our lift doesn't work,' he said, stupidly. 'It's been condemned for years.'

'Quite right too,' Clare said. 'Dangerous thing, hanging by a thread.'

111

Lizzie heard something – a door, opening, closing – *downstairs*. She jolted with hope, felt the big old lift shiver correspondingly, and froze again.

Footsteps, coming up.

Whose?

'Lizzie?'

Robin's voice.

Thank God.

'Robin, I'm trapped,' she called out to him. 'In the lift shaft.'

'Jesus,' his voice said.

Lizzie smiled in the dark for the first time, forgot her pain and fear.

'You need to be very careful,' she called. 'The gate's open on the top floor, and I'm about two floors down, on the lift's roof.'

'God almighty,' she heard him say.

And then, suddenly, his head and shoulders appeared in the open gateway above, staring down at her.

'Be careful,' she told him again.

'Shame no one said that to you,' Allbeury said.

Lizzie's smile was tremulous. 'How did you know I was here?'

'Clare Novak told me.'

'She *pushed* me,' Lizzie said, her voice quivering. 'She said she'd killed before, Robin.' She bit her lip to stop herself crying. 'She said she knew about Christopher, what kind of husband he is.' The words were spilling out in a rush. 'And when I asked her how she knew, she said I should ask *you*.'

Allbeury was silent for a moment.

'Why did she say that, Robin?' she asked. 'Did you tell her?'

356

'Of course not.' He paused. 'Lizzie, are you hurt?'

'Not too badly, considering.' She took a breath. 'Better now you're here.'

'Thank God for that, at least,' he said, then surveyed the scene. 'Don't suppose you're up to rope climbing?'

'It's cable, not rope,' she said. 'And it all looks a bit dodgy, I don't trust it.'

'Hm,' he said.

'Robin, why did Clare Novak say that about you?' Lizzie found she couldn't let it go, felt she needed to know, now, right away, if this man was to be trusted or not. 'How could she know about Christopher?'

'She could have found a little information – a *very* little,' Allbeury said, 'on my computer. She's been breaking into my files, Lizzie, and I think she's probably been doing the same to other people.'

Vaguely, in the back of her mind, Lizzie recalled something odd that Christopher had said to her after the pimp had beaten him up, about someone snooping in the files at the Beauchamp clinic.

'Oh, God,' she said, felt suddenly as if she were drowning, and then, looking up, she saw that Allbeury had vanished.

'Robin, don't go!' she called out, panicking.

'Not going anywhere,' his voice said. 'I'm going to come down to get you.'

'You can't,' she told him urgently. 'The lift's very shaky – I'm not sure it can hold you too.'

'Of course it can,' Allbeury's voice dismissed. 'It might be a bit decrepit, but it was designed to hold freight as well as people, and it only feels shaky because you're sitting on its damned *roof.*'

'So what do you do now?' Clare's voice was growing fainter. 'Your wife sitting here beside you, bleeding, your baby dying by inches.'

'Stop it, Clare.'

'Your friend Robin about to risk his life to save a woman who's too pathetic to *deserve* to live.'

Novak stared at her again, disbelievingly, then got to his feet, his legs like jelly. 'Where's that fucking ambulance?'

'But maybe they'll both be okay.' Clare began rocking again.

'Maybe the lift won't crash, or even if it does, we're hardly talking skyscraper heights, are we? So they'll probably be fine – unless that steel rope splits and the live wire zaps them.'

'The power's turned off,' Novak said.

'Maybe,' his wife said. 'Unless I turned it on at the box before I left.'

112

Keenan had just reached Lamb's Conduit Street, was looking for the Novaks' address, and he'd decided to hedge his bets, follow up on Shipley's hunch, but by himself, not fancying making himself a laughing stock just yet.

There was the building.

He found the flat number and buzzed.

No reply.

He buzzed one of the other numbers, then another.

'Who is it?' a man's voice asked.

'Police,' he said. 'Let me in, please. Just to the building, not your flat.'

There was a second's pause, and then the door clicked open.

The Novaks' flat was on the first floor.

Keenan rang the bell and knocked.

No grounds for kicking the door in.

He bent and peered through the letter box and listened.

Nothing.

113

'The only safe thing to do,' Lizzie said, 'is call the fire brigade.'

'I was going to do that anyway,' Allbeury told her.

'And once you've talked to them,' she added, 'it might be an idea to get a doctor, because I think I've probably broken my left arm.'

'Why didn't you *tell* me?' His head and shoulders appeared again, backlit, in the gateway. 'Christ, Lizzie, you said you were okay.'

'I was just so happy to see you,' she said, feeling foolish, 'I forgot.'

'Your left arm?' he checked. 'So I can tell them when I phone.'

'And some of my fingers,' she said. 'Clare trapped them in the gate.'

'Christ,' Allbeury said again, and went to dial 999.

Clare had finally ceased talking, and there was no more laughter now, nothing at all, and suddenly she slipped sideways on the bench.

'Clare.' Novak moved back beside her, felt for her wrist, her pulse. '*Clare*.'

He looked at the restaurants behind them, at the brightly lit All Bar One and the sweeping Pont de la Tour frontage, thought again about getting Clare inside.

Better not to move her.

Reaching a decision, cursing the ambulance people – cursing Allbeury again – he drew his leather jacket away from her shoulders, lifted her feet so that she was lying on the bench seat, partly sheltered by the large planted box attached to it, and laid the jacket over her.

'I'm going to get help,' he said, loudly, clearly. 'We can't wait any longer.'

She gave a small moan.

'I'll be as quick as I can,' he told her.

He ran, oblivious of the tears on his face, into the closest place, the bar, into brightness and music and normality, scanned the long bar for a phone, saw none.

'I need help,' he said loudly to anyone in earshot.

Eyes veered to him, a waitress carrying bottles, drinkers and diners on brown leather sofas and at long narrow tables, all startled.

'I need a *phone*.'

'Sir.' A waiter hurried towards him. 'How can I help you?'

'I need you to call an ambulance.' Novak had an urge to grab the young man, to propel him to a phone. 'My wife's outside – she's losing our baby . . .'

Over the music and chattering voices, he heard it at last.

The siren.

114

'Shouldn't be much longer now.'

Allbeury was sitting by the open lift gate trying to keep Lizzie's spirits up, but she was getting colder, and he'd dropped his jacket down to her a few minutes before, and even that slight added weight had made the lift shift a little, scaring her more. He was growing increasingly anxious for her, knew that in addition to her own predicament she was wretched about not calling home, and he'd told her he'd spoken to Gilly earlier and that the children had been okay then (not that he actually knew that for sure), had offered to call again on her behalf under some pretext, but Lizzie had said that both Jack and Edward were more than likely, in the circumstances, to see through any tale and imagine something dreadful.

'I just don't understand,' she said now.

'What don't you understand?'

'Why someone like Clare – you called her a nice woman, I think, when we had dinner that night . . .'

'I remember,' Allbeury said wryly.

'What could happen to a woman like that to make her *do* such things?'

'Try not to think about Clare now,' he said.

'How can I *not*? She's the reason I'm in this mess.' She winced, could feel her left arm swelling and her fingers growing more numb, and that was another reason for talking about Clare Novak, because it stopped her thinking about the pain.

'Is it very bad?' Allbeury asked.

'Not too bad,' she said. 'Talk to me, Robin.'

'What about?'

'About Clare and her—'

A new sound from above – like something *tearing* – silenced her.

'What was that?' she asked after a moment, her voice hushed.

'I don't know,' Allbeury said uneasily.

The lift shuddered, and Lizzie let out an involuntary cry. 'I didn't move, Robin. I didn't even *move*.'

He was already on his feet.

'What are you doing?' she asked edgily.

'Going to find something,' he said. 'Something to lower down to you, like a lifebelt, to hold you.'

'In case the whole thing goes,' Lizzie said.

'It's not going to go,' he said. 'So long as you stay still.'

'No argument there.' He disappeared. 'Keep talking to me, please,' she called.

'Will do,' Allbeury called back.

Nothing in the office appeared to have changed since he and Novak had left after Shipley's fall, and abruptly he remembered promising to follow her to St Thomas's, but that would have to wait a while longer now.

'Robin, what are you doing?' Lizzie's voice asked from a distance.

'Looking around,' he told her.

He looked at the computer monitor he'd wrecked, shook his head, then saw the cables at the rear. Strong, but not long enough, though maybe if he tied them to the length of cable behind the printer, and to the phone wires and all the other flexes in the office . . .

'Hang on, Lizzie,' he called. 'I've got something, but it's going to take a few minutes to put together. You just hang on.'

'Poor choice of word, Robin,' her voice said.

At eight-fifteen, Keenan was stuck in traffic near Fenchurch Street, and he didn't know what the *hell* was going on in the city tonight, and maybe he'd just been influenced by the over-intense Helen Shipley, but his own gut was telling him that something bad was going to happen if he didn't get the fuck *moving*.

And he was just beginning to wonder if he'd been very wrong trying to deal with this on his own, and if maybe he ought, after all, to try and rustle up some local help, when, miracle of miracles, the jam ahead of him cleared away, and he put his foot down hard.

'I can't come with you now.'

Standing in Curlew Street, Novak read the faces of the two paramedics as he said that just after they'd put Clare into the ambulance, and he knew they thought him callous, and Clare, her face half hidden by an oxygen mask, eyes open again, made no further attempt to speak.

'I'll be there as soon as I can,' he told her.

As they closed the ambulance doors, Clare was looking straight at him, and Novak had a great urge to howl.

Instead, he turned and ran.

115

Allbeury's hands were shaking with tension and effort, but he had completed the knotting, working near the lift shaft, talking to Lizzie as he laboured, filling her in on what he was doing, and now he was back in the office seeking something more solid than himself to which to tie one end of his makeshift rope.

'Filing cabinets are heavy,' he called to Lizzie, 'but they're a bit far in, and anyway, they'd probably tip over.'

'What about the office door?' Lizzie, glad of the diversion, had been trying to work things out too. 'That must be reasonably solid.'

He went to take a look. 'Not sure about the hinges.'

'Right,' Lizzie said.

'I'll just have to use my weight,' he said, 'find some way to anchor myself. It'll be fine, and anyway, the fire people should be here any second now.'

He found one end of his cable rope and tied it around his waist, realized that if it were actually to be used it would rip through his shirt and flesh, but that was just too bad.

The lift gave another groan. Despite herself, Lizzie whimpered.

'Right.' Allbeury crouched beside the open shaft. 'I'm going to lower this contraption to you now, Lizzie. I've attached my belt at your end, cut a few more holes in it so it'll fit.'

'It'll still need pulling though, won't it?' she said. 'I'm sorry, but I don't think I could manage that with one arm and my fingers the way—'

'God, I'm a bloody idiot,' Allbeury exclaimed. 'Of course you can't manage that.' He stood up again, began untying the rope around his own waist. 'It's okay, though, I just need another minute or two.'

The cable-rope thudded to the floor at his feet and he fumbled with the belt, and it wasn't easy, even for him, with the cumbersome heavy lengths attached to it, and he was sweating now, silently cursing the emergency services for taking so long.

'How's it going?' Lizzie's voice enquired from below.

'I'm making a kind of harness that we should, with a bit of luck, be able to get over your head and shoulders, and if I get this *knot* right . . .' He grimaced with concentration. 'I'm hoping it'll tighten automatically if need be.'

'If the lift crashes,' Lizzie said.

'Shut up, Lizzie,' Allbeury said.

'Were you ever a scout?'

Lizzie remembered that Jack had once said he wished he could join the movement after hearing his brother talking about it, but then the very next day Edward had changed his mind, and Lizzie and Christopher had both known it was only because he hated Jack feeling left out of anything. Lizzie smiled now, tried to lift her right hand to wipe the tears away, but her fingers were too painfully swollen.

'I asked if you were ever a scout, Robin,' she said.

'Shush,' his voice said.

She heard it then, too.

Footsteps on the staircase, then a muffled curse.

'Is it them?' she called.

'Up here!' Allbeury shouted. 'Top floor, and get a *move* on!'

'It'd help if the damned lift was working.'

Allbeury recognized the voice even before he saw him.

'DI Keenan,' he said. 'Hoped you were the fire brigade, but you'll have to do.'

'Thanks very much.' Keenan, out of breath, arrived on the landing, stared at Allbeury and the coils of cable in his hands. 'What the bloody hell is going on?'

'Short version,' Allbeury said. 'Woman trapped in lift shaft with broken arm and fingers.'

'*Probably* broken,' Lizzie added from below.

'Bloody hell,' Keenan said again.

'I second that,' Lizzie agreed.

'That's Lizzie Piper,' Allbeury said.

Keenan scratched the back of his head. 'The cook?'

'That's me,' Lizzie said.

The policeman went gingerly to the open shaft. 'You sound in good spirits.'

'I'm all right,' she said. 'Or I would be if this lift would stop shaking.'

'Christ,' Keenan said.

'It's probably sounder than it seems,' Allbeury told the DI, 'but just in case . . .'

Keenan looked at the cable rope. 'You were planning on getting that down to her?' He took a look. 'Good idea.'

'With two of us to anchor it,' Allbeury said, 'it should do the job.'

Keenan nodded. 'Streets are gridlocked – probably why the brigade's not here yet.' He bent to check that the belt end, around the other man's waist, was secure. 'The Novaks not here, I take it?'

'Last I saw of them,' Allbeury said, 'they were by the river below my place.' He paused, looked into the DI's face. 'Just so you know, it was Clare Novak who did this to Lizzie.'

'She said she'd killed other people,' Lizzie called up. 'She told me.'

'But she wasn't, I gather,' Keenan said, still absorbing the information, 'the one who shoved DI Shipley down the staircase.'

'What staircase?' Lizzie asked.

'Nothing to do with this,' Allbeury said, and raised a finger to his lips.

Keenan got the message, nodded.

'Fill you in later,' Allbeury said quietly. 'How is DI Shipley?'

'Broken leg.' Keenan checked the knots on the harness end. 'St Thomas's.'

'Who's DI Shipley?' Lizzie asked.

The lift groaned.

'Do you think,' she said, 'you could hurry?'

'Any minute now,' Allbeury said.

'Back up,' Keenan told him. 'Other side of the door, and hang on tight – hook your legs round something if you can.' He watched as the other man backed away. 'Tell me when you're secure.'

Allbeury vanished into the office, the cable-rope stretching behind him.

367

'Ready,' he called.

'Good.' Keenan approached the lift shaft again. 'Lizzie, I'm going to try getting this thing down to you now, all right?'

He glanced sideways, put out his right hand, gripped the gate firmly, stood with his feet apart and not too near the edge, then lowered the noose-like harness, grunting loudly as it dropped.

'What's wrong?' Allbeury called, hearing the grunt.

'Nothing,' Keenan said. 'Just heavier than I expected.'

'You okay, Lizzie?' Allbeury called.

'So far.'

She looked up, saw the thing hanging, swinging.

'Think you'll be able to get it over your head and shoulders?' Keenan asked.

'Don't know,' she said. 'I'll try.'

'You still secure, Allbeury?' Keenan called.

'Okay this end.'

Keenan lowered more rope.

'That's enough,' Lizzie said. 'Let me see if I can reach it, hook my wrist through it, maybe . . .'

She lifted her right arm, stretched a little, cried out in pain and then fear as the lift shifted again, *groaned* again.

'It's moving,' she said warily.

They all heard it then – another sound.

The door down below crashing open, feet on the way up, *running* feet.

'Don't touch the *cables*!' Mike Novak's voice bellowed frantically.

Keenan, Lizzie and Allbeury all froze.

'The *power's* on!' Novak yelled.

In the distance, coming swiftly, mercifully, closer, they all heard sirens.

116

The power, they later learned, had not been on.

That had just been Clare, almost at the end of herself, twisting the knife in Novak one last time. Lizzie, extricated by the firemen with relative ease, had been taken to St Thomas's, temporarily euphoric from pain relief and the sheer joy of being alive, Allbeury beside her in the ambulance, holding her hand.

Keenan had driven Novak to the hospital to see Clare, talking to him as they drove, working to sort facts out in his own mind in order to pass them on with a degree of clarity to the local boys.

'She's ill,' Novak said. 'The Clare I know would never, ever have hurt anyone.' He paused, shaking his head. 'She's a nurse, the gentlest person I've ever known.'

'She told you about it, did she?' Keenan asked gently.

Novak nodded.

'What exactly did she tell you?'

'About Robin's friend, Lizzie,' Novak said. 'About trying to hurt her.'

'Lizzie Piper,' Keenan said. 'Mrs Wade.' One bit of confusion, at least, that had already been tidied for him by Allbeury.

'And others,' Mike Novak said, softly.

'Yes,' Keenan said, still gently. 'She told Mrs Wade about them too.'

He could only begin to imagine Novak's agony at that confirmation, wondered exactly how much he did know – very little, he suspected – and knew that now was not the moment for pushing, that it would all come soon enough.

'I'll see what I can find out about your wife,' he said when they reached the hospital.

He returned soon after, sat beside the shattered man, and added fresh grief to his load. 'She lost the baby,' he told him gently. 'I'm very sorry.'

'Where is she?' Novak asked.

'In theatre, having a D&C.' Keenan paused. 'They said she'll be fine.'

Novak nodded.

They let Novak see her afterwards, when she was out of recovery and in a side ward, allowed him to go in first, before the police alerted by Keenan went in to formally arrest Clare on suspicion of the attempted murder of Elizabeth Wade.

Her face was very white.

'Clare?' He put out his hand, covered hers with it, and she didn't pull away, just lay still and silent, not looking at him. 'They told me about the baby.'

She went on looking at the ceiling.

'I'm so sorry,' Novak said.

He thought, was not certain, that she shook her head, very slightly, but after that, again, there was no response.

'Clare, I still love you,' he told her in despair.

She looked at him then, no expression in her eyes.

'Don't,' she said.

Allbeury had stayed with Lizzie through admission, waited while they X-rayed her arm and hands, then sat with her in a cubicle during the next bout of waiting, gave her his mobile phone to use when she felt sufficiently composed, so that she could call Gilly and ask her to tell the boys and Sophie that she'd had a minor fall, but was fine and would speak to them in the morning.

'I need to tell you something,' Allbeury said when she'd finished.

He told her about Christopher apparently following him to the agency, about his terrible, uncontrolled rage, about his knocking Helen Shipley down the stairs and subsequent escape.

'I thought,' he said, 'I should wait till after you'd called home before I told you, in case one of the children asked you about their father and you weren't much good at telling lies.' He smiled. 'But after hearing you call that nightmare a "minor fall", I'm not quite so sure.'

'Practice,' Lizzie said, very quietly and wearily. 'Years of it.'

117

Christopher was found, late that evening, by a dentist collecting his car after a night out from the multi-storey garage below Cavendish Square.

The news of his death was not brought to Lizzie till next morning, after she'd phoned Gilly again, confessing that she was in St Thomas's with one broken arm and several fingers. She thought, at the time, that Gilly sounded strange, but then Edward came on the line, followed by Sophie, then Jack, desperate to know if she was *really* okay, and Gilly left her mind.

It was Angela who brought her the news.

Who sat with her, ready to help with tissues when she wept, but was confronted only by her daughter's white and stony face.

'Better,' she said, from long-ago but bitter experience, 'to let it out, if you can.'

'I expect I will,' Lizzie said.

'When you're ready,' Angela said, red-eyed.

Lizzie nodded.

'The children don't know,' her mother said, 'obviously.'

'No,' Lizzie said. 'I spoke to them earlier.'

'We thought,' Angela continued, unnerved by the continuing calmness, 'Gilly and I, that you would want to tell them yourself.' She shook her head, impatient with herself. 'Not *want*,' she said. 'Stupid thing to say.'

'I know what you mean, Mum.'

'The thing is though,' her mother went on, 'with you stuck here . . . We can't risk waiting too long in case it gets out.' She snatched a breath. 'Gilly's doing all the right things, keeping them busy, keeping the TV off and the boys away from their computers, and there's nothing in the papers yet, thank goodness—'

'I'll go to them now,' Lizzie said abruptly.

'You can't,' Angela said. 'Look at you.' She paused. 'I was thinking, perhaps, I should go and fetch them, drive them into town.'

'No.' Lizzie was adamant. 'Absolutely not.'

Her surgeon disapproved, but finally gave in, making Lizzie sign a release, then telling her, quite paternally, that she should keep in mind her own physical and emotional ordeal, and that while she might temporarily find the strength she needed for her children, at some later point this was all bound to take its toll on her.

Robin Allbeury arrived with a bouquet while she was waiting for the private ambulance that the surgeon had advised for her journey.

'Dear God,' he said, visibly appalled by the news about Christopher.

Lizzie saw something very like guilt in his eyes.

'Not your fault,' she told him, almost crisply. 'Don't think that for a second.'

'He came after me,' Allbeury said quietly. 'The thing with DI Shipley was wholly accidental, but he must have—'

'He didn't do this because of DI Shipley,' Lizzie said. 'And certainly not because of you.' She turned her face towards the door. 'You know, better than anyone else, why he did it.'

They sat for a few moments, in silence.

'Anything you need,' he told her. 'Any time, day or night.'

'You've done more than enough for me,' Lizzie said.

'Not as far as I'm concerned,' Allbeury said.

118

Both Angela and Gilly were on hand when Lizzie broke the news to Edward, Jack and Sophie.

Each so different in their reactions. Sophie sobbing, letting out her heartbreak, wanting to be held, to be comforted, and then, several times, like a much younger child, wanting to be told that it was not really true, that her daddy *would* come home again. Edward wholly bereft but struggling for courage, finding, if not consolation, then a degree of spurious control in anger, lashing out when Lizzie tried to embrace him with her good arm.

And Jack, utterly silent, wheeling himself into his bedroom, remaining there for hours. Neither hostile when Lizzie or his grandmother or Gilly came to check on him, nor crying. Just sitting.

Angela came upon Lizzie, early on Saturday evening, at the bottom of the garden, finally weeping.

'That's good,' she said quietly.

'I'm not crying for me,' Lizzie said. 'Or for Christopher.'

'For the children,' Angela said.

'God, yes,' Lizzie said.

Her mother held out her arms, and Lizzie came into them.

'I don't know,' she said, 'if Jack will bear this.'

'I think he will,' Angela said. 'He is a remarkable person.'

The letters were not found for several more days. Lizzie agonized about whether or not to give the children theirs, since to both Edward and Jack, and probably Sophie too, they would be clear proof of their father's suicide, a fact which had not, to date, been discussed.

'It's too much,' she said to Angela.

'I think the boys already know, more or less,' her mother said.

'It's too big a burden,' Lizzie said. 'We could invent something credible.'

'More lies,' Angela said, without condemnation. 'Catch up with you eventually.'

Sophie, presented with her letter, appeared afraid to touch it, asked her mother to read it to her, then snatched it from Lizzie and ran sobbing to her room.

'I'm not sure,' Edward said, a bit later, to Lizzie, 'if I'm going to read mine yet.'

'When you're ready,' she said. 'It's up to you, my darling.'

'Have you read yours?' he asked her.

'Yes, I have,' Lizzie replied.

'Was it awful?' Edward asked.

'No,' she answered. 'Not awful at all. Filled with love.'

'Like Dad,' he said.

Jack, who had by then emerged from his self-imposed isolation, found Lizzie in her study and offered her his letter.

'I thought,' he said, 'it might help.'

'Are you sure?' Lizzie asked. 'Isn't it private?'

'I think I'd like you to see it,' Jack said. 'If you don't mind.'

Her tears came again while she was reading it, holding the paper between the two good fingers of her right hand.

'It's rather beautiful, isn't it?' she said when she'd finished. 'Just very, very sad.' She looked at Jack. 'Did it help you at all?'

'A bit.'

She had the sense, then, that he wanted, at last, to talk to her.

'It's terribly hard, isn't it, my darling?'

Jack nodded, hesitated. 'It's all of it,' he said.

She knew he was remembering the last night, waited for him to go on.

'I keep feeling . . .' He stopped.

'What, my love?'

'That it's my fault.'

'Of course it isn't,' Lizzie said, appalled.

'But he left because of me.' His mouth worked. 'I made him go.' He shut his eyes, and tears squeezed between his lashes and rolled down his cheeks. 'If I hadn't gone for him like that . . .'

'No.' All Lizzie's anger with Christopher returned full force. 'Absolutely not, Jack, do you hear me?'

He opened his eyes. 'But it's true, Mum.'

'It is *not* true,' she told him, hating Clare Novak for depriving her of the ability to properly hold her son when he needed her most. 'Jack, you have to listen to me on this, you have to believe me.'

'But don't you blame me?' he asked her.

'How could I possibly blame you for trying to protect me?' Lizzie picked up the letter again. 'Even your father felt proud of you for it – he knew you were right.'

'But that's only because of how I am,' Jack said. 'Because of *this*.' He looked down at the chair, at his useless legs, and the tears were angrier now, fiercer.

'Please tell me you don't mean that,' Lizzie said quietly, all her pain gathering in a hot ball in her chest. 'Jack, *please*, I mean it – tell me you know that isn't true.'

'He said he supposed it wasn't,' Lizzie told her mother later that night. 'But I think he was saying that just to make me feel better.' She paused. 'I get the feeling that Jack wants to know, to really try to understand what happened that night.'

'And all the other nights,' Angela said quietly, still shattered by what Lizzie had finally, after so many years, shared with her about Christopher, her perfect son-in-law.

'I won't tell him that,' Lizzie said decisively. 'Not now, or ever.'

'What about Edward?'

'I don't think Edward will want to know,' Lizzie said.

'But if he does?'

'I don't know.' Lizzie paused. 'Perhaps, if he asks me when he's older.' She looked at her mother. 'Jack's only ten years old,' she said. 'God knows he's been robbed of so much already, has more than enough suffering ahead of him.'

'I know,' Angela said, gently.

'I'll be damned if I'll allow every last fragment of childhood to be stolen from him,' Lizzie said passionately.

'No,' Angela said.

'You do agree with me, don't you, on this?' Lizzie asked.

'Of course I do,' Angela said.

119

Christopher's funeral, on the third Monday in November, a day that dawned foggy, then cleared into an almost perfect late autumn afternoon, was small and private, but deeply moving, having been arranged by Lizzie and Guy Wade, in consultation with the children. 'All Things Bright and Beautiful', chosen by Sophie; 'Jerusalem', by Jack, because he knew his father had loved it; and a reading by Guy, of 'Funeral Blues' – Edward's choice, because he and Christopher had both wept right through it in *Four Weddings*.

'I expect you'll be organizing a memorial service in a while,' Dalia Weinberg said afterwards, back at the house.

'I'm not sure yet,' Lizzie said.

'I think you may have to,' Dalia pressed. 'So many people are going to want a chance to pay their last respects.'

'They'll have to wait—' Guy came to her aid '—depending on the children.'

Guy had been a rock to Lizzie after she had, at last, decided to confide in him over his brother's weaknesses.

'I remember him telling me once,' he'd said one afternoon while Moira was rehearsing for a concert in London, 'about some dope-induced romps at university. But I never guessed for a second that he had any kind of real problem.'

'It's all just conjecture now, isn't it?' Lizzie said.

'I do know one thing for certain,' Guy said. 'His love for you and the children was utterly real, Lizzie. Knowing he was hurting you must have tormented him.'

'Maybe if I'd left him long ago,' Lizzie said, 'it might have been better for him.'

'I'm not sure he could have stood that,' Guy said. 'And we both know why you felt you had to stay.'

'Yet now the children have to go on without their father anyway.'

'His fault,' Guy said. 'Not yours, Lizzie.'

'I know,' she said.

'You do believe that, don't you?' Guy asked her.

'Sometimes,' Lizzie said, and smiled at him.

Ten days after the funeral, at lunchtime on a school day, Allbeury came to call. Others had visited in the past few days; Susan Blake and Howard Dunn, and the Szells, and a couple of the children's friends, and, on official business, Jim Keenan.

But Allbeury had stayed away till now.

They spoke, for a while, in the drawing room filled with memories of life with Christopher, about the children and how they were coping, and Lizzie told him it had been Jack's eleventh birthday at the weekend, and Allbeury said that he couldn't begin to imagine how rough that must have been for him.

'Beyond rough,' Lizzie said.

'How about you?' he asked. 'How are you doing?'

She raised her plastered arm and fingers. 'Not easily.'

'And otherwise?'

'Thinking about the children helps a lot,' she said.

He asked, a while later, how much she had been told about Clare Novak and the prequel to what had sent her plunging into that lift shaft.

'Not too much,' Lizzie said, 'because I may have to testify against her – if they feel she's fit to stand trial.' She paused. 'Detective Inspector Keenan came to see me. With a woman detective.'

'Helen Shipley?'

'No,' Lizzie said, with a wry smile. 'No broken leg.'

She knew now, of course, how close her brush with death had been, knew at least a little more about the two women with whose murders Clare Novak had now been charged. And she knew, also just a little, about Allbeury's links with those women.

'DI Keenan said you'd been trying to help them.'

'Much good I did them,' Allbeury said quietly.

'He said they were both in marriages with violent men,' Lizzie said. 'Marriages they felt trapped in.'

'That's right.'

Like me, she thought, but did not say.

'He said he thought you were trying to help them escape.' She paused. 'He's under the impression it's something you've already done for other women.'

The room was silent but for the faint ticking of the carriage clock on the mantel.

'Why?' She knew this was one of the questions she needed answered, if their friendship was to continue. 'Why do you do that, Robin? Why do you *want* to do it?'

Allbeury sat for a moment or two, then took a breath. 'A number of people have asked me that over the years,' he said. 'But you're the first I've wanted to answer.'

Lizzie said nothing, just waited.

'My mother committed suicide when I was twelve,' Allbeury said. 'Because she felt she had no alternative. She thought she was beyond help, that because most people thought my father a decent man – which he was not – no one would believe she had a right to be unhappy.' He paused. 'She had no real life of her own, no career, no money to speak of. No escape.'

Still, Lizzie did not speak.

'She told me all about it in a letter. She left me feeling that I ought to have known, to have found a way to stop her, help her.'

'You were twelve,' Lizzie said. 'You couldn't have helped.'

'I know that now, but not then.' He paused. 'It did some damage, I suppose, perhaps even stopped me marrying. I'm not like my father, thankfully, but that hasn't prevented me from being afraid I might possess the potential to wound, as he did.' He shrugged. 'It did some good, too, I hope. Years after my mother's death, after I'd become successful, made more money than I needed and learned a few things about power and influence, I found myself in a position to try and help women like her.'

Lizzie sat very still for a second and then said: 'Like me.'

'In one sense, perhaps just a little like you.'

'Is that why you befriended me, Robin?' she asked. 'Did you think I might want to escape?'

'I thought it, yes,' he said. 'But it wasn't what drew me to you.'

'Are you?' Lizzie asked. 'Drawn to me?'

'Very much so,' Allbeury replied.

'I can't help wondering,' Lizzie said, 'what you think of me, for staying in my marriage.' Her head was aching, and she rubbed her right temple with her two good fingers. 'I have enough money to be independent. I could have left.'

'You stayed because of the children,' he said.

'I did,' Lizzie agreed. 'And see where it's got them now.'

'You couldn't have known,' Allbeury said.

'Couldn't I?' she asked him painfully. 'Clare Novak told me she'd killed other women "*like me*—" ' that phrase again '—and isn't this what she meant?'

'Clare's very sick,' Allbeury said. 'Very disturbed.'

'Of course,' Lizzie agreed. 'But wasn't it surely always on the cards that my children would find out the truth about their father one day, regardless of my lies?'

'Maybe,' Allbeury said. 'But you were only hoping to protect them from the pain for as long as possible.'

'I think,' Lizzie said, 'I've been a dreadful coward.'

She waited until they were in the entrance hall as he prepared to leave before she asked one of the other questions gnawing at her.

'Why were those things about us on your computer, Robin? For Clare to hack into, to steal?'

'I did some research into you,' Allbeury said simply, 'because I liked you, and you intrigued me, and I'm a curious man, and I wanted to know more about you.' He paused. 'And then I found that I was worried about you. No other, more sinister reason.'

'What about Christopher?'

'That was different,' Allbeury admitted. 'I'd sensed that something was amiss with you both, and, frankly, I suddenly realized that I didn't trust him.'

Lizzie said nothing, still too shaken.

'I'm so sorry, Lizzie,' he said, softly. 'I know very well that if I'd minded my own business, Clare might scarcely have known of your existence.'

She had to wait another moment before she felt steady enough to speak.

'If I hadn't asked you that,' she said, 'would you have told me?'

'I think so,' he said, 'in time.' His smile was small, wry. 'Maybe only because I knew it would probably all come out in due course, anyway.'

'That's honest of you, at least.'

'I suspect,' Allbeury said, 'that if I weren't honest with you, Lizzie, I could have no hope of any long-term friendship with you.'

Lizzie looked straight into his face.

'You're right about that,' she said.

120

Allbeury went to visit Shipley – still on sick leave – took her flowers, pleased by the warmth of her smile when she accepted them and somewhat touched by the rather embarrassed way she limped about her small, chaotic flat hunting out a vase in which to put them. Over a pot of tea and chocolate finger biscuits, he learned from her that John Bolsover had now been released, but that, however devoutly Shipley and Lynne's sister, Pam Wakefield, might hope for him to be rearrested for his true crimes against Lynne, that would not now happen.

'I gather,' she told him, 'he had a fairly grim time inside.'

'Some small comfort for Lynne's sister,' Allbeury said.

'She says she's going to go on keeping a close eye on the kids,' Shipley said. 'And at least, from what she's told me, it seems he never laid a finger on them.'

He asked her what she had heard regarding Clare Novak.

'Is that why you came?' Shipley asked. 'I did wonder.'

'Not at all,' Allbeury said. 'I rather enjoyed our spats, your conspicuous dislike of me and your tenacity.'

Shipley shrugged. 'I can't tell you much about Novak,' she said. 'You probably already know she's being assessed in Rampton. Jim Keenan might know more.' She smiled again. 'Doubt he'll tell you much though.'

Keenan did know more, was still learning, most of the information coming his way via the specialists from the IT department at the forensic laboratory analysing both the computer at Novak Investigations, and the one belonging to Nick Parry, Clare's patient, who had, it was now becoming clear, helped his carer –

enjoying the challenge – to hack into any number of systems, and was, as things stood, more likely to face charges relating to computer security than Clare was, ultimately, for murder.

She was, Keenan was reasonably certain, insane, though the disturbingly cool calculation of her crimes and, until the end, her sheer efficiency, might yet speak against that insanity. Clare had been highly manipulative, using Mike and the agency, first and foremost, and their client Robin Allbeury (of whom she had written in a password-protected file that she considered him a user of women, possibly sick and probably perverted). She had used her own skills plus Nick Parry's isolation and passion for computers to invade hospital systems and, when that had been inadequate, she had wheedled facts out of Maureen Donnelly or visited A&E departments where she was known and trusted, scooping up titbits of information on cases that interested her.

'Cases.' DC Karen Dean noted the plural at one of their meetings.

'So there could be more victims,' Terry Reed said.

'She'd certainly shown interest in many more women than Patston and Bolsover,' Keenan confirmed.

Dating back to her breakdown, it seemed that Clare's PC had become her only truly trusted confidant. In it, she had kept detailed, regularly updated records relating to her targets, her *cases* (including Lizzie Wade) – all neatly referenced with what seemed to be partially dates of birth – all of whom, Clare wrote, had lacked moral courage. They had all married brutes, yet *they*, she claimed, were the really guilty parties for remaining with their husbands and perpetuating the risk to their children because they were too afraid of what leaving might entail.

'And,' Keenan said, 'in Lynne Bolsover's case, the husband had bullied her into having an abortion.'

'Maybe,' Dean said, visiting the possible motivation that Helen Shipley had previously ascribed to Allbeury, 'she believed she was giving the children a chance. Getting rid of their weak mothers, then getting the men put away.'

'You should be a shrink,' Reed said disparagingly.

No one had, as yet, been able to dredge up any deep-rooted motivation for the crimes. Malcolm Killin, her father, a tired, sick man, had no tales of trauma to offer, other than the death of his own wife when Clare was still a young girl. They had her history of breakdown and depression, her premature departure from nursing and, most significantly, the loss of her first baby.

Keenan had unearthed the newborn infant's post-mortem report and the transcript of the inquest into the death, both making it clear that, whatever Clare had told Mike Novak about killing their child, it had to have been a lie.

'How she must have hated him,' Dean said, sickened, 'to lie about that.'

'Unless,' Keenan had said, 'she was doing her best to make him hate her.'

'What a fucking fruitcake,' Reed said.

'What a bloody tragedy,' Keenan said.

Another tragedy had been exercising Keenan's mind – a nightmare replaying over and over in his memory – that of little Irina Patston being taken away from Sandra Finch.

He'd seen Joanne's mother several times since that day. Tony Patston was awaiting trial for offences relating to the illegal adoption, and the file regarding his probable assaults on the child had been sent to the CPS, but Sandra's anguish continued undiminished.

She had pleaded with Keenan to tell her what he could about Joanne's death, and he had, since it was just a matter of time till she heard it at the inquest, shared with her, off the record, some of the details they had gleaned from Clare Novak's PC.

That it had been Clare who had phoned Joanne that last morning, identifying herself as Novak's partner, telling Joanne that Allbeury urgently needed her to sign last-minute papers relating to her escape with Irina. That after Joanne had left Irina with Sandra, she had gone to meet Clare on the green outside the library in Hall Lane, where Clare had suggested it might be safer if Joanne filled out the forms in the privacy of her car and away from passers-by. That Clare had brought a flask with her, from which she had poured Joanne a cup of coffee laced with diazepam. That the tranquillizers had acted swiftly enough for Clare to drive Joanne into Epping Forest, then drag her to the spot where she had stabbed her – using her own medical expertise by piercing the jugular first, then covering that skill by inflicting the other wounds.

'Thank you for telling me,' Sandra Finch had said, when Keenan had finished.

'I wish,' he had said, 'there was something more I could do for you.'

'You can,' Sandra said. 'Help me get Irina back.'

'I don't think I can do that,' Keenan said.

'Surely *someone* could help.' The grandmother's eyes were tormented. 'How can anyone believe it could possibly be better for her to be with strangers, let alone be sent back to Romania?'

'I don't know,' Keenan had said.

121

Novak felt wrecked, at a total loss, directionally and emotionally.

Trying to go on, keeping the agency running, because that was what well-intentioned people kept telling him he needed to do, both for therapeutic and financial reasons.

And perhaps work might have been some sort of remedy, he accepted, had he felt he were doing something worthwhile. If he had not, via the agency, via Robin Allbeury, helped to draw two innocent women to their deaths.

If he were not reminded, each time he walked into the office and saw Clare's unoccupied desk, and his own gleaming new computer, of *everything*.

Allbeury had paid for Winston Cook to help extract all the non-evidential data from their old hard disk, and having the young man around in the office was helping to distract him just a little. But though it was tedious, painstaking work that would take Cook weeks, ultimately Novak knew that he would be alone again, waiting for Clare to allow him to come and visit her, for ever since she had been taken into custody his rights as her husband seemed to have been brutally cut off.

Most people, he knew, might not understand why he should *want* to see her. But then they couldn't know that the woman he'd first met, the one who'd stitched the head wound for him in A&E more than five years ago – the compassionate nurse who'd found her daily routine of other people's sufferings too much to bear – was not the same woman who had done those monstrous things, been cold-blooded enough, in one case, to go back and plant the murder weapon in her victim's husband's garage, had then logged it all with such clarity and precision on her computer.

Novak wished he could hate that Clare. Maybe he would, eventually, when the time came for him to endure all the facts at the trial. If she was found fit to *face* trial.

If he became certain that the old Clare was never going to find her way back through all that hate and torment to the surface.

Maybe then he would be able to hate her.

122

Allbeury found himself thinking about Lizzie and her children for too much time every day.

He had rung Susan Blake once to ask if she had seen her, and Susan had told him that she'd visited twice, that they spoke quite regularly and that Lizzie's plan was to stay close to home for the present.

'She can't cook properly until everything heals,' she had said, 'which is bugging her quite a bit, I'd say.'

'What about writing?' Allbeury had asked.

'I don't know,' Susan had said. 'I haven't asked, because I don't want her to feel under pressure, not professionally, at least.'

He waited another week before returning to Marlow.

She welcomed him with a degree of reserve, but still, he was glad to note, with warmth. Her arm was in a lighter cast, which was making life somewhat easier, and only two of her fingers remained bandaged, though the hands were by no means back to normal.

There was a Christmas tree in the drawing room, cards on the mantel and a fire blazing in the hearth.

'We look the part, anyway,' Lizzie said.

'Have you managed any gift shopping?' Allbeury asked.

'Some, thanks to my mum and Gilly.' She paused. 'Gilly's out with the children now, doing just that, I think.'

'How are they all?'

'A little better, I think.' Lizzie paused. 'Inquest still to come, of course.'

'They won't have to be there, will they?'

387

'No,' Lizzie said. 'But they'll know about it.'

Allbeury shook his head.

'What?' she asked.

'Just that everything I seem to want to say is a cliché.'

'The resilience of children, you mean,' she said. 'Time, and all that.'

'I'll shut up,' Allbeury said.

'No,' Lizzie said. 'Don't do that.' She paused. 'I'm much too pleased to see my rescuer again.'

'Except I didn't,' he said. 'Rescue you.'

'You tried.'

'I've a confession,' he said.

'Yes?' She waited.

'You asked me, that day, if I was a scout,' he said. 'And I wasn't.'

For a moment she looked blank, and then she remembered. 'The knot,' she said. 'You mean, if the lift had crashed . . .?'

'It might have held,' he said. 'With luck.'

'Were you just trying to keep my spirits up?' Lizzie asked.

'And my own,' he said.

He came, a while after that, to one of his main reasons for coming.

'Jim Keenan's been to see me. To ask for my help, off-the-record.'

'What sort of help?'

'It's about Irina Patston,' he said.

'How did you know,' Lizzie asked, 'that she's been on my mind?'

'I wasn't sure you knew much about her,' Allbeury said.

'DI Keenan told me the whole story.'

'When?'

'He came again last week.' She smiled. 'He really is very nice, isn't he?'

'Knows what he wants, too,' Allbeury said.

Lizzie had, even before Keenan's second visit, begun to feel a kinship with both murdered women, strangers as they were. But the case of little Irina, swallowed up in the general horror and in danger of being forgotten, had begun to haunt her.

'What,' she asked now, 'does Keenan think you can do?'

'I think he was hoping,' Allbeury said, 'that I could perform some not-strictly-legal magic trick and spirit Irina back to her grandmother.'

'Which you can't?'

'Unfortunately not.'

Lizzie waited a moment.

'Why are you here, Robin?' she asked finally.

'Because I think this is one for the media,' Allbeury said.

'I'm not a journalist,' Lizzie said.

'But you are a TV personality,' he said. 'And a writer.'

She held up her hands. 'Not doing much of either just yet.'

'You could manage some two-finger typing, couldn't you?'

Lizzie wiggled her fingers. 'Bit better than that, maybe.'

'Good physio, probably,' Allbeury said.

'What am I supposed to be writing?'

'You're the best judge of that, don't you think?'

'I don't know,' she said. 'Letters to MPs, perhaps?'

'Articles, too,' Allbeury said. 'The bigger and splashier and noisier the better.'

'Thought you were leaving it up to me,' Lizzie said.

He leaned forward in his armchair. 'So you will help?'

'Of course I will,' she said. 'Or at least, I'll give it a bloody good try.'

'Thank you,' Allbeury said.

'Haven't done anything yet.' She thought about it. 'We are quite sure that Irina's still in the country, aren't we? That they haven't already sent her back to Romania?'

'From what Keenan says, they don't even seem to be all that certain now that she necessarily *came* from Romania in the first place. Tony Patston's told them all he can – hoping it'll help when his case comes up – about the woman who sold Irina to them.'

'Sold,' Lizzie echoed, softly.

'Joanne Patston was desperate to be a mother,' Allbeury said. 'If it hadn't been for her bastard of a father, Irina would have been very lucky to have her.'

'Presumably there's no hope that they'd let the grandmother adopt her legally?'

'Too old,' Allbeury said.

'What about fostering?'

389

'Exactly what Mrs Finch suggested to Keenan.'

'Good.' Lizzie nodded. 'Seems like the best approach, don't you think?'

'Whatever you think.'

'You'll help too, won't you?' Lizzie asked.

'Try stopping me,' Allbeury said.

123

On a windy but sunny afternoon in April, three months after the first of Lizzie's articles hit the *Daily Express* and Irina Patston's case became the paper's latest *cause célèbre*, a six-year-old girl with large, wary, almost-black eyes, small for her age, but otherwise sturdy, was led by the hand into her new foster home.

Sandra Finch, who had been allowed to see Irina several times during the past few weeks, had, nevertheless, been apprehensive of the moment, afraid lest Irina, having endured so much upheaval and trauma in her young life, became unnerved or upset.

She had no need to worry.

The hallway of the house had been decorated with balloons and flowers, and with some of the countless cuddly toys that *Express* readers had sent in, but the instant Irina caught sight of the woman she had known for most of her life as her grandmother, nothing else mattered.

'Grandma!'

Sandra Finch opened her arms to greet her.

The party thrown the following weekend by the newspaper was smaller than they had first envisaged, because Lizzie had put her foot down for the little girl's sake, and the editor had seen her point.

'No one else gets photos,' he said.

'Except family,' Lizzie said.

'Goes without saying.'

Lizzie and the children were at the party, especially appropriate since they all – and and most particularly Jack – had become heavily involved in the fight to get Irina back where she belonged.

Jim Keenan and Karen Dean had both turned down their invitations, lest their presence bring back painful memories for the young guest of honour. As had Anna Mellor, Christopher's friend, who had, once Lizzie's campaign had begun, come forward with a substantial offer of help, remembering that the Patstons had once come to her with Irina, recalling, too, guiltily, how bothered the husband had been by the baby's crying, and how she had laughed off his concerns.

'Where's Robin?' Edward asked Lizzie twenty minutes after their arrival.

'I don't know,' she said. 'Perhaps he can't make it.'

'He'll be here,' Jack said.

Lizzie glanced at him, surprised by the conviction in his tone.

'I just said he'll be here, Mum, that's all,' Jack said.

Less than a minute later, the doorbell rang.

'Told you,' Jack said.

Sandra went to answer it, Irina still clutching her hand.

Allbeury was not alone. He had, cuddled in his arms, a very small King Charles spaniel puppy.

Irina stared up at him, her eyes larger than ever.

'Yours, I believe, Irina,' Allbeury said.

'You knew about this, didn't you?' Lizzie said to Jack, accusingly.

And then she looked back at Allbeury, and smiled.